Fighting the Inevitable

J C GORDON

Copyright © 2015 J C Gordon

All rights reserved.

ISBN:1512138762
ISBN-13: 978-1512138764

DEDICATION

This book is dedicated to my dad, Gordon Edward Irvine.
28 Aug 1936 - 4 Oct 2014

You were a true inspiration to me growing up.
You were my ultimate hero.

I love you dearly, Dad, and miss you every day.

REVIEWS

I can't recommend this book enough! Ms Gordon weaves two love stories throughout this tale, and shows how a small twist of fate can change a life forever. Fighting the Inevitable is filled with memorable characters and introduces us to a world we all want to visit time and time again. Fair warning - chances are, once you start reading it, you won't be able to put it down. ~ Lana St. Louis

~~~~

J C Gordon draws you into this spellbinding tale of love, loss and the universal struggle for acceptance in the unforgettable first book of this tale. Her sumptuous writing has you right beside the characters as they feel, love and lose themselves in a world that has been irrevocably changed - whether for better or worse, only time will tell ~ Stephanie Passmore

~~~~

As an avid reader, I found that I could not put Ms. Gordon's Fighting the Inevitable down. This book is indeed well worth losing a night's sleep over. The world and characters she has created will draw you into their lives, making you want to be part of it all." ~ Aisie Lynn

ACKNOWLEDGMENTS

Special thanks and my eternal gratitude must go to

my wonderful cover art designer Kelly Shorten

and

my lovely editor Aisie Lynn

Also, to my KBF, Evan Guillemette, for his unfailing friendship, and constant support of all of my writing projects. You are the best!

Huge hugs to Jennifer Cothran for the tremendous work she put into helping me get FTI to publication. I couldn't have done it without you, sweets!

And finally, much love and a special thank you goes to the all amazing people who helped make this book possible #yourock

Tonya Ramey • Andi Downs • David Franden • Jennifer Cothran • Aisie Lynn • Angel N Disguise • Mistress of Shadows • Dave Dennis • Flora Thomas •Amey Hooten • Jackie Worrall • Samantha Darvin • Tabatha Adamson • Preshina Naicker • Maria Plaud • Elizabeth Gates • Jennifer J Willams • Artish Bell • Letitia Flanders • Sharon Kinnier •Natalie Liao Jen • Carrie Edgerton-Thompson • Mez Tunney • Wendy Burgess • Aimee Martin • Sherry Walsh • Stephanie Cobb • Marion M. Putman • Mary Wisniewski • Carolyn Dunnewijk •Shannon Porter • Isabele Smith • Jessica Aldridge • Gladys Settle • Bonni Rice • Mardi Atkinson • Rita Mutlow • Joe Smith • Stephanie Clark • Remi Akintunde • Donna Wyatt • April Taylor • Misty Turner • Scott Way • Amanda Archer • Toni Stockstill • Crystal Hood • April Mechtly

CHAPTER ONE

Demetri Bozic looked up from the delicious little brunette who was secreted in the back of the dark booth beside him. A scent teased his nostrils, and his deep green eyes searched the darkness until the object of the scent became visible. He smiled and nodded, turning back to the woman in his arms. He knew his friend would join them, but for now, his attention was firmly on his companion.

She really was quite delectable, her face flushed with her arousal, her lips swollen from his ravishment. What really stirred his lust was the pale creamy breast that was bared to his intent gaze. The hardened nipple was mouth-watering, and he bent his head again to suckle on the tasty morsel. He returned his hand between her thighs, and pressed his fingers back into the wonderful warmth of her body. As she moaned in ecstasy, his fangs elongated, and he bit into her breast, swallowing down the sweet nectar that was her life giving blood.

He heard his friend approach, sensed him slip into the booth across from them. The sound of wineglasses being placed on the table brought a pause to his feeding. He always enjoyed a little red wine after a meal. He didn't raise his head though, Caleb could wait until he was finished. He suckled harder against the creamy breast in his mouth, closing his eyes as he savoured the sweet nectar dripping down his throat.

~~~~~

Caleb allowed his golden brown gaze to flicker over the sight before him. He preferred privacy when he dined, but Demetri didn't hold to most conventions, especially when his bloodlust was upon him. He sipped at a glass of wine as he watched his friend ride the girl's body with his fingers, as he fed liberally at her breast.

It was an erotic sight and Caleb knew it wouldn't be long before he would have to feed his own dual lusts. For the moment, he continued to watch the show, his lips curling in a small smile as he admired his friend's finesse.

The brunette suddenly stiffened and gasped out her pleasure. Locked in her moment of orgasm, she was barely aware that Demetri sealed the wound on her breast with a swipe of his tongue and then peeled his fingers out of her body. The human would have no idea that she had just fed an Ancient vampire. All she would remember was the intoxicating pleasure Demetri had given her.

"Thank you, chérie," the dark haired vampire purred, kissing her lips lightly before hustling her out of booth. He sucked at his damp fingers as he watched her go, satisfaction etched across his inhumanly beautiful face.

"Enjoy your dinner?" Caleb Ryder's voice was light and teasing, with a hint of huskiness about it. His body was hard and aching. Watching Demetri indulge himself was an intensely erotic experience, and he hadn't been with a woman for almost a week. He really would have to satisfy his urges soon.

"She was delightful," Demetri laughed throatily, accepting a glass of wine from the other man. "A little appetiser. I'm still hunting my main course."

Caleb laughed loudly at the wicked expression on his friend's face. His people were an extremely hedonistic race, indulging themselves liberally, but Demetri always took things that little bit further than most. After his main course, Caleb wouldn't be surprised if his friend sampled a little dessert too. Taking three women in the one night wasn't beyond the dark haired Ancient if he was in the mood. It appeared from the glint in his eyes that tonight he was.

Caleb's eyes ran slowly around the dimly lit nightclub, looking for something to take his fancy. He was a partner in Karpathia's along with Demetri, though he was more of a silent partner. Demetri ran the club and he left him to it. They were joint business partners in a number of technology companies as well.

They had been friends for two thousand years, their different personalities often causing some of their people to wonder how they managed to maintain such a tight relationship. Demetri was wild, unforgiving and utterly deadly, while Caleb was more reserved, appearing slightly more civilised than his friend.

The truth of the matter was simple for Caleb. He trusted Demetri with his life and vice versa. His friend would die to protect him and he would do the same. Demetri was his family though they had been born countries apart.

Their friendship had been forged in blood, when humans were still animals and wars and persecution had run rampant. He had saved Demetri's life, though some would perhaps argue that point. He'd been barely a decade old to this life, a Youngling defying his Sire when he had found Demetri dying from a sword wound.

It had been during one of the many wars that had ravished the world at the time. Caleb had been hungry, the scent of blood calling him. Dead blood was unsatisfying so he looked through the battlefield for the dying. They could sustain him while he could ease their pain by injecting his soothing toxin into their system as he drained what little blood they had left.

It hadn't been a sexual act. Caleb loved woman and wasn't tempted by the flesh of men, and that was why he had been surprised when he found the dying dark haired soldier and felt an affinity for him which he couldn't explain. Demetri's deep green eyes had opened as he'd fed from his wrist, bright and shiny for one who was so close to death.

"What are you?" The words had been whispered softly, but Caleb had heard them because of his enhanced hearing abilities. He had stopped feeding, surprised at being addressed in his native tongue. It showed the man below him was of considerable intelligence if he could speak a language other than his own.

"A vampire," he answered, smoothing back blood soaked hair so he could look again at this exotic man who had piqued his interest.

"I don't want to die!"

There has been such vehemence, such hunger to live that had shone in those green eyes that Caleb had smiled slowly, impressed with the will of his current meal.

"Very well."

He had drunk deeply at the dying man's wrist, listening to his heartbeat falter. Then he had healed the sword wound and ripped open his own wrist, pressing it to the other man's mouth. He'd had no idea if he was doing it right. He was only a Youngling, and not supposed to be Siring anyone until he reached Elder status. However, he had done it anyway, knowing his Sire would be furious with him.

Perhaps it had been because Caleb remembered what it was to be human. He remembered how he hadn't wanted to die either, how his refusal to succumb had led to his Sire granting him immortality. If this man wanted to live that badly too, then he deserved the same gift.

No one living knew of Caleb's connection to Demetri. They never spoke of it; he never used his hold over his friend. Demetri knew he could walk away at any time he wanted, and Caleb would let him go. Perhaps that was one of the reasons that he stayed.

Now they sat together, two thousand years older and so closely bound together that they often thought as one, moved as one. Nothing could separate the allegiance they had for each other, even when they had their rare disagreements and tried to beat the crap out of one another.

Female eyes were automatically drawn to the booth they sat in, and Caleb's lips twitched slightly as his shrewd gaze continued the search for his evening's entertainment. He knew what women saw when they looked at them, how their physical aura alone could draw every woman in the room's attention.

The two men were of similar height, Caleb being the taller by one inch, standing at six foot one. While Caleb's colouring bordered on an almost Grecian look with long flowing golden brown hair, his friend Demetri had shoulder length thick hair that was as black as sin itself. His complexion had more of an olive tint too. He was a mix between European and Slavic, a deadly, seductive combination.

Both men were powerfully built as well as incredibly tall. Broad shoulders supported wide, well-muscled chests tapering down to trim waists and taut, flat stomachs. Long muscular legs and thick muscled arms strained in their clothing as they lounged in the booth. They were both dressed fairly casually. Demetri had opted for tight black jeans with a midnight blue silk shirt; while Caleb was poured into the tightest pair of black leather pants he owned, and completed his outfit with a black silk shirt.

The men practically oozed sex appeal as well as power and a substantial hint of danger. They were predators of the most deadly kind, the top of the food chain and with the haughty arrogance of knowing it.

Caleb sighed deeply as he ran his bored eyes around the dimly lit nightclub. He watched barely dressed women bump and grind with horny males and wondered once again if he was getting too old for all of this. Not so long ago he would have been the one on that dance floor with some lithe little beauty in his arms, grinding his hardness against her soft body, letting her know in no uncertain terms what he planned to do with her once they were off the dance floor. Tonight, it just left him feeling cold, his only spark of interest being Demetri's earlier little display.

Not one woman in the room sparked his lust, and he had to admit he was slightly concerned about his lack of interest. There had always been two constants in Caleb's life. The first was the need to feel the sweet taste of blood in his mouth, and the other was the need to slide his body into a hot, willing female. So far this week he had done neither and didn't feel the urge to, either.

Running a large hand through his hair, he gave his third sigh in under five minutes and was rewarded with a deep growl.

"For fuck's sake, Caleb, will you get into the party spirit?" Demetri said tersely, his cool, green eyes flashing as he regarded his friend with a hint of annoyance. He was starting to grate a little on the warm buzz running through Demetri.

"I'm bored," Caleb grumbled quietly. "There isn't one decent woman in here tonight." His tone did sound bored and also slightly jaded.

Demetri quirked an eyebrow though he wasn't really that surprised. He'd noticed his friend becoming ever quieter in the last few weeks, especially when they were out hunting. He was quiet and restless and out of sorts which was unusual for him.

"You want to try somewhere else?" he asked, just as the main door to the club opened and the scent of jasmine and lavender assaulted his senses. He saw Caleb stiffen slightly, and he turned his head to look at the woman who had just entered.

"Fuck me!" Demetri breathed softly, a huge compliment coming from him because he wasn't easily impressed with a woman's looks.

Caleb was quite literally stunned as he watched the woman come into the club. Fuck, was she even old enough to be in a nightclub? She was so tiny that for a moment he thought she surely had to be underage but the bouncers were strict at Karpathia's.

They most definitely would have carded the girl and asked enough questions to be reasonably certain she was old enough to be allowed in.

Her little purple sandals must have been at least four inches high; that would put the woman at five feet tall in her bare feet. Her ankles looked delicate and her calves were shapely as his eyes slowly worked their way up her body.

He found himself taking his time as he perused her. He didn't want to miss a thing as his gaze swept passed her knees and came to the shimmering deep purple and diamante little slip dress she was wearing. The hem came to mid-thigh and he got a good look at the pale, satin smooth skin of her thighs before he took in her softly rounded hips, flat stomach, and delicate waist.

His gaze continued its upward movement, and he stopped when he reached her breasts. The two perfect orbs were full and pert, a bit large for her small frame but not as buxom as a lot of women tended to favour these days. His keen eye could tell that he'd be able to completely enclose the soft flesh in his large hands and he felt an itch to do so right there and then.

His body hardened and he growled softly as his gaze continued his upward movement enjoying the swell of her breasts peaking daringly out of her dress before he sighed as he took in her slender little neck bare of all jewellery. Her shoulders were practically bare too with the exception of two thin strips of material that held her dress up.

His body twitched again in his leather pants as he finally got to her face. Fuck she was stunning to look at. Her little heart-shaped face seemed so delicate. Her eyes were a strange lavender colour and framed by long, thick black lashes, which gave her a mysterious look. Her colouring stirred something in his memory, but he pushed it ruthlessly away. He didn't want to be distracted by anything but the sight of her beauty.

Her skin was pale and soft, her little upturned nose giving her a slightly haughty appearance. Her lips were the most spectacular pair of lips he could ever remember seeing. They were wide and generous and deliciously plump, enhanced by the amethyst lipstick she was wearing.

Her best feature though was the glorious mane of waist-length auburn curls, which tumbled down her back like a living flame.

There wasn't one thing about the girl Caleb didn't like. She was total perfection.

"I think we'll stay here, Demetri," Caleb said quietly, belatedly answering his friend's question as he watched the girl head over to the bar and slip onto one of the high bar stools.

Demetri chuckled lightly as he watched his friend's intense expression. He was a little regretful that he wouldn't get a chance at the auburn haired beauty, but this was the first time in weeks he'd seen Caleb express any genuine interest in a woman so he wasn't about to queer his pitch.

~~~~

Rhianna steeled her nerves as she took a seat at the bar, her hands shaking slightly. She had no idea what had compelled her to come out tonight. Perhaps it had been the fact she'd just had the worst day of her life and she needed some kind of distraction. Perhaps she just needed to be surrounded by noise, and strangers; people who didn't know or care who she was. Whatever the reason, she was here now, signalling the bartender for a glass of red wine. He set it down in front of her, and she was just raising the glass to her lips when she felt someone slide onto the stool next to her, and she turned her head to the left.

Her eyes connected with the buttons of a black silk shirt and slowly moved upwards. Her breath hitched in her throat as she found herself looking at the most stunningly beautiful face she'd ever seen. The man was so stunning she actually considered whether a God had descended from the heavens and sat down next to her.

Warm golden brown eyes roamed over her face as she took in the strong, rugged jaw line, thin, straight nose, and high chiselled cheekbones. He seemed to blink in slow motion, long lashes hiding his glittering amber eyes before revealing them again as a slow smile curved his wide generous mouth.

He wore his hair long to his shoulders and it looked shiny, thick, and so incredibly soft. Her breath caught again as she took in his wide shoulders and chest, all rippling with hard muscles. The man was clearly enormous and she felt even smaller than usual sitting next to him.

The most astounding thing about him was he made her *feel*. After a week of total emptiness, it was an incredible sensation to stare up at him and feel attraction towards him. She gripped that emotion tightly and held onto it for dear life.

"I'm Caleb," he said, and his rich deep voice sent a shiver down her spine as she gazed open mouthed at him. He could have uttered the most ridiculous sentence in the world and she still would have shivered as his voice whispered over her. She felt a sharp stab of pleasure in her stomach and she blinked in surprise that a simple introduction could affect her so badly.

Rhianna watched his luscious lips curve into a wider smile as he leaned closer and inhaled deeply at the side of her neck while she sat there like a stunned rabbit in the headlights of a car about to mow it down.

"And you are?" His sexy voice whispered against the shell of her ear and her breath hissed out as another shiver went through her and the pleasure magnified in her stomach.

"Rhianna," she answered breathlessly, almost crying out in disappointment when the man, Caleb, pulled back from her and sat straighter on his stool.

"It's my distinct pleasure to meet you, Rhianna," He gave her another bone melting smile, and he really did sound genuinely pleased to meet her.

Rhianna stared into his gorgeous eyes and saw his pleasure mixed in with a healthy dose of blatant sexuality. She dragged her gaze away from his face, looked down self-consciously, and then stifled a moan as her action brought her eyes lower down his body to the skin-tight black leather pants he wore and the very obvious bulge.

She issued a startled gasp and dragged her gaze back up to see Caleb watching her with an amused expression on his face, not in the least embarrassed about his body's reaction.

"I was just about to leave when you walked in," he said conversationally. "I took one look at you and my body hardened instantly."

Rhianna felt her cheeks flush scarlet at his forthrightness, and she picked up her glass of wine and took a large slug, struggling not to choke as the tart liquid slid down her throat. She heard him chuckle lightly as he watched her, and she felt liquid heat slide through her body at the sound.

"You shouldn't be embarrassed," he said with more than a hint of amusement. "You're a very beautiful woman and I like very beautiful women. It's only natural my body would react to seeing someone I want."

If he thought to ease her embarrassment, he was going about it in the completely wrong direction. Her cheeks reddened further. "You like to move fast, don't you?" she asked, keeping her eyes firmly on her glass of wine, and pleased to hear she didn't sound as gauche as she was feeling.

She could almost sense him shrug beside her. "What's the point in beating about the bush?" he countered. "I know what I want and I'm not afraid to come right out and ask for it. Tonight I want you, Rhianna. Will you come home with me?"

Her hands shook around the stem of the glass. He was incredibly handsome and he had the most amazing body she'd ever seen on a man. She was sure he would be a very skilled lover. She could imagine many a woman taking him up on his offer to go home with him. However, she wasn't many a woman. She just didn't do things like this. It was completely out of her comfort zone.

Rhianna turned to tell him so and found herself locked in his heated gaze. She hesitated, biting her bottom lip nervously and saw his eyes drop to her mouth when she did so, a sharp intake of breath coming from him. This beautiful man truly did want her, and there was something about him that called to her very being.

She could lose herself in his strong arms so very easily. She could almost imagine what his mouth would feel like on her body as he pleasured her. She wanted to forget about everything tonight. She didn't imagine she'd be thinking of anything other than Caleb if she went home with him. He could make her feel the most incredible sensations, and she heard herself saying yes before she'd even realised she'd made the decision.

As she uttered the word, she saw a flare of intense male satisfaction cross his face as he leaned forward slowly, halting when his lips were barely a fraction of an inch from hers. "You won't regret your decision, Rhianna," he whispered quietly just before his tongue snaked out and very slowly licked along her bottom lip.

The thoroughly intimate gesture stole her breath away and she stared into his eyes with a slightly startled expression. He moved back once more and smiling, slid from his stool and helped her from hers.

Rhianna knew that it wasn't the wisest course of action, but she allowed him to lead her from the nightclub and settle her into a very expensive looking silver Porsche sports car.

CHAPTER TWO

Caleb drove fast but expertly. Rhianna didn't think he obeyed one speed limit the entire twenty minutes it took to reach his big white mansion on the outskirts of town. Still, she hadn't been afraid by his driving. It had been fast and almost wild, and just the thing she needed tonight. She wanted to be wild and uninhibited.

"You drive fast," she said, her voice sounding breathless as she allowed him to help her from the car.

He chuckled low in his chest and kept a hold of her hand as he tugged her towards his front door. "I do lots of things fast," he laughed, his amber eyes twinkling suggestively. "I also do lots of things slow too." His voice had dropped to an intimate level as he opened the door and pulled her inside.

"Oh, wow," Rhianna said softly, taking in the large open hallway with beautiful white tiles on the floor. The entranceway was the full height of the building, a huge, ornate chandelier hanging from a dark wood beam just below an impressive glass skylight.

Caleb watched the little redhead's face light with pleasure as her eyes ran slowly over the hallway. He smiled as he watched her, feeling strangely pleased that she liked his home. In all truthfulness, coming home didn't have the same effect on him. Oh, he felt as if he was coming home but he didn't notice the beauty of it as he once had.

He tugged her hand and pulled her into the sitting room, which harked back to a more gothic time. The room was full of thick furnishings and dark woods, the fireplace open and blazing.

He wasn't quite sure where he wanted to indulge in her beautiful body. It was always nice to have a soft bed beneath him, but he found himself reluctant to take the girl to one of the cold, empty bedrooms he usually used when he brought his women home.

He had no intention of allowing her into his own bed. No woman entered his private place, but he did want something slightly more intimate than usual with the little beauty beside him. When they'd spoken in the nightclub he had caught a hint of deep sadness about her before she'd quickly forced it away. He didn't know why she was so sad and hiding it, and to be truthful, he didn't particularly want to know. He didn't do *'relationships'* and wasn't about to get emotionally involved with a woman. He just wanted to enjoy her body and take them both to heaven and back.

Caleb settled on tugging her towards the fire, pulling her down onto the thick brown rug before it. She came hesitantly, a hint of doubt in her eyes as if she was reconsidering her actions.

He smiled slowly and his eyes glinted as she knelt before him. There would be no backing out for her tonight. He would have her, and she would enjoy every single moment of it. She was the first woman he'd truly wanted for months now. He wasn't letting her slip through his fingers when need was ravaging through his body so viciously.

"Caleb," she started to say hesitantly, but he stopped her by placing his right index finger to her lips.

"Don't think," he whispered softly. "Just feel."

He trailed his finger from her mouth down to the side of her neck, pausing at her throbbing pulse, and closing his eyes to enjoy the steady beat against his skin. Her pulse was strong and vital, so full of life and the delicious sweet blood his body hungered for. It was all he could do not to lean forward, sink his fangs into her neck, and feed deeply from her.

His cock strained hard against the confining leather of his pants, and he was filled with a need to see her totally naked. "Stand up and take your dress off," he whispered silkily, his tone both gentle and commanding at the same time. She stiffened slightly as if to deny him his request, and then she stood up and slowly peeled her dress from her slender frame.

Caleb's breath hitched in his throat as he watched the material pool at her feet, his greedy gaze sliding over her soft skin. Her breasts were perfection, their tips already reacting to the cool air around them. There wasn't a blemish on her creamy white skin. It looked pale and silky soft and crying out for his touch.

He wanted to do such deliciously wicked things to her body. He wanted to drive her mindless with pleasure until she writhed and screamed her ecstasy. He just wasn't sure where he wanted to start first. His gaze slid down to her gently rounded hips and to the scrap of purple lace between her legs. "Take them off," he said huskily, his voice deep and gravelled, as his lust escalated higher than it had in a very long time.

She hooked her fingers in the waistband of her panties and soon they joined her dress at her feet and he got his first glimpse and smell of her enticing womanhood. Caleb's eyes darkened to almost black as he stared at the feminine perfection before him. He had a perfect view of her slick folds already wet with her arousal, her musky aroma teasing him delicately.

He leaned closer, but didn't touch her. Instead, he inhaled deeply and let the sweet scent of jasmine and lavender and the heady mix of her arousal sweep over him. She smelled just as good as she looked, and he knew she would taste even better.

He reached out and tapped the back of her right knee, gently forcing her to lift her leg so he could slide her dress and panties from her foot. He did the same with her left knee and moved back to fold her clothes neatly and place them on the sofa closest to them.

Caleb looked at her heels and decided to leave them on. Depending on how lost he became in her body she may need the additional height the heels gave her later on. In addition, they looked sexy as hell on her. She was shivering slightly as he continued to just gaze at her perfect body, and he smiled again and raised his eyes to hers.

"If you want me to undress, you need to persuade me to do so," he said huskily, delighting in the confusion that crossed her beautiful face. Loving a woman was a true art form, and Caleb liked to discover what a woman really wanted from him. At the moment, he was being slightly dominant with her, but not overly so. Not whips and chains type of domination, more a subtle, mental kind.

"It's very easy to get my clothes off, Rhianna," he smiled gently at her. "Just spread your beautiful legs and open yourself up so I can get a proper look at what you have to offer."

It was endearing the way her cheeks blushed scarlet and his smile widened at the heated blood flowing through her. He could tell she liked what he was doing even if she didn't want to like it. Her innocent shyness was warring with her arousal, which was deepening by the moment from the wonderful bouquet of aromas coming from between her legs.

Rhianna stood before the kneeling man and slowly opened her legs wider, her hands hesitantly moving over her flat stomach. She couldn't believe she was actually doing this, but the heated look of total worship in Caleb's eyes was making her so hot and wet she couldn't seem to stop herself. She used two fingers to tease herself open to his greedy gaze as he slowly raised his hands to his shirt and began to unbutton the silk material.

"Very good," he sighed with pleasure, and inhaled deeply again.

He could feel the heat coming from her body; see the moisture gathering across her pink flesh. For a moment, Caleb was concerned at her size. He was well endowed, and much larger women than Rhianna had had trouble taking his size and girth. He could hurt her if he tried to take her too soon, and he didn't want to do that. He'd need to be very careful with her, ensure that she only experienced pleasure when they finally came together.

He peeled his shirt from his body and smiled when she moaned at the sight of his lightly haired chest. He knew he had a body to make women swoon, hell he did it regularly; however, it was always gratifying to hear a woman's moan at the first sight of his well-muscled physique.

"Show me how you pleasure yourself," he ordered quietly. "Climax for me and I'll take off the rest of my clothes."

Rhianna bit her lip at his demand, her cheeks flushing scarlet even as she found herself instantly obeying him. She wanted, no, she needed to see him completely naked. She moaned and closed her eyes, lightly stroking her body, her hips moving at the brief caress. She breathed in deeply and stroked again, moaning louder as a jolt of pleasure spiralled through her body.

She could hear Caleb's breathing quicken, and she began to move faster, a feeling of power coming over her, as she knew her actions were making him hornier than he already was. She wanted him to feel as hot as she did standing before him in nothing more than her sandals, touching herself.

Caleb groaned and quickly snapped open his leather pants, his eyes never leaving the little hand stroking against her sex. Her breathing was coming in little pants as her hips bucked into her hand and she soared higher and higher towards her orgasm. He tugged his boots off and peeled the leather from his body, a sigh of relief escaping him as his enormous cock sprung free.

Rhianna was almost at her release judging from her sharp cries and the frantic movement of her fingers. He decided to help her over the edge and leaned forward just enough so he could slide his tongue against her flesh and get his first taste of her sweet honey.

She screamed and shuddered wildly as she came hard at the first touch of his tongue inside her. His mouth filled with the sweet taste of her release and he licked greedily at her nectar, his large hands spanning her waist to keep her from falling as her knees buckled.

He held her firmly as she shook, his mouth ravishing her body, his lust spiralling as she filled his mouth with her heavenly taste. Fuck, she tasted even better than he'd imagined she would. He couldn't remember a time when a woman's pleasure had felt so satisfying.

"You taste divine," he complimented her, watching a blush steal across her face. "I want some more."

His lips curved in a satisfied smile as he watched her with intent eyes. Her mix of innocence liberally sprinkled with hot, spicy lust was incredibly erotic, and he felt his body throb painfully with appreciation. This beautiful woman was delightful and he was going to enjoy every inch of her sexy body before the night was over.

Rhianna tried not to scream out aloud when he put his mouth to her most intimate place again. She couldn't hold back the cry or stop her fingers from threading in his thick hair to hold him in place, even though she was still trembling from her first release.

He devoured her, licking and nibbling, teasing her heated flesh with light flicks of his tongue before diving in for a deeper taste of her juices. She felt tension coil in her stomach, her breath catching in her throat an instant before she did scream loudly, her body shaking with the violence of her climax.

Caleb kept licking at her, her sweet taste intoxicating as she shuddered from her pleasure. Her release was like an aphrodisiac and he sipped at her body greedily until she slowly calmed. He had known she would taste heavenly and she did, so much so he wanted more, but knew he had to give her some respite. Perhaps tomorrow morning before she left, he could taste her once more.

He had never wanted to indulge a second time with a woman before, but something about this particular woman had him thinking of a second time and possibly even a third. It was something he would need to examine more carefully later. For the moment, he was aching with need for her and all his senses where attuned to that feeling.

He allowed her to sink to her knees before him, running his hands lightly up to cup her luscious breasts and squeeze gently. His thumbs played with the hard peaks as he watched her pupils dilate with pleasure, her breath rasping out in little pants.

Caleb's own breath was becoming ragged as lust clawed at him. Her scent swirled around him, heady and intoxicating, the pounding pulse in the side of her neck making his mouth water. He was so close to losing all control that he was startled at how badly she affected him. He was hard-pressed to remember a time when a woman had enticed him so badly.

"How did you like the appetiser?" he laughed softly, Demetri's words coming back to him from before. He liked to indulge himself just as much as his friend did, only he sampled from the same table, in this case, the stunning redhead before him.

Rhianna stared up at him, her body still coming down from the incredible pleasure he'd just given her. She flushed scarlet at his words and the lazy way his eyes roamed over her as if she belonged completely to him.

"You seriously didn't think we were finished, did you, Rhianna?" he laughed softly. "Your body is quite slender, and I am a large man. You need careful preparation before I can slide inside your beautiful little body."

Her gaze automatically slid down his body to his thighs and she gasped out loud when she saw his cock resting proudly against her thigh. He chuckled at her startled expression and stroked her cheek again.

"Yes, it is rather a monster, isn't it," he smiled proudly, his amber eyes twinkling as he drew her gaze back to his. He rolled over her, positioning himself between her legs, and pressing his throbbing cock against her stomach. His hair fell forward framing her face like a curtain as he lowered his mouth and kissed her for the first time.

Her lips were as intoxicating as the rest of her, his tongue seeking entrance into her mouth to dance seductively against hers. Was there any part of this woman that didn't send him wild with need? So far, he had yet to find it.

Caleb could feel the tenseness in her body and he slowly pulled his lips away from hers and trapped her gaze with his. "Relax, Rhianna," he whispered softly. "I won't hurt you, I promise. I take no satisfaction from sex if the woman beneath me is not enjoying it just as much as I am."

She stared at him with wide lavender eyes, her trepidation plain to see. "You're too big," she whispered back. "It'll hurt."

He sighed and sat up, resting on his knees, and pulling her up with him until she was astride him, his amber gaze intent in her face. "Did someone hurt you?" he asked softly, correctly guessing the reason for her sudden fear. He saw the answer in the way that her eyes turned away quickly.

"I've only done this once before," she heard herself say, flushing with embarrassment when she realised she'd just blurted it out.

Surprise crossed his face and his eyes narrowed slightly. "Why?" he asked in a gentle, almost hypnotic voice.

"I wasn't very good at it," she answered, flushing a darker shade of pink and biting her lip nervously. Would he send her away now that he knew she was a disappointing lover? The thought of going home, going back to the world that she so desperately wanted to stay away from almost made her burst into tears.

Caleb felt a stirring of rage deep within him. He found himself feeling strangely angry that a man had hurt this beautiful woman in such a way that she was now afraid of her sexuality and the pleasures to be found by joining with a man.

Only a very inept lover would leave a woman feeling she was inadequate in bed, he knew that from years of experience. This stunning woman had given the precious gift of her virginity to some man and been left wanting at the end of the experience because of his ineptitude.

"We are all novices at the start, sweet one," he breathed softly, stroking his fingers lightly over her neck. "The true art of lovemaking is the choosing of your partner so they can teach you the joy of expressing yourself openly and with passion. It sounds to me that you erred in your judgement when you chose your first lover."

She blinked slowly at him, feeling a slight smile tug at her lips. He sounded so condescendingly arrogant in his statement. He was obviously trying to make her feel better, but was doing a piss-poor job of it. It was almost as if this sensual man knew the art of making love but had no concept of the emotions behind it. It was as if he viewed it as a skill he ticked off; one that he was proficient at. It made him kind of endearing, and it didn't stop her wanting him.

"Trust me," Caleb whispered, and then gave into the temptation to lick against the raging pulse in her neck. She shuddered at his touch, another sexy moan leaving her lips, and he suckled harder, fighting the urge to bite deep.

Rhianna moaned again, feeling her fear evaporate as her desire rose swiftly once more. She was aching to feel him slide deep inside her, to have him move within her and stroke her erotically. She shouldn't be responding to him like this, she was confused by her reactions, and the fact that she was actually naked in his sitting room, waiting for him to claim her.

Moreover, it would be a claiming. It would be outright possession and she knew it. Making love with Caleb would be like nothing she had ever experienced before and probably never would again after this one night.

"So exquisite," he murmured softly, stroking a long finger slowly against her cheekbone. His amber eyes were burning with desire, his jaw clenched as if he were struggling to hold himself back.

She shivered in pleasure, her breath rushing out in a harsh gasp. "Can you teach me, Caleb?" She wanted so badly to know the pleasure he'd hinted at earlier. She was certain that he was the correct choice of lover to show her what her body was capable of experiencing.

His eyes flared brightly, his lips curling sensually. "Did you really think your statement would make me change my mind about having you?" he asked with a hint of incredulity in his voice. "Rhianna, you won't be leaving this house until I have pleasured you into exhaustion."

The stark promise in his words made her stomach flip over and her breath rush out loudly. The heat in his eyes was an inferno, and his hand was suddenly at the nape of her neck, pulling her towards him. He stopped when their lips were a hairsbreadth apart.

"I'll show you pleasure you've never dreamed existed," he breathed against her lips.

Then he kissed her and she forgot who she was. His lips slanted over hers, his tongue brushing her lower lip boldly before slipping inside her mouth to taste her leisurely. She moaned into his mouth, her tongue reaching to taste him as he was tasting her.

Caleb's head spun as their lips touched, and lust coursed through his body. He had never tasted a woman so intoxicating before. Her lips were so soft, her tongue hesitant against his but quickly becoming bolder as she surrendered to his kiss. He was instantly caught in a dual lust. His fangs threatened to elongate and he had to fight his bloodlust hard to prevent her finding out what he was.

One kiss and he was at the edge of his control. Her mouth was more delicious, more deadly to his senses than the sweet taste of her body he had already indulged in. It was astounding that this woman could bring him, an Ancient, to the point of almost revealing his race by such a simple touch. Nevertheless, she was and his instincts were kicking in wildly, his hand tightening around the back of her neck.

He was an Ancient of his people, but he was also a Council Enforcer, called upon to take on Assignments to protect their race when humans came too close to discovering their existence. He was proficient in the art of mind control, slipping into fragile human minds and steering them from the course they were on. However, sometimes that skill was worthless. Sometimes more direct methods were required when a human had a natural shield that prevented him from using his abilities. When that occurred he had to use other means to protect his people. Violent means.

Caleb Ryder could kill with no hint of remorse. He had done so before, and would most probably do so again. A human life was a small price to pay to keep his people safe. He took no pleasure from the killing, but he felt no guilt for it either. Vampires didn't have emotions. Not for humans or Weres. They could form deep attachments to their own kind but the other races meant nothing to them. Weres were despised and humans were simply food and sexual release.

If a vampire became attached to a human then they Sired them into their race. On a very odd occasion, they would leave them human and choose to take them under their protection, but that practice was almost non-existent now. Humans had such short life spans none of his kind were willing to suffer the pain of losing them when they died after a few short decades.

The woman in his arms was threatening his control. He was seconds away from revealing himself to her and endangering his race. His thoughts were clouded, too disjointed to test her mind to see if she was one of the compliant ones. His fingers tightened fractionally around her nape. One little burst of strength and her neck would break, snapping like a twig.

Caleb realised what he was doing and slowly released his hold on her, easing back and taking a deep breath as he fought to get his feral side under control. He was better than this. He didn't go around losing control like a new-born Youngling. What was it about this woman that affected him so much?

A few deep breaths and he was in control again, his feral nature hidden deep within himself. He was reluctant to destroy the innocent creature before him. She piqued his interest, and stirred his blood as no other.

He could slip into her mind now his control was back, and yet he didn't. He was afraid to in case he found she was a natural shield. If he discovered that then his choices would be taken from him. No, he had to maintain the cold discipline he was famed for.

He stared into Rhianna's face for a long moment and then he kissed her again slowly.

This time his control held, and he savoured her softness, running his hands slowly down her body until he cupped her breasts gently. Relief washed through him, followed swiftly by the deep hunger she spurred in him. Slowly and methodically, he teased her to arousal, brushing his thumbs over her taut peaks until she cried out softly and shivered against him.

His lips trailed over her heated flesh, sliding lower as he kissed every inch of her creamy white skin, licking and nibbling as she moaned softly and clutched at his shoulders. His natural dominance loved how she clung helplessly to him. It was a primal thing, so intrinsically male that it spanned all races, human, vampire and Were. Having a woman submit to the pleasure a man gave them brought out the predator in a man, he became the hunter, and the female became the prey.

The beautiful redhead under his hands was indeed his prey, and he intended to mark her delectable body so all others would know he had claimed her. The thought surprised him, and he stiffened for a moment, before her sweet scent captivated him again, and he continued down her body.

Rhianna surrendered to his touch, her hands sliding down to his chest as his fingers stroked her body relentlessly. His muscles contracted under her fingers, a low animal sounding growl erupting from his throat sending a thrill through her body.

Caleb's head rose, and there was something so feral in his expression that her heart fluttered wildly and she moaned softly, liquid heat scything through her to gather between her thighs. She was embarrassingly wet down there, could see his nostrils flaring as his eyes darkened to a rich, deep shade of amber. He was scenting her arousal. She had noticed that scent played a large part in Caleb's life by the way he had scented her neck earlier, the way he had inhaled so close to her body before his wicked mouth had ravished her until she had shuddered and cried out her pleasure.

He used all of his senses to full effect when he made love, which was probably why he was so damned good at it and she was a quivering wreck, almost at the point of begging him shamelessly to complete the act, to come inside her body and drive her wild with pleasure.

She leaned forward and pressed her lips to his chest, delighting when another throaty growl escaped him and his hand threaded in her hair and held her to his hot skin. His taste filled her mouth, hot, heady, primal and masculine. Her tongue flicked lightly against his nipple and he shuddered.

"Harder."

Another order, another demand that made her shiver with pleasure as she realised that her touch was as heady to him as his was to her. Any nerves she'd had about not being good at this faded, and she rasped her tongue more boldly against him.

"Bite," he ordered, his voice sounding strained, his body taut with need.

Rhianna scraped her teeth against the hard peak and a deep groan left him, his fingers digging almost painfully into her scalp. She repeated the caress and then moved across his chest and treated his other nipple to the same fierce nip.

Caleb shuddered wildly at her soft teeth scraping over his skin. Her hot mouth was sending fire spreading through his body, his imagination running rampant at the thought of how her sweet lips would feel against other parts of his body. He could feel his feral side rising again, and knew if he lost control, he could possibly hurt her. He didn't want to hurt this delightful woman, this strange blend of innocence and passion with a hint of fragility which ran deep within her.

Reluctantly he pulled her mouth from his body, bearing her back against the rug to loom over her. His need was at fever pitch and so was hers. The time for play was over; it was time to possess, to claim, and to indulge the dual lusts that drove him.

Caleb watched her face as his fingers danced down her luscious body, sliding between her legs to feel her wetness, to stroke against her molten heat. He pressed a finger deep inside her, watching her arch up to his touch, a sweet cry leaving her lips. Her pleasure was written all over her exquisite face, her lips parted, her cheeks flushed with colour as he moved his finger deep within her. He pressed another digit inside, teasing her body into readiness for his. She made the most incredibly sexy sounds as he stroked her, his cock throbbing with each throaty moan.

Gripping her hips firmly, he positioned himself at her opening, no longer able to deny himself. He had to slide deep inside her, had to feel her tight warmth embrace him. Her eyes flew open and he saw a hint of hesitancy in their stunning lavender depths.

She still felt doubt. Her body reacted with desire, but her mind still held back. It angered him that she couldn't let go completely, couldn't allow herself to just feel. The brief burst of anger soothed almost instantly as another emotion came over him, one he didn't recognise but reacted to instinctively.

"I would never hurt you," he said softly, moving his hands under her back to raise her up. He sat back on his knees again, pulling her astride him, their bodies touching but still not yet joined. Her wet heat caressed him and he groaned softly.

"What if I disappoint you, Caleb?" she whispered, burying her head in the side of his neck, her breath caressing his skin and making him shudder.

His arms held her tightly, raising her body until she was aligned with his. "You could never disappoint me." The words came out with little thought to what he was saying. He was pulling her onto him as he pressed up to begin his journey into her body.

Caleb found he had no control over his reactions to her. What should have been a night of satisfaction of his two basic urges was turning into something he didn't understand, and didn't want to understand. All he knew was he wanted to pleasure the beautiful redhead in his arms as much as he wanted to take pleasure from her.

He pressed deeply, pulling her onto him until they were fully joined. The heat that exploded through him took his breath away. She was perfection, made for him. Holding her tightly, he stroked into her body, her sweet cries filling the air along with her intoxicating scent.

He moved with long, deep strokes, taking her gently until he was sure her doubts were completely gone, that she was lost in the heady bliss of their bodies riding together. Then he bore her back to the rug, increasing the pace of his movements, his lips feverish against the side of her neck as his bloodlust rose swiftly.

He needed to feed. The deep rich scent of her blood was pulsing through him, making his gums ache with the need for his fangs to be buried in her sweat slickened skin. His tongue rasped over her body, sliding down to her breast to lick and nibble at the hard tip.

Rhianna was mindless with pleasure, her body humming as Caleb did such wicked things with his hands and mouth and the hard, thick masculine heart of him. She moved with him, clutching onto his shoulders as he suckled at her breast and moved harder and faster within her. She couldn't breathe, tension surrounding her, coiling deep inside her as she felt herself climbing steadily higher towards a fall which she knew would be exquisite and yet terrifying as well. Caleb had the power to give so much pleasure that everything would pale into insignificance afterwards. She knew she would never be the same again after this one night with him.

His bloodlust hit critical point. Caleb's fangs elongated as he felt Rhianna reach the peak of her pleasure. She shattered with a lusty scream and in that moment, he pierced the fragile skin of her breast. His soothing toxin immediately took away the brief sting of pain and heightened the intensity of her climax. Her rich, warm blood filled his eager mouth, and he suckled hard, his head spinning from the combination of her body gripping his so painfully tightly, and the intoxicating flavour of her life essence trickling down his throat.

Caleb ground into her hard and pulsed deeply, ecstasy rippling through his body as he bathed her with his seed, enhancing her own pleasure with his. He pulled against her breast once more and then carefully extracted his fangs, instantly healing the small wounds with his tongue as he shuddered once more and surged deep within her.

His heart thundered hard in his chest as he rested against her body for a moment before he withdrew slowly and lay beside her on his back. He couldn't remember the last time he'd taken such pleasure from a woman. It had definitely been a long time, of that he was sure.

He lay there with his eyes closed, savouring the pleasure he'd received and the feel of her hot blood coursing through his veins. His reaction to Rhianna had been out of the norm, and he knew he would need to address that, but for the moment he was too sated to care. She had been totally amazing, so utterly fascinating, engaging him on a level he hadn't expected. His big body still hummed with the sweet bliss she had given him and a slow, satisfied smile curved his sensual lips.

He finally turned his head to the side and saw Rhianna had fallen asleep beside him. It was to be expected after the way he had ridden her body and pleasured her. In addition, he had exhausted her even further by feeding from her.

He slowly ran a hand down her side and over her hip but she didn't stir. His fingers tangled in the silky softness of her luxurious hair, and he trailed it slowly threw his fingers. It was like a living flame in the glow of the firelight, rich and deep, and so soft he found it hard to let go.

Smiling contently, Caleb rose from the rug. He didn't bother dressing again. He was only going to bed, so it was pointless doing so. He grabbed a thick woollen throw from over the sofa and placed it almost reverently over the sleeping woman. She would be comfortable enough on the rug, it was thick and the heat of the dying fire, plus the throw, would keep her warm enough until morning. Grabbing his clothes, he headed upstairs to his private rooms, feeling more satisfied than he had in a long time.

Rhianna woke when the first rays of sunlight filtered into the room through the large French doors. For a moment she lay there, completely disorientated, wondering where she was. Then her memory returned and she gasped and blushed, sitting up straight and groaning softly at the slight discomfort between her thighs.

She looked around the room seeing no sign of Caleb. Her face burned hotter as she thought of what they'd done the night before, of what she'd done. She had actually gone home with a complete stranger and had sex with him.

She couldn't believe she had behaved so wantonly, so out of character for her. It didn't help that she'd enjoyed it so much either, that she'd actually participated so eagerly in her own ravishment at the hands of the stunningly beautiful man.

The pleasure Caleb had all but ripped from her body had been the most mind-blowing experience of her life. Her one time with her ex-boyfriend had been painful, made her feel dirty, and used, but she didn't feel that with Caleb. He had pushed her to orgasm after orgasm, before he'd taken his own pleasure from her. It had been hot and wild and so incredibly erotic.

Groaning again, she jumped up from the rug looking for her clothes. She found them where Caleb had left them the night before, folded neatly on the sofa. She dressed hastily feeling less exposed once she had done so. What was she supposed to do now? What did women do in these circumstances? Should she wait for Caleb to wake up or should she just leave? She didn't even know if she wanted to see Caleb again.

She muttered a curse under her breath and looked for her purse. It was on the sofa too, so she quickly grabbed it and dug out her cell phone. It was just after six am and she knew Millie would kill her, but she phoned her friend anyway.

"What!" Millie yelled down the phone, her voice thick with sleep and irritation.

"Millie, it's me," Rhianna whispered. "I need you to come get me."

"Annie?" her friend said incredulously. "Honey, what's wrong? Where are you? Has something happened to you?" Her tone was immediately concerned.

"I'm fine, Mills," Rhianna said reassuringly. "I just need a lift home. I kind of went out last night to a club and did something a bit stupid. I'm now at some guy's house and I need to get home now." Total silence greeted her and for a moment she thought her friend had gone back to sleep.

"Have you lost your fucking mind?" Millie gasped in shock, now sounding fully awake and also very angry. "You said you'd taken a sleeping pill. You lied to me! How did you know this guy wasn't some kind of raving lunatic?"

Rhianna sighed. "Can we dissect my behaviour later, Mills?" she asked patiently. She knew her friend was right and that her anger was justified. She had done an incredibly stupid thing, so out of character for her. Moreover, she had never once lied to Millie. She knew that would hurt her friend deeply because they were all each other had now.

"I'm at the big white mansion on Forrester Road. Will you please come and get me?"

"I'll be there in twenty," her friend answered, and the phone disconnected.

Grabbing her jacket, which she found on the hall table, Rhianna slipped quietly out of the house and headed down the long driveway to await her friend.

CHAPTER THREE

"Just exactly what did you think you were doing?" Millicent Cooper demanded as Rhianna pulled open the passenger door of her run down Ford Fiesta and climbed in.

She sighed loudly as she turned to look at her irate friend. Millie's black curls were in wild disarray around her head and it was obvious she had only run her fingers through them rather than brushed her hair. Her cobalt blue eyes were sparkling with anger and disbelief at Rhianna's reckless behaviour.

Even rumpled and still wearing her pyjamas, Millie looked stunning. She had a classical beauty that invariably drove men wild and generated lots of date offers, which she normally refused. She was much taller than Rhianna, standing at five feet seven inches with a generously curved body, which suited her height perfectly. She wasn't heavy in any fashion, just curvy in all the right places.

"Can we just go, Mills?" Rhianna said quietly, glancing nervously at the white mansion, half-expecting to see Caleb appear in the doorway.

"Fine," her friend grumbled, "but don't think for one minute this conversation is over. I can't believe you lied to me last night. If you wanted to go out then you should have told me. You know I would have gone with you."

She paused for breath and then started again. "Annie, I know things are tough for you right now," her voice faltered, and she swallowed to contain her emotions. "But you're not behaving naturally. This…this…Christ, I'm picking you up from a total stranger's bed!"

"Rug," Rhianna corrected her, staring out the side window as they drove down the forest road.

"What?" Millie asked perplexed, her rant cut off by her friend's interjection.

"We didn't use a bed; we fucked on a rug before an open fire."

Millie sucked in a deep breath, worry shivering through her at the lifeless note in Rhianna's voice and the coarse way she spoke about herself. Annie didn't talk like that; she very seldom cursed and it was usually the milder imprecations she used when she did.

"Annie, talk to me. Please. I'm worried about you. I don't mean to yell but I can't think of any other way to get through to you right now."

"Maybe I don't want you to." The flat answer that came back broke Millie's heart and she wished for the thousandth time she could think of a way to reach her friend.

Her failure made her angry again, and her voice was sharp when she next spoke. "I don't ever want to hear you talk about yourself like that again, Annie," she said through clenched teeth. "You're not some promiscuous slut who has sex at the drop of a hat. Don't denigrate yourself that way. You're obviously not acting as you normally would at the moment."

Rhianna let her friend's angry words wash over her as she leaned back against the car seat and closed her eyes. She knew everything her friend was saying was true. She had done a very foolish thing going home with Caleb last night but that didn't mean she'd lost her moral compass. Thankfully, he hadn't turned out to be a weird axe murderer but the possibility had been there.

Taking risks wasn't her speciality. Millie was the one who was more outgoing, more adventurous, and more spontaneous. She knew her friend's anger was based out of concern for her, so she didn't take it personally. All she wanted to do was go home and have a nice long shower before she had to start dealing with reality again.

Millie had stopped ranting by the time they got home and was giving her the silent treatment as they walked upstairs to their apartment. Her shoulders were rigid with disapproval as she marched up the stairs in front of her and Rhianna couldn't help but smile slightly. She could almost see the steam coming out of Millie's ears she was so mad.

She waited for her friend to unlock the apartment door and then brushed swiftly passed her, heading into her room and locking the door behind her before Millie had enough time to register her intent. She heard her friend banging loudly on the door as she headed into her en-suite bathroom and started the shower.

"Open this door," Millie yelled. "Don't think you can hide in there from me, girl! You and I have a conversation to finish and I'm not going away until we do!"

"I'm having a shower," Rhianna yelled back. "I'll be out in a bit!" She closed the bathroom door and stripped quickly, stepping under the hot spray so she couldn't hear Millie any more. She stayed in the shower for a long time, gently soaping her aching body.

She had light bruises on her hips and deep love bites on the curve of her breasts. She hadn't even been aware of Caleb being so rough with her last night. The deep ache between her legs actually felt deliciously pleasant as well as tender. He had been so big and full inside her. She was still wet from his seed and she suddenly stifled a gasp. He'd come inside her, and she wasn't taking any contraception. Even worse, he might have some disease she didn't know about.

She groaned loudly, and rested her head against the cool tiles as the hot water sprayed over her back. Reckless wasn't the word for how she'd behaved last night. Downright irresponsible summed it up so much better. Crap, she'd have to go to the doctor for a prescription for the morning after pill. Her cheeks flushed scarlet at just the thought.

All because she had gone home with a man she didn't even know. A man who made it more than plain he didn't want to know her either. All he had wanted was sex and she had quite happily given it to him. Okay, so it was the best sex she'd ever had, but it still didn't make what she did any more palatable.

She was vaguely aware her hand was still between her legs and she felt a little shiver of pleasure course through her as she remembered Caleb pushing into her body. She moaned softly as she remembered how it felt to have Caleb thrusting hard and fast into her aching body. She had wanted him so badly, needed to feel him taking her forcefully. He was an extremely virile man, and he almost seemed to read her mind as he took his pleasure from her whilst giving her the most incredible pleasure in return.

She had just wanted to *feel*, and he had made her feel so alive she had soared through the sky on a wave of pure bliss. The ice around her heart suddenly cracked under the memory, as Millie's words resounded in her ears, and the smell of the trees returned from when they'd driven through the final place Rafe had walked.

A deep shudder wracked her body as his smiling face quickly came to mind. Sweet, gentle, loving Rafe. He was big brother, mother and father to her all rolled into one, and now he was gone. She would never see his deep brown eyes sparkle with humour again. Never watch the lazy smile curl over his wide lips. Never complain when he ruffled her auburn curls as if she was still six years old.

Rhianna turned the water off as a deep well of pain built up inside her. She grabbed a towel as the first deep sob wracked her body and she sank down onto the cold tiled floor, the towel clutched to her chest.

Rafe was gone. He was never coming back.

In a blink of an eye, her perfect life had turned upside down by a simple knock on the door. A knock that had shattered her so completely, she didn't know if she would ever be able to rebuild herself again.

The sounds that ripped from her throat resembled an animal in deep pain as she rocked on the bathroom floor, the ice wall she'd constructed so perfectly, crumbling completely within her. With no defences to protect her, she threw her head back and wailed out her anguish.

She was vaguely aware of Millie screaming loudly and banging on her bedroom door, her voice no longer angry, instead frantic with worry, but she couldn't drag herself up from the floor. She threw her head back again, and screamed her agony into the air, her tears flowing wildly down her face.

Not Rafe! Not her gentle, big brother whose only goal in life had been to make sure she was safe and cared for. He didn't deserve this. He deserved so much better in life than to die at the hands of some feral animal, alone, screaming in an agony that matched the one she was going through right now.

A loud crashing sound echoed into the bathroom, but she paid it no mind. She sobbed loudly, rocking in anguish as she felt Millie wrapping her arms around her and holding her tightly.

"I'm here, Annie," her friend whispered tearfully, stroking her wet hair and rocking with her. "You just let it all out, honey. I've got you."

Rhianna didn't know how long she sobbed and railed against the total injustice of losing Rafe. It must have been a long time, because her voice was hoarse by the time she was finished, and she had no more tears left, just a deep ache where her heart was.

Millie's face was streaked with tears too, her own grief coming out at the loss of the hulking man who had been as much of a big brother to her as Rhianna was her sister at heart. Getting the phone call this morning had shocked her and worried her so badly she'd yelled at Rhianna and forced her more into herself instead of opening up to her. The haunting wails coming from the bathroom had terrified her and ripped at her very soul. She'd never heard anyone in so much pain before.

When her friend's sobs subsided, Millie helped her to her feet, grabbing her bathrobe, and helping her into it.

"Sorry, Mills," her friend said numbly, her face a mask of grief.

"You've nothing to be sorry for, honey," Millie answered gently. "It's me who should be apologising." She led her into the bedroom and Rhianna gasped in shock as she stared at the ruin that had formally been her bedroom door. Lying on the floor was a large sledgehammer.

"Like I said, I should be the one apologising," Millie said sheepishly. "I kind of killed your bedroom door, hon."

Rhianna felt a bubble of laughter escape her as she stared at the ruins with wide eyes. "Rafe to the rescue again," she smiled sadly, looking at the large sledgehammer which belonged to her brother.

Millie's smile echoed hers. "Good old Rafe, always there when you need him." she sighed softly.

"I don't know what I'm going to do without him, Millie," Rhianna said tearfully sinking down onto her bed. "He's taken care of me all my life. He's always been there to pick me up when I fall."

"I know, honey. I'm kind of trying to figure out what I'll do without him too," Millie sighed sitting beside her and putting an arm around her shoulder. "He had such a big, kind heart. Didn't think twice about adopting me as his little sister too when we became friends. It's a bloody tragedy that someone so kind and gentle gets taken from this world when there are so many evil bastards out there."

Rhianna sat quietly, staring blankly ahead as she tried to get a grip of her erratic emotions. So this was what grief felt like. She didn't like it one bit. It was white-hot pain and terrible cramps in her stomach. It was her heart slowly shattering into a million pieces never to be the same again once it put itself back together.

"I'm sorry if I scared you by staying out last night," she finally said quietly. "I just couldn't face dealing with it, Mills. I just wanted to pretend it hadn't happened. Just for a little longer. I know it was stupid and reckless. I promise I'll never do anything like it again."

Her friend sighed and scooted under the covers, pulling her with her and cuddling into her back. "You have marks on your skin," she commented. "The man you were with last night, he didn't hurt you?"

Rhianna shook her head. "No, he didn't hurt me," she answered with a deep sigh. "It was actually pretty incredible if I'm honest about it."

She went silent, staring at her bedroom wall with unseeing eyes. "Do you think I'm so terribly bad, Mills? Am I some kind of heartless person because I took pleasure in sex last night when I've just lost Rafe?"

Millie hugged her tightly, hearing the deep pain in her voice. "You couldn't be bad or heartless if you tried, honey," she whispered softly. "It's not uncommon for people to seek some kind of affirmation of life when they lose someone they loved so much. Don't feel bad for needing the comfort of a man last night. Rafe wouldn't want you to ever feel guilty for being alive, Annie."

She held her friend tightly as she began to weep again, more softly this time, the raw animalistic pain now spent, replaced by a deep aching sadness. She whispered comfortingly to her, stroking her auburn curls gently until she finally cried herself to sleep.

~~~~~

The scent of coffee on the air was prevalent, and it brought a smile to his face. It was hard not to be happy when he was in the company of the two most precious people in his world, Annie and Millie, his baby sister and her lifelong best friend.

Millie was grumbling and giving him dirty looks for having woken her up so early, but he knew she didn't truly mind. Annie was face deep in the mocha he'd greeted her at the door with, the chocolaty coffee concoction a sure fire way to earn her forgiveness for the early hour.

The need to see them before he headed off on his camping trip had been overwhelming. He wasn't used to being out of contact with them for any length of time despite the fact they didn't live with him anymore. He guessed he would never get used to not having his Annie living in his home. He'd been her primary guardian since their parents had died when she was only three and he had just turned eighteen.

His happiness was complete, his love for the two extraordinary women in his world absolute...but something was tugging at him, something was pulling him away from the warmth and contentment, something dark and insidious, something wild and feral.

NO! He wanted to stay with them. He didn't want to leave! He tried to cry out, he tried to call their names, but they were fading before his eyes, and they didn't appear to notice he was disappearing....Annie, come back! Millie, can you hear me?

A low, deep growl was the only answer, an agonising burst of pain along every joint in his body the only thing he could feel. They were gone and so was he, in his place a feral animal howling and growling. Blood! Kill! Blood...Kill...

~~~~

The moment passed, how long it had taken to pass he didn't know, but he was more himself - at least he thought he was. It was night now, and the scent of the wilderness was all around him. He was camping; one of his favourite activities and one he'd had to give up when it was clear Annie and Millie were not the camping kind of girls.

He hadn't minded really, he knew he would one day go back to communing with nature when the girls grew up. He had always loved nature and animals, he had been about to go to university to study to be a Vet when his parents had died and he'd been left to care for Annie instead. Again, it was a sacrifice that he had never regretted having to make. He wouldn't trade his time with Annie for anything in the world, his baby sister who was more like a daughter to him than a sibling.

Now he was in the trees, listening to the sound of the nocturnal animals around him. Something was off though, something didn't feel right. He swung his flashlight around in a wide arc, hearing a noise behind him as he did.

A prickle against the back of his neck was all the warning he received. He started to turn just as the animal at his back sprang with a feral snarl sounding through the cool night air. Insane yellow eyes were all that registered before sharp teeth sank into the muscles of the forearm he'd raised instinctually to protect himself.

He felt shock rock through his body, followed by pain so sharp he thought he would pass out instantly from the sheer intensity of it. Fear swiftly followed the other sensations. He was being attacked by a wild animal, and the brief glance he'd had of its eyes told him the wolf was feral.

He lashed out with his other hand, hitting the animal with the flashlight he still carried as he cried out in agony as a chunk of flesh was ripped from his arm. His eyes watered, his vision swam, and he felt his knees give way.

Self-preservation kicked in instantly. He was on his knees before the wolf, a sitting target for its next strike. He lashed out furiously, catching the animal on the side of its head as it sprang again. His blow was powerful, but nowhere near strong enough to cause any real damage to the wolf. It backed off briefly, but only so it could launch another attack from a different angle.

He screamed as powerful jaws clenched around his shoulder, biting deep into the meaty part of his flesh, effectively rendering that arm useless. Even insane, the wolf had enough intelligence to work out how to render its prey helpless, and he knew he had only moments left. Blood was pouring profusely from his wounds and he was starting to lose consciousness. The instant that happened, the wolf would go for the killing blow- his throat.

Tears ran down his face as he fought to stay awake. His sudden inexplicable need to visit his girls before his trip came to mind. Had he somehow known it would be the last time he would see them?

He was terrified of dying, not for himself, but for his Annie. She was so young, so innocent, and fragile. His death would crush her tender spirit in such a way she may never fully recover. He cursed himself for being so overprotective of her, for sheltering her so much. Maybe she wouldn't be so shattered by his death if he'd allowed her to be more independent, less reliant on him.

Millie would be distraught but she was a fighter. Her tough childhood had hardened her to the blows that life meted out from time to time. He could only pray that Millie would be strong enough to help his baby girl through the nightmare that was coming their way.

More searing agony rocked his body as the wolf ripped into his torn flesh. "Annie," he groaned, coughing up blood as his vision swam. "I'm so sorry."

~~~~~

Rafe Armand opened his eyes and wondered why the pain was gone. He lay still against the warm padded floor of the very white room, his deep brown eyes trying to adjust to the brightness around him. Where was he? What had happened to him? He knew the memories were there somewhere, but he couldn't seem to reach for them no matter how hard he tried.

He sat up gingerly, waiting for the pain to come again, but his shoulder didn't ache the way it had the other two or three times he'd woken up. Memory returned slowly and he looked around the white padded room slowly. He *had* woken up in the same room before, he was sure of it. There was no furniture, just endless white padding covering the floor, the walls and even the ceiling. Hell, even the door was padded in thick whiteness, only this time there were deep gouges in it as if some wild animal had clawed madly to get out.

Once more, he was naked as he had been every time he'd awakened. How long had he spent in this padded cell? Time didn't seem to make sense to him at the moment. He started with surprise when he heard a key in the door, and moved swiftly back into the farthest corner he could, his big body coiling protectively around him. This was new. No one had come in the door before. He was tense and alert, and extremely wary as a large man entered the room and closed the door quickly behind him.

The man was over six feet tall and very broad in the shoulders and chest. He was dressed completely in denim and had long black hair, which was tied at the nape of his neck. His deep blue eyes were sharp, and showed a keen intelligence as well as a hint of wariness as he regarded Rafe. He held his hands up in a gesture, which plainly said he meant no harm. He didn't come any further into the room, merely rested against the door.

"My name is Jared Hanlon," he said quietly. "Can you tell me your name?"

It seemed such a silly question to Rafe. Why would the man think he wouldn't know his own name? "Rafe Armand," he answered carefully, his eyes intent on the man.

"Pleased to meet you, Rafe," Jared said with a slight curve of his lips as if he were pleased about something. "I know you're probably feeling pretty confused right now. You must be wondering why you're here in this room. It's for your own protection. You're going through some...changes at the moment. The changes can be pretty violent at times so the padding is to ensure you don't hurt yourself too much."

"What kind of changes?" Rafe growled. "And why am I naked? I want some clothes." He looked up at the video camera in the corner above the door. They were watching him, and he didn't like the fact he was naked for anyone to see.

"You'll only destroy the clothes we give you," Jared replied, his tone patient. He'd had this exact same conversation too often in the last six months. Finding the rogue was starting to become a real issue.

The man before him was the fifth forced turning so far and the first that looked like it might reach a suitable conclusion. The other three men and one woman had gone insane and died. Rafe must have a strong character to be able to converse intelligently with him. He must have a very strong desire to live.

"I want clothes," Rafe persisted. "You want to spy on me with your camera? You're not getting any sick pleasure out of my nakedness!" He could feel his temper bubbling under the surface, a need to rip out the throat of the man before him. The thought stunned him as soon as he had it and he blinked slowly.

"What have you done to me?" he whispered horrified. "There's something inside me, something evil that wants to take over me! What have you done?" He literally screamed the last words at the man and saw him tense, his gaze becoming even more wary.

"Be calm, Rafe," Jared said firmly, using his Command tone and hoping it would register with the furious man before him. He watched him blink again and frown slightly as the command washed over him, but he seemed to settle slightly.

"We haven't done anything to you, Rafe," he said calmly raising his hands again to help ease the man down a bit further. "You're right about something being done to you, however it wasn't us. You were bitten while you were camping. We found you and brought you here to try to help you."

The moment Jared mentioned being bitten Rafe's memory flooded back, and he groaned in fear and shrank further into the corner. He'd gotten up to pee. The night had been well lit due to the large full moon in the sky but he'd taken a flashlight anyway. He'd finished relieving himself and was about to go back to camp when a wild animal had flown at him, knocking him down.

The memories crashed within him, the gut wrenching fear, the excruciating pain. Knowing he was weakening and about to die. The last thing he remembered was seeing Rhianna's face before him and whispering her name. He knew it would break her heart when he died. Then there was only blackness until he first woke up in this white room.

"Annie," he whispered, his eyes filling with tears as he turned to look at the man called Jared. "How long have I been here? Does Annie know I'm okay?"

Jared frowned and stifled down a deep sigh. This was going to make things more difficult. Rafe obviously had someone he cared about in the outside world. "Rafe, I need you to listen very carefully to me," he said. "The wolf that attacked you was no ordinary wolf. He was what you would most probably call a werewolf. He is part man, part wolf. When he bit you, he passed the infection onto you, changing you. You are what we call a forced turning. Someone who had been turned into a Were against their will."

Rafe stared at him blankly, slowly shaking his head in denial. There were no such things as werewolves. They were a figment of someone's very active imagination. Why the hell was this man standing there feeding him this garbage? He wanted clothes, and he wanted to go home to Rhianna and no one was going to stop him.

He growled low in his chest feeling something stir deep inside him. He was leaving this room even if he had to go through the man in front of the door to achieve his goal. He tried to stand up but found he couldn't. The man was talking again, and he felt something tug in his head, but he shook it to get free of it. He moved forward dropping onto his hands and knees and staring in shock as he watched his hands start to change a fraction of a second before he felt a deep pain inside him.

He threw back his head and tried to scream, but instead issued an agonised howl as his face started to ripple and change. He felt bones being pulled and tugged in every direction, loud popping noises occurring in time with the pain. He whimpered and fell to his side, letting out another long howl as his body shifted around him. Then mercifully the pain was gone, and he tried to stand up.

He fell down immediately, his mind registering complete shock as he realised his feet weren't there anymore. In their place were paws, four big enormous paws completely covered in dark brown fur. He lifted a paw, and held it up to his face and touched a long snout. He whimpered again, threw back his head, and howled for what felt like forever.

When he finally stopped howling he turned to the man Jared, but instead of a man he found a large black wolf before him, deep blue eyes watching him intently.

"*Be calm, Rafe,*" he heard Jared say in his head, and he looked around for the man but only found the wolf before him.

"*What?*" he gasped, hearing his throat rumble but no words come from it. He couldn't talk!

"*I can hear you, Rafe,*" Jared said patiently, his tone soothing as he sensed the wolf's panic. "*You can talk to me like this too. Just think what you want to say.*"

"*I'm a wolf,*" Rafe half sobbed. "*I'm not human anymore.*" The full impact of the changes that had befallen him almost crushed him. He wasn't human anymore; he was some kind of wild beast now.

The black wolf approached him carefully and lay down so as not to intimidate him.

"You are a Were now, Rafe. You are not some mindless, wild beast," Jared said soothingly. *"When you learn control, you will be able to call your wolf form at will and will no longer be subject to these uncontrolled shifts. You are doing very well. This is the third time you've reverted to wolf form and the first you have been coherent enough to understand what has happened to you and be able to communicate with me. The other two times you were pretty mindless and acted on instinct to get out of the room."*

"Who are you?" Rafe asked miserably, lying down across from the other wolf.

"I am Jared Hanlon as I told you, and I am the Alpha of the Hanlon Pack."

"Alpha?" Rafe queried. *"Is that like the boss or something?"* He blinked when the large wolf raised his head slightly and grinned at him. A wolf could actually grin? For some reason Rafe found that even weirder than everything else that had happened so far.

"I suppose Boss is one way of terming it," Jared answered. *"I lead the pack, yes. I am the Alpha and everyone is beneath me. They do as I say when I say it. You are now part of my pack, Rafe. You cannot return to your old life, it would be too dangerous. It takes a lot of training to learn to control your wolf. Your forced turning makes you particularly volatile. If you were to return to your old life you might accidentally harm those you care about. I am sure you wouldn't want to harm Annie in any way."*

Rafe growled loudly and jumped up, pacing away from the black wolf. The thought of even accidentally scratching Rhianna, of possibly turning her into the monster he now was, made him want to howl loudly. He could understand the wisdom in the Alpha's words but his heart was breaking too.

"I'm all she has, Jared," he said forlornly. *"I've taken care of her since she was three years old and our parents died. I've dedicated my life to ensure she was always safe and happy. Her heart will break when she knows she will never see me again."*

Jared could feel the other man's pain and he really felt for him. He didn't want to add to his pain but he believed in being totally honest with his pack. *"I'm sorry, Rafe, but you should know that she will already have been informed of your death. You've been here three weeks already. There was enough of your flesh for the police to find and perform a DNA test on. Your Annie will have most probably buried you by now."*

The shock of his words rocked Rafe to the core, and his pain washed over him at the thought of Annie and Millie arranging his funeral, crying as an empty casket was lowered beside their parents' graves. The wolf howled within him and retreated, and he was once more a man lying balled up on the floor, weeping for the life now lost to him forever.

Jared left Rafe to his grief and shifted back to human form before knocking on the door to be let out. Aaron waited outside with a pair of jeans for him. He slipped them on silently with a wry smile. He hadn't expected to have to shift today otherwise he'd have worn an old pair of sweats before entering the safe room. He hated ruining a perfectly good pair of jeans, but it was part and parcel of the life of a Were.

"Arrange some sweats for him," he told Aaron, "and socialise him a bit more. Have different people entering with his food and water. A small amount of small talk is permissible, but no direct answering of any questions regarding pack life or what's happened to him. I'll deal with those questions. If he asks for me, let me know as soon as possible."

Aaron nodded and gave his Alpha a tight smile. He'd been working the safe room ever since the man had been brought in, and he couldn't help being impressed with Rafe's progress. Being coherent during a shift so early on boded well for his chances. "He's one big wolf, boss," he said to Jared who nodded his agreement.

"I think he may be an Alpha," Jared sighed. "He was able to shake off my command when he was shifting." He met Aaron's light blue eyes and saw a note of concern in them. He understood his friend's concern.

There could only be one Alpha in a pack. If Rafe truly was an Alpha, then it could create major problems once he joined the pack properly. He could even challenge Jared for his role as Alpha. He turned and walked away leaving his beta to take care of Rafe.

~~~~

Rhianna didn't know how she'd made it through the last few weeks. Millie had been there for her constantly. She had helped her every step of the way and they had spent many a night huddled in either hers or Millie's beds crying out their joint grief.

Letting her friend in had opened up a floodgate of emotions that threatened to cripple her, and yet she knew she had to work through her grief. Still, she felt so alone. She knew she had Millie, but Rafe was her last blood connection in the world and she couldn't help but feel completely orphaned. She knew she had to start pulling herself together, had to start thinking about going back to work and getting on with life, but it just felt insurmountable.

She alternated between having good days and very bad days. On the bad days, she could barely drag herself out of bed and even Millie couldn't reach her. The insistent ringing of the doorbell dragged her out of bed on one of her bad days. Millie was at work and Rhianna tried to ignore the bell, however, whoever was there wouldn't give up. Cursing loudly, she pulled on her dressing gown and all but ran to the door. She yanked it open furiously.

"What the fuck do you want?!" she screamed at the strange man on her doorstep.

Jared Hanlon actually took a step back from the tiny red-haired woman screaming at him. He blinked in surprise as he stared down at her. She was in her nightclothes, and her long auburn curls were tumbling wildly about her pretty face.

Lavender eyes flashed at him, and he could see the deep pain within them, could see the tiny lines of grief around her eyes and mouth. He could also see the resemblance to Rafe in the woman before him, and he struggled not to show any sign of recognition. "Pardon me, Miss, but I'm looking for Rhianna Armand. Is she at home?" He kept his voice level and very neutral.

Rhianna stared at him open mouthed, and then suddenly blushed scarlet. She had just screamed at the man and yet he was so polite to her, acting as if she hadn't just behaved like a screaming banshee. She swallowed slowly. "I'm Rhianna Armand," she managed to get out. "What can I do for you, Mr....?"

"Hanlon, Jared Hanlon." The gorgeous man responded. "I'm here about the estate of your brother, Rafe Armand. Would now be a convenient time to discuss this with you or would you prefer for me to make an appointment for another time?"

The mere mention of Rafe brought tears to her eyes and she looked down to hide them from him. She stepped back and allowed the man to enter her apartment. "Have a seat," she said quietly. "If you'll just give me a few minutes, I'll get dressed."

She didn't even stop to see his reaction, she turned and fled into her bedroom and closed her new door behind her. She doubled over and let the tears come. There was no point in fighting them, they would come whether she wanted them to or not. Smothering her sobs with her hands to muffle the sound, Rhianna headed into her bathroom and closed the door.

Jared's enhanced hearing could pick up Rhianna's sobs and he sighed sadly at her pain. He'd promised Rafe he would check up on his sister, make sure she was okay. He had also told him he'd provide financially for the girl until she could get back on her feet.

Rafe's closeness towards his sister was clearly reciprocated. The girl was in immense pain at the loss of her brother, and he truly wished there was something he could do to ease both of their pain, anything other than revealing the truth that was.

He put down his briefcase and took off his jacket when he heard the sound of the shower going on. He headed across the open plan great room into the kitchen area and decided to make some coffee for both of them. The next half hour or so was going to be difficult for him, and probably excruciating for Rhianna. A coffee seemed the least he could do.

He was sitting at the breakfast table sipping his coffee when she finally left her bedroom. She stared at him for a long, silent moment, before she crossed the room and sat down in front of him.

"I didn't know what you take so I left it black," he said as she looked down at the cup of coffee before her.

Rhianna flushed with embarrassment and look at him. "I'm really sorry about that screaming stuff," she said self-consciously. "I'm still trying to come to terms with...you know...and some days are more difficult than others."

Jared smiled gently at her, his blue eyes warm. "Think nothing of it, Miss Armand."

Rhianna rose and went to put a sugar and some milk in her coffee. "Please, it's Annie," she finally said as she sat back down.

"And I'm Jared," he smiled. "I'm sorry if appearing out of the blue like this upset you, Annie. I've been trying to get in touch with you for a couple of weeks now and haven't been able to. I really did need to get the estate sorted out as soon as possible."

Rhianna frowned as she looked at the gorgeous man across from her. He didn't look like a solicitor or whatever the person was who dealt with death estates. He had more of an untamed look about him even if he was wearing an Armani suit.

"You keep mentioning an estate, Jared. I went through all of Rafe's paperwork and there was nothing there to indicate he'd taken out any kind of insurance policy. He was only thirty-six years old and had no family apart from myself. He probably hadn't seen a need to think about that kind of thing."

Jared was prepared for this, and smiled gently at her. "He'd lodged the paperwork with a firm of solicitors," he lied smoothly. "When his obituary appeared in the paper they located the paperwork and approached me about the pay-out. You were listed as the sole beneficiary of his estate which I believe you have already cleared so therefore the cheque is all yours."

She nodded numbly, only half wondering why Rafe had never told her about it. He usually told her everything when it came to financial matters. She managed a weak smile as she sipped at her coffee.

"I can't imagine it will be that much," she said quietly. Rafe had worked labouring jobs. The money was reasonable but not exactly the kind of money which would allow a huge life insurance policy.

"On the contrary, Annie, your brother appears to have been very concerned about your well-being should anything untoward happen to him," Jared answered. He clicked open his briefcase and pulled out some legal documents and a cheque. "Rafe insured himself for the sum of one million dollars. I just need you to sign these legal documents and the cheque is all yours."

Her mouth dropped open and she stared at him in shock. The man wasn't looking at her, his head staring down at the documents before him as he quickly leafed through the sheets of paper. "Did you just say one MILLION dollars?" she stammered, her eyes wide, her mind whirling madly as she blinked at him.

He looked up at her in surprise. "Yes, one million dollars," he repeated slowly.

"There has to be some mistake," Rhianna gasped, jumping up from the table and beginning to pace in agitation. "There is no way on the planet Rafe could afford to take out a policy with that kind of pay-out. I know my brother very well and I know he couldn't have afforded something like that." She turned to look at Jared, her eyes narrowing at his surprised expression.

He rose slowly. "I can assure you, Annie, your brother did take out the policy and that was the agreed upon amount of life coverage he requested. If you read through the documents you can see for yourself."

"But how?" she asked, clutching at her stomach. "This just doesn't make sense!"

Anything he was about to say was cut off by the sound of a key in the front door and Millicent Cooper walking in. The instant the tall, curvy dark haired woman entered the apartment Jared's wolf howled loudly and he stiffened in shock.

Millie looked from her friend's anxious expression to the tall handsome man looming over her and she actually growled. An honest to goodness growl erupted from her throat, and she flew across the room to pull Rhianna behind her protectively.

"Who are you? What are you doing here? And what the hell are you doing upsetting my friend?" she barked at the man who was looking at her as if he was completely stunned. She tried to ignore just how gorgeous he was, how his deep blue eyes seemed to be peering right into her soul, and how her heart was practically skipping as she took in the sheer size of the man.

Her actions seemed to shake Rhianna out of her shock, and she stepped from behind her friend and placed a hand lightly on her arm. "It's okay, Mills. This is Jared Hanlon. He came to speak to me about an estate Rafe left."

Millie dragged her eyes reluctantly from the gorgeous man before her and turned to look quizzically at her friend. "Estate? We went through all of Rafe's papers. There was nothing there."

"It appears he lodged the paperwork with a solicitor. Jared was just telling me that I am now the proud beneficiary of one million dollars."

Millie's eyes went round with shock, and she slowly sat down on one of the chairs at the breakfast table. Rhianna sat back down beside her and so did Jared after a moment. "You're shitting me, right?" Millie managed to get out, shaking her head in disbelief. "How the hell could Rafe afford a policy like that?"

Jared watched the new woman who was obviously Millicent Cooper as per Rafe's information. His wolf was howling *'mine'* repeatedly, and he was seriously having to battle hard to calm him down while still appearing to act normally in front of the two women.

He wanted to howl himself. If things weren't bad enough already, they had just become so much worse. Here he was lying his ass off to Rafe's sister, and it turned out her best friend was his mate!

How could he rip the only other person Rhianna Armand had in her life from her after all she had been through? However, he would have to do so, because it was impossible to deny his wolf. Millicent Cooper was his mate and he had to have her. No one could fight the mating instinct.

CHAPTER FOUR

Caleb strangled down a deep sigh and tried hard not to drum his fingers on the boardroom table. The CEO from Belmont Industries was droning on and on and he was bored with the man. He was only half listening to the fat, balding human, letting his mind wander to what he'd do once he finished work.

He sensed Demetri shoot a quick glance in his direction, and realised he'd actually started to drum his fingers. It was a shocking loss of control, one he wasn't used to. His mind had been wandering constantly for weeks now, and it was immensely irritating. He stopped immediately, and tried to pay attention to the proposal the other company was outlining.

"Can you at least try to look interested?" Demetri said sarcastically inside his head. *"This will be an excellent deal for the company, Caleb. All these meetings will be for nothing if you piss off Arthur Belmont."*

"The man's a moron," Caleb retorted acidly. *"Look at him. He's so full of his own self-importance he's about ready to explode. If you want to kiss his ass then go ahead, Demetri. Quite frankly he's doing my fucking head in."* He could feel his friend's shock through their mental link.

"What the fuck is up with you? You've been a bear with a sore fucking head for the last month. I think the last time I saw a smile crack your face was when you picked up that little redhead at the club."

Caleb barely stiffened, but knew his friend would pick up the movement, though the others in the meeting would be none the wiser. He had tried very hard to put that night out of his head, but without much success. He didn't need Demetri bringing it up and waving it under his nose. The strength of his disappointment at finding Rhianna gone when he woke up had stunned him. Never in his very long life had he ever felt such regret at finding a woman gone from his home. Usually he was relieved not to have to face them the morning after.

It was different with the delightful little redhead though. He had woken up and smiled as he walked downstairs to find her. He had wanted to see her lying before his fire, her beautiful face sleepy, her long auburn curls tumbling wildly around her head.

His body had hardened at the image, and he'd begun thinking of how he could love her delectable little body before driving her home. Instead, he'd been greeted by an empty room, and a fierce rage settling deep within his soul. His feral side had kicked in and he'd wanted to start hunting immediately.

Her scent had still been in the air, as had the heady scent of the sex they'd had, but the girl was gone; his throw folded neatly on the sofa. A quick check had shown she'd even re-locked his door and posted his keys through the letterbox. For some reason that tiny gesture had soothed a lot of his feral nature, and had brought a slow smile to his face.

It was a very considerate thing to do. She wasn't to know that no one within a hundred miles would have dared to enter his mansion if the door had been unlocked. Animals and humans alike could detect a dangerous predator instantly. Even the mail carrier wouldn't walk up his drive, hence the reason for having a mailbox outside the main gates as well as one in the actual door.

What frustrated him so much was that he didn't even know her last name so he couldn't look her up to try to find her. He had gone back to Karpathia's every night hoping she would appear once more, but she hadn't. It was as if she had vanished completely.

His restlessness was starting to gnaw at him, and he was finding it increasingly difficult to concentrate on everyday things like work. He knew he was testing Demetri's patience to the limits, but he couldn't help himself. He craved the little redhead so badly he hadn't been with another woman since their night together.

Denying his physical release also denied him the chance to feed from source. He was an Ancient and the need to feed was not as essential for him. He could go months without the hunger twisting his guts into knots, though he didn't usually leave it that long.

There was no point in deliberately torturing himself and, up until now, he had always had a ready supply of willing women to enjoy. If his current dry spell with women continued he would have no choice but to feed from his private stock of chilled blood.

Times had changed greatly since the old days when the only way to satisfy his hunger was to find a warm, lusty woman and drink from her as they indulged their passion. Feeding from source was more recreational now than a necessity for his kind. There were ample sources of blood available from the blood banks run by his kind. Granted, chilled blood did not taste nearly as intoxicating as the hot, sweet essence of a woman in the throes of her passion but it satisfied the hunger.

He stifled down a sigh as thoughts of feeding stirred his bloodlust, and drew his mind back to the little redhead and how sweet she had tasted in his mouth. He felt his body start to stir, and he smothered down a curse. He couldn't sit here any longer listening to the fat old man waffle on. His annoyance was ratcheting up so quickly he might be tempted to silence Belmont forever. "I'm sorry gentlemen, if you could please excuse me. I'm not feeling too good." His words were abrupt as he rose quickly.

He caught Demetri's glare as Arthur Belmont stuttered in surprise, but he ignored them both. "Please, continue the meeting with Demetri. He has my complete trust and is authorised to make all decisions on my behalf."

He didn't wait to see the reaction. He strode determinedly out of the room and headed to his office. He blocked Demetri from his head, not willing to listen to his angry mutterings. It didn't need both of them to attend the meeting anyway. They'd already discussed and agreed on the proposal prior to meeting with Belmont Industries. The finer points were just a formality and his friend could deal with them.

An hour later, a furious Demetri crashed into his office, slamming the door hard behind him. Caleb watched his friend with a slight smile tugging at his lips. Demetri was impressive with his green eyes and midnight black hair, but he was glorious when he was in a fury. He was like some avenging angel spewing forth his wrath, and was he spewing right now! Caleb tuned out most of his words letting him rant on until he got his anger out of his system.

"Talk to me, Caleb. Tell me what the fuck is going on with you right now because I don't have the first clue!"

Demetri threw himself into the chair in front of Caleb's desk and yanked the leather thong from his long hair so he could rake his hands through it. His friend's erratic behaviour was causing him serious concern. It was so unlike him.

Caleb leaned on his desk and sighed deeply. "I wish I knew, my friend," he said quietly. "I feel so restless, so off-kilter right now. No woman attracts me, I don't want to feed from source, and I can't be bothered with work. There's only one thing I want to do and that's find Rhianna, and yet, I can't do that because I don't know anything about her."

Demetri stared at him open-mouthed. "All this because of the redhead?" he asked incredulously. "Caleb, I know she was hot but come on, she's just a human, nothing spectacular."

Caleb glared at his friend and narrowed his eyes. "That's a matter of opinion. I don't know what it is about her but I need to see her again, at least one more time so I can see as clearly as you can that there is nothing spectacular about her."

He couldn't keep the sarcasm out of his tone as he said that last part. He objected to his friend saying there was nothing spectacular about Rhianna. There was something about the woman, the way her mouth shaped as she talked, the feel of her soft skin under his fingertips, the way she fit his body so perfectly as he slid deep within her.

A hot, clawing hunger overwhelmed him, and his body tightened instantly. He bit back a curse, anger warring with need as his perfect memory replayed their night together. This need, this craving for the redhead, was dangerous. He had almost lost control once with her. If that happened again he might be forced to do something he would actually feel some regret over.

Caleb wasn't used to being out of control, wasn't used to experiencing emotions. No woman had ever been able to get under his skin the way Rhianna had. Was there something of the otherworld about her? Had she cast some kind of spell over him? He had enemies just like everyone else. He'd lived a long time, was considered the top of the food chain among his own people even though he didn't get involved in the politics that shaped his race. Was someone using Rhianna to weaken him?

He hadn't sensed anything unusual about her. She was fully human, he was almost positive about that. He had scented her deeply and endlessly that night, enthralled by her exotic aroma that had rushed over him like a tidal wave. His body tightened further and he uttered a strangled groan.

Demetri sighed as he watched the struggle on his friend's face. Caleb would only be this unguarded when he was alone with him. Demetri could sense his conflict, sense the onslaught of lust and wondered regretfully just what it had been like for his friend to lay with the little redhead. She had to have been good for Caleb to want to see her again.

He closed his eyes for a moment before opening them and looking at his friend intently. "Okay, let's see if we can find Rhianna and you can then do whatever it is you need to do to get her out of your system so life can get back to normal. What can you remember from the night at the club?"

His tone held a weary note but also a hint of amusement. There was something quite entertaining about seeing Caleb so riled up, even if it was concerning. He would have endless decades of teasing his friend about this, once he had satisfied his urge for his human and she was once more gone from their lives.

Caleb thought back to the night. He was blessed with an eidetic memory so it wasn't hard for him to remember their entire conversation in Karpathia's. They hadn't really said anything which didn't directly relate to him picking her up and taking her home. He frowned suddenly and leaned forward. "She was very sad," he said quietly. "I saw it in her eyes. It was there for a moment and then she hid it, but for a brief second her eyes were filled with such pain and sadness."

Demetri pursed his lips and tapped a long finger against his lips. "What makes humans sad?" he mused, tapping slowly as he pondered. "Maybe she had just broken up with her boyfriend?"

Caleb shook his head slowly. "She hadn't been with a man in a very long time. There was no male scent on her." He felt his temper spark at the thought of another man sleeping with the girl even though he knew of her relative inexperience of other men. He was quite certain that if he learned she had been with another man after their night together, he would walk the fine line of the killing edge. This was irrational because she didn't belong to him in any way and he didn't want her to.

"Maybe she'd just lost her job?" Demetri tried again but Caleb shook his head in the negative once more.

"There was pain and sadness. She wouldn't have been that upset about losing a job." Not with the level of pain he had witnessed. Something tugged at his heart at that memory, some primal instinct deep within him that sought to comfort the woman who had captured his interest.

"Perhaps someone she cared for had just died? Humans are so fragile. They're always dying," Demetri sighed dramatically, waving one large hand gracefully in the air.

Caleb blinked slowly at him, feeling instinctively that his friend was on the right track. "You might be onto something there, Demetri. Something like a death could have explained her sadness." He picked up his phone and dialled Beth Hollis, his PA.

"Beth, can you check all obituaries in the last six weeks. I'm looking for any mention of a woman named Rhianna." He hung up and wondered if he should have given her slightly better information to work with. She'd probably be checking for a woman dying called Rhianna.

He sighed and left it to her. Beth was very good at finding out information. He was sure she'd check every death notice for any mention of the name Rhianna. He turned his gaze back to his friend. "Did the deal go through?" he asked quietly, and saw his friend nod.

"You just need to sign both copies of the agreements and courier Belmont's over to him," Demetri answered with a slight smile.

"Fine, get them to me and I'll get it done," Caleb said with a bit more life in him at having a new avenue to pursue in his quest to find Rhianna. "Sorry I left you with the meeting. I was mentally thinking of how many different ways I could kill Belmont so he'd stop talking. I thought it was more prudent to leave."

Demetri laughed loudly, amusement dancing in his eyes. "How many did you come up with?" He could understand the other man's irritation. Belmont was challenging to have to deal with, but the deal was lucrative.

"Too many." Caleb's response was clipped, cold and decidedly unfriendly. "Maybe you should deal with him for a while until I get my loathing for him under control?"

The request wiped the amusement from Demetri's face. Out of all of them, Caleb was the most civilised, the one least likely to give into his feral side. The cold, hard edge to his words was surprising.

Demetri watched him shrewdly for a long moment. His friend's reaction to Rhianna was an anomaly. If the girl proved to be a danger to Caleb then he would have no qualms in making sure she disappeared for real. He protected Caleb from everything, including himself.

He uncurled his big body from the chair and stood up to leave. "I hope you find your girl soon, Caleb. You're driving me insane at the moment." He headed out of the office deep in thought. If Caleb's behaviour became too erratic he would consider his options, until then he would keep his own council.

Beth Hollis stepped into Caleb's office just before four pm. She was a pretty woman, tall and lithe standing at five foot nine with blonde hair and green eyes. She'd been Caleb's PA for four years and probably knew him almost as well as Demetri. She didn't know his true nature because she was human, but she knew everything else about him.

"I couldn't find anything about a woman called Rhianna passing away, but I did find one obituary about a Rafe Armand who was killed while on a camping trip. He was survived by his sister Rhianna Armand." She placed a printout on Caleb's desk. "It made the local paper so I e-mailed you the online link. There's a photograph of brother and sister in the article."

Caleb smiled broadly as he looked at the obituary printout. "Thanks, Beth! I don't know what I'd do without you. You're a genius." He knew this was his Rhianna, the woman who haunted his dreams every night. He didn't need to see the photograph but he would look at it anyway, just to make sure.

"You could give me a raise," Beth laughed with a cheeky grin as she turned and walked out the office.

Caleb opened his e-mail and clicked on the link Beth had sent him. It took him directly to the online story about Rafe Armand's passing, and he sucked in a deep breath when he looked at the picture of the laughing couple.

It was her - Rhianna. She was laughing as she looked up at a tall, beefy man with dark brown hair and brown eyes. Her brother was a giant compared to the little redhead, and he was laughing too as he gazed down at his sister with open adoration. It was obvious for all to see how close the siblings were.

He felt a stab of pity for the petite redhead. She looked so carefree in the photograph, completely different to how she'd looked that night in Karpathia's when she hadn't guarded her expression. From the date of the article, it would appear her brother had died the week before they'd met. She'd probably still been in denial that night, trying vainly to convince herself it hadn't happened.

Armed with a name, he now had enough information to track her down. He felt a thrill of anticipation course through him, his heart starting to kick up a beat as he stared at the photograph. He had to see her again. It was a gut-wrenching ache deep within him to scent her, hear her voice, and touch her fragile skin.

The clawing need was back, assaulting all his of senses. Rhianna Armand had some kind of hold over him that he couldn't understand. It was exciting but it was also throwing up warning signals. He'd seen the look in Demetri's eyes before he'd left. It was cold, calculating, and utterly feral. His friend was concerned about his reaction to the girl. He was under no illusions that Demetri would make Rhianna disappear if he felt she was a danger to them.

He could understand his friend's concern because he felt it too; his reaction to her could prove lethal for their kind. Demetri would kill her if he felt it was justified. The question was…would Caleb let him.

~~~~~

Rhianna was sitting on her sofa trying to work out what she was going to do with her life. She'd already quit her job, figuring she now had the financial backing to allow her to do something she really wanted to do, rather than be forced into doing a job to meet the bills.

The last week had been so surreal. Jared Hanlon had left not long after Millie had come home. Her friend had automatically taken a dislike to the man and had all but chased him from the apartment. For some strange reason, Jared had been disinclined to leave, but Millie had been persistent about it. He'd called three times since then, always asking for Millie, but her friend had either been out or refused to take his calls. When Rhianna quizzed her about her reaction to the man, she just smiled and brushed it off as if it was nothing.

That left Rhianna sitting alone, wondering what she was going to do now that she was a millionaire. She was still stunned about Rafe having the policy, but the paperwork Jared had shown her looked above board so she had signed it and deposited the cheque. Now she just needed to think about what she would do with the money.

The ringing of the doorbell brought her out of her reverie, and surprised her. She wasn't expecting anyone, and though she often forgot her keys, it couldn't be Millie because she wasn't due back from work for another couple of hours. She opened the door and stared in complete shock. "Caleb."

Caleb looked down at Rhianna and instantly saw the sadness in her expression. She was as stunning as he remembered, but her lavender eyes were sad and he could see tiny lines of grief in the corner of her eyes and the tight pinch of her lips. She appeared completely shocked to see him, but not necessarily annoyed about him being there.

"May I come in?" he asked quietly, fighting the urge to reach out and touch her. Her scent was washing over him, her fragility making him want to reach out and take her in his arms. He held himself rigid and watched as she shivered slightly.

Lord, the man's voice still had the same effect as it had the night they'd met in Karpathia's. Rhianna couldn't believe he was here and that she was actually pleased that he was. She stepped back wordlessly and let him into the apartment.

"How did you find me?" she asked, more curious than annoyed. They hadn't shared any personal information with each other. Sure, he'd taken her home so she at least knew where he stayed, but he had only known her first name.

She watched him look around the great room slowly before he moved to sit on the sofa. He was dressed in an Armani business suit and his luscious golden brown locks were tied back by a leather thong at the nape of his neck. He looked just as gorgeous as he had in Karpathia's and she felt a stab of desire course through her body.

"It was difficult," he answered, a small smile tugging at his lips as his eyes roamed over her face. There was a slightly predatory look in his amber gaze as he watched her walk over to one of the armchairs and sit down across from him. "That's why it's taken me so long to stop by. I only managed to track you down this afternoon."

Rhianna was surprised he'd been looking for her. He hadn't struck her as the type of man who was looking for anything other than one night of passion with a woman.

"You look tired, Rhianna," he said, his gaze intent on her face. "Tired and so very sad. I remembered you looking sad in Karpathia's that night. That's how I tracked you down. I'm sorry about your brother."

She blinked at him slowly a few times, trying not to let the tears come again. He sounded so genuine, as if he truly was sorry about Rafe, and she had to fight the urge to throw herself into his arms and cry like a baby. She stood up abruptly. "Can I get you something to drink?" she asked, unconsciously clutching a hand to her stomach. "Coffee, tea, a glass of wine?" She turned and hurried into the kitchen area, needing a moment to try to get herself under control.

Caleb felt his gut wrench at the abject misery that crossed her face when he mentioned her brother. He had said the words by rote because that was what humans expected someone to say. He hadn't actually meant them, but her reaction to it was so profound he found himself feeling angry that she was hurting. He could see she was fighting to hold back tears and it was plain to see her wound was still raw. She retreated from him and he couldn't stop himself from following her.

The need to touch her, to comfort her was almost an ache within him. Long dead emotions clawed at him viciously, incited him to react. He wanted to take her pain away like he'd never wanted anything before in his life. He caught her shoulders and pulled her back against his chest, sliding his arms around her.

"No, I don't want anything to drink," he breathed into her hair as she trembled against him. "I want to help you, Rhianna. I want to offer you comfort." His reaction to her pain stunned him. He meant every word he was saying. He had come here wanting to know why he couldn't get her out of his mind, wanting to know why she was different from all the other women he'd been with, and instead of answers he was only creating more questions. Why did it matter to him that this tiny, fragile woman was hurting so badly?

The damned tears came again. She tried hard not to cry but his gentleness, the genuine tone in his voice broke through her battered defences and she twisted in his arms, buried her head against his silk shirt, and started to sob quietly. Rhianna was vaguely aware of him picking her up effortlessly and carrying her back to the sofa. His strong arms enfolded her tightly as he sat her in his lap and held her while she sobbed out her grief and misery. He didn't speak; he just held her and stroked her hair as she cried.

Rhianna was unaware of how long she'd cried. All she knew was she felt safe in Caleb's arms, safe and protected. It was as if he was silently lending her his strength. After a while the tears stopped, and she just rested against his chest absent-mindedly toying with one of the buttons on his shirt.

"Do you want to talk about it?" Caleb asked quietly. Her distress was wrenching at his gut. He could tell this was a common occurrence for her. The thought of her doing this night after night since they had been apart made him want to hit something. Hard.

His feral nature was on the rise and it was difficult to tamp it down, to remain gentle with her. He was overcome with the need to protect this fragile human, to ensure no harm ever came to her again. It was confusing but it was there. He couldn't stop himself from reacting as he was. He decided not to fight the instinct, and tightened his hold, letting her know she was safe.

"Nothing really to talk about," she mumbled against his chest. "Rafe is gone and I just have to try and find a way to get on with life." Her voice sounded so defeated.

"You were very close?" His fingers had a mind of their own, lightly stroking against her curls. The thick, heavy weight of the luxurious locks soothed his beast so he repeated the caress, finding it was soothing her too. She appeared to be very tactile, reacting favourably to his touch.

"Our parents died when I was only three," Rhianna said after a long pause and a deep sigh. "Rafe was quite a bit older than me. He had just turned eighteen when they died and was about to start university. He gave up his studies and took a job as a building labourer so he could look after me. He devoted his entire life to making sure I was loved and cared for. He was everything to me and now he's gone."

Caleb breathed in deeply and tightened his hold. Her brother sounded like a selfless kind of person. He could now understand the depth of Rhianna's grief. "He sounds like a pretty cool guy," he said softly. "I'm sorry I never got the opportunity to meet him."

Rhianna smiled slightly and pulled her head back so she could look up at his face. "You would have liked him, Caleb. Everyone liked Rafe. He was so easy going, never had a bad word to say about anyone. Took each person as he found them, warts and all. When I met Millie in grade school and started hanging around with her, Rafe just adopted her as his second little sister. Her parents didn't give a crap about her and she was hurting pretty badly at the time. Rafe just started looking after her the same way he did me."

Her eyes filled with tears again and she dropped her gaze back down to the buttons on his shirt. "It's just so unfair that someone so good can be gone like that, Caleb. Just when I was old enough to take care of myself and Rafe could finally start living his own life, this has to happen. It's just not fair."

Caleb hugged her tightly and kissed the top of her head. "Life has a habit of doing the most unfair things," he said softly. "I really am truly sorry for your pain, Rhianna, but you have to ask yourself if Rafe would want to see you like this?"

She stiffened for a moment, and then relaxed against him. "He'd sit me down and have a 'talk' with me," she admitted with a wry smile. "He'd tell me not to dwell on the bad things but to remember the good things. I do try to, Caleb. Every day I think of one happy memory of being with Rafe and it helps a little, but sometimes the grief just takes hold and I can't shake it."

He kissed the top of her head again. "Let me guess, you've cocooned yourself inside this apartment since it happened, haven't you?" he asked gently.

She nodded against his chest, closing her eyes and leaning on him as she took a deep shuddering breath. She was vaguely aware that it should feel odd sitting here with him like this. It wasn't as if they were friends or going out. They had only spent one night together and she had been so sure at the time it had been a one-night stand.

"Maybe it's time to be getting out and about again?" Caleb suggested. "Why don't you come out with me tonight? We can go to a movie or have dinner; whatever you want to do. Just get out of the apartment for a couple of hours."

Rhianna sat up straight and Caleb allowed his arms to drop so he could reach up and wipe away her tears. She truly was beautiful, even with her eyes red from crying.

"You mean like a date?" she asked breathlessly, her lavender eyes staring intently into his.

"Do you want it to be a date, Rhianna?" he asked huskily, his thumb gently tracing along her bottom lip as he kept her gaze locked with his. "I'm willing to just be your friend for now, if that's what you need at the moment. I know our first meeting was rather intense. I understand the reasons behind it, too. I'm willing to take this, whatever it is we have together, as slowly as you want."

Rhianna could feel her face blushing scarlet as he mentioned their night together. She tried to look away from him but was trapped within his golden brown eyes. "I don't usually do things like that," she said quietly.

"I know," he smiled softly. "I don't regret our night together, Rhianna. I don't want you to regret it either. You needed me. I was glad to be there for you."

She sighed and rested her forehead against his. "I just feel so out of control right now, Caleb," she admitted quietly. "I feel as if I've lost direction. I don't know what to do anymore."

"Well, you can come out with me tonight for starters," he said with a small smile tugging at his lips. "Getting out of the apartment will be good for you."

She managed a shaky laugh and gave in to the sudden urge to touch the side of his face. She pulled back slightly so she could watch her fingers stroke lightly over his cheekbone and down to his strong jawline.

She heard his sharp intake of breath and felt something stirring underneath her bottom. She smiled and brought her eyes back to his, which had darkened. "Okay, I'll come out with you tonight," she agreed. She slipped from his lap before the sudden tension between them could get any stronger.

She wanted to lean forward and kiss him. She knew he wanted to kiss her too, but her normal reticence was back. She wasn't about to jump into bed with him again, not when she knew nothing about him except he lived in a fancy mansion on the outskirts of town.

Caleb smiled with pleasure as he watched her scoot back to her armchair. Her hesitancy really was quite endearing. He had surprised himself when he'd offered her friendship. He was aching to throw her down on the sofa and slide into her beautiful body once more, but her sadness had touched him deeply and he was willing to wait until she was ready.

He stood up. "I'd better get home then, and change," he said, his amber eyes glowing with pleasure. "Dinner? I can pick you up about seven?"

Rhianna walked him to the door. "Seven's fine," she answered feeling a little bubble of excitement deep inside her. "Will it be a dress up dinner?"

He smiled down at her, lightly brushing her curls back from her face. "Wear something totally stunning," he sighed softly. "I may be forced to behave like a gentleman tonight, however I can at least get to admire you as I behave myself." His tone was light, teasing, and ever so slightly husky.

Rhianna couldn't help but laugh at his words. "I'll make sure I knock you dead then," she quipped lightly and then sucked in a deep breath when he leaned down and brushed his lips across her cheek.

"See you at seven," he said huskily before he let himself out.

CHAPTER FIVE

Rhianna actually found herself humming under her breath, as she got ready for her date with Caleb. It was the first time in weeks she'd felt even slightly happy, and it surprised her. She didn't know why she reacted so strongly to the gorgeous golden-haired man. They had barely talked the first time they met. Today, he had been so understanding, so comforting, and it had felt good to have someone strong to hold onto.

She supposed he must remind her a little of Rafe. He was big and intimidating in appearance, but was quite kind and generous underneath the buff exterior. Okay, maybe the first time they met she'd been intimidated by him. He had been so self-assured, so determined in getting what he wanted, which had been her at the time. Today though, he'd been completely different, almost tender as he'd comforted her as she'd cried all over his silk shirt, probably ruining the expensive item.

She heard Millie coming home as she finished the last touches to her make-up. She smiled as she admired her appearance in the mirror. She'd chosen a strapless deep purple dress in chiffon and lace. The bodice was tight around her breasts and waist before the skirt flared out around her hips in yards of wispy material. The skirt ended at mid-thigh and she pulled on a pair of black lace thigh high stockings that didn't require a garter belt. She topped off her ensemble with the same four inch purple heels she'd worn the first night she met Caleb.

She opted for leaving her hair loose. Caleb seemed to like it loose and she was trying to knock him dead as promised. A light touch of make-up and she was ready for him, and looking as good as she'd ever managed to look before. She wondered if he'd approve, as she slowly smoothed her hands over her dress before she stepped out into the great room.

"Oh. My. Fucking. God!" Millie practically yelled, her blue eyes going wide as she looked up from the breakfast table at her friend.

Rhianna blinked in surprise and looked down at herself with a frown. "Do you think it's too much, Mills?" she asked worriedly.

"Too much?" her friend spluttered. "You look positively stunning, Annie! What's the reason for this? Are you actually going out tonight?"

Millie had been truly worried about her friend and the level of depression she kept sinking into. She understood Rhianna's grief and did her best to counter it, but she'd been unsuccessful most of the time. She'd been expecting another quiet night in with her friend, watching crap movies and stuffing their faces with too much ice cream.

Rhianna smiled, her face flushing slightly. "Remember that guy Caleb I met a few weeks ago? He managed to track me down, showed up today, and invited me out for dinner. He must have seen my picture in the newspaper article about Rafe. He seemed to think it would be a good idea for me to get out and about again, so I said I'd go to dinner with him."

She watched Millie's face carefully as she spoke. Her friend had been quite guarded around her lately, and she really wanted to hear Millie's honest opinion about going out with Caleb.

Millie pursed her lips, surprise clearly showing on her face. "You don't really know anything about him, Annie," she said doubtfully.

"Well that's why people go out on dates, Mills, to learn more about each other, and it's just dinner and nothing else. I won't be going back to his place again like the first time. He said he's willing to be friends for now."

Millie burst out laughing and shook her head. "You seriously think any man could look at you dressed like that and just want to be friends?" she asked incredulously. "Annie, you'll be lucky to make it to dinner, girl."

Despite her concerns, Millie couldn't help but be pleased that there was a little bit of light shining in Rhianna's eyes, a small hint of excitement. It was the first time in weeks she'd seen her friend smile, let alone laugh. This Caleb guy must be something pretty amazing to get this type of reaction from Rhianna.

Her friend was frowning doubtfully again as she looked down at herself for a second time. "He said to wear something stunning. Said if he had to behave like a gentleman, he could at least admire me whilst doing so. I don't have time to change, Mills. He's going to be here any second." She was unconsciously biting her lower lip with concern.

"You look perfect, Annie," Millie sighed, crossing over to her friend to give her a big hug. "I'm only teasing you. I'm so happy you're going out on a date, honey. It's time to start getting back into the swing of things. You go and enjoy yourself. You deserve a little bit of fun."

Rhianna smiled slightly and couldn't deny that her heart was thumping a bit louder than usual as she anticipated Caleb arriving. As if on cue, the doorbell rang and she jumped slightly, her heart pounding a little bit harder.

"I'll get it," Millie said gently. "Give you a minute to collect yourself and me a minute to check out this Caleb." Before Rhianna could answer, her friend was striding quickly towards the front door and pulling it open.

Caleb smiled down at the tall, dark-haired woman who opened the door to him. He kept his expression carefully neutral, not giving even the tiniest hint he'd heard the tail end of their conversation because of his enhanced hearing abilities. That skill wasn't exactly something normal human males possessed.

"Hi," he said pleasantly. "You must be Millie. I'm Caleb Ryder." He politely held out his hand to the woman and watched her blink up at him slowly before she took his hand and shook it firmly.

"Pleased to meet you, Caleb," she said cordially. "Please, come in. Annie's almost ready."

She turned her back and must have made some kind of gesture, because Caleb caught a flush of colour in Rhianna's cheeks before his golden brown gaze slowly roamed over her. He had to stifle a deep groan as his body stirred with a healthy appreciation of the perfection he was viewing. He'd told her to wear something stunning and she'd promised to knock him dead. She'd managed to do both in one fell swoop. He was quite literally willing to drop to his knees and promise her anything if she would agree to let him peel that beautiful dress from her body and let him lose himself in her.

He realised he was literally standing there on the doorstep practically mute, and gave himself a mental shake. He stepped into the apartment, walking slowly over to Rhianna so he could lean down and graze her cheek lightly with his lips. He also took the opportunity to breathe in her heady scent before he whispered in her ear, "Just as well you have a chaperone or dinner would most definitely be out the window right now."

Rhianna shivered delicately as his husky voice whispered across the shell of her ear and she had to smother down a moan as she felt a trickle of liquid heat rush through her body. He was obviously very pleased with her choice of dress, and she had to admit he was looking spectacular too. He was wearing another black Armani suit coupled with a black silk shirt. He'd forgone a tie and his long, silky golden brown locks were loose around his shoulders. He looked good enough to eat.

"Shall we go?" Caleb asked, straightening up and placing a hand lightly on the small of her back to usher her from the apartment.

Rhianna grabbed her wrap and purse, and smiled at her friend. "I won't be late, Mills," she said, and almost laughed when Millie rolled her eyes at her, giving her a 'yeah, right' look.

"Enjoy yourselves," she answered, smiling. "Nice to meet you, Caleb."

"And you, Millie," Caleb smiled, genuinely liking the dark-haired woman on first meeting. The bond she had with Rhianna was obviously something special. He found it hard to dislike someone who cared about the woman at his side.

He stifled down another groan as he escorted Rhianna from the apartment and down to his waiting Porsche. Had he really offered to just be friends for now? Was he insane when he had? There was no way on the planet he could ever simply be friends with Rhianna Armand. He wanted her far too much to deny himself the pleasures of her body.

Caleb helped Rhianna into the car and then climbed in himself and waited until she'd buckled up her seatbelt. He watched her with a slight smile tugging at his lips. Who would have thought a seatbelt could be so erotic? She obviously sensed his eyes fixating on the way the strap lay over her breasts and he had to give himself a mental shake when he caught her arching an eyebrow at him.

"Are we going, Caleb?" Lavender eyes searched his face intently as she tensed slightly.

He smiled and looked away, taking a deep breath and regretting it immediately when the sweet scent of lavender and jasmine assaulted his nostrils. His body twitched and he managed to keep his expression as neutral as possible as he started the car.

The enclosed space inside the car was going to be a problem. Her scent was incredibly intoxicating and his photographic memory was kicking into gear and replaying their night together at his mansion. Caleb felt like an untried youth trying to overcome his excitement at the prospect of his first sexual encounter instead of a man with over two millennia of experience to draw upon. It would have been highly amusing if it were happening to someone else.

He pulled away from the apartment and tried to turn his mind to something else. "So, Millie calls you Annie," he commented as he drove through the residential neighbourhood. "Is that your preference?" It sounded like such an asinine thing to ask but it was something to say.

Rhianna could see the tension in him and was going to ask what was wrong, but the heated look in his eyes a moment ago rather answered the question for her. His attraction to her was evident and she couldn't deny it sent a little shiver down her spine knowing he found her so attractive. "Rafe and Mills always called me Annie," she answered after a brief pause. "At school I was more commonly called Rhia. I don't really mind either. Whatever you're comfortable with."

Caleb pursed his lips thoughtfully for a moment as he ran the names over in his mind. "I like Annie," he finally answered and glanced quickly to see her reaction. She was staring out the windscreen and a slight smile curved her lips when he spoke. She approved of his choice; that, in turn, made him smile too.

"I don't know very much about you, Caleb," Rhianna said, turning to look at him. "What kind of work do you do?"

"I'm a partner in a few technologies companies and also a silent partner in Karpathia's," he answered carefully. This was one of the reasons he didn't have relationships with women. They invariably asked questions and he had to be exceedingly careful with his answers.

"You part own the nightclub," she repeated slowly, a hint of surprise in her tone. "I find that surprising for some reason. I can imagine you working in a big company with your suits and all, but owning a nightclub seems a bit out of character for some strange reason."

He laughed and shot her an amused glance. "You don't think even high flying businessmen need an outlet to let their hair down?" he asked. "My partner Demetri sees to the day to day running of the club. I tend to just go there to let off steam after a particularly hectic day in the boardroom."

He watched her out of the corner of his eye as he turned onto Old Forest Road. "I went back to the club every night after we met. I was hoping you'd come back."

Rhianna sighed and closed her eyes, leaning her head against the headrest. "I had to go back to reality," she answered, a hint of sadness in her tone. She couldn't help feeling a thrill at his words though. A beautiful man like Caleb actively trying to find her again was quite a heady thought.

Caleb took his eyes off the road for a fraction of a second so he could look at her unobserved, and in that exact moment a shape blurred out of nowhere, crossing the road in front of them and crashing into the car.

Caleb's first thought was for Rhianna. His arm shot out across her chest to keep her firmly in the seat even as he automatically began to correct the hard slide as the car spun around. They were in the middle of nowhere, the forest on either side of them, and he had to work hard to stop the car from hitting any of the trees.

A startled cry escaped Rhianna's lips as the car spun completely around and then half way again. Caleb gripped the wheel tightly, now using both hands to halt the slide and shift down into neutral as the Porsche finally came to a halt. He was snapping off his seatbelt even as he turned to Rhianna.

"Are you okay?" he asked tersely, his eyes quickly running over her as he spoke.

Rhianna placed a hand to her chest as if doing so would slow her thundering heart. "I think so." Her voice shook slightly and her words came out sounding breathless. "My heart feels like it's going to burst it's going so fast. What was that, Caleb? Did we hit something?"

Caleb's sharp gaze was staring at the large grey shape in the road. Fuck, it was a wolf and he was in the Hanlon Pack area! This was not good. Jared Hanlon would not be happy with him if he'd just killed one of his pack. He looked back at Rhianna's anxious face. "Stay in the car, Annie," he said tersely. "I'll go check it out."

Jared's wolf was quite literally pissed at him and it was making life a tad difficult. He sighed and rubbed a weary hand over his face as his wolf howled and raged inside him. "Stop," he groaned in exasperation. "You don't think I want to go over there and throw her over my shoulder and bring her home with us? It's not that simple and you know it!"

Millicent Cooper was driving both Jared and his wolf insane. She was their mate and they couldn't get anywhere near her. She had quite literally tossed them out of her apartment that day and had so far refused to take any calls. His wolf wasn't willing to accept her actions. He was the Alpha and she was his. It was so black and white to the animal part of him. Jared had to contend with the practical side of things though. Yes, Millie was his mate and he wanted her so badly sometimes it felt hard to breathe without her. She was also Rhianna Armand's best friend.

He'd taken an instant liking to Rafe's little sister the moment he'd met her. He felt protective of her and extremely guilty that she was going through such a hard time over the loss of her brother. It didn't help that Rafe was very much alive and living with his pack and he couldn't let her know that. He had to think of the wellbeing of the pack first. Their dual nature had to be protected at all costs.

Then there was Rafe to consider. He was a dormant Alpha, of that Jared was now sure. He appeared to be content just to be another member of the pack though. Jared surmised the man must have had a gentle nature when he was still human. Not all Alphas wanted to lead a pack. It was a hard role to take on and often required very difficult decisions that ultimately led to deaths. Rafe's nature seemed to shun the violent part of being a Were.

If Jared brought Millie here to the pack, he didn't think Rafe would maintain his current docile state of mind. He was adapting slowly to joining the pack proper, now he was in better control of his shifts, but he would know his sister would be in pain at the loss of Millie as well as himself. There was no accounting for what he'd do if his sister was hurt by any actions of the pack and more importantly, his Alpha.

He sighed deeply again and leaned on his desk, dropping his head in his hands. He had to have Millie. He could only deny his wolf so long. She was his. His wolf howled again inciting him to go and get their mate and Jared had to struggle hard to push him back down.

"I can't," he said, his voice anguished. "Do you want to lose your Alpha status? You know Rafe will challenge for leadership if we bring Millie here."

His wolf huffed, growled and sent him images of them ripping out Rafe's throat, before jumping on Millie and dragging her into their bed.

"I'm glad you're so confident," he smiled at the animal. "I, on the other hand, am not. Rafe is the biggest wolf in the pack. His lack of experience of pack life will not hamper him much should he choose to challenge."

It wasn't that Jared was afraid of the challenge. It was part of pack life and, if he was not strong enough to meet any challengers, he didn't deserve to be Alpha. His issue was the people involved in the whole mess. He genuinely liked Rafe and Annie and he didn't want to hurt them because Millie was his mate. He had to find some other way to work through this so that no one got hurt.

He heard a ruckus outside and then his study door opened and Aaron strode in. "The rogue's been sighted, Jared," the tall blond man said with an edge of excitement in his voice.

Jared stood immediately. "Gather the pack, Aaron. The rogue dies tonight."

"What about Rafe?" There was a note of concern in his number two's voice.

Jared paused for a second and then nodded. "Rafe too. He has to understand the animal nature of the pack. He may not like it but it's necessary. Plus the rogue may be the best way to introduce him to it. He deserves to get a chance at punishing the Were who did this to him."

Aaron nodded and left the room as Jared followed him out. The hunt was on.

Rafe was not happy at being made to shift into wolf form to hunt the rogue who had forcibly turned him. He was given little choice in the matter by the Alpha. Jared had been firm and resolute when he'd balked at the very idea. Pack life hadn't been as bad as he'd expected up until now. He was basically left alone to do his own thing when he wasn't being taught the pack laws. He could now change at will and no longer lost it when he got angry at the changes happening to him. The rest of the pack seemed to treat him with some kind of special status at the moment and left him alone.

Well, the males did. The females strutted up and down outside the small log cabin he was currently staying in. They were usually naked when they did this which was rather disconcerting to say the least. The whole pack setup was a complete culture shock to him.

The Alpha had his own private residence set a bit apart from the other buildings in the compound. It was an imposing wooden building that served as his office as well as his home. Rafe had been inside it a few times and was surprised how modern the inside was. From the outside, it looked as if it was just a larger cabin but inside it was clearly a proper home as well as a place of work.

The rest of the pack seemed to live more communally, with sometimes two or three families occupying some of the bigger cabins dotted around the compound. Meal times were a communal event, taking place in the largest building in the centre of the compound that served as kitchen and dining room as well as meeting room for the pack.

Rafe knew he was lucky to have his little cabin that only consisted of two rooms: a sitting room and a bedroom with an adjoining bathroom. He knew Jared was allowing him some privacy as he gently eased him into pack life. In addition, the cabin was right next to Aaron's, who appeared to be his minder and was one of the handful of betas who had yet to mate.

Getting the hierarchy right in his head was a major confusion for Rafe. The alpha and his betas seemed almost guaranteed to mate for some reason and therefore automatically had their own private dwellings. They still ate in the communal dining room but essentially, they had more privacy than the rest of the pack.

Clothes seemed to be optional in the pack but most people wore something to cover their nakedness, usually. It just seemed to be the females who liked to bare all in front of his modest home.

He had asked Aaron about it and his friend had laughed loudly and started talking about the very sexual side of pack life. Rafe was rather shocked at the level of promiscuity which went on in the pack. He wasn't exactly a prude. He'd known his fair share of women before the change, but he'd always been discerning with his partners. He preferred to have relationships rather than one night stands as a lot of men did.

From what Aaron had told him, he would have numerous women coming on to him until he 'mated'. Rafe didn't like the sound of being mated. It was just so animalistic and he still wasn't comfortable with the wolf half of his nature. He didn't want to be ruled by a mating instinct. He was a man first and a wolf last. He wanted to choose his partner or 'mate' with his human side.

The Alpha chuffed loudly breaking into his reverie, and he turned to him as did the rest of the assembled pack. Aaron stood beside Rafe and nudged him slightly with his long snout. His friend was impressive in wolf form. Not as large as Jared or himself but his markings were beautiful. Aaron's wolf was a light brown with golden highlights. His markings made him very popular with the females.

Rafe would have sighed in resignation if he could have in wolf form. He nodded to Aaron and followed the rest of the pack into the forest. His wolf was in control and he wanted to howl his pleasure at running through the densely packed trees. Rafe reminded the wolf that the Alpha would not be pleased if he alerted the rogue to their presence.

Rafe couldn't help but enjoy the feel of the rich soil beneath his paws as he ran, or the way the wind whistled past his ears. The moon was full tonight and it called to his beast. Maybe being a pack member wasn't so bad after all if he could run free with the moon guiding his path. It felt so liberating.

The scent of the rogue was soon caught and the pack stepped up a gear, low growls coming from those around him. Rafe was surprised to hear himself emit a low growl as a stab of pure rage surged through him. He recognised the scent of the rogue. It was most definitely the one who had done this to him, who had taken him from his beloved Annie.

Rage he'd never before experienced overcame him and he took off, flying past the rest of the pack. He was going to catch the rogue; he was going to rip its fucking throat out. He was going to tear it limb from limb as it howled its pain into the night.

He was vaguely aware of the Alpha calling to him but the red mist of rage fogged his mind. He heard a loud bang ahead of him, heard the sound of squealing tires as he scented blood and heard an agonised howl. He burst through the trees and onto the hard surface of a road.

~~~~~

Caleb knelt down beside the grey wolf and checked it over carefully. He sighed deeply and ran a hand through his hair. It was dead and it was most definitely a Were. Hanlon was going to be pissed at him. It wouldn't matter to the Alpha that it hadn't been his fault. The stupid Were had come out of nowhere. Even if he had been watching the road he wouldn't have been able to avoid the bloody thing.

"Caleb, is it dead?" Rhianna asked nervously, stepping out of the car and taking a couple of hesitant steps towards him.

Caleb's head snapped round quickly and he frowned deeply. "I told you to stay in the car, Annie," he said tersely. "Go back to the car now."

Rhianna blinked at him in surprise for a second, and then she frowned. Who the hell did he think he was talking to? She wasn't a child to be ordered around. His tone shocked and hurt her, and she took another step closer to him in defiance just as a large ball of some kind of wild animal burst through the trees.

"Annie!" Caleb shouted, momentarily at a loss to what to do. He had time to get to her side but in doing so he'd reveal his nature. The enraged Were who was bounding out of the trees could be the mate to the one he'd killed, which would seriously endanger Rhianna's life.

Rafe scented the vampire kneeling beside the rogue's carcass as he cleared the trees and growled loudly. His wolf reacted instinctively to the danger the other predator posed and his strong body immediately prepared to defend itself. He was vaguely aware the vampire wasn't alone, but he didn't scent the human female properly until he heard her name being shouted.

"Annie!"

The wolf recoiled, the red mist of fury shattering around him as Rafe clawed his way up frantically as he barrelled towards the petite female.

No! He screamed silently inside his wolf's mind as it fought with him for control. His wolf scented danger, fear and death, and he didn't want to give up his control.

No! Rafe roared the word hoarsely; his claws digging into the hard surface of the tarmac as he brought himself to a shuddering halt less than a foot from the human female who was staring at him with a look of abject horror on her face.

He sniffed slowly and let out a low whine as his Annie's unique scent engulfed him, lavender and jasmine with a hint of coconut. She must have showered with the coconut buttermilk gel he'd bought her for her last birthday. She loved the disgusting smelling stuff that he'd always hated. It took a fraction of a second for these thoughts to seep through his rage and then he whined loudly again. His Annie was right in front of him and she was terrified at the sight of him in wolf form. He wanted to shift to human, to go to her, tell her everything was going to be okay but he knew he couldn't.

He was amazed he was managing to hold down his wolf without automatically reverting to being human. He had been practising this with Aaron for the last week, the delicate art of being in wolf form whilst having his human consciousness in control. Apart from the very first time he'd spoken to his Alpha, he had been unable to do so, either changing back to human or being fully the wolf. Perhaps necessity was the key to his mastering this skill? He just knew he couldn't allow his wolf to hurt his sister, and he couldn't reveal himself to her in his human form.

"*Oh, Annie,*" his heart cried as he stared into her beautiful lavender eyes and whined for a third time.

Rhianna let out a deep breath as the enormous brown wolf whined as it looked at her. Her terror was slowly starting to abate, as the wolf appeared to not want to rip her to shreds as she'd first thought it was going to. It simply stood there regarding her with large brown eyes and whined repeatedly.

"Don't move, Annie," she heard Caleb say as he stood slowly and took a step towards her. The wolf's large head swung towards him and it bared its teeth and growled low in its throat, halting Caleb's forward movements instantly.

"I don't think it wants to hurt me, Caleb," she said shakily and the wolf turned back to her and whined again before it lay down very slowly in front of her and rolled over onto its back and thrust its head back against the tarmac.

Caleb watched the wolf intently, ready to dispatch the Were in an instant if he even looked like he was going to hurt Rhianna. The consequences of doing so would be enormous. There would be no hiding what he was from her if he had to protect her from the Were. He would most likely start a war with the pack too if he deliberately took out one of their own. It would be a complete headache to sort out but he was ready to do what he must to protect Rhianna.

He tried to relax when he saw the wolf's posture though his heart was still pounding with concern. It appeared the Were did not want to hurt Rhianna, but Weres could change at the blink of an eye when in wolf form. He moved a step closer and the wolf turned its large head and growled low again. He caught the sharp intelligence in the animal's eye and he relaxed a bit more as he saw the human persona in control of the huge animal.

The Were was less of a danger when its human was in control. The fact it was apparently submitting to Rhianna was curious and strange. He had only ever known a male Were to submit to its mate or its child, never a total stranger in the middle of a road.

He decided to step closer again and test the wolf's reaction. If the dog thought the redhead was his mate he would instantly attempt to attack him. Despite growling again, the wolf remained prone so Caleb took the last step needed to reach Rhianna's side. He didn't touch her, merely stood as close as he could without enraging the wolf.

"Why is it lying there like that, Caleb?" Rhianna asked hesitantly. The enormous animal didn't appear dangerous at the moment, but she was still a bit frightened of it.

"He's submitting to you, Annie," Caleb said calmly, keeping his tone non-threatening to the wolf. "In the wolf world, this is the sign of letting another wolf know he will not hurt them and that he submits to their dominance over him."

Rhianna stared down at the wolf in shock. This huge beast was submitting to her? He was telling her that she was dominant over him? Why on Earth would he do that? She started when the wolf's head moved to look at her and he whined again deep in his chest.

"What do I do, Caleb?" she asked, not taking her eyes from the wolf.

"Very gently touch his stomach and then his neck," Caleb instructed. "Let him know you accept your position as being above him and you mean him no harm. He is effectively baring his most vulnerable areas to you. To accept him, you must touch those areas without causing him any injury."

Rafe listened to the vampire talking to his Annie. It was obvious the golden haired male knew of Were life. He didn't like the scent of him but his Annie appeared to trust him, so for now he would do so as well. He whined and tried to will Rhianna to accept his gesture. He needed her to know that he would never hurt her. This was the only way he knew how to do so when locked in his wolf form.

He chuffed lightly as she slowly knelt down beside him and pressed a trembling hand to his exposed belly. Her touch was so hesitant at first, but then it firmed as she slowly ran her hand up to his neck. She held her hand against his neck for a long time as he lay docilely before her, feeling the first true moment of happiness since he'd been forcibly turned.

"Your fur is so soft," Rhianna murmured with a delighted smile on her face. "You are so big and strong, Wolfie, but I think underneath all that brawn you're really a big softie at heart, aren't you?"

Rafe chuffed again and tried to grin at her without looking too ferocious. She was accepting his wolf and he wanted to howl for joy, though he wasn't overjoyed with the 'Wolfie' part of her words.

"I'm sorry if we hurt your friend over there," Rhianna said soothingly. "It was an accident. He seemed to come out of nowhere. There was nothing Caleb could do to avoid him." She was worried all the whining the wolf had been doing was because of the one they'd hit.

She moved back slightly when the wolf rolled over and looked at the grey beast in the road. Caleb automatically slipped an arm around her waist and pulled her tightly to his side when the wolf moved, but the animal merely stared at the dead Were and growled loudly and then swung its big head back towards her.

"I'm glad he wasn't a friend of yours," Rhianna said softly, correctly guessing this beautiful animal was not unhappy with them about the demise of the other wolf.

A sudden noise from the trees made them all tense and the brown wolf jumped swiftly to its feet and placed itself in front of Rhianna and the other wolves that had cleared the tree line. He growled loudly at the large black wolf that walked slowly towards them while the others hung back.

To say Jared was pissed at Rafe taking off was an understatement. To find him standing protecting his little sister was beyond surprising. How in hell had something like this come about? His quick gaze took in the dead rogue, damaged car and Caleb Ryder eyeing the pack warily whilst shooting glances at the little redhead behind Rafe.

This was just unbelievable. A bloody car accident took out the rogue and the people in the car just happened to be Annie and one of the resident vampires? Someone somewhere must be having a laugh at his expense.

Rhianna didn't appear to be afraid of Rafe and Jared knew this meeting was going to give him an endless headache. He had to get Rafe back into the pack and he had to do it swiftly and without a challenge.

"Rafe, your place is no longer at Annie's side," he sent telepathically. *"You must come back to the pack now."*

Rafe growled and tossed his head wildly. *"No! I'm staying with Annie. She accepts me in wolf form. She's my sister. I must protect her. She's with a vampire of all things. She needs me to look out for her."*

"I know this vampire," Jared said firmly. *"He is honourable for his kind. He will not hurt Annie. You must come back to the pack now, Rafe."*

"I will not," Rafe growled angrily, feeling his rage start to build at the mere thought of losing connection with his sister again.

Rhianna watched the two wolves chuff at each other. It was clear they were having some type of conversation and whatever was going on was quite bad because all the other wolves were watching them intently as if waiting for something to happen.

She stepped to the side of Wolfie and placed a hand on his trembling head. The growls he'd been omitting silenced immediately and he whined softly and turned to look at her with large sad eyes. "I don't know what's going on, Wolfie, but it's a bit frightening all that growling and stuff," she said softly. "I'm guessing really, but I think the big black wolf wants you to go home with them?"

Rafe whined and chuffed, lowering his head in misery.

The huge animal seemed so miserable Rhianna felt her heart tug painfully. He didn't look like he wanted to go back with his pack. "Don't be sad, Wolfie," she said wrapping her arms around the wolf's thick neck impulsively and sensing Caleb's hands reaching for her. She shook her head at him and his eyes darkened in anger. Reluctantly, he did drop his hands, though he remained tense.

"They're your pack. Your place is with them," she said soothingly as she stroked the beautiful animal's soft fur. "You didn't think I could take you home with me, did you?" she asked with a wry smile at the thought of Millie's face if she came home with this beast at her side.

"I think you're the most beautiful animal I've ever seen and I've been privileged to get the opportunity to meet you, but it's time to go home now," she sighed softly. "Old Blackie there doesn't look too happy at the moment and I really don't want to see you get into trouble. Please, Wolfie. Go home to your pack. For me."

She had no idea why she knew she was doing the right thing at the moment; she just knew it was somehow important that the enormous brown wolf went home with his pack.

Rafe whined loudly, his eyes glistening with unshed tears as his beloved Annie spoke with such wisdom for her tender years. He knew he couldn't go home with her. He knew he couldn't endanger the pack either. He just wanted one more moment with the girl who was more a daughter to him than a little sister.

"Listen to her, Rafe," Jared said with a hint of kindness in his tone. *"You know what she's saying is true. You belong here now, in our world, not in hers."*

Rafe whined one final time and stepped away from Rhianna and towards the pack. He turned and looked over his shoulder at his little sister and then turned and ran into the trees howling his misery.

Wolfie's abrupt departure surprised Rhianna. A chuff from the black wolf sent a golden brown wolf careening into the trees after him. Another chuff sent four wolves over to the body of the grey animal. They picked it up with their teeth and dragged it into the trees.

Caleb watched Hanlon closely as he wrapped his arm protectively around Rhianna. He knew the Alpha well and wasn't expecting any trouble from him, but he was still prepared to defend the girl if he had to.

Jared shook his head at the familiar way Ryder held Rhianna against him. The touch screamed intimacy and he was surprised and a little concerned. He felt a small bubble of hope well up inside him. If the girl had feelings for a vampire then perhaps things would not be as difficult as they currently were. He bowed his head at the couple and then chuffed loudly and the pack turned on their heels and sped into the forest.

Caleb relaxed slowly when the pack moved off. He turned his head, looked down at Rhianna and frowned deeply. "What part of 'stay in the car' didn't you understand?" he asked, unable to keep his anger out of his voice.

Rhianna looked up into his furious face and swallowed loudly. She was in big trouble and for a moment, she wished she'd disappeared into the trees with the wolves…

CHAPTER SIX

Caleb didn't quite know what to do with Rhianna. Half of him wanted to pull her into his embrace and kiss her senseless, while the other half wanted to punish her for scaring him so badly. He was vaguely aware that he needed to address what it meant for him to have felt such fear, but he wasn't willing to do so now.

Instead, he opened the car door. "Get in the car, Annie, and stay in it this time." It took all his self-control not to take the door off its hinges when she did as he asked.

He slammed it closed, took five long strides away from the car, and struggled to calm his anger. The car was a write off and wasn't going anywhere. He dug his cell phone from his pocket and hit speed dial.

"Demetri, I need a car out on Old Forest Road, about half-way down heading into town. I hit a wolf and the car's a write off."

"How'd you manage to hit a wolf?" Demetri asked with a healthy dose of surprise in his voice. A vampire's reflexes were phenomenal. His friend should have been able to avoid the Were.

"I don't have time to go into it," Caleb sighed. He could just imagine his friend's laughter if he admitted he'd been too busy mooning over Rhianna at the time of the accident. "Have someone else follow you out so you can get a lift back. I've got Rhianna with me and don't want any additional passengers."

Demetri whistled loudly. "So, you managed to track her down. I'm impressed."

"Demetri, just get here as soon as you can," Caleb said tiredly, running a hand through his hair. "This night has been a complete disaster and I just want to get it over and done with."

His friend laughed and hung up after promising to be there within the half hour. Caleb turned his head to peer back at the car and noted that Rhianna had remained safely inside. At least she was listening to him this time.

He kept his distance from the car, not trusting himself near the petite redhead. His thoughts were in turmoil and the longer he ignored them the worse his rage was becoming. The blind panic and fear that had coursed through him as the brown wolf charged out of the trees had stunned him and left him immobile for a fraction of a second.

He was still dithering over what to do when the wolf stopped of its own accord in front of Rhianna and then the weirdness had really started. Caleb instantly knew the wolf was a Were. He knew the animal had clear, rational thoughts and was, therefore, less of a danger to Rhianna than a normal wolf.

Still, the way the Were had submitted to the girl enraged him even as he was relieved the animal wasn't going to hurt her. Male Weres only ever submitted to their mates or children. The thought that this Dog was even contemplating mating with Rhianna brought a deep rage bubbling up from within. He had wanted to rip the wolf limb from limb at the sheer audacity of it even deigning to think of mating with his woman.

That thought had stunned Caleb even more. First the fear for Rhianna, and then thinking of her as his woman. The emotions of fear and jealously were completely alien to him. He had never had this type of reaction to a woman before and he didn't like it one bit. In a matter of weeks, she had turned his life upside down until he couldn't think straight and was feeling emotions he didn't want to feel.

He had to find some way to break her hold over him. He should just take her home and stay away from her. She was human and he was a vampire. She was short-lived and fragile. He could never tell her what he was. She was already mentally fragile enough because of the loss of her brother. How the hell could he turn around and tell her he was a vampire? He'd most likely send her completely over the edge and she'd end up in some mental institution.

Caleb sighed, and put his hands in his pockets. Still, she had adapted to the wolf quickly. Granted, she had no idea she was stroking the belly and throat of a man who was only an animal part time. Would she have adapted so easily if she'd known the wolf was a Were? It was a moot point anyway. The Weres had left and the night was ruined. She'd probably never speak to him again either after the way he'd slammed the car door on her.

Rhianna watched Caleb covertly as he stood in front of the car with his hands in his pocket. He seemed pissed at her. So pissed he didn't even want to be in the car with her. He'd called someone. Probably arranging a car to pick them up.

She was pissed at him too. He had no right to order her about as if she were a child. She was a grown woman and able to make her own decisions. The lovely warm feeling she had from meeting the large brown wolf had melted away in the face of Caleb's anger. It had been such a magical moment for her. She had felt such a strong connection to the wolf once she'd gotten over her initial fear. Now she just felt tired and disappointed. She just wanted to go home and forget she'd ever met Caleb Ryder. She closed her eyes and didn't open them again until the glare of headlights alerted her to an approaching car.

Caleb met Demetri as he stepped out of the car. His friend ran an experienced eye over him and grinned broadly. "Trouble in paradise, Caleb?"

"Fuck off," Caleb grunted, taking the keys from him as a second car pulled up. "Just arrange to get the car towed and mind your own business."

He turned back to his car and strode over to it, opening the passenger door. "Come on, get your things." He kept his gaze averted as she gathered her purse and wrap, and got out the car.

He escorted her over to the black Volvo and opened the passenger door. Once she was seated, he made sure to close this one with a lot less force than before. He ignored Demetri and didn't bother making any introductions. His friend just laughed and walked forward to inspect the damage to the Porsche, his eyebrows rising as he took in the little car.

Caleb climbed into the Volvo, fighting down his irritation at Rhianna as best he could. At least Demetri had come from the opposite direction they'd been travelling in so he didn't have to turn the car around to take Rhianna home. That was one less minor irritation to deal with.

The tension in the car was almost tangible. Neither spoke as Caleb shifted through the gears almost violently as the Volvo travelled at excess speed through the night. He didn't consciously decide to turn towards his house, it just seemed to happen. Before he realised what he had done, he was pulling up outside the mansion.

"I thought you were taking me home," Rhianna said in a small voice, staring out the windshield at the large white mansion before her.

"So did I." Caleb unclipped his seatbelt and stepped out of the car. He walked around the bonnet and opened the passenger door, waiting patiently as she hesitated before getting out.

He closed the door and headed up the steps into the house, leaving her to follow behind at her own pace. He was still furious and wanted some extra moments to try to control his anger. He had no idea why he'd brought her home. It would have been better to take her back to her place so he would have more time to calm down.

Rhianna watched Caleb warily as she stepped into the magnificent hallway. It had astounded her the first time she'd come here, but this time she barely registered the grandeur. She was too concerned about the barely controlled anger rolling off Caleb in waves. Though she didn't think he would physically hurt her, she didn't really know that much about the man. That uncertainty sent a shiver of fear coursing through her body.

Caleb noticed the motion and the slender control he had on his temper broke. His eyes narrowed dangerously. "You fear me? You insult me by fearing me? You, who all but rolled in the road with a fucking animal who could have ripped your throat out in a blink of an eye?" His anger was palpable, his tone harsh as his golden brown eyes flashed dangerously.

"Wolfie would never have hurt me," Rhianna said defensively and realised instantly it was probably the worst thing she could have said to him at that moment.

His hand snaked out so quickly she barely saw it move. One moment he was a few feet from her and the next his big hand was circling her neck and he was right before her, looming threateningly as a loud hiss escaped his throat.

She froze in panic; a little whimper of fear bubbling out of her throat as he leaned down until his face was barely an inch from hers.

"You did not know that," he hissed quietly. "When I tell you to do something you will obey me instantly, Rhianna, or suffer the consequences."

His hand wasn't squeezing her neck; it was simply holding her in place and making sure she could not back away from him. His golden brown eyes burned into her and she whimpered again as she tried to look away but found she couldn't.

Her fear infuriated him. It shamed him too. She was terrified of him and he had no one to blame but himself. The admission tore through him and his hand moved slowly, lightly stroking over the curve of her fragile neck as he took a deep breath and dampened down his rage, his expression softening.

He moved that last inch closer to her and his mouth found hers. Her startled gasp opened her soft lips so he could stroke his tongue inside her moist heat and taste her amazing sweetness again. He groaned and gathered her into his arms, his mouth becoming more demanding as he opted to kiss her senseless rather than choke the life out of her. He could never hurt this human no matter how much she infuriated him.

Caleb's kiss stunned her for a second and then she was responding to him, her tongue searching for his, stroking him lightly over and over again as he pressed his hardness against her. Her fear melted into deep, heady pleasure as his kiss deepened further. She clutched at the lapels of his jacket to keep herself from falling.

Not that he would have allowed it. Caleb's strong arms were so securely around her he would have caught her if her knees buckled as they were threatening to do.

Her memories of their night together seemed to pale in comparison to this hot, wet, luscious meeting of lips. She swooned under the assault of his mouth even though she knew she should be fighting him. She should be giving him a piece of her mind at the chauvinistic way he was behaving. However, to do that would mean taking her lips away from his and she didn't want this wonderful feeling to end.

Caleb reluctantly pulled his lips from hers to allow her the opportunity to breathe. He rested his forehead against hers and took a deep ragged breath as he fought for a new kind of control-- the control needed not to throw her down on the floor and ravish her beautiful body the way he so badly wanted to.

"I'm sorry," he whispered quietly. "For a moment I thought that wolf was going to hurt you and I felt a fear I've never experienced in my life before. I reacted badly to that fear. I know that doesn't excuse my subsequent behaviour, Annie. I'm not trying to justify myself. I'm just explaining why I acted the way I did."

Rhianna let out a long, shaky breath and swallowed hard. Caleb sounded oddly vulnerable in his admission and that tugged at something inside her. He was always so confident, whether he was making love to her or pissed at her. Never before had he ever seemed so hesitant, so unsure of himself as he did right now.

"Caleb, I'm a grown woman," she said softly. "All my life I've had my brother at my side, helping me make my decisions. He's gone now and I'm left in the position where I have to learn how to stand on my own two feet. I don't need another man to come into my life and start making my decisions for me. Yes, it probably would have been wiser if I stayed in the car tonight but I chose not to. Meeting Wolfie was a wondrous experience and you spoiled it for me with your caveman behaviour."

Caleb sighed and straightened up, moving away from her and putting his hands in his pockets to stop himself from dragging her back into his arms. "I'm sorry, Annie." There really wasn't anything more he could say. Her disappointment was palpable and he was the cause of it.

She watched him silently for a moment, warring with the need to give in to him, to grant him forgiveness, but she knew if she did then she would be silently giving him permission to behave like that again. "I'd like to go home now, Caleb," she finally said quietly.

Caleb wanted to refuse, wanted to demand she stay with him, but her set expression told him it was the wrong thing to do. "I'll take you home," he sighed, running a hand through his long hair. "Will you let me make this up to you, Annie? Can we try again to go out for dinner or a movie or something?"

Rhianna frowned slightly as she looked up into his face. He seemed sincere in his request but she wasn't sure if she wanted to see him again. She didn't need another man to come into her life and take over. She loved Rafe and missed him terribly, but he had sheltered her far longer than he had needed to and that was why she had taken his death so hard. She had been at a loss at how to go on without him. It was time she learned to take care of herself.

"I'm not sure, Caleb," she said with a deep sigh. "I'll have to think about it. I need some time to decide what I'm going to do with my life. I'm not sure if you're someone who fits in with what I want my life to be from now on."

She watched him digest what she said and saw displeasure cross his face before an expression of resignation took its place. "I understand," he said quietly before turning towards the door to take her home.

~~~~~

There was a feeling of jubilation among the pack as the rogue was finally brought to heel. They didn't even seem concerned by the fact that it had been stopped by a vampire mowing it down with his car rather than the pack putting it down. The men and women of the pack were just happy it was finally dead and there would be no more forced turnings.

Jared was also relieved but angry. He had to deal with Rafe and he wasn't looking forward to it. He had felt the man's deep pain at having to walk away from his sister. He nodded to Aaron and headed inside his house to put on a pair of jeans and a shirt.

Ten minutes later Aaron and Rafe entered having changed into clothes too. Jared's intent gaze took in Rafe's misery and he struggled not to empathise with him. He had endangered the entire pack tonight and he had to be punished.

"Leave us, Aaron," he said tersely and waited for his beta to depart before he ordered Rafe to sit down in the chair in front of his desk. He sat down behind the desk and glared at the man.

"You endangered the pack tonight, Rafe."

The other man's head shot up and he met his eyes defiantly. "How did I do that, Jared? I remained in wolf form. I did not reveal myself to Annie. I came back to the pack as ordered." Rafe's tone was terse, fury in his eyes. He was still reeling from having been so close to his sister and being forced to leave her.

"You came back to the pack when your sister told you to!" Jared barked out. "You ignored my direct order to return to the pack. I am the Alpha! You obey me at all times, not when it's convenient!" He slammed his hand down hard on the desk to emphasise his words.

Rafe dropped his gaze from his Alpha and bowed his head. Everything Jared said was true. He had disobeyed his Alpha and he knew enough about pack law to know this meant he was in serious trouble.

"What is my punishment?" he asked with a weary sigh. Whatever it was, he would endure it. Having that brief moment with his sister was worth whatever punishment his Alpha was going to mete out to him.

"Do you think I want to punish you, Rafe?" Jared uttered a muffled groan. "Do you think I don't understand how painful and hard it was for you tonight to be so close to Annie and have to walk away from her? I see right inside you, Rafe. I understand she is more your child than your sister. You have cared for her for so long, and I understand how your relationship with her has changed because of it."

He stood up and began to pace around the study. Dealing with Rafe presented the Alpha with so many unique challenges. He didn't want to break the man's spirit. Heavens above, he'd already been through so much through no fault of his own! Jared had to try to maintain authority whilst tempering his judgement to reflect the rather unique circumstances of Rafe's forced turning. He didn't want to lose him from the pack.

He stopped pacing, raking a hand through his hair as he threw himself into his chair. "Your circumstances make things difficult, Rafe. If you were an ordinary member of the pack, I would simply have you flogged for disobedience and then set to the most menial tasks for a prescribed period. I find I cannot do this with you. Doing so would only increase your hatred of pack life and you would slip further from us, possibly even going rogue."

Rafe stared at him in shock and tried to swallow down the sudden fury engulfing him. "I will never turn rogue! I will never be like that animal who did this to me! Decree your punishment, Jared. Flog me and set me to the menial tasks. I will accept your judgement."

Jared frowned at him and then a wry smile crossed his face. "Yes, you would accept the punishment and go right ahead and disobey me all over again You'd gladly accept any form of punishment just to experience that brief moment with Annie again."

Rafe looked away from his Alpha. It was true. The damned man really could see right inside him.

"You leave me no choice," Jared sighed. "It pains me to do so but I am promoting you to Beta. Perhaps if you experience some responsibility for having to care for the pack, it will instil a sense of belonging in you and you can understand the need to follow the correct chain of command."

Rafe growled and jumped from his chair. "No, you can't do this! I don't want to be a beta!" He understood the enormity of Jared's punishment. Aaron was a beta and he was Rafe's closest friend here. He routinely watched Aaron settling minor disputes, taking charge of various parts of pack life, of being responsible for every single Were beneath him.

"You have no choice," Jared drawled with a smug smile. "Well, you do have one choice," he amended. "You can either accept your promotion or you can challenge me for the position of Alpha."

The look of complete horror that crossed Rafe's face satisfied Jared's wolf. The hulking man before him had no wish ever to be Alpha, even though he was more than capable of being one. Rafe Armand would never challenge Jared for leadership.

"That is not a choice," Rafe finally ground out, his shoulders slumping in defeat.

"I'm sorry, Rafe. I know this is not what you want. I know you wish you could return to your old life as if none of this had ever happened. It has happened, though, and cannot be changed. Aaron will begin your training as a beta and you will accept the huge responsibility that is now on your shoulders. You will protect this pack with your life as we all do."

Rafe bowed his head and mumbled his agreement. He turned and left the Alpha's house with a heavy heart.

Aaron was waiting not far away, his handsome face concerned as he saw the dejected figure approach. "What was the Alpha's punishment?" he asked, concerned for his friend. He was aware of Rafe's struggle to adapt to his circumstances. "Are you to be flogged?"

Rafe's tortured gaze met his and he shook his head miserably. "You are to teach me how to be a beta."

Aaron threw his head back and laughed loudly as he slapped Rafe on the back. "The Alpha is truly evil at times, my friend. Don't look so woeful. Being a beta has many benefits as well as much responsibility. You will make an excellent beta, Rafe."

Rafe seriously doubted it but he had no choice in the matter. Jared was forcing him more fully into the pack and he was helpless to fight it.

CHAPTER SEVEN

Rhianna smiled as she drove her car along the dark road surrounded by large, looming trees. She found herself smiling often whenever she drove along Old Forest Road. It had been a week since the night she'd met Wolfie and she always found herself looking out for the hulking beast as she travelled the road. She watched her speed, too, just in case any wolves shot across her path. She didn't want to accidentally run one over.

Her smile slipped a little as her thoughts invariably turned to Caleb. It was hard not to think of him as she drove along this road. He'd taken her home that night and waited until she was safely inside before driving away. She hadn't heard a word from him since and she felt a mixture of relief with a deep longing to see him again.

She knew it was for the best. She couldn't seem to think straight when the man was around her. His overt sexuality overwhelmed her at times. She found herself giving in to him with little or no fight at all. The man was also a mass of contradictions. He could be loving and kind at times but terribly frightening at others. So many things about him scared her witless, and yet, she still longed to see him again.

She smiled ruefully and rolled her eyes. He probably hadn't given her a passing thought since he'd dropped her at home. He had most probably moved on to someone who was a lot less high maintenance than she was. Noting her surroundings, Rhianna slowed the car on impulse when she recognised the area they'd hit the wolf. She pulled over and climbed out of the car, peering into the dark at the tree line. She couldn't really see that far into the trees but she still peered intently looking for any sign of movement.

"Wolfie?" she called quietly, holding her breath to see if she could detect any sign of movement. "Are you there, Wolfie?" She was conscious of just how incredibly stupid and possibly dangerous it was to stop in the middle of the forest at night and look for a wild wolf. Caleb would be pitching a fit if he could see her right now, but she felt pulled toward the wolf in a way she just couldn't explain. She had even dreamed about Wolfie a couple of times in the past week.

The strange connection she felt towards the animal was confusing. She liked animals well enough, and had even had a dog when she was younger, but she wasn't as fond of them as Rafe had been. He had been the true animal lover in the family. So why did she feel this need to stop and see if Wolfie was around?

Rafe watched Annie from the shelter of the trees. He'd come here every night over the last week hoping to catch one more glimpse of his little sister. He thought he'd seen her car passing by a couple of times, but she'd never stopped before. He ached to break the cover of the trees and let her know he was there.

He knew Jared would be on him like a ton of bricks if he did. Even now he could feel his Alpha approaching as if he could somehow sense his beta was up to no good. He broke cover of the trees just long enough for his beloved Annie to catch sight of him for a brief moment. He whined softly once and then turned and slunk back into the trees.

Rhianna was sure it was Wolfie she'd just seen. He had only been there for a short moment before disappearing again, but she was sure it was her wolf. She stood silently hoping he would come back but he didn't. The chill in the night air sent a shiver down her spine and she got back in her car and carried on home.

Millie was in a stinking mood when she arrived. Her usually even-tempered best friend was banging noisily in the kitchen as she muttered dark threats under her breath.

"What's wrong, Mills?"

"What's wrong?" her friend practically shrieked. "*Jared bloody Hanlon* is what's wrong! That man had the barefaced nerve to call me at work today. Work of all places. He knew damned well I would have to hold my tongue because I was in the office."

Rhianna smothered a smile. Jared called Millie daily, much to her friend's disgust. She managed to avoid most of the calls; and the few that did reach her, she would bluntly tell him where to get off before hanging up. Rhianna liked the big man. He had been very kind to her after Rafe's death. She couldn't understand why Millie was so upset by such a gorgeous specimen of a man being interested in her. It wasn't as if she was still dating that guy from her work she'd been seeing briefly when Rafe died.

"Why don't you go out with him?" she asked her friend, and then ducked quickly when a saucepan sailed in her direction. "I was only asking, Mills. If you went out with him once, then maybe he'd stop calling you." Her eyes lit up with amusement.

"You could make yourself out to be the world's worst date like that movie we watched the other night. The one were guys paid a man to date their exes and be such an ass to them they ran back to their old boyfriends." She couldn't remember the movie's name but it had been kind of funny in a cringe-worthy way.

Millie blinked at her for a long moment and then slowly smiled. "Maybe that would work," she said, brushing her black curls out of her face. "Annie, you could be a borderline genius."

Rhianna laughed and picked up the saucepan, which had landed on the sofa. "Only could be?"

"You'd need to sort out your own love life before you could definitely be a genius," Millie laughed, flushing sheepishly as she accepted the saucepan back. "Sorry about that."

"I don't know why you're so angry at Jared." Rhianna sat down at the breakfast table and slipped off her shoes. "The man is tall, dark, and gorgeous. He has the body of a Greek god and he's charming to boot. What isn't there to like about him?"

Millie groaned and sat down next to her. "I don't know, Annie. There's something about the man that sets me on edge. He's so cocky and sure of himself. It's almost as if he thinks all he has to do is crook his little finger and I'll melt into his arms and do whatever he tells me. I'm not that kind of woman, Annie. I don't submit to that macho male crap."

Rhianna smiled and shook her head. She could kind of understand where Millie was coming from. She had practically run from Caleb when he'd tried his macho crap on her, only she had been with Caleb and knew just what she was missing by running from him. Millie was running and she hadn't even had the chance to sample the delights of Jared Hanlon.

She found herself trying to imagine what Jared would be like as a lover. He oozed the very same sexual confidence that Caleb did. He was probably just as skilled as Caleb in the bedroom; and yet, despite all the things going for Jared, he did not spark one single bit of interest in her. He was just a very handsome, charming man to Rhianna. A friend and nothing more.

"What are you thinking about?" Millie asked curiously.

"I was trying to imagine Jared as a lover." Rhianna smiled, her smile broadening at the unconscious look of displeasure that crossed her friend's face and the slight tensing of her body. So, Millie wasn't interested in Jared? Yeah, right!

"I couldn't imagine it though," she continued, as if she hadn't noticed her friend's reaction. "I keep thinking of Caleb instead."

"You really liked him, didn't you?" Millie asked, shooting her a sympathetic smile. She didn't know why her friend had stopped seeing the gorgeous man. Rhianna had been very tight lipped about their short-lived date the previous week.

Rhianna's thoughtful expression was broken by a smile. "I still do. He was just exhibiting some of the macho male crap you so disapprove of, and I needed a bit of time to decide if it was something I could put up with or not."

"And?"

"And I'm going to go and see him tonight," Rhianna announced slowly, as if she had only just made the decision.

Millie was surprised at her announcement and also pleased. Her friend had no idea just how animated she became when she talked about Caleb. He seemed to be one of the few people who could make Rhianna smile these days. He seemed to be good at pissing her off too, but that was healthy. Laughing and temper tantrums were all part of living and finally Rhianna was starting to live again.

"Maybe you should give Jared a chance too, Mills. You never know, you may be pleasantly surprised." Rhianna couldn't help smiling as indignation crossed her friend's face, along with a healthy dose of doubt. She decided not to push it any further and rose from her chair to head towards her bedroom. "Oh, have a look in my bag, Mills. I've been working on an idea and I've done up a business plan. Let me know what you think."

Millie had a big smile on her face as she read Rhianna's business plan for her bookshop. She pouted her lips at the name 'Armand's Bookshop'. It felt impersonal, lacking the intimacy of the proposed type of bookstore her friend was envisioning.

Bookstore was definitely better than Bookshop. She pondered it some more and then slowly smiled. Hunting for a pen, she scrolled across the top of the first page of the business plan. 'Create Your Own Happiness Bookstore'.

It sounded a bit clichéd, but it had been one of Rafe's favourite sayings whenever they were sad about something. He would sit them down and gently tell them that they created their own happiness. It had always made them feel better. She wondered if Rhianna would like it.

Her friend appeared out of her room ten minutes later. Millie's smile widened as she took in the little black skirt and purple halter neck top Rhianna was wearing.

"Smoking hot, girl," she laughed, and made her best leer face.

Rhianna threw her head back and burst out laughing, her long auburn curls swaying around her as she did. "Let's hope Caleb thinks so too," she smiled, as she sat down at the table beside her friend.

"So, what did you think of the bookshop?" She grabbed an apple out the fruit bowl and bit into it.

Millie's cobalt blue eyes shone as she smiled her approval of the idea. "I thought the name was a bit impersonal, but apart from that it sounds really fantastic, Annie. I'd be up for offering my services as a storyteller at the weekends." She passed the plan over to Rhianna and watched her friend's face intently as she read her scrawled writing across the top of the page.

Rhianna looked up at Millie and her lavender eyes gleamed wetly even as her smile was radiant across her face. "It's perfect, Mills," she whispered. "It's all of us together forever."

Millie returned her smile and squeezed her friend's hand gently "That's what I thought when I wrote it."

"Crack open that bottle of red, Mills," Rhianna said with a big smile. "Let's have a toast."

Her friend jumped up and opened the red wine, pouring out two very generous glasses and handing her one.

"To new beginnings and creating your own happiness." Rhianna smiled.

"Amen to that, Annie!" Millie laughed, as they clinked glasses together.

Rhianna finished her wine, then grabbed her wrap and purse and headed for the door.

"Call Jared, Millie," she called over her shoulder. "Take a leap of faith!"

Millie grunted, but laughed as the door closed behind her friend. Maybe Annie was right. Maybe she should take a chance. She considered it briefly and then frowned. She was not ready to give in to Jared Hanlon. Not yet.

Rhianna took a cab. She had two choices of where to head, either Caleb's mansion or Karpathia's. She opted to try Karpathia's first. It was Friday night and most people went out to wind down after a long, hard week at work. She gave the cab driver the address and sat back for the short ride to the club.

She tried to calm down her heart, which had suddenly started beating loudly. What if Caleb wasn't interested anymore? What if she got to the club and found him wrapped in some other woman's arms? Well, it would be her own damned fault if that was the case, but she wouldn't know if he'd moved on if she didn't at least try to find him.

~~~~~

Caleb was lounging in the shadows. His bored gaze ran across the crowded room as he wished he'd ignored Demetri's incessant bullying to come out tonight. He was tired and cranky and he just wanted to go home and put his feet up.

He'd tried to slip out a couple of times but Demetri had appeared at his side, halting his escape with a deep frown and a long lecture about how it was time for him to give up on Rhianna and get back into the swing of things. Caleb caved in both times just to shut his friend up. His constant nagging was driving him insane.

He was just about to make his third bid for freedom. Demetri was sitting in a booth with a lithe little brunette tucked up in his lap, so the chances of Caleb getting out this time were more encouraging than the last two attempts. He watched Demetri move in for another long, lusty kiss with the brunette, and took a deep breath, getting ready to move. He froze where he stood.

Lavender and jasmine assaulted his nostrils and his eyes widened as he slowly turned his head towards the club door. He blinked slowly as Rhianna walked in, her gaze quickly sweeping around the room.

God, she was so stunningly beautiful she astounded him. His greedy gaze ran over her body, and he smothered a groan at the sexy outfit she was wearing. The material clung to her body like a fitted glove, showing off all her wonderful assets and making his body harden instantly.

He knew she couldn't see him in the shadows. It was one of the reasons they kept this part of the club so dimly lit. They could hide within the shadows and survey the entire room unobserved. Rhianna was definitely looking for someone. Was she looking for him? He didn't dare hope she was but he did remember telling her he was a silent partner in the club. Surely she must be looking for him? She wouldn't be so cruel as to arrange a date with another man in the very place she knew he would most likely be?

~~~~~

Rhianna couldn't see Caleb and she struggled to hide her disappointment. She would have to try his mansion then. If he wasn't there, then she'd just go home. At least she would have tried to catch up with him. She was just about to turn to leave when something drew her eyes to a couple in the booth across from her and something about the man caught her eye.

He was gorgeous and had long flowing black hair which obscured his face slightly. Even so, there was something about him that convinced her she knew him from somewhere. She stepped a little further into the room just as the woman on the man's lap brushed his hair back from his face and she got a better view.

He was the man who had come out with the Volvo when Caleb's car was struck by the wolf. He was a friend of Caleb's, she was sure of that, though she didn't know his name. He would probably know where Caleb was, but he appeared to be a little busy at the moment.

Rhianna's eyes went wide as she saw the man run a hand up the woman's thigh and slide it under her short skirt. Was he really touching her intimately in the middle of a club? Her cheeks flushed scarlet, and she looked away and nervously clutched at her stomach. She couldn't very well walk over there now and ask where Caleb was, and yet, if she didn't she may lose her nerve and never try to find him again.

Squaring her shoulders, she walked determinedly over to the booth. The man and woman ignored her, continuing to kiss as if they were somewhere private. Rhianna felt her embarrassment mount. She timidly cleared her throat whilst trying to look anywhere but at the couple.

Demetri growled low in his throat as the human woman's scent washed over him and her little throat noise interrupted his very pleasant moment with the woman in his arm. "I'm busy," he grunted, not even bothering to look up. "Come back later if you want some action."

Rhianna gasped at his abrupt tone, and his automatic assumption that she wanted in on the 'action'. She felt her temper spark, and though her embarrassment deepened, she couldn't stop her tart response. "Oh, please! I have much better taste than you!"

Her tone literally dripped with derision and Caleb found himself smiling from his spot in the corner as she knocked Demetri down a peg or two.

Demetri stopped kissing the brunette, and looked up with a hint of surprise in his cool, green eyes. He scrutinised the woman before him, and then he slowly smiled.

"Well, well, well, if it isn't the little redhead," he drawled, pushing the woman from his lap as he sat up straight. "Give me a moment, darling." He shooed her away with a hand, his full concentration on Rhianna.

"So, what can I do for you, Rhianna?" he asked with a mocking smile. "I suppose you're looking for Caleb? Feel the need to do a little more emasculating of my friend?"

His words were nasty, cutting, and totally undeserved. She stared down at him and felt an itch in her palm. She clenched her hand so she didn't smack his smug face the way she wanted to.

"What goes on between Caleb and I is none of your business," she answered frostily, squaring her shoulders against his glacial green gaze. "You're hardly one to talk about what's appropriate anyway. Not after what I've just witnessed. You do know there are public indecency laws? This is a public place and what you were doing to that poor woman just now was outrageous."

She knew she sounded stuffy and prudish, but something about the man rubbed her up the wrong way. It didn't help she was embarrassed and nervous about seeing Caleb again, too. The combination of emotions was making her lash out, though he didn't seem the least annoyed about it judging from his expression.

Demetri threw back his head and laughed loudly. "Who the fuck are you, Martha Stewart? Believe me, darling, that little filly was most definitely not complaining about what I was 'doing' to her. On the contrary, she loved every single second of it."

Rhianna felt her face flushing scarlet again, but she held her ground. The man may be gorgeous to look at, but he had no redeeming qualities whatsoever. "Fine, I'm not going to argue with you," she snapped. "I just want to know where Caleb is. Is he here tonight?"

Demetri glanced in the corner and saw Caleb glaring at him with a murderous expression on his face. He knew his friend could hear every word being said, and was not at all pleased with what he'd heard so far. He sighed deeply and looked back at the redhead. If he didn't apologise to the girl, his friend would most probably try to rearrange his face for him. He sighed deeply again.

"My apologies, Rhianna. You caught me at an inopportune moment and my manners were severely lacking. Yes, Caleb is here tonight. Do you wish me to tell him you're looking for him?"

She was taken aback by the complete change in the man and she looked around quickly to see if she could spot Caleb anywhere near them. She didn't see him and turned back to the booth.

"I'm sorry too," she said thawing slightly. "You have me at a disadvantage. You appear to know who I am, but I have no idea who you are other than you brought the replacement car out to Old Forest Road last week."

"Demetri Bozic, proprietor of this fine club and Caleb's business partner in many a venture." He smiled, holding out his hand.

Rhianna accepted his hand and shook it quickly. "Pleased to meet you, Demetri. Sorry I ran my mouth off just now. I'm not used to such public displays and to be honest I'm a bit nervous, too. I'm not usually such a bitch."

Demetri smiled and stood up. "No apology necessary," he answered with a dismissive wave of his hand. "Come; let me buy you a drink. I'll track down Caleb for you and send him over."

She allowed him to escort her to the bar and told the bartender to give her a drink of her choice on the house. He waited until she was talking to the bartender and quickly slipped into the shadows beside Caleb.

"If you ever speak to Annie like that again you and I will have a serious issue," Caleb growled in his ear.

"Peace, Caleb," Demetri said soothingly. "You've been impossible to live with for weeks now. Forgive me if I find it hard not to blame the girl for the cause of your shocking behaviour. I apologised to her and she accepted my apology. Let it go at that."

Caleb dampened down his anger as his gaze turned to Rhianna sipping at her glass of red wine as she turned around to survey the room. He wanted to go to her, but now the moment was here he was afraid to. Her rejection the last time he'd seen her had been hard to take.

She had come looking for him though. He had seen her mortification at Demetri's lewd acts with the other woman, and she had still approached him to ask if he was in the club. She must want to see him pretty badly to endure the embarrassment and then Demetri's tirade on top of it.

"Well, are you going to go to the girl?" Demetri asked with a tinge of irritation in his voice. "She is the reason you've been moping around all this time. She's here willingly. Go to her."

Caleb turned to his friend and raised an eyebrow at him. "I thought you didn't like her, Demetri."

"Not like her," Demetri chuckled. "That girl has spirit! Can't remember anyone giving me lip like that before. I'm almost annoyed I let you have her the first night she came in."

Caleb growled at him again, and Demetri's chuckles increased. "I said almost. I prefer my women to know the boundaries, Caleb. Can't be bothered with all this touchy feely crap you're letting yourself in for."

Demetri gave his friend a level look. "If you want the girl then go get her. I have no wish to spend the next century watching you mope around because you were too much of a coward to take a chance."

With that Demetri melted back into the room, and went hunting for his brunette. She was waiting for him in the booth they'd been sitting in and he slid gracefully onto the plush leather seat, gathering her back into his arms.

Rhianna saw Demetri come back from wherever he went to and looked around for Caleb but there was no sign of him. She took Caleb's lack of appearance as a sign he wasn't interested anymore.

Quickly finishing her wine, she went to slide from her stool only to feel a strong arm snake around her waist to prevent her. She gasped and looked up to find herself staring into Caleb's eyes.

"Surely you're not leaving already, Annie?" he asked with a small smile tugging at his lips. "Not after coming all this way to find me."

"Caleb." His name came out breathlessly, and she flushed at how gauche she sounded. "I didn't think you were going to see me." She flushed again as she blurted the words out without thinking.

Caleb stared down at her, his heart thumping wildly in his chest now that he was so close to her. He read the uncertainty on her face, saw the flush of colour creep across her cheeks and he smiled and leaned closer so he could inhale her delicious scent.

"As if I could stay away," he murmured against the shell of her ear, hearing her heartbeat start to race as she sucked in a sharp breath. His lips brushed against her ear before sliding slowly down the side of her neck. "I didn't think you'd come looking for me, Annie. Not after our last conversation."

"I told you I needed some time, Caleb, to decide what I wanted to do with my life." Her breath coming out sharply as his lips moved back up to her ear and he nipped lightly at her earlobe.

"I presume you've decided what it is you wish to do?" His lips teased along her jawline, his greedy gaze memorising every single feature on her beautiful face. He was pleased to see the little lines of grief looked less pronounced now, as if she'd begun to come to terms with the death of her brother.

"I've made a start," she smiled softly. She was so tempted to turn her face slightly so their lips would meet, but she didn't want to appear too eager. He could probably already hear how hard her heart was beating as his lips trailed across her skin.

He pulled back so he could meet her gaze. He smiled at her, his golden brown eyes warm. "And what have you decided, Annie?"

"That if I wanted to be happy I can't sit around and wait for it to happen. I have to make it happen," she answered slowly. "As soon as I decided that, I changed and came looking for you. It seemed like the next logical step to take."

Caleb closed his eyes and inhaled her sweet scent again. He knew he should stop this before it went any further but he couldn't resist her any longer. Demetri was right. He would be a complete pain if he didn't explore whatever this was between them. Despite all the unexpected emotions, the inherent difficulties of being with her, he had to have her in his life.

"Do you think I could make you happy?" he asked softly, his lips a hairsbreadth away from hers, her hot breath fanning across his face and making him ache with the need to kiss her.

"I think you could, Caleb." Annie knew she was being bold but her reward was a flash of joy that crossed his face a second before he leaned forward and captured her lips with his. Her lips trembled as he gently rubbed his mouth against hers in a kiss so tentative and yet so full of promise.

The tiniest of moans escaped her throat, and he deepened the kiss before he reluctantly pulled away. He really didn't want to stop kissing her but he knew she was more inhibited than he was. Once she realised she was sitting at the bar in full view of everyone, she would feel uncomfortable about their kisses and he didn't want that. He sat up straight and signalled the bartender for two more glasses of red wine.

"So, I believe we have a dinner date to reschedule?" Caleb asked, reaching down to brush a finger over her cheek. He saw the surprise on her face and knew she had expected him to drag her from the club back to his place so he could ravish her. He was sorely tempted to, but he wanted to do this slowly. He wanted to date her the human way. It would help him to adjust from his normal way of doing things too. He had to learn how to be with a woman and not just indulge in the pleasures of a woman's body.

"Okay, dinner it is," Rhianna laughed, and leaned her head on his shoulder. If Caleb wanted to do this right then she wasn't going to stand in his way. She was actually very touched he was being so considerate. It gave her hope they could build something worthwhile together and that they wouldn't just have a few months of wild passion before it fizzled out into nothing.

"How about tomorrow night?" Caleb reached for his glass of wine and took a sip. He watched her face trying to gauge her reaction. "Or we could meet for lunch and then maybe do something afterwards? It is Saturday tomorrow and I don't have any other plans."

Rhianna grinned broadly, as she sat straighter and reached for her glass of wine. "That sounds perfect, Caleb. I do have something I need to do in the afternoon but you can help me with it."

Her lavender eyes were bright with excitement and Caleb couldn't stop the smile which tugged at his lips. Whatever she needed to do it was something that truly excited her.

"Okay, you've piqued my interest. What do you have planned for the afternoon?" He blinked in surprise when she told him.

"Property viewing?" he repeated. "Are you moving?"

"No, silly. Can we go sit somewhere else, Caleb? I feel kind of on show here at the bar. I wouldn't normally sit at a bar if I was going out with friends."

Caleb slid gracefully from his stool, wrapping an arm around her waist to help her down. He nodded imperceptibly to one of his kind in the booth across from them and the man moved from the booth as Caleb escorted Rhianna across the room.

Her lavender eyes sparkled with mischief as she slid into the booth. "I hope you're not as naughty as Demetri is in these booths, Caleb."

Caleb chuckled and slid in beside her, dropping a quick kiss on the side of her neck. "I'll only be as naughty as you allow me to be." He laughed against her soft skin, and she shivered and let out a throaty laugh which went straight down his spine and made him suck in a deep breath before he straightened up.

"Behave, woman." He laughed, shaking his head. "I'm trying to be on my best behaviour here." His body was hard and aching with need and he wouldn't have minded a little discreet fun in the booth, but he really didn't think she would be up for it.

"This slow dating thing, Caleb, you're not going to do the whole 'friends' thing like you suggested the last time?" Rhianna asked, her hand moving to his silk shirt to rest against the hard muscles of his chest.

Caleb swallowed and stifled a groan at her touch. "I don't honestly think I'd be able to keep my hands off you to just be friends, Annie." His voice came out sounding hoarse. "I won't lie to you and say I don't want you in my bed because you know I do, but I want to do this right. Normal couples do a lot of kissing when they're dating though so we'll have enough fun together while we get to know each other better."

Rhianna smiled up at him and reached up to brush her fingers through his hair as it fell forward as he looked down at her. "I'm glad to hear that." She smiled impishly and raised her face for his kiss.

Caleb groaned and bent down as his arms wrapped around her and pulled her onto her knees so she was closer to him. His mouth was hard and demanding against hers, his teeth nipping at her bottom lip until she opened her mouth to him and their tongues met in a feverish duel. Her sweet taste overpowered his senses, his hands sliding down her back to her hips as he twisted her body until she was sitting in his lap. He devoured her sweet lips.

"You taste so amazing," he whispered. "You feel amazing, and you smell amazing."

Rhianna laughed, and leaned her head against his chest. "I think I'm getting the message, you think I'm amazing."

Caleb's laughter joined hers and he leaned back against the leather seat and cradled her in his arms. He couldn't remember a time when he'd ever felt this almost blissful feeling of happiness. This petite woman in his arms had somehow wormed her way through every one of his defences and now he was open and exposed to her in a way no one had ever been able to manage before. It felt liberating and terrifying at the same time.

"So, this property viewing?" he queried.

Rhianna smiled as she played with one of the buttons on his shirt. "I'm going to start my own business. A little old-fashioned bookstore where people can buy books, then sit down, and read them as they drink their coffee or tea. It'll have a combination of old and new books with the option to trade second-hand books. Too many people have forgotten the joy of reading, Caleb. I want to give people that joy back."

"Sounds nice," Caleb smiled, and it did sound nice. He was an avid reader himself, always had been. If he'd ever found a bookstore like the one Annie was describing, he'd have spent many an hour inside such a place. "So, you're going to look at property space to rent?"

Rhianna sat up and reached for her wine glass. She took a long sip and put it down again. "I did consider renting but then I realised my landlord could decide to not renew my lease, so I'm opting to buy instead."

Caleb blinked in surprise. "You can afford to buy? The properties in town are quite expensive."

"I know," Rhianna sighed. "I've already looked at a couple. They weren't right though, and were too expensive like you said. The ones I have lined up for tomorrow are off the main drag and a bit cheaper."

Caleb's mind was whirling as he listened to her. He owned property in town. He knew just how expensive they could be even off the main drag. "Annie, I hope you don't mind me asking but how can you afford to purchase property in town?"

She slid off his lap and turned to look up at him. "Why do you want to know, Caleb?" she asked carefully. "Are you after my money?" She made it sound like a joke but he could see wariness in her lavender eyes.

He sighed deeply. "Annie, I have more money than I know what to do with. I can assure you, I have no interest in yours. I was just curious as to how you had the funds to purchase property in town."

"Rafe left a life insurance policy with a solicitor. I knew nothing about it until Jared showed up at the door a few weeks after Rafe died." She didn't notice the expression that crossed Caleb's face as she cuddled back into him and rested her head against his chest.

Caleb felt his blood run cold and knew the expression on his face would be murderous. He struggled hard to change it to a more neutral expression. He toyed with Rhianna's curls as a way to soothe his sudden rage. "Jared," he said carefully. "That wouldn't be Jared Hanlon, would it?"

Rhianna sat up and smiled widely. "Oh, do you know Jared? He was very kind to me when he dropped by. I was having a bit of a bad day and I screamed bloody murder at him. Thankfully he forgave my appalling lack of manners, which I thought was really kind of him."

Caleb had carefully schooled his features and he hoped Rhianna didn't notice his smile didn't quite reach his eyes. "Yes, I've known Jared for a very long time. We go way back."

"He's got a thing for Millie but don't let her know I told you about it," she said in a low voice. "He calls her every day insisting she go out with him and she keeps refusing. I told her to at least go on one date and see what happens, but I don't know if she will."

He listened to her prattle on about Jared's pursuit of her friend and the icy feeling inside him deepened with every word. He was glad Rhianna didn't notice his detachment. He was glad she didn't notice his barely controlled fury. If she had any inkling what was going through his mind right at that very moment she would have run for the hills and never looked back.

Caleb spent the next hour with her fighting hard not to go over to the Hanlon Pack and rip the dogs to shreds until he finally reached Hanlon and 'Wolfie'. He now completely understood the strange behaviour of the brown wolf. He knew exactly who he was and he wanted to kill him for the pain he'd put his woman through, the pain she was still suffering. Rafe Armand had a lot to answer for, as did Jared Hanlon.

Not content with taking Annie's brother from her, Hanlon was now lining up to take her best friend too. He would kill him before he allowed him to hurt his Annie again.

He smiled and nodded, answered questions by rote, as he fought with himself to contain his rage. His Annie sat cuddled against him, completely unaware of his turmoil, and he was grateful for it. He didn't want to lose her again.

He finally closed his eyes and pulled her up against him so he could kiss her soft lips, taste her sweetness, and lose himself in her innocence. It was the only way he could calm the raging beast within. When he kissed Annie, all the anger melted away and the danger point receded for a short time.

He decided he wouldn't kill the dogs. That would hurt Annie too much. He would be having serious words with Hanlon though. As soon as he could arrange it.

CHAPTER EIGHT

"Give me a second while I have a quick word with Demetri." Caleb smiled and ran a finger down Rhianna's cheek before heading out of the booth and looking for his friend.

The instant the dark-haired vampire saw the expression on his friend's face, he tensed and quirked an eyebrow in query.

"Meet me on Old Forest Road in half an hour. I'm taking Annie home and then I'll meet you there."

The coldness of Caleb's tone had Demetri's interest piqued. "The wolves? What's going on?"

His friend cast a glance behind him, smiling at Rhianna before turning back. "I'll explain when we get there. Just make sure you're there to back me up." He turned to walk away but a hand on his arm stopped him. His pointed look had Demetri removing his hand with a deep sigh.

"If there's going to be trouble out there then maybe we should bring some more backup." Demetri didn't even attempt to phrase it as a question. "I can call the twins…"

"Leave those two out of it," Caleb interjected, frowning deeply. "We'll have all-out war if they're there." He considered for a moment and then sighed. "Bring a couple more people, just enough to show I'm serious."

Demetri nodded. "I don't know what's gotten you so riled up, my friend, but you know I'll stand beside you. The Council will not be happy if you start a war though." It was unusual that he was the one advising caution, but the expression on Caleb's face was one he hadn't seen in a very long time. His friend was beyond furious about something and that didn't bode well for the Weres.

"Leave me to deal with the Council if it comes to that." Caleb didn't wait for Demetri to respond, turning and heading back to Rhianna.

"Ready to go?" He smiled, helping her from the booth and waiting patiently as she collected her purse. Tucking her under his arm, he escorted Rhianna from the club, listening as she chattered away beside him. The sound of her voice helped soothe him, as did the feel of her body pressed against his side. By the time they reached her apartment some of his tension had eased and he was sure that the petite redhead at his side had no inkling of the darker thoughts running through his head.

He was somewhat perplexed as to why figuring out Hanlon's deceit had infuriated him so much. Turning to glance at the woman at his side had him tracing the small lines of grief just beginning to lessen at the corners of her eyes. Remembering how she had cried in his arms earlier had his fury ratcheting back up a notch.

Why Rhianna's pain tugged at his soul was a mystery but he knew he couldn't walk away from the rage within. Hanlon and her brother had hurt her and he couldn't let that go. This fragile woman had somehow becomes his to protect and heaven help anyone who hurt her.

Rhianna was tired but had a big smile on her face. The evening with Caleb had been fun and like the first time they'd met, she had been able to forget about losing Rafe for the few hours while she was in his company. There was something about Caleb Ryder that soothed her soul in a way no one else could. Was she falling in love with him or were her emotions confused because of the tragedy she'd recently suffered? Rhianna found she didn't want to examine the question and smiled up at the man who made everything seem that bit easier to deal with.

"I really enjoyed tonight, Caleb. Thank you for a lovely evening."

"I enjoyed it too, Annie." He smiled back, reaching over and brushing her curls from her face. "I'm already looking forward to spending the day with you tomorrow." He wasn't surprised to find that he meant what he said. Despite everything that was about to happen, his thoughts were already straying to spending the next day with her. For the first time in a long time, Caleb was actually looking forward to time passing.

Walking her to her front door had him feeling disquiet at the thought they were about to be parted. "I'm going to miss you the moment you go inside," he sighed softly.

His words brought a smile to Rhianna's face and she looked so beautiful, he had to reach for her and pull her into his arms. She melted against him and he lifted her up so she could wrap her arms around his neck as he kissed her. His sudden need appeared to surprise her and she pulled back and looked at him quizzically, but he just smiled and placed a gentle kiss on her mouth before her set her down again.

"Get inside before I forget I'm supposed to be a gentleman." His tone was lightly teasing as he pushed her inside.

His smile melted instantly when she closed the door. Spinning around, Caleb took the steps three at a time to get to his car and speed away from the apartment. Black rage filled his soul as he sped all the way down Old Forest Road until he came to three park cars. Demetri was already standing outside his car waiting for him. Caleb signalled the other vampires to stay in their cars for now and turned to face the trees.

"Hanlon!" he roared at the top of his voice and Demetri looked at him with a concerned expression.

"Caleb, are you going to tell me what the fuck is going on?" his friend asked. "If I need to back you up then at least clue me the fuck in so I know why I'm about to start a war with the dogs!" His friend's unusual behaviour was unsettling him. He figured it had to have something to do with the redhead because until Caleb had met her he'd been pretty level-headed.

Caleb didn't answer him. In truth, he was too furious to speak. He glared into the trees, knowing there would be wolves around who would have reported that they were there waiting for the Hanlon Alpha to appear. Demetri had called him anyway at Caleb's instigation. If Hanlon didn't show up quickly he'd go looking for him, and the Alpha knew it. Jared Hanlon wouldn't want a vampire in the middle of his pack compound.

Finally, the enormous shapes of half a dozen wolves appeared, the big black Alpha leading the way. Caleb saw the brown wolf close at his side and his fury escalated as he watched it with narrowed eyes. The wolves surveyed the vampires intently for a moment and then Jared shifted and rose to his feet standing naked before him. "What's this all about, Ryder?" he asked tersely. "Why did you have your lackey call and demand this meeting?"

Demetri rolled his eyes and leaned against his car. He was way too old to let a stupid dog goad him into losing his temper. Better dogs had tried and failed. His gaze remained fixed on his friend who was ignoring the Alpha and glaring at the large brown wolf at his side.

Caleb pointed at the brown wolf and growled, "Change!"

Jared took a step forward, his hands clenching at his sides. "You don't get to order my pack around, vampire."

"I'm not talking to a member of your pack, I'm talking to the brother of the woman I intend to spend the rest of my life with," Caleb hissed. He glared at the wolf as it growled loudly at him. He didn't even register what he had just admitted to but Demetri did and was staring at his friend in shock. "Change! I want to look the bastard in the eye that broke my woman's heart and then played with her here on this road. Change, Armand, or so help me God, I will rip your throat out where you stand. You're already dead to Annie. She'll never know you died twice!"

Demetri straightened as loud growls echoed through the trees. "Caleb, calm yourself. I understand your anger," he paused and then smiled wryly. "Actually I don't understand it, but are you really willing to start a war with the dogs over this? Do you really think this would be what the redhead wants? You can't be killing her brother, my friend. She'll be very put out about it."

Caleb turned his head and shot his friend a murderous look. "Did I ask for your opinion?"

Demetri stepped back and put his hands up. "I'm only saying, Caleb. Maybe you should calm down a little first and think things through. I'm more than happy to help you with the dogs. I just don't think Annie will be mighty impressed about it when she finds out."

"If they're all dead then she'll never have to find out." Caleb voice was cold, his gaze once more swinging to the brown wolf.

"There are more of us than there are of you," Jared countered calmly. "You should listen to your friend, Ryder. Go and cool your head. Come back when you can be reasonable about things. If you truly cared anything for Annie then you'd know what he says is true. She will find out and she'll hate you until the day she dies."

Caleb felt his rage boil over as he turned to the Alpha. "Don't you dare pretend you give a flying fuck about Annie, Hanlon," he roared furiously. "If it wasn't bad enough you took her brother from her, now you're sniffing around her best friend!

"Do you know how cute Annie finds your pursuit of Millie? She thinks it's so romantic you won't give up despite being rejected time and time again. She's actively encouraging Millie to go on a fucking date with you; she thinks it's so romantic. She has no idea that you're planning to steal the only family member she has left. She knows nothing about Weres and their mating. She doesn't understand that when Millie finally agrees to mate with you, she'll never see her friend ever again!"

Rafe let out an agonised howl and shifted into human form. "You bastard," he roared at Jared. "You fucking sneaky, lying bastard! You said you'd take care of Annie. You said you'd make sure she was okay, when all the time you were plotting on how to get your hands on Millie!"

"Rafe, it wasn't like that." Jared used a soothing tone, signalling to Aaron to flank Rafe on his other side in case the big man started to go rogue. There was only so much a forced turning could take in a short period, and Ryder's revelations could prove to be the final thing that pushed him over the edge. "The vampire is twisting things to his advantage, Rafe. Don't let him push your buttons."

"He's the only one talking any sense here." The words ground out of Rafe, hate and self-loathing layering his tone. "He is right to be furious at me. I let you keep me here when every instinct said to go home to Annie. I let you convince me it had to be this way; that the pack had to be protected. The pack was never in any danger from my sister. She would never have told anyone about us. To do so would have endangered me and she would never do anything to cause me any harm."

"Rafe, the protection of the pack is paramount. You've been with us long enough to know that. We can't start picking and choosing who someone thinks can be trusted to know our secret. It just doesn't work that way. Eventually the wrong person would be chosen and all of us would be in danger. It's a pack law and a pack decision. Everyone has agreed to it."

"I never agreed to it," Rafe yelled. "I didn't ask to be made into one of you. You let one of your kind go mad and run around attacking people and killing them. I wish to God that the rogue had killed me too. It's your fault I'm like this. Your laws fucked up somewhere, you didn't protect innocents like me, and do you give a shit about it? No, you don't. Not only am I punished by becoming a Were, I have to lose the most precious thing in my life too!"

Rafe suddenly broke. "You wouldn't even let me be with her in my wolf form." Tears welled up in his eyes as he looked at his Alpha. "She knew me, Jared. Even as a wolf, my Annie knew me somehow and you wouldn't even give me that!"

Jared frowned deeply as Rafe broke before his eyes. The man's anger petered out as quickly as it had arrived and he sank to his knees to the ground weeping inconsolably. Aaron chuffed loudly, rubbing his head against Rafe's shoulder, using the power of a wolf's touch to try to soothe his distraught friend.

"Are you happy now, Ryder?" Jared asked coldly, turning to Caleb. "Months of painful, hard work has just been pissed down the drain because of you. You may not think much of us or how I run this pack, but you've no right to destroy one of mine just because you want to bed his sister. Get the fuck off my land. If you come back here, we will take it as a declaration of war." He turned his back to the vampires and helped Rafe to his feet. He murmured low to the weeping man as the wolves flanked them as they disappeared into the trees.

Caleb watched them go silently, pursing his lips. He'd learned a lot from the encounter and not everything to his liking. Rhianna's brother was in deep torment. A torment he had increased greatly tonight. He had expected to feel some kind of satisfaction but instead he felt hollow inside. She'd hate him for hurting her brother. It wouldn't matter how angry she was at Rafe, she would still hate him for what he'd done this night.

"That was a roaring success." Demetri's dry remark had him hissing through clenched teeth.

"Fuck off, Demetri. I'm going home. Stay away from the pack until I decide what to do."

Demetri barked out a laugh without humour. "You want to decide? Maybe you should let me decide, Caleb, because so far you're fucking everything up. What the hell is all this 'the woman I intend to spend the rest of my life with' shit? Has the redhead cast some kind of spell on you because since you've met her you haven't been behaving normally?"

Caleb bristled, his eyes going flat as he pinned his friend with his gaze. "Her name is Annie. I suggest you use it. What goes on between us is none of your business either, so keep your comments to yourself. Now, I'm going home."

"Caleb..." Demetri tried once more to get his friend to talk but he walked away ignoring him, climbing into his car and speeding off down the road. He watched the car retreat, sensing Stephan approach.

"What's going on, Demetri?"

He turned to look at his friend, meeting puzzled eyes. "The hell if I know, Stephan. Whatever is going on is done for tonight. Go home. I'll keep an eye on Caleb." As he headed over to Caleb's, Demetri's thoughts were once more on the woman who was the centre of the current storm. If Caleb continued to act aggressively out of character, then he would have to step in and protect his friend. He would do what needed to be done to protect not only Caleb but also his people. If Rhianna Armand proved to be a threat, he would have no qualms about neutralising that threat.

~~~~

Caleb didn't sleep well. He tossed and turned most of the night trying to think of some way to make things right. He'd wounded Rhianna's brother gravely. His ignorance of the events leading up to Rafe's turning was no excuse. Sighing loudly, he got up and headed in for a quick shower. Pulling on a pair of old faded Levis and a silk shirt, he knew he had to do something to repair the damage he'd caused. His erratic emotions were making life difficult to say the least.

He was so used to always being in control. He didn't know how to handle the extreme mood swings he was now subject to. It was all Rhianna's fault. He'd been just fine up until the night she'd walked into Karpathia's. Now he had all these raging emotions deep inside him, and it was disconcerting to say the least.

Caleb shook his head as he pulled on his boots. He wondered if Demetri had gone home or stayed the night so he could continue with his berating of him first thing this morning. His friend had been livid last night, screaming furiously at him about starting a war with the Weres.

That had been an unexpected turn of events. He hadn't expected Hanlon to react so aggressively. They'd managed to co-exist for over two centuries, which was pretty good going considering the natural loathing Weres had for Vampires. Hell, he'd even become somewhat friendly with the Alpha over the years.

He dug out his cell phone and called Hanlon. He had to nip this talk of war in the bud before it got out of hand. "We need to talk."

"Didn't you do enough of that last night, Ryder?"

Caleb strangled down a deep sigh at the animosity in the Alpha's tone, and counted to ten. "Just meet me in half an hour, Hanlon. I'm coming alone." He disconnected the call, knowing the Alpha would show up. Although, the call was frosty to say the least, Jared Hanlon didn't want a war any more than he did and he would meet him on the Old Forest Road. Glancing at his watch, he saw it was barely six am, so he had time to meet with Jared before he went to pick up Rhianna for lunch.

Caleb was early, leaning against the hood of his new Porsche, waiting for Jared to appear. He wondered if he would come in wolf form or human. The form he chose would be a good indicator of just how furious the Alpha was. He waited for half an hour staring sightlessly in front of him with his arms crossed, Hanlon obviously making a point by showing up late. His head turned to the trees as he scented a human approaching and Jared strode from the trees in a pair of old denims and a denim shirt.

Caleb schooled his expression carefully and tried not to let the Alpha see his sigh of relief.

"What do you want, Ryder?" Jared's bark was aggressive as he came to a halt a few feet away from him and folded his arms across his wide chest.

Caleb's golden brown eyes regarded the Alpha for a long moment before he dropped his carefully constructed mask and let his true weariness show. "A way out of this sorry mess, Jared." He saw some of the tension leave the Alpha's body as the Were walked closer. Caleb moved over slightly and Jared rested his long body against the hood beside him.

"You were out of control last night, Caleb," Jared finally said with a deep sigh. "I've never seen you so wild before, not in the whole two centuries I've known you."

Caleb nodded his head in agreement, his lips twitching in a rueful smile. "I surprised even myself last night," he admitted. "I appear to be caught up in a situation I'm at a loss to deal with.

Rhianna, she's like no one I've ever met before. I find myself experiencing strong protective instincts over her, being subjected to emotions I haven't felt in a long time. This whole feeling thing is a complete minefield to me. I don't understand it and I don't know what to do with it."

Jared swung his head around and regarded Caleb's intently. "You love her?" He couldn't keep the incredulous note from his voice. The finer feelings in life were a bit sparse when it came to vampires. Some of them did remember enough of their former humanity to be able to bond emotionally with others, but usually it was all about sexual gratification with no strings attached.

Caleb frowned, his brow furrowing deeply as he pondered the question. Was he in love with Annie? Was he even capable of love? He knew there were a select few in his life that he did have deeper emotions for, but they were all vampires. Never had a human interested him.

He stared down at the road trying to work out how to respond. "I don't know," he finally sighed. "It's been so long since I've felt the emotion I don't know if I'd recognise it. All I am sure of is, at this moment in time, she is all I think of. From the very first moment I met her I've craved to be with her. Her scent, her beauty, her blood, her body, every single part of her calls to me. I want her and yet I give her space to get to know me first. Usually I just take what I want."

Jared chuckled, shaking his head in amusement. The situation wasn't really funny but seeing the bewilderment on the vampire's face made him laugh. "Sounds like love to me, Caleb. It explains your shocking behaviour last night too."

Caleb met his gaze. "We were at the club last night. She was telling me about her little bookstore she was going to open, mentioned the unexpected life insurance policy her brother had and the very kind man Jared Hanlon who had given her the news. It wasn't hard to work out that 'Wolfie' was her brother. You're a good Alpha, Jared. You always make sure families are taken care of when you add to your pack."

He shook his head, offering a wry smile. "I lost it, my friend. Her pain and grief at losing Rafe is so deep. I was infuriated that he was alive and with your pack when she was suffering so because of his loss."

Jared felt a stab of guilt. He could understand the vampire's reaction because he too felt for Rhianna's loss and the fact Millie was his mate. However, protection of the pack was paramount. Personal feelings didn't come into it. The pack had to come first. He sighed and heard the sadness behind it. He hoped his friend would understand.

"You know how difficult it is for us to maintain our secret, Caleb. Do you think I want Annie to be suffering like this? I barely know the girl and yet I like her immensely. I can see why Rafe has struggled so hard with joining the pack, why he craves to return to her. She is sweetness, innocence and kindness all rolled into one. I take no pleasure in her pain but it is necessary to protect the pack."

Caleb shifted, standing straight and stretching his long legs. "I understand your dilemma even if I disapprove of it, Jared. I can't condone anything that hurts Annie, but I do understand it. I know your pack laws forbid outsiders from knowing your true nature. I know you can't break the laws, not even to save Rafe."

Jared nodded his head sadly. "He's the only one of five innocents to survive a forced turning. It took three weeks for him to be coherent enough to begin to understand what had happened to him. Many days I thought he would lose the battle, but he fought hard to live. I believe he fought for Annie's sake. I think somewhere deep inside him, he wanted to return to her."

He turned to his side so he could look directly at the vampire. "He's a latent Alpha, Caleb. His nature is too gentle to allow him to lead. He abhors violence and that has been an added reason why he's struggled so hard to be one with the pack. His last meeting with Annie when he was in wolf form seemed to help him to integrate more. He seemed more at peace with himself and even began to take women to his bed. That was until last night."

Caleb looked down at the road and pursed his lips thoughtfully. "How is he today?"

"We put him in the safe room last night just as a precaution, but apart from weeping, he maintained enough control so I let him out after a few hours. Aaron is his closest friend so he stayed at his house last night. Aaron says he is quiet and withdrawn but appears stable enough. He reckons Rafe will work out his issues in his own mind and find a balance eventually."

Jared straightened and took a few steps from the car, automatically letting his eyes roam over the surrounding area for any signs of movement. He had come to the meeting alone, but he wouldn't put it past some of his pack to be hanging around just in case there was trouble. He didn't see any of them but he knew they were there.

Caleb watched him with a slight smile on his lips. He, too, knew the other Weres were about but he didn't take it as an insult. After last night, it was only right they were wary of him and why he wanted to speak to their Alpha.

"Jared, the only way I can see out of this mess is for Annie to know the truth." He watched the other man tense, and held up his hand as the Alpha spun around to face him. "Hear me out first. You can't tell her of your existence but I can tell her of mine. I hadn't planned on letting her know my true nature so soon, but it would appear it's necessary for the truth to come out. Once she knows of vampires, she will find out about Weres. Once she knows of Weres, there will be no reason to keep Rafe from her."

Jared frowned, digging his hands in his pockets. "That's just semantics, Caleb, and you know it. It doesn't matter who tells her about Weres. It's the fact she would know of our existence."

"What do you think your mate will say when she finds out about all of this?" Caleb countered, watching the Alpha tense further. "Do you think she'll agree to stay with you knowing your part in her friend's misery? I've only met Millie once but I could sense her deep attachment to Annie. She will not roll over and agree to mate with you, Jared, you know that yourself, otherwise you would have taken her for your own by now."

Millie's beautiful face sprang to Jared's mind and his wolf howled loudly and began to pace restlessly. What Caleb said was true. His Millie would fight him tooth and nail over Annie and Rafe. He didn't need the vampire to tell him that. He sighed and his frown deepened.

"This is what I will agree to, Caleb. You reveal yourself to Annie and we'll see how she handles that bombshell. If she's willing to accept you for who you truly are then I'll meet with you again and we can discuss whether or not she can be trusted with the knowledge of our existence. If I feel she can handle it, I'll take it to the pack and we'll put it to a vote. I can't make this decision arbitrarily, my friend. I have over two hundred lives to protect here. They deserve to have a say in this."

Caleb regarded him intently for a long moment and then finally nodded his agreement. "Will Rafe be strong enough to hold on until a decision is reached?"

Jared's eyes turned sad. He genuinely liked the big man and it pained him greatly to lose him. "I don't know." He had to be honest about it. "You have to understand, Caleb. I can't risk the lives of two hundred for the sake of one, no matter how much I like him. If Rafe isn't strong enough to work this out then…"

He didn't complete the sentence but then he didn't have to. Caleb knew exactly what the outcome would be if Rafe went rogue. Walking over to the Alpha, he held out his hand. "I understand, Jared."

Jared clasped Caleb's arm in a firm grip and managed a crooked smile. "I'm relieved I do not have to go to war with you, Caleb."

"As am I," Caleb smiled, before turning and striding back to his car. He slid in quickly and tore off down the road.

CHAPTER NINE

Rhianna dressed casually for her lunch date with Caleb. She didn't think he'd be taking her anywhere too fancy as they were going property viewing afterwards. She pulled on a pair of comfortable jeans and a summer top in deep purple. She picked up a button down sweater just in case the afternoon turned cooler and hurried downstairs to wait for Caleb.

He arrived five minutes later in a brand new flashy Porsche that looked exactly like his old one. She smiled when he pulled up and quickly opened the door before he could get out and come around to her, as appeared to be his usual habit so far.

"Hi!" She smiled, trying not to cringe as her voice came out sounding breathless. Seriously, he was going to think she was an airhead the way she gushed every time he came near. She couldn't resist running her gaze over his face, noticing the slight tightening of his mouth.

"I would have come up for you." The words came out a tad sharper than Caleb meant them too and he had to bite the inside of his mouth to contain his annoyance. Rhianna merely continued to smile at him, her lavender eyes twinkling.

"I know you would have but this is the twenty-first century, Caleb. We delicate little women have had the vote and independence for a very long time now. We don't need men to open car doors and escort us downstairs anymore."

Her easy smile and teasing tone wiped the slight frown from his face as he leaned towards her and inhaled her sweet scent before brushing her lips with his. "But I like doing those things for you, Annie." Their breaths mingled and it felt so natural his lips curved in a smile.

"Call me old fashioned but I like the woman I'm with to be treasured and treated with respect when I'm with her."

She pulled back a fraction and gave him another little smile that tugged at his heart. "All your women or just me?" She was teasing him, laughing at his choice of words. That small gesture made his heart flutter. No one had teased him in a long time, except for Demetri, but he didn't count. Having Rhianna's sweetness and laughter washing over him was refreshing.

He caught a handful of her curls and raised them to his face so he could inhale the fresh clean bouquet of her shampoo. "I see no other woman when I'm with you. I see no other woman when we're apart either. I see only you, Annie."

Her lips brushed his softly and she sighed with pleasure. "You say all the right things, Caleb," she laughed, her voice breathless once more, as she sat back in her seat and put on her seatbelt. He was positively sinful with his sexy voice and all the right words.

"I merely speak the truth." His smile was wide as he started the car and headed off into the traffic. He'd opted for an informal lunch spot, choosing one of the local burger bars. It would be quick and then they could start looking for a place for Rhianna to start her business. He watched with fascination as she polished off a burger and fries with a large diet cola.

He toyed with his own burger, managing to force some of the rare beef into his mouth. It wasn't that he couldn't eat human food; all vampires could to keep up appearances. It just didn't taste of much to him so wasn't all that enjoyable an experience.

He saw Rhianna's gaze slide to his plate a couple of times and he forced another mouthful of beef into his mouth, chewing slowly. He'd eat the food for her if it made her happy. Soon she would know the truth but for a short time, he wanted to appear normal. He was surprised when he actually finished the burger and found it hadn't been half as bad as he'd imagined it would be. Maybe it was because the beautiful little redhead across from him was smiling so sweetly at him. Her pleasure seemed to radiate out towards him and he couldn't help but bathe in it.

Caleb paid the bill and stood up, grabbing her hand in his. "So which property are we going to view first?" He smiled as Rhianna began to all but hum with excitement as they walked down to their first viewing. Everything about her was infectious and he couldn't remember a time he'd enjoyed himself more.

Two hours later and her bubbly excitement had waned considerably as they came out of the last property on her list. None of the buildings had been exactly what she was looking for and the one she had quite liked was so expensive it was completely blown out of the water.

Her disappointment wrenched at Caleb's heart and he hugged her to his side and dropped a kiss on the top of her head. "I've got a suggestion, Annie," he finally said. "Will you promise to hear me out and not get mad at me?"

Rhianna stared up at him curiously. His expression was so serious and he seemed to be nervous as he gazed down at her. "Okay." She was quickly coming to realise that Caleb was a man like none she had ever met. His attentiveness was old school and he was used to being in charge. Seeing a hint of uncertainty about him was intriguing.

Caleb smiled and tugged her into the next street. He stopped in front of an old shop that was currently empty. He watched Rhianna's face light up as she took in the traditional Victorian front of the shop and then her expression dropped.

"I don't think I'll be able to afford this place, Caleb." She said it doubtfully, biting her bottom lip.

"You promised to hear me out first." He smiled, pulling out a set of keys and unlocking the front doors and pushing them wide open. He entered the building and waited for Rhianna to join him.

The space was huge and very dirty, but the potential for the exact kind of bookstore Rhianna wanted to open was there. "It's a great space, Caleb," she said, her eyes running to the stairs that led to the upper floor. "I could put the second hand books and café area up on the top floor and have the storytelling area by the big bay window just over there."

She walked further into the large room checking out the back storeroom area with the small kitchen and full bathroom. She turned back into the main room and looked at him. "I can't afford this."

"No, you can't," he agreed with a tight smile. "It would take up most of your budget to buy this place, which wouldn't leave much over to equip it and have a cushion for any lean times in the business. However, if you leased it, you could afford it."

"I told you I didn't want to lease a building." Rhianna shook her head in the negative, determination in her voice. "My landlord could pull the lease out from under me at any time. I don't want to be at the mercy of a possible bad landlord."

"I could negotiate an extremely good lease for you," he argued gently. "For as long as you want with no get out clauses for the landlord."

He watched her lavender eyes narrow slightly as she looked at him. "What landlord would be stupid enough to agree to something like that?"

It was hard not to smile as she stared at him so suspiciously. He could almost see the wheels turning in her head as she worked out what was going on. Caleb closed the gap between them and pulled her into his arms. "One whose only concern is your happiness."

"You own this building," she finally said, her gaze intent as she searched his face.

"I would give it to you but I know you wouldn't accept it." Caleb stroked her cheekbone lightly. "I know you want to do this on your own, Annie. I promise you I'll charge you the correct market rate for the lease. The only thing I'll give to you freely is the length of time you want to be here. If you want a thirty-year lease or a fifty-year lease, it's yours. I'm not using the building for anything else anyway."

She gaped up at him stunned, unable to say a word as she took in what he was saying. Her eyes fell from his and she looked around the room slowly, feeling a bubble of excitement welling up inside. "You would seriously have given me this beautiful building?" she asked incredulously.

"I still would if you'd accept it from me," he told her with a tight smile. He knew she wouldn't accept it, not as a gift. The bookstore was her dream and she needed to do it on her own. He just wanted to be part of her dream, to have some deeper connection with her.

"You know I'm not going to do that," she smiled and he nodded his head.

"You will consider leasing it from me though?" Caleb was surprised at how anxious he was to have her agreement to the idea. It meant a lot for her to see the wisdom in his proposal.

Rhianna pulled out of his embrace and walked around the large room, her eyes beginning to shine again with excitement. "How soon can you have the lease drawn up?" she finally asked and was rewarded with a beautiful smile crossing his face.

"I've already had it drawn up, just in case you agreed to my suggestion. It's in the car." He crossed the room, pulling her into his arms again so he could kiss her soundly on the lips. "I'll help you as much or as little as you want me to, Annie. Just let me know what I can do and I'll do it."

They stayed inside the building for another half an hour while Rhianna talked through her ideas and Caleb offered suggestions. He couldn't remember a time when he'd been more enchanted listening to someone talk about a new project they were interested in.

Sure, the bookstore was small fry compared to the large corporate deals he was usually involved in, but because this was Rhianna's dream, it was suddenly the most important thing in his world. Her excitement and enthusiasm was infectious, and he found himself smiling as he listened to her.

It was amazing how this woman was turning his life so completely topsy-turvy. It frightened him even as it exhilarated him. He didn't want it to ever end and yet he knew he had to reveal his true nature to her and soon. Would she still want to be with him when she knew the truth? He couldn't imagine his life without her anymore. She had to be strong enough to accept him for who he was. If she wasn't, he didn't know how he would be able to go on without her.

Caleb argued with himself internally over whether or not to have her sign the lease before he told her the truth. His selfish side wanted to tie her to him any way he could and he was almost amused at the inner debate going on inside his head. A few months ago, it wouldn't have been an issue. He'd have done what he wanted and to hell with the consequences. Now he was arguing with himself about doing the right thing rather than what he wanted.

"Do you mind stopping off at my place before going home?" he asked Rhianna as he locked up the property. He heard her sharp intake of breath and hid a smile. He wondered what was going through her mind right now. Did she anticipate his request meant he wanted to have his wicked way with her? He most certainly did, but he'd added another condition to his now lengthy list of conditions he was applying to himself where she was concerned.

He wouldn't make love to her again until she knew exactly who she was laying with.

"No problem," she said quietly, as she climbed into the car as he held the door open for her.

Rhianna was not as oblivious to Caleb's erratic mood shifts as he thought. She was conscious of the fact he had something on his mind. He lapsed into long periods of quiet thought as she talked about her ideas, though he smiled and nodded as if he was paying complete attention to her. She felt a slight feeling of apprehension settle over her, especially when he asked if she'd go back to his place. He had something to tell her and whatever it was made him nervous and uncertain. This didn't bode well for whatever it was he was about to tell her.

They were at his mansion a lot quicker than she really wanted to be. The closer they got to his home the quieter and more intense his expression became. His mood triggered something inside her, and she found herself becoming more unsettled too.

Caleb was mentally working out where he would tell her. Not the drawing room. If he took her in there he'd most likely chicken out and take her before the fire as he had the first night they met. The kitchen was too cold and sterile and the bedrooms were out for similar reasons to the drawing room. That only left the library.

He tugged Rhianna by the hand, feeling her feet drag slightly as she began to tense as if sensing something momentous was about to happen. He tried to smile reassuringly at her, but he knew his smile didn't reach his eyes and was probably more of a grimace than a true smile.

Rhianna barely noticed the room he took her into it. She sank down onto the leather sofa he led her to and then watched as Caleb began to slowly pace in front of her, as if he was in some internal debate with himself. "Whatever it is, Caleb, just say it," she finally said as the tension in the room became almost tangible. "I mean, it can't be that bad, can it?"

She watched him stop pacing and turn his head to look at her. His expression frightened her slightly, and she swallowed nervously. "What is it, Caleb? Oh God, please don't tell me you're married!" The look of outright shock that crossed his face almost made her laugh.

It wasn't just the shock, he looked completely stunned at the very notion of being married. Rhianna tried not to sigh with relief. If he'd been married she would have had to stop seeing him. She wasn't about to become the 'other woman' in a relationship.

"No, I am not married." Caleb's voice was low and slightly pained.

Rhianna tried to lighten the mood a bit. She managed a little laugh. "Well, it can't be anything worse than that," she quipped lightly and was rewarded by a deep frown from him. She felt her disquiet grow stronger as she stared at him.

It was worse than being married? What could be worse than that? Her mind strove to come up with something, anything that would cause her more heartache than finding out he belonged to someone else. He spoke suddenly and Rhianna felt her heart stop dead in her chest.

"I'm a vampire, Annie."

Four little words. That was all it took to stop Rhianna's heart for a fraction of a second. The anguish in his golden brown eyes, the tense way he held himself before her, she knew without a single doubt what he said to her was true. It didn't even cross her mind to laugh at him, to deny the existence of such a mythical creature. Caleb announced he was a vampire and she believed him instantly.

She tried to suck in a deep breath but her lungs wouldn't obey her request for air. Her lungs or her brain, one of the two organs, was ignoring her but she wasn't really sure which one. Only a fraction of a second had passed since Caleb had spoken, but it felt like an eternity had gone by.

Work brain, work heart, work lungs. The words tumbled around in her head and suddenly she felt her heart thud loudly in her chest, and her lungs allowed her to suck in some much needed air. She wasn't going to die today after all, not here on Caleb's leather sofa in his library? Yes, she was in his library. That's what you called a room with large bookcases and loads and loads of books.

Rhianna felt hysterical laughter starting to bubble up inside her. Her boyfriend had just told her he was a vampire and she was admiring his bookshelves? It was now official. She was clinically insane.

"Say something, Annie," Caleb pleaded, frightened by her silence and the increasingly wild look in her lavender eyes. He didn't know how he'd expected her to react to his admission but this silence was terrifying.

Rhianna turned her gaze back to him and she wondered what there was to say. Her brain was still slow in catching up with the rest of her body and she said the first thing that came to mind. "You ate a burger!"

Caleb blinked slowly at her, a look of deep concern crossing his face. "Yes, I ate a burger." He grimaced. "It was…challenging but I did it for you, so you wouldn't feel uncomfortable eating alone."

"You did it for me?" She repeated his words, dropping her eyes from his and staring down at the coffee table before the sofa. She was at a loss at how to react to his announcement. She could see his concern and knew she was acting strange at the moment, but then this wasn't exactly a normal situation.

"I don't know how to react to this, Caleb," she said in a small voice. "It's not the normal run of the mill confession a boyfriend suddenly dumps on his girl. This is….this is…it's just so off the wall."

Caleb approached her slowly, sitting down beside her, but giving her enough room so she didn't feel crowded. "You believe me." He had mentally prepared himself for her laughing at him at first. This quiet acceptance quite literally threw him.

She laughed suddenly and there was a slight note of hysteria to it. "I should be jumping up and telling you you're insane but instead I find myself believing you. I don't know why but I just do. I don't think you would ever lie to me, Caleb."

The simple trust she placed in him with that sentence tore at his heart. He would never lie directly to her, she was right about that, but he would lie by omission. Was it the same thing? Was keeping Rafe's secret from her for a little longer the same as lying to her? "Annie," he breathed quietly, his hand reaching tentatively for hers. She let him take her hand and he felt a little hope at this simple act.

"I know this is a shock to you. It's a lot to take in. I know you'll probably need some time to come to terms with it. I'm willing to wait for you, Annie. Take as much time as you need.

Just promise me you won't make any snap decisions. Think about what you truly want before you decide one way or another whether you still want to be with me."

Rhianna closed her eyes and let herself succumb to the feeling of his thumb caressing the back of her hand as he spoke so passionately beside her. Her mind was finally getting into sync with the rest of her as she heard the fear in his voice as well as the incredible longing.

Caleb was a vampire. Her boyfriend was a vampire and he was terrified she wasn't going to accept him. She could hear it in every word that came from his lips. She could hear the slight catch in his voice towards the end of his little speech. She breathed in deeply and slowly opened her eyes, turning to look at him. "I don't need time to think about it, Caleb," she said and his expression turned fearful and his fingers pressed against her mouth lightly.

"Please Annie," he whispered, his voice rough. "Please don't do anything rash without really thinking it through."

He was actually shaking beside her, his fingers trembling against her lips. It was just so wrong that this beautiful, confident man could be so easily brought to his knees. Rhianna was astounded she had this level of power over him. She pulled his hand from her mouth and looked deep into his panicked eyes. "I don't care if you're a vampire, Caleb," she said firmly and wasn't surprised to find she really meant it.

"What you are doesn't define you; it's who you are that does. I'm assuming being a vampire isn't a new condition and you were one when we first met. I liked you then and I haven't changed my mind just because you've told me what you are. I don't need to think about it, Caleb. I know what I want and it's you."

She took a deep breath and searched his face intently. Hell, if they were going down the whole 'tell the truth' road she may as well do so too. "I have a confession to make too. I'm in love with you, Caleb. I have been from probably the first night we met but I didn't have time to explore my feelings for you because of Rafe."

Caleb blinked slowly, trying to take a deep breath and wondering why his heart was pounding so loudly in his chest. Her lavender eyes were locked to his, waiting for his reaction and he was quite literally speechless for a moment. "This isn't quite how

I expected this to go," he finally said with a bemused smile on his lips.

"Let me guess you thought I'd run screaming out of the room?" Rhianna asked dryly.

Caleb laughed lightly. "Something like that," he admitted ruefully. "I didn't expect you to so readily accept what I am and then just turn around and say it doesn't matter, and I most definitely didn't expect you to say you are in love in me."

She frowned. "Does that bother you, Caleb? Me being in love with you? Is it just sex you're looking for from me?"

"God, no, Annie," he groaned, pulling her into his arms. "I'm just so stunned you love me. You are so sweet and pure and I'm….well, I'm the proverbial monster humans are so terrified of. I find it so utterly unbelievable you can see something in me worth loving." He buried his head in the crook of her neck and clutched her tightly to him, afraid she would change her mind and opt to run screaming from the room after all.

"What's not to love, Caleb?" Rhianna's voice was husky, her arms snaking around his waist. "You're beautiful both inside and out. Everything about you calls to me. I miss you so much when we're apart and when I'm with you I feel safe and protected and happy again."

"I don't deserve to have someone as wonderful as you loving me," he whispered into the side of her neck. "I've not always been the man you see before you today, Annie. I've done so many terrible things in my life. I've been empty and shallow and only interested in my own needs for such a long time. Even now, I'm still struggling with all the new emotions you make me feel. Sometimes I do the wrong things for the right reasons and I don't know how to stop doing them."

Rhianna could hear the struggle in his voice, hear the longing to be someone better than he had been and it made her heart melt. "Oh Caleb, don't you think the rest of us do that too?" she asked with a little laugh. She raised his head up so she could look into his beautiful face. "We all make mistakes, Caleb, even me. The only thing you can do is try and learn from your mistakes so you don't make the same ones twice."

His expression turned fierce and his eyes glittered as he cupped her face gently. "You're perfect. I can't ever imagine you doing anything to deliberately hurt anyone." He felt a wave of guilt wash through him about Rafe and he dropped his eyes from hers. She would be very angry with him when she learned about the pain he had caused her brother.

"What is it?" she asked softly and he shook his head at her.

"I can't say," he admitted. "It's not my secret to tell. I have to speak to someone else before I can tell you."

Her lavender eyes were intent on his face and then she slowly nodded. "Okay, Caleb. I can understand that. Whatever it is, don't beat yourself up about it too much. You may as well wait until it comes out in the wash before you give yourself such a hard time about it."

Her words made him feel even worse. She was such a generous soul. She was half forgiving him even though she didn't know what it was she was forgiving him for. He truly didn't deserve this beauty before him but he was going to take her and make her his anyway. He couldn't let her go.

His heart thundered as he looked down at her, a riot of emotions coursing through him. "Is this love I'm feeling, Annie?" His question came out sounding timid and so at odds to what he was usually like. His uncertainty was clear in his voice, his expression confused.

"Tell me what you're feeling."

"My heart is racing in my chest and my hands are shaking. I want you so badly and yet I want to wait until you're ready to come to me. I ache to hear your laughter and I ache to see your beautiful smile, which causes me to suck my breath in every time I see it. I want to kiss you, hold you and make love to you until you are so exhausted you fall asleep in my arms. I want to give you all of your heart's desires and I want to keep you safe from anything or anyone who would hurt you."

The words just tumbled from his mouth until he was almost breathless from talking. He wasn't used to being so open and honest with anyone. It was refreshing and scary as hell, but he felt strangely liberated telling her every feeling deep inside him.

She smiled her beautiful smile at him and leaned up to brush her lips against his. "Sounds pretty much like love to me," she sighed against his mouth and he groaned and gathered her body into his lap so he could feast on her mouth the way he ached to. He parted her lips and teased his tongue inside her warm heat, licking leisurely, drinking in her soft moan of pleasure and feeling his heart expand to almost bursting point. "I love you, Annie," he whispered against her lips, a radiant joy filling his soul as he uttered the words. "I'll love you forever, my beautiful woman."

She wrapped her arms around his neck and pressed her tongue into his mouth, drowning in his declaration, astounded this wonderful man, this vampire, could feel such depths of emotions for her. She twisted in his arms until she was sitting astride him and he had to tilt his head back slightly to look up at her. She ran her fingers through his luscious locks, letting the silky strands run through her hands slowly.

"You are so gorgeous, Caleb," she breathed softly. She traced her fingers lightly across his brow and down his strong nose, across his cheekbones and down to his hard jaw. Her lavender eyes shone with appreciation as she stroked his face so gently, her touch was like a feather brushing against his skin.

"Make love to me," she whispered. "I want to feel your hands and mouth on my body, caressing my skin so arrogantly the way you did the night we met. I want you to take me and make me yours, Caleb."

Caleb's nostrils flared and his body hardened as his hands tightened on her waist for a fraction of a second before he stood up swiftly, forcing her to hold onto his neck and wrap her legs around his waist. They both groaned when her heat pressed against his hardness.

He couldn't deny her. He could deny himself but he could never deny his Annie. He carried her from the library and upstairs, striding into his private rooms. He kept his gaze on hers looking for any sign she might change her mind but all he saw was acceptance and a hot need in her eyes. He slowly lowered her down his aching body and he smiled wickedly at her when she moaned as he stepped away from her. They were in his bedroom standing beside his enormous four-poster bed.

"So, you found my touch arrogant, did you?" he laughed, his golden brown eyes twinkling with excitement. "Did you like it, Annie? Did my arrogance make you hot?" He walked around behind her and slid his hands into the heavy weight of her long curls, lifting them away from her slender neck. He leaned down and ran his tongue slowly from her collarbone all the way up to her throbbing pulse point in the side of her neck.

She moaned softly and he licked at her pulse again. She tasted so good, so much better than he remembered. The heavy pulse of her essence flowing through her veins teased him mercilessly and he had to fight to control his blood lust. The urge to sink his fangs into the side of her neck was pretty high and he didn't want to frighten her.

"You haven't answered my question, Annie," he whispered against the shell of ear and she moaned again and leaned back against his chest.

"Yes," she moaned softly. "Your arrogance made me very hot, Caleb." She heard him chuckle and the sound sent a shiver right down her spine. A bolt of pure pleasure began in her stomach and flowed quickly down between her thighs. She heard Caleb inhale deeply and let out a little sigh.

"The scent of your arousal is a true aphrodisiac," he whispered against her neck. "My sense of smell is so much more enhanced than yours. I can smell everything on your skin. I can smell lavender and jasmine. The sweet tang of coconut, the honey in your shampoo. I can smell that little bead of sweat that is slowly trickling down between your breasts right this very moment and I can smell the heady musky aroma of the juices pooling between your thighs. The combination of sweet scents is making my mouth water and my body rock hard with anticipation."

He moved back from her and walked back around her. Her beautiful face was flushed with passion, her lavender eyes darkening to almost violet, her lips parting as her breath rasped out deeply. His eyes slipped down her little summer top and he watched her breasts rise and fall with each deep breath she took. His palms itched to hold her soft flesh but he maintained his distance, slowly raking his eyes over her heated flesh.

"Take your clothes off, Annie," he ordered softly. "Show me the sweet delights you have to offer to me." He heard her breath hitch in her throat as her eyes met his. He smiled was almost wolfish, his eyes shining brightly with barely concealed need.

Rhianna saw his wicked smile and she smiled back at him. This was the man she remembered, the cocky one so sure of himself and his own sexuality. So sure of the pleasure he was about to give her. She pulled her top off and quickly removed her jeans and panties, leaving them in a pile on the floor as Caleb's heated gaze raked over her naked body.

She heard him groan and his hands clenched into fists at his side. He took a step closer and she swayed wanting to feel his arms around her. His hands moved to her hips and held her steady, keeping a slight distance between them. His grip was tight and she knew she'd probably bruise from his touch but she didn't care.

He lifted her by her hips and laid her sideways across the bed, her legs hanging down to the floor. He dropped to his knees and lightly slid his hands up the back of her calves until he reached her knees. His touch firmed and he pushed her legs up and wide open, baring her throbbing sex to his greedy gaze. He inhaled deeply at her core and then blew softly against her heated flesh.

She moaned and spread her legs wider, offering herself up to him as tiny goosebumps shivered across her body. She waited breathlessly for him to touch her but he stayed still and simply breathed in deeply again. "Caleb," she moaned trying to press her body up to his mouth but his grip on the back of her thighs held her immobile.

"In a minute," he laughed softly. "I'm not finished smelling you yet. Scent is very important to a vampire. It transmits so many different messages to one of my kind. Right now, your scent is telling me just how turned on you are. I can see your flesh practically pulsing with desire. Your lips are swelling so beautifully as your blood rushes to your very core in anticipation of the pleasure which awaits you."

He inhaled once more and watched the tiny beads of moisture begin to seep from her body, as the scent of her arousal grew stronger. He finally lowered his head and teased her with some light kisses along both inner thighs. His lips moved closer and closer to her core but never quite got there causing her to moan her disappointment even as her stomach tensed and relaxed with anticipation. He laughed again and nipped playfully up her thighs until she was tossing her head on the bed.

His own desire took over and he ended his teasing when his need to taste her became too overwhelming. He licked boldly against her flesh and she cried out hoarsely at his touch. He licked again, long bold strokes teasing her as he nibbled against the tiny bundle of nerves that drove her wild.

Her sweet honey was delectable and he coated his tongue with her sweetness again, choosing to dive into her tight canal this time to sample more of her delights. Her wetness drenched his mouth and he rumbled his pleasure.

She couldn't move against him and it was driving her insane. She wanted to grind her body onto his wicked mouth and tongue but he held her so still it was impossible to do so. "Caleb," she moaned hoarsely. "I need to move."

He chuckled lightly and looked up from his feast. "No, you need to be quiet and stop interrupting my feast," he laughed. "I'll let you move soon enough but for now, be quiet and let me finish tasting you."

His arrogance sent a bolt of pure pleasure straight between her legs and she moaned loudly as he licked and lapped, nipped and nibbled every single inch of her most intimate place and then started working his way slowly from the bottom to the top again.

Her first orgasm hit her out of the blue. There was no slow build up to it. His teeth rasped unexpectedly on her clit and she came with a loud scream, her entire body shaking with the sheer intensity of the pleasure exploding inside her.

Caleb growled continuing to pleasure her as she shattered against his mouth. God, she tasted of the sweetest nectar. Her total abandon stirred his blood as no other had ever done. His touch gentled as he coaxed her down from her release and he smiled his pleasure as he took in the flush of colour creeping over her breasts.

Rising, he pressed her further onto the bed, kneeling between her legs as he slowly took off his shirt as he watched her fast breaths begin to calm. Her eyes opened and she looked up at him with a lazy, very satisfied smile and her impish expression brought a low chuckle from his chest. "Did my lady enjoy her appetizer?"

"Should I not be asking you that question?" Rhianna laughed breathlessly as she stretched her arms above her head making her full breasts jiggle very temptingly.

"Oh, I thoroughly enjoyed my appetiser," Caleb smiled wickedly. "I enjoyed it so much I'm thinking of having seconds." He stripped the shirt from his shoulders and growled as her lavender eyes flared with excitement as they ran over his tightly muscled chest.

He moved from the bed so he could strip his jeans and boots off as his woman watched him with an almost feral expression in her eyes. He loved how she didn't try to hide her lust from him. Her gaze raked his body with a healthy appreciation of what she was viewing.

"Caleb, when we made love the first time, did you bite me?" she suddenly asked and he blinked slowly and then gave her a wide grin.

"I bit you many times, sweet Annie," he sighed softly. "Do you not remember my marks on your beautiful breasts? I remember them well. Your creamy flesh decorated with lovely hues of reds and blues and deep purples from my love bites."

She sat up as he moved back onto the bed, her face close to his, her eyes intent on his. "I didn't mean loves bites," she said seriously. "I meant did you bite me? Did you feed from my body, Caleb? Did you drink my blood?"

Her question caught him off guard and he didn't know what to say. He didn't want to lie to her and yet he didn't want to repulse her either. He lowered his eyes to her left breast and reached out to run a finger slowly around her nipple. She gasped and her skin puckered so erotically under his touch. He brought his eyes back to hers and he circled her nipple once more.

"I fed from here," he confessed. "I only wanted a little taste of you to see if your blood tasted as wonderful as all the rest of you did."

Her breath caught and her teeth worried her bottom lip for a moment before she took a deep breath and smiled. "And did it?"

His golden eyes burned with heat as he stared into her face and saw only curiosity there, no condemnation or loathing at his admission. "It surpassed everything I've ever tasted," he whispered. "Your essence is the sweetest, most wonderful flavour in the whole world, Annie. It's thick and hot and so incredibly satisfying."

His answer seemed to please her because her beautiful smile danced across her face again and his heart melted as he watched her. "Will you taste me again, Caleb?" she asked softly. She rose to her knees and cupped her breast in her left hand while her right hand threaded into his silky locks and pulled his head down to her. "Take what you need from me, my beautiful vampire," she whispered.

A deep growl erupted from Caleb's throat and his fangs elongated as his mouth connected with her tender breast. He couldn't have stopped himself if he wanted to and he didn't want to. She was offering herself to him and the call of his blood lust was strong.

He gripped her breast around her hand and looked up into her face quickly to make sure she really wanted this before he growled again and sank his fangs into her areola. She stiffened in momentary pain and then he released his soothing toxin and her back arched with pleasure as he took a long, hard pull on her breast. Her thick, hot life's blood poured into his mouth and they both moaned at the same time.

Caleb let his mouth fill completely, savouring her intoxicating sweetness on his tongue before he swallowed her precious life's blood with another deep groan. He lost himself in her sweet taste, drawing deeply at her breast and swallowing her essence with relish. He heard her cry out and felt her body shake as his feeding brought her to a quick second orgasm. Reluctantly he withdrew his fangs and licked the tiny pinpricks closed as he cleaned up any stray traces of blood.

"Annie," he breathed softly, pulling her face to his and waiting for her to open her eyes. He searched her face intently as she smiled a dreamy smile at him and threaded her hands in his hair.

"Wow, that felt amazing," she gasped with a little laugh.

He laughed and shook his head in wonder. "You're the one who's amazing, Annie." He held her close as they knelt together on the bed, their mouths meeting in a long, slow, very wet kiss which had them both fighting for dominance with their tongues.

He finally decided enough was enough and he flipped her onto her back and loomed over her. "I'm in charge in the bedroom," he growled softly. "You can twist me around your little finger anywhere else, my Annie, but the bedroom is my domain." He dropped a hard kiss on her lips and smothered a laugh when she gasped in surprise. Well, she had asked for arrogance. It was her own fault if she was suddenly unsure of it.

He raised his head again and gave her a wicked smile as he cupped the soft flesh of her breasts and tugged on their hardened peaks. She arched up into his hands and he rewarded her by tugging a little harder on her nipples. "I can't make up my mind if I'm still hungry or if I'm ready to slide into your beautiful body."

Rhianna laughed and looked down at his substantial erection with a raised eyebrow. "I think you're ready enough," she said cheekily and then groaned when he gave her nipples a particularly hard tweak.

"Don't get mouthy with me." His voice was a rough growl but his eyes twinkled with laughter and his lips twitched with a smile as he lowered his head and gently soothed her tortured nipples with his lips and tongue.

He teased her mercilessly ignoring his own body's needs. He wanted this to be for her pleasure, not his. She was welcoming him into her bed and into her heart and his love for her overwhelmed him and made him want to kneel before her and worship her as a goddess.

He suckled and nipped and licked all over her hard peaks until she cried out his name and writhed beneath him. Her scent was overpowering him and his cock was ready to burst by the time he finally settled between her thighs and slowly rubbed his hardness up and down her wet heat.

"Caleb, please," Rhianna moaned. "No more teasing. Please take me."

"As my lady commands," he breathed against her lips and pressed forward. He took his time, slowly rocking back and forth, sliding inch after inch into her body as her hips rose to meet him half way. Finally he was buried to the hilt and he lay above her and inside her, pausing for a moment to savour the feel of being sheathed so tightly in her body. It was amazing how she could take his entire length. It had amazed him the first time he had lain with her, and it amazed him this time too.

She moaned and rolled her hips slowly and his breath hissed out at the sweet pleasure her movement caused inside his body. He moved ever so slowly, taking his sweet time easing from her tight heat before sliding just as slowly back inside.

Her sexy little moans stoked his fire but he refused to move faster. He wanted this to last and he refused to be rushed. He captured her clutching hands and secured them above her head with one hand. The other hand he hooked under her right leg, spreading it further apart and raised it slightly so he could get a better angle into her body.

Then he truly began to torture his lover. He took her with long, slow, unhurried strokes as he held her pinned beneath him. He ignored all her attempts to make him move faster, ignored all her little moans and pleas for more. He just moved in and out of her sweet body with a level of self-control he didn't know he possessed.

The fire in Rhianna's veins was burning her up inside as she pleaded with Caleb to moved faster, to take her harder. He only laughed huskily and silenced her pleas with hard kisses as he moved so achingly slowly inside her. She was ready to beg, plead, promise him the Moon if he'd only put out the flames deep within her body.

Caleb continued his slow torture until Rhianna was almost sobbing with her need for completion. Her pleas turned to curses and he was impressed with her inventiveness. Some of the things she came up with shocked even him and he'd heard a lot in his very long life. His woman had a bit of wild side about her. He'd have to hide the knives when he finished making love to her. He preferred his cock firmly attached to his body and he wasn't so sure she might not seriously be tempted to carry out some of her more dire threats.

He finally gave in to their bodies' demands. His next thrust was shorter and harder and caught her completely by surprise. She screamed and threw back her head as he picked up the pace, growling his pleasure.

Hot sweaty skin slapped against each other as they danced the ancient dance of love. He kissed her wildly, his body moving hard and fast as her muscles tightened around his aching cock as she shattered in his arms, a long howling wail escaping her as her orgasm crashed over her.

Her release was all he was waiting for. He took his own pleasure, his release triggering another orgasm. Caleb was lost in the sensation of utter bliss, Rhianna's pleasure increasing his own pleasure tenfold. The room was filled with the harsh sounds of ragged breathing as Caleb tensed with his release and then slowly collapsed and lowered his forehead to hers as he supported his weight on his elbows.

The scent of sex was heavy on the air as was the delicious scent of their sweat slickened bodies slowly starting to cool after the strenuous workout they'd both just received. Rhianna's breathing was harsh and laboured and her little heart was practically thrumming in her chest.

Caleb smiled his satisfaction and rolled onto his side, pulling her body flush against his as he dropped little butterfly kisses on her trembling lips. He wrapped his arms securely around her and closed his eyes, basking in this one, perfect moment. He didn't know how long he'd have to enjoy this wonderful feeling of peace but he would hold onto it for as long as he could.

CHAPTER TEN

Caleb pulled the heavy, chocolate brown comforter over Rhianna's body and half draped his lower body too. He didn't feel the cold the way humans did but he had felt a slight shiver run through her body as she slept against his chest. She'd been sleeping for over an hour while he simply lay there basking in the afterglow of their passion. She stirred and he dropped a kiss on the top of her head and ran a large hand lightly down her hip until she settled.

Rhianna's total acceptance of what he was astounded him and humbled him at the same time. He knew she would never reveal his true nature to anyone. He was certain she would never do anything to hurt him. Her capacity to handle the unusual was quite amazing in one so young. Perhaps Rafe's death was the reason she was so accepting. As far as she was aware she had already lost someone she loved dearly. She wouldn't want to open herself up to that kind of heartache again.

Caleb sighed, concerned about her reaction when she learned the truth. She was going to be hurt and most probably pissed. At Rafe, at Jared and at him too. He wasn't looking forward to it. He didn't want to be the one who caused her even a moment's pain or anger.

Her luscious red curls spread across his chest and he toyed with a long lock. He was certain her temper would match the fieriness of her colouring, just as her passion did. He could almost hear her voice rising sharply to almost screaming range.

He chuckled softly as he felt his body twitch the moment he thought of her screaming. She certainly gave vent to her feelings when in the throes of passion. God, she made such sexy, erotic sounds when he pleasured her, from the low moans to the sharper cries and then the loud lusty screams. It was enough to drive him insane with need for her. She stirred again, and her small hand stroked his chest lightly and he swallowed hard as his body reacted more.

"What are you laughing at?" Her sleepy voice was low and husky, which only served to harden his cock further.

"I was thinking about how lusty your screams are when you climax," he admitted, his voice turning husky too as he tilted her chin up so he could memorise his first look at her sleep-filled face. His breath caught in his throat as her sleepy eyes opened to stare up at him, her lips parted and still swollen from his kisses. A delicate shade of pink stained her perfect cheeks and he smiled feeling tenderness well up inside.

"Don't ever be embarrassed about enjoying your pleasures, not with me, Annie. I love it when you become so uninhibited and lose yourself against me. It's the most beautiful, erotic thing ever." He leaned down and brushed her lips with his trying to will his body to behave itself and not react to her closeness. He had worn her out already. She needed time to recover from their lovemaking.

She laughed against his lips and reached up to brush his hair from his face. "Is that an order, sir?" she asked impishly, her lavender eyes sparkling with amusement.

He chuckled again and pulled her over him, settling her along the full length of his body. His hands moved slowly down her back and gently cupped the soft round flesh of her bottom. He made a show of looking around the room and then he looked back at her and smiled wickedly.

"As far as I can tell we are still in the bedroom, my lady, which means I am still in charge, so yes, it is an order. I order you to scream long and very loudly when I ravish your beautiful body."

Rhianna burst into peels of light, tinkling laughter and tapped a finger against his lips. "I think, perhaps, you're taking your arrogance a step too far, sir," she teased. "I will only scream if you're up to the job of making me."

She shrieked in surprise when he rolled quickly and pinned her body beneath his. "Are you casting doubts on my ability as a lover, my lady?" Caleb's voice was low and husky, his golden brown eyes glinting with a slight edge to them. "Do I need to give my lady another example of just how adept I am at finding every single pleasure point on her beautiful body?" He pressed his aching cock in the juncture between her thighs and watched as her eyes darkened and her succulent nipples tightened hard.

"Perhaps later, sir?" Rhianna giggled with a breathy little moan. "I think you loved me just a little bit too good the last time. I may need some time to recover."

Caleb groaned and rolled off her pulling her back against his side. "I'm sorry, Annie. Was I too rough?"

"No, love, you were prefect," she sighed snuggling against him, loving the feel of his hard body against her softness. "I just need to do some pesky human things like eat for one. You may not have to eat at regular intervals but I do."

He was instantly contrite, sitting up and pulling her onto his lap. "Sorry Annie, I didn't stop to think. It's been hours since lunch time. You must be ravenous." It had been so long since he had been human. He could only imagine how awful it must be for her to need to eat and not have any food. Was it like the hunger he felt when he waited too long between feedings? He hoped not because that kind of hunger was crippling for him.

"I'm not quite that bad, Caleb," Rhianna laughed seeing his worried expression. "I'm just hungry. It's not as if I'm going to die because I haven't had dinner yet."

His expression cleared and he hugged her tightly against him. She was so precious to him. He just wanted to make her happy and see to her needs. He saw her eyes slowly take in his bedroom and wondered what she was thinking.

"You like the colour brown," she remarked with a slight smile as she took in the deep chocolate accent wall, the dark wood furniture and the brown and black bedding on the dark wood four-poster bed.

"As you like purple," he countered with a chuckle. "Every time I've seen you, you've been wearing something purple. The colour suits you but then I honestly think you could dress in filthy rags and still look stunningly beautiful."

Rhianna smiled, oddly pleased he'd noticed her favourite colour. It was such a little thing but it made her insides feel warm and mushy. She sighed and rested her head against his shoulder. "I suppose this room must have seen its fair share of women." She bit her lip, wondering where the hell that thought had come from and cringing because she had actually said it out loud.

Caleb tilted her chin up and captured her gaze with his amber eyes, his expression very serious. "This room has known only one woman within its walls, Rhianna. You are the first woman I have ever let into my private room and you will be the only woman ever to lie with me in this bed."

His words were spoken with such sincerity she believed him instantly. "So where did you take all your other women?" She was curious and surprised when he frowned and moved to settle her back onto the bed. She instantly missed the closeness of his body heat and shivered.

He stared at her for a moment and then pulled the comforter around her to enclose her body. Caleb felt uncomfortable about Rhianna's questions. He didn't want to think of any other woman when he was with her; it was like he was being unfaithful in some way. He knew it was irrational but he couldn't help the way he felt.

"Caleb?"

An expression of uncertainty crossed Rhianna's face and he instantly felt bad and reached for her, wrapping his arms around her body swallowed up inside the thick comforter. He pulled her wrapped body back into his lap and bent his head to kiss her softly on the lips. "I don't want to think about them. They no longer exist as far as I'm concerned. There is only you in my head and in my heart, Annie."

Rhianna stifled down the smile that threatened to burst across her face. He was so strong and arrogant, so tender and loving, and so incredibly naïve if he thought he could simply dismiss a part of his life because he willed it so. It was quite endearing to see this naivety about him. It made him seem less intimidating, less out of her league.

Because he felt as if he was way out of her league sometimes. She had no idea how old he was, how long he had lived for. She knew he was obscenely rich because he'd told her so. His mansion screamed his wealth, as did his choice in motorcars and his clothing. She felt so young, so insignificant compared to how ancient he must be.

"How old are you, Caleb?" she asked, her voice coming out sounding hesitant. She felt and heard him suck in a deep breath before he slowly released it and kissed the top of her head.

"I was twenty eight when I was turned to the life of a vampire," he answered slowly. "That was over two millennia ago, Annie."

Two thousand years! She had expected maybe two centuries or a little longer but over two thousand years old? That was totally mind blowing. "Wow, that's pretty old," she managed to get out and was pleased to hear only a light trace of shock in her voice. "I must seem like a child to you."

His chest rumbled as he chuckled into her hair and dropped another quick kiss on the top of her head. "Oh no, you feel like all woman to me, my precious one," he laughed throatily, his large hand slipping inside the comforter to cup her right breast firmly and give it a rough caress.

She let out a little moan of appreciation and then a deep sigh of disappointment when he removed his hand and tucked the comforter securely around her again. She could feel his hardness pressing against her bottom and she knew he wanted her again. She wished he would just take her and ravish her until she screamed his name in ecstasy. Her stomach rumbled and she groaned with embarrassment when he laughed.

"I know what you want," he whispered against her ear, "and I know what you need. Go and have a shower while I fix you some food. I'll satisfy your other hunger after you have eaten." He nipped her earlobe lightly and pushed her from his lap so he could slide his jeans and shirt on. He really wanted to join her on the bed and satisfy both of their needs, but she required food and he was determined that he was going to provide for her.

Caleb left the bedroom and headed downstairs and into the large kitchen. It was one of the very few, ultra-modern rooms in the mansion. It was all stainless steel appliances and shiny white cupboards with black, granite work surfaces. Along the nearest wall to the doorway was a large wooden oak table with four oak chairs around it.

Despite being a vampire and not needing to eat human food, he used the kitchen daily. His people enjoyed drinking most beverages and his weakness was coffee. He loved the taste of the rich, bitter liquid and had a state-of-the-art coffee machine which made every type of coffee imaginable. He smiled happily as he moved to the machine and started to make a cappuccino and a mocha. Rhianna had opted for a mocha earlier when they had been waiting for the real estate agent to arrive to show them the properties she had short-listed.

He frowned suddenly and stopped making the coffees. He should probably cook first, that would probably take the longest time. It was a bit weird having to think about things so carefully.

He headed to the refrigerator and was glad he had brought in some human food. He had done so on impulse after speaking with Jared this morning, just in case Rhianna came over and he needed to feed her. He pulled out the two steaks and wrinkled his nose. He could probably eat his 'blue'. It would be a bit more palatable.

However, Rhianna probably wouldn't be too impressed with watching him eat a steak swimming in blood. It would doubtless put her off her own food. Rolling his eyes, Caleb grabbed his newly acquired cookbook and hunted out the steak recipes. He quickly settled on peppered steak. The burgers earlier were peppered and she had seemed to enjoy hers immensely, so she should like peppered steak.

He was soon lost in the new intricate art of creating a meal. He was surprised to find he was actually enjoying the experience and put it down to his desire to cater to his woman's human needs. Taking care of her made him feel warm inside and he was soon serving up peppered steak and fries with a green, leafy, side salad to go with it along with crusty garlic bread and the hot coffees he'd started preparing earlier.

He set the plates on the dining table and smiled proudly. He had even managed to get the dishes to look exactly as they did in the cookbook. He hoped that was a good sign and her dinner would taste exactly the way it should.

~~~~

Rhianna showered as quickly as she could, taking care not to get her hair wet. She didn't know if Caleb had a hairdryer and all their exercise had made her famished. She dressed quickly and tried to remember the route back down to the lower floor. She hadn't been paying that much attention on the way up, but after a few false starts, she finally found the stairs and hurried down them towards the wonderfully delicious smells coming from the kitchen.

She stopped in the doorway and stared in surprise at Caleb sitting at the huge dining table sipping at a cup of coffee while he waited for her to appear. There was a feast on the table and she quickly noted he had cooked for himself as well as her.

"You didn't need to do that, Caleb." A small smile tugged at her lips as she slid into the place that was patently meant for her.

She saw him frown quickly, his eyes dropping to the plates on the table.

"The food isn't to your taste?" he asked starting to rise. "I can make something else."

Rhianna reached out and stopped him by placing her hand on his. "The food is amazing, Caleb." She smiled to reassure him. "It looks and smells heavenly and my mouth is watering to taste it. What I meant was, you didn't need to prepare a plate for yourself. It really won't bother me at all to eat alone."

Caleb relaxed and smiled at her, twisting his hand so he could capture her delicate one in his and raise it to his lips for a quick kiss. "I want to eat with you, Annie." His breath whispered across the back of her hand and he inhaled deeply of her wonderful sweet scent. He did truly want to eat with her, even if it had no taste to him.

She laughed and pulled her hand from his so she could reach for a slice of garlic bread. She loved garlic bread and was a little surprised it was on the menu. "Garlic?"

His face broke into a wide smile and he took a slice of the bread too. "Myth." Caleb bit into the pungent smelling bread. He chewed slowly as he watched her enjoy her own bread with obvious pleasure on her face. He tried hard to see the appeal of the garlic bread but it did nothing for him, still he ate it anyway.

At least his coffee erased the pungent taste from his mouth. "Most of the things you've seen and read about vampires are nothing but myths, Annie. We have to let you humans feel safe by ingraining our immortality with 'get out' clauses like garlic and silver and holy water, not to mention the old sun burning us to a crisp and a stake through the heart turning us to ash. Humans would never be able to sleep at nights if they didn't have the comfort of believing they could kill us so easily."

His tone was matter of fact, with a large hint of amusement in it. Rhianna watched his face as he spoke and literally answered a large portion of the questions she was dying to ask him. "You can't die at all?"

"Everyone can die, Annie." Caleb's tone was low. "Some of us can just live a bit longer than others. If we are burned badly enough, it can kill us or if someone takes our heads, we will die. We naturally try our hardest to avoid those circumstances." His smile was wry as he watched her assimilate his words. He really wished she would just eat her food and not ask the one question he wasn't ready to answer.

She seemed to consider it, he could almost see her mind whirling as she debated internally whether to ask, and then she appeared to come to a decision and she picked up her knife and fork to cut into her steak.

They ate in a companionable silence. Caleb managed to eat most of the steak before his iron control finally rebelled, and he set his utensils on the plate before rising to make another coffee. He emptied his plate into the bin and set it in the sink before crossing back to watch Rhianna finish her meal.

"Will you stay with me tonight, Annie?" He didn't want her to leave. He wanted to lie and watch her sleep, to listen to her deep even breathing as she rested at his side. He wanted to wake up in the morning with her lying beside him in his bed so he could slowly kiss her awake and make sweet, passionate love to her again.

"I can't, Caleb," her tone was regretful. "I need to get home soon. Millie will start to worry and I don't have any clothes to change into anyway. It's not that I don't want to because I do want to stay. I just need to be slightly better prepared for staying over."

He nodded his understanding but he wasn't happy about it. Now he had found her he never wanted to let her go. She belonged to him. She belonged with him forever but he couldn't push her into anything too quickly. He had to give her time to become used to him, to want to be with him the way he wanted to be with her.

Rhianna could see his disappointment. His gentle smile didn't quite reach his eyes but he didn't protest her decision, and if she hadn't already been in love with him, she knew she would have fallen in love with him that very instant. She gave him a big smile and reached over to take his hand in hers. "Take me home now," she smiled. "I have a couple of things I need to do, but I'll come back later tonight and stay with you."

Caleb's face lit up with such joy she was glad she had changed her mind. He squeezed her hand gratefully and tugged her from her chair and into his lap. "Thank you, Annie," he sighed, burying his head in the crook of her neck, his hard lips whispering gently across her shoulder. She fit so perfectly in his arms, her skin tasted so wonderful against his lips. He nibbled at the spot where her shoulder joined her neck and she moaned with pleasure.

"Come on, the sooner I take you home the sooner you can come back to me, sweet Annie." He smiled raising his head and standing up, his arm steadying her as she slipped from his lap onto her feet. He bent his head and kissed her with a deep need, his body craving hers badly. Soon she would be back in his arms and in his bed. He was content to let her go for now knowing she would be back before too long.

He was surprised when she asked if she could take the property lease home with her. He had forgotten all about it. "I don't suppose there's any chance you will let me give you the shop?" he asked with a smile. "Now that we're a proper 'item'?"

She laughed and shook her head. "Not a chance and don't even think about trying to get arrogant about it. You are not in the bedroom now, mister."

He laughed at her sass and then had to kiss her one more time. She was just so adorable he couldn't keep his lips from hers. It was Rhianna who ended the long, slow, kiss that had them both breathless by the end of it.

"Take me home, Caleb," she breathed against his mouth, her lips curving in a little smile when he protested her withdrawal. "I'll be back so much quicker if you stop messing about."

Groaning he rolled his eyes and grabbed her hand, practically running out of the house with her as she laughed loudly.

CHAPTER ELEVEN

Rafe lay quietly, feigning sleep on the large bed in Aaron's guestroom. He had been pretending to be asleep for the last few hours, wanting to alone, and shunning contact from Aaron and his Alpha, who kept stopping by to see how he was. Their concern grated on his nerves.

Why they even gave a damn about him was a mystery. He didn't deserve their concern or their pity. The vampire had been so right about him, he was a bastard. A cold heartless bastard who had broken his sister's heart and then allowed himself to be persuaded out of going to her time and time again.

The pain inside him cut deeply. He wanted to go to Annie, to look after her, protect her and hold her as he had done for so many years. The pack wouldn't let him. His Alpha wouldn't let him.

The pack crowded him. They were always there flaunting their nakedness and lust, battling each other with sharp bloodied claws and hellish teeth. The scent of blood sickened him. The violence sickened him. The lust sickened him. It was all around him and it was deep inside him.

His wolf revelled in it even as his human side cried out against it. His dual nature ripped him apart inside until he was screaming silently in his head. Only when he was with Annie did the terrible duality ease and he could find some small measure of comfort from the pain.

This life wasn't for him. He wasn't a wolf and he could never be one. The violence made his soul scream in agony and he longed for the escape from his endless suffering. He had to get away from the pack but where would he go? If he went to Annie, Jared would only come looking for him and there was the chance his sister would not be able to come to terms with what he now was.

He could run away from the wolves but he would never be free of them, his wolf would always be there inside him clawing to get out. Would his need to suppress his wolf cause him to go insane? Would the wolf break free and subjugate his human side, turning him into a rogue like the man who had done this to him?

The thought of that happening terrified him. He didn't want to hurt anyone.

Rafe sighed and shifted on the bed, making the appropriate sleepy movements a person made, just as Aaron popped his head around the door to check on him again. He settled down as if going back into his deep sleep and waited until his friend left.

He had made up his mind. He knew what he was going to do. He rose stealthily from the bed and stripped off his clothes. Naked, he pried the window open and slipped silently from the wooden house. He shifted as he jumped and carefully kept his mind blank so Jared wouldn't sense him.

He took off into the trees and began to run as fast as he could. He knew it wouldn't be long before they noticed him gone. Aaron's frequent checking had become shorter and shorter in interval and he knew he had little time to get his head start on his Alpha. He flew through the trees, his one goal firmly in his mind. He was going to end this torment finally.

He heard Jared roar into his mind and he felt the crushing weight of the Alpha's command pressing down on him. *"Stop, Rafe!"* Jared bellowed, but Rafe shook his head knowing he could shake the command off. He'd done it once before and he could do it again. Nothing was going to stop him. Nothing!

He broke through the trees at full speed, seeing the open tarmac in front of him. He prayed for a car, any car to come speeding down the road towards him. The pack was behind him, they were all trying to crowd into his head trying to pull him back to them. He howled an agonised sound and shot into the road just as a car barrelled towards him.

"Yes!" he howled triumphantly as the speeding hunk of metal raced towards him just as Jared and the pack hurtled out of the trees. Only a few more moments and his torment would be over. A car had ended the rogue's life and so a car would end his and he would finally be at peace.

"No!" Jared roared in anguish as he read the full intent in Rafe's mind. *"Rafe, no!"*

~~~~

The wolf appeared from nowhere and it was only Rhianna's careful speed and quick reflexes, which helped her stop before she hit it. The squeal of protesting tires screeched through the night as she performed her first emergency stop ever and her car halted mere inches from the large brown wolf in her headlights.

Shaking and white faced, she stared into the big brown eyes of Wolfie as her heart hammered a staccato beat in her chest. Her fear turned to uncontrolled rage, as she fumbled for her seatbelt, yanking it undone, and opening the car door. She stumbled out on shaky legs, her breath coming in short, sharp pants.

"You fucking idiot!" she screamed at the wolf, her fury spurred on by the adrenaline coursing through her veins. "You stupid fucking animal! Are you out of your mind? I could have killed you! Fuck, you could have killed me! I could have lost control of the car and crashed into one of those trees. What the fuck were you thinking, Wolfie?"

She was vaguely aware that she had most probably said the work fuck more times than she had ever said it in her life but her anger was at boiling point and she didn't care if her language was vulgar. She had been in her own little world, happy to be returning to Caleb's and the almost-accident had scared the life out of her.

Rafe stared at his sister in shock, her words piecing right through him as the enormity of what he had just done sunk in. He had wanted to be free from this life so badly he hadn't stopped to think of the potential danger he would be putting the person who was driving the car in.

He had almost killed Annie, his baby sister! He threw back his head and howled his agony into the night. Once he started, he couldn't stop and he howled repeatedly, his anguish more than he could bear.

The terrible agony from the wolf wrenched at Rhianna's heart and her fury evaporated before he had howled the second time. She felt tears in her eyes as she ran to the huge wolf and threw her arms around his wide neck. "Wolfie," she whispered. "Oh Wolfie, what is tearing you apart so badly? Please don't cry my beautiful wolf. Please, Wolfie."

The wolf howled mournfully and slumped to the ground in front of her, his entire body shaking wildly. Rhianna fell to her knees and tried to comfort the poor animal as the agonised sounds from him ripped deep into her soul. He was in so much pain, so much agony.

She heard a sound to her left and she looked up to see what looked like fifty wolves standing close to the grass verge, the large black one standing slightly in front of them. She stared into the deep blue eyes of the leader of the wolves and she felt her anger spark again.

"What have you done to him?" she screamed at Old Blackie. "Why are you doing this to him?" She didn't know why she felt he was to blame for Wolfie's pain but she just did. "Why aren't you helping him?" she sobbed. "Make him stop hurting. Please!"

Rafe's anguish was ripping through Jared just as much as it was ripping through Rhianna. The pain was filtering down to all of the pack, even the wolves with a lesser connection to the big man.

Jared couldn't believe Rafe had tried to end his life. If anyone other than Rhianna had been travelling this road, then the gentle wolf would now be dead. He was sure of it. He pondered the coincidence of it being Annie who had been driving towards the tortured man in the road. Was this a sign of some kind?

He turned away from them and looked at his pack. He had to protect them at all costs. Personally, he would trust the petite redhead with their secret but it wasn't a decision he could make alone, even as Alpha.

"Tonight Rafe has tried to take his life," he said to his pack. *"You all feel his pain. You all know how he has struggled to join the pack and come to terms with his new life. As Alpha, I must put the needs of the pack first even though it pains me greatly to lose Rafe. He is kind and gentle and we could use the diversity of thought he brings to the pack. You all know it is his sister who cradles him and weeps over his wolf. She, too, has the same kindness of heart her brother shows.*

"On a personal level, I trust Rhianna Armand with my life. I believe she is the one person who can save Rafe and help him come back to the pack. I know some of you hold firmly to the survival of the fittest ethos and see Rafe as weak. I see Rafe as an opportunity to remind us of our humanity, which is just as important as our wolves."

He ran his eyes over the assembled pack trying to gauge their reaction, but they stood still and silent. *"As Alpha, I call for a vote. I propose we allow the human woman, Rhianna Armand, to know our true nature so she can care for her brother and bring him back to the pack. You know she runs with vampires already.*

"*I have spoken with Caleb Ryder and he has revealed his true nature to her and she has accepted him. Her love for her vampire means she cannot allow any harm to come to him therefore, she keeps his secret. Her deep abiding love for her brother will mean she will protect our pack. Even in wolf form she unconsciously recognises him. Therefore, I ask my pack to grant me the permission to try to save Rafe Armand in the only manner I can think of. I ask as your Alpha and as your friend. What say the pack?*"

Wolfie had stopped howling and was looking at Old Blackie with tortured eyes. All the other wolves were watching him too and there was a lot of chuffing noises and odd barks coming from the large black wolf. It was almost as if he was talking to them, the way they all looked so intently at him. He stopped chuffing and stood still.

For a long endless moment there was total silence in the trees, and then one by one the gathered wolves gave one solitary bark. The air was thick with tension and Rhianna sensed something momentous was happening but she had no idea what it was.

The more barks that sounded, the more Wolfie trembled under her hands. She began to feel very afraid for him. Were they passing some kind of sentence on the wolf? Or where they casting some kind of sentence on her? She was only just beginning to realise in what a perilous situation she was in. She didn't have Caleb here to help her either if the wolves decided to attack her.

Slowly Old Blackie turned to look back at her and Wolfie and she tried to gauge his intent. His didn't look angry, but then, would she really know what a wolf looked like when he was angry? He chuffed at Wolfie and her wolf howled. Old Blackie stepped a little closer and chuffed again. Wolfie's response was another long howl.

Rhianna blinked slowly as she watched the large black wolf, a small frown creasing her brow. Did Old Blackie really just give a look that appeared to convey bemusement? He chuffed once more and then he seemed to ripple all over and the black wolf was suddenly gone and kneeling naked on the grass was Jared Hanlon.

She blinked again, and then once more, as her startled mind tried its best to register what it had just seen. The wolf had changed into a man and not just any man, one she knew. Jared Hanlon was a wolf. She repeated it to herself as Jared looked down at her in all his naked glory and it was most definitely glory. She would have to be blind not to notice how gorgeous his body was. It was as vibrant and as beautiful as Caleb's was and yet it didn't instil the same lust within her.

She wondered if he was going to speak but he stood there silently looking at her, and she realised her mouth was hanging wide open and she was still ogling his body like a teenager seeing her first naked man. She blushed scarlet and closed her mouth, swallowing loudly. She supposed she should say something to him and so she opened her mouth and said the first thing she could think of. "You're stark bloody naked, Jared!"

Jared had been giving Rhianna time to come to grips with what she had just witnessed. Her face was a riot of emotions ranging from shock to appreciation and then embarrassment. He had tried to convince Rafe to change into his human form but the man had refused, which left him rather bemused. The gentle wolf had literally begged to see his sister again and the moment the chance had been granted he had balked at the idea.

So he had changed into his human form himself. He felt a great pride for his pack's understanding and their resounding vote of yes to allow Rhianna into their secret. There had only been two votes of no and one abstention, which had allowed the vote to be passed by the majority rule.

The petite redhead's first words to him made him throw back his head and laugh loudly. Caleb had said she was good with the paranormal and it certainly appeared she was. He turned to Aaron who was hovering close to him in wolf form.

"Run and bring two sets of sweats," he told him before turning back to Rhianna. "You'll have to forgive me, Annie," he smiled. "Clothes do not transform when we do so we tend to go around naked most of the time when we're shifting."

"Are you a werewolf?" she asked timidly, her wits a bit sharper.

"I am a Were, which is effectively a shape shifter of some kind. It just so happens we shift into wolves. There are many other types of Were who shift into different animals. I must admit, you're taking this more calmly than I anticipated. Caleb said you were very accepting of him, but I thought you would possibly have more of an issue with us."

His mention of Caleb surprised her and then she realised they knew each other. She supposed it was only natural vampires would know about Weres.

"I am aware of Caleb's true nature, so you will not be harming him in anyway by anything you say, Annie." Jared said reassuringly as the wolf with golden streaks ran up and dropped clothes at Jared's feet.

Rhianna was relieved when Jared slipped the sweats on and approached with another set of sweats in his hand. He tossed them beside Wolfie and sat down on the grass. The implication of what he had just done didn't escape her and she looked down at Wolfie and gasped in surprise. "You're a man too, Wolfie?" Her hand slipped out of his fur as she moved back a few inches from him. Wolfie howled and bowed his head.

It appeared he was a man, however it was the wolf that lay so dejectedly before her and he tugged at her heart. "What's wrong with him, Jared? He just ran into the middle of the road. I was barely able to stop in time and then he just kept howling in such horrible pain."

"Are you going to tell her?" he asked Rafe with a deep sigh, and the wolf whined low in his throat. Jared sighed again and looked at Rhianna. "I just want you to know that I'm really sorry, Annie. I hope you'll be able to understand why I did what I did."

He looked back at Rafe hoping he would change and reveal himself of his own volition but he remained resolute and kept his head lowered. "Why don't you move your car to the side of the road and I'll try my best to explain everything," Jared said to Rhianna before he looked at the wolf. "You… Get off the road now or I'll have the pack drag you off kicking and screaming." His tone was firm and brooked no argument.

Rhianna watched Wolfie stand and head over to the grass where he threw himself down again, his body language miserable. She hurried to park the car in a safe spot and then sat down close to Wolfie but not touching him. It wasn't that she didn't want to comfort the wolf because she ached to do so. It was just knowing he was a man too made it seem almost perverted for her to stroke him the way she had been.

Jared sat on the other side of Rafe preferring to be away from Rhianna's fists just in case she reacted with anger when she learned the truth. In addition, he wanted to be close to Rafe in case he tried to throw himself under any further passing cars.

"Annie, revealing ourselves to you tonight is an unprecedented event for our kind," Jared began. "It is our pack law and the pack law of all Weres to ensure that no human ever learns of our existence. I am the Alpha of this pack and each and every person under me is my responsibility to protect."

"I'll never breathe a word about you or your pack, Jared." Rhianna's tone was sincere. "I swear it."

"I know you won't, Annie. It's why I asked the pack to vote tonight to allow me to reveal ourselves." Jared smiled proudly at her. "You already swear to protect us and you don't know what it is you are protecting. I knew I was right about you, Rhianna Armand."

His comment was rather cryptic and she wanted to ask him what he meant by it, but she had a feeling it would all come out soon so she held her tongue and let him continue.

"The Were Caleb killed with his car the other night, he is what we call a rogue," Jared said. "He had gone insane and lost himself within his wolf form." He noted Rhianna's surprise at hearing the dead wolf was one of his kind. "Don't feel too bad about it, Annie. He was wild, vicious, and attacking innocents. He killed four humans and severely wounded a fifth before Caleb unwittingly solved our problem for us.

The man who survived is your Wolfie here. It took three weeks for him to become sentient and stop shifting and trying to kill anyone close to him. Once he was coherent enough to understand what was happening to him, he took the changes he was experiencing hard. He wanted to go back to his human life, but I couldn't allow that."

Wolfie whined loudly and Rhianna's heart melted and she reached out and stroked his head. He seemed to settle a bit but he was still so melancholy it was pitiful to see. At least she could sort of understand why he was hurting so badly.

"I couldn't let him go home, Annie," Jared said quietly. "He was legally dead and a danger to himself and his family. I tried to integrate him into the pack but he has such a gentle nature and pack life is quite rough. He's fought me every step of the way. I've tried my best to help him but he is slowly dying inside. He pines for those he's been forced to leave behind."

"Is that why he comes to me?" Rhianna asked her tone curious. "Do I remind him of one of his family members?" She stroked Wolfie's head as he whined softly and began to tremble wildly.

Jared took a deep breath and looked her directly in the eyes. "He comes to you because you are his family, Annie," he said as gently as he could. He watched her lavender eyes widen with shock, saw her hand still on Rafe's fur as the big wolf howled loudly between them.

Rhianna dropped her gaze from Jared's and let it fall on the trembling wolf beside her. Those deep brown, all seeing eyes. The instant connection she had felt towards the wolf. The way he rolled over and submitted to her the very first time they met. Jared showing up with the unheard of insurance money. She stared in shock at Wolfie and felt fresh tears start to brim in her eyes as her hands began to shake.

"Rafe?" she whispered. He whined and turned his head towards her. His tortured brown eyes seemed to plead with her as he whined again and his trembling reached fever pitch.

Her heart thundered hard in her chest as she looked into Wolfie's eyes and saw Rafe looking back at her. She burst into loud sobs and threw her arms around his wide neck. "Rafe," she choked out between sobs. "My Rafe!"

CHAPTER TWELVE

Rhianna sobbed against him, her tears soaking the fur on the back of his neck as she wept uncontrollably. His Alpha had moved off a bit to give them some privacy and Rafe could only tremble and whine as his little sister sobbed. He wanted to hold her and comfort her and tell her how sorry he was but he would need to shift to do that and he was too afraid to look at her with his human eyes.

She wept on and the longer she wept the worse Rafe felt. It was sheer agony to hear her heartbreak and he howled loudly once more before he shifted beneath her and wrapped his arms around her trembling body. "Don't cry, Annie. Please don't cry. You're breaking my heart with your tears. I'm so sorry, Annie. I'm so sorry I've done this to you!"

Rhianna heard the rich timber of her brother's voice and felt the steel bands of his strong arms crushing her tightly against him. She cried harder, trying to speak, trying to tell him of the sheer joy she felt at finding him alive but the tears wouldn't let her. She settled on kissing him instead. She twisted in his arms, grabbed his face and planted kiss after joyful kiss on every single part of his skin she could reach.

He went rigid with shock for a moment and then he slowly relaxed and he was kissing her back, his big hands brushing at her wet cheeks so gently as if afraid he would hurt her. "Annie," he breathed softly. "My baby girl!"

"I can't believe you're alive, Rafe," she finally managed to get out. "I can't believe you're not really dead." She was crying and laughing at the same time, hugging him tightly one minute and then kissing his face the next.

Rafe could feel the joy radiating from her and he felt such shame. How could she be so happy he was alive when he had put her through such pain and misery? "Why don't you hate me, Annie?" His voice broke as he spoke.

Rafe's misery finally penetrated through Rhianna's happy haze and she drew back and looked into his anguished face. She knew her expression must be one of complete shock because that was how she was feeling inside. "I could never hate you," she whispered. "How can you even think that, Rafe? You're everything to me. You always have been." Her lavender eyes saw the denial in his and she really looked at him and saw the deep lines of abject misery on his face.

She turned to find Jared, and the dark haired man approached them slowly and sat down beside them. He placed a hand on Rafe's shoulder and she watched her brother flinch from the contact. "Be at ease, Rafe," Jared said, his tone soothing. "I am not going to take you away from your precious Annie."

Rafe's broad shoulders relaxed and he nodded his head to his Alpha as Rhianna quickly ran through what Jared had told her about Wolfie just before she found out he was her brother. Her heart broke at the thought of how hard Rafe was finding it to adjust to his new life. She could understand his pain. Her big brother was even more tender-hearted than she was. He refused to swat a fly or stomp on a spider. He would always find some other way to deal with the little pests. Having a wild wolf inside him would be so hard for him to come to terms with.

"Why did you run in front of my car, Rafe?" she asked suddenly and she saw the truth before he was able to slide his ashamed gaze away from her. "No, Rafe." Rhianna felt her stomach clench with fear. She squeezed her eyes shut and shuddered before she took a deep breath and opened them again.

"What happened to you create your own happiness, Rafe?" she asked softly. "You always told me that. You brought me up telling me to never give up no matter how hard things became. It's what helped me get through the pain of losing you. How could you give up, Rafe? How could you stop fighting?"

He bowed his head in shame. She was so right. He had given up. He had stopped fighting. "I don't know how to make myself happy being what I am now, Annie," he replied brokenly. "I don't know how to be at peace with the wolf inside me."

Rhianna met Jared's troubled eyes and she saw the deep concern he had for her brother. He was worried Rafe would try to kill himself again.

"The pack needs your help, Annie," Jared said quietly. "I need your help. You are all Rafe thinks about, the one person he thinks of over himself. We want him back in our pack but not until he is ready to return willingly. Will you help him, Annie? Will you mend his wounded soul so he can one day come home to us?"

The plea in Jared's voice touched her. He genuinely cared about her brother. The whole pack obviously did, otherwise they would never have broken their laws and revealed themselves to her. "Where can I take him?" she asked. "I can't take him home, Millie is there. She'll ask questions which neither of us can answer."

She thought of Caleb's mansion as she spoke. She could take him there. She didn't think Caleb would mind. If Rafe was there, then she would be spending a lot of time there too, and she knew Caleb wouldn't be averse to her spending as much time with him as possible.

"I can take him to Caleb's," she decided before Jared could answer. "He's got plenty of spare rooms."

Jared arched an eyebrow at her. "Don't you think it would be a wise idea to ask first?" His remark came out drolly. "I mean, Caleb's okay for a vampire but Weres and vampires don't usually get on that well."

Rhianna snorted. "I don't care about that," Her expression was determined. "Love me, love my family. He'll just have to like it or lump it." She didn't feel half as confident as she sounded, but she needed somewhere safe to take her brother and Caleb's was the only place she could think of.

"Come on, Rafe." She stood up. "Can you put those sweats on? You are naked." She turned her back while her brother quickly pulled on the sweats.

Jared smiled warmly at her. "Caleb really doesn't know what he has let himself in for, does he?" he laughed softly.

"I think he has a fair idea," she laughed back and then she turned serious again. "I'll take good care of Rafe, Jared. I'm not angry with you or your pack. I understand why you did what you did and I know you only have my brother's best interests at heart. I have already sworn once I would keep your secret. I mean that tenfold now. No one will ever learn from me of your existence."

On impulse, she wrapped her arms around Jared's big body and gave him a tight hug. He hesitated briefly and then hugged her back. "Thank you for trusting me, Jared. Thank you for giving me my brother back." She stepped back and turned to look at the wolves sitting patiently just outside the ring of the trees surrounding them. "Thank you," she called loudly. They regarded her solemnly for a moment and then the golden streaked wolf chuffed lightly in her direction.

"Aaron says it is you we should be thanking," Jared translated. "He is Rafe's closest friend in the pack. He has fought as long and hard as I have to keep your brother well."

"You have my eternal gratitude, Aaron," Rhianna said quietly to the beautifully marked wolf. "I will keep him well." The wolf grinned at her and bowed his head.

She turned to her brother, who was staring silently off into the distance as if trying to detach himself from the wolves around him. She gave Jared one more smile and then turned away. "Come on, Rafe." Rhianna pulled on his arm to move him over to the car.

Rafe was silent as she drove towards Caleb's mansion. Her mind was whirling as it tried to assimilate everything that had happened. She was anxious about Rafe. The depth of his depression was scary. She had promised to keep him well but she didn't know if she even knew where to begin.

"Your vampire will not be happy that you're bringing me to his home." Rafe broke the silence and she was surprised at him speaking and the certainty in his voice.

"I'll talk to him."

"He wanted to kill me last night." Rafe's tone lacked emotion.

"He what?" Rhianna couldn't stop the shocked gasp escaping her lips. Caleb knew? He knew Rafe was alive and he hadn't told her? Her hands tightened hard on the steering wheel and she felt a deep anger begin to pulse inside her. She couldn't believe Caleb could keep something like this from her. How could he say he loved her but leave her grieving for her brother who was still alive? She felt Rafe's eyes on her and tried to relax some of the tension from her body.

Rafe sighed loudly and leaned his head against the headrest. "Don't be angry with him, Annie. He didn't find out until last night. Something you said to him led him to put the pieces together as he knows the Alpha well. He came to Old Forest Road with his people. He was beyond rage, furious on your behalf. He demanded justice for the pain our pack had caused you. He was quite magnificent actually." His tone still lacked emotion but it was the most he'd said.

"He should have told me!" she blurted out and then she remembered their earlier conversation about how he couldn't tell her something because it was someone else's secret. How she had told him not to worry about it. She felt her anger lessen slightly and took a deep breath.

"He would have started a war if he had," Rafe told her quietly. "He almost started one last night. The vampires would have decimated the pack even though they were in smaller numbers. They are faster than us and their bite is deadly to us. He agreed with the Alpha to reveal his true nature to you, so he could prove you were able to accept the truth and protect those you cared for. He risked losing you so he could convince the Alpha to agree to tell you I still lived. It would be rather mean and petty of you to be angry with him after he did all that for you. Don't you think so?"

He opened his eyes and looked at his sister. She was biting her lip hard as she listened to what he had to say. Her hands relaxed more around the steering wheel and her lips tugged in a slight smile. "Maybe just a little," she finally agreed.

Rhianna was reeling at the information she had just learned. Caleb had almost started a war because of her? He really needed to work on learning how to handle his newfound emotions. A small part of her was flattered too. He had told her he loved her but she hadn't understood just how much. He was willing to lose her so she could have her brother back? That was huge!

"Rafe, don't worry about Caleb." Rhianna felt the need to reassure her brother as she pulled up outside the mansion. "He really is a wonderful man. He's still learning how to control his emotions, so he may be a bit erratic at expressing them from time to time, but his heart is kind even if he doesn't quite believe it yet."

She smiled at him and stepped out of the car. She opened the back door and pulled out her overnight bag, waiting for her brother to decide he was getting out of the car. She waited patiently as Rafe just sat there.

Long moments passed and she began to bite her lip. She didn't want to press him too hard but she couldn't just stand on the driveway all night. The sound of the front door opening behind her drew her eyes and she took a deep breath as Caleb stepped out of the house.

Caleb's quick gaze took in Rhianna's tearstained face and her anxious expression as she looked at him and then back at the huge man sitting half-naked in her car. He tensed and felt his anger start to boil up. Had the man hurt his Annie? He took one threatening step forward and then stopped as suddenly as he had moved.

He recognised the man from the night before. He watched Rafe Armand intently as he sat staring straight ahead. Annie's brother was truly wounded to his core. It was plain for all to see. Caleb stepped forward again, keeping his tread light. He opened the passenger side door and looked down at the man.

"Welcome to my home, Rafe," he said quietly. "You are welcome to stay for as long as you need."

Rafe turned his head and looked at the vampire who had captured his sister's heart. He didn't look half as intimidating as he had the night before. He sensed no intent on the vampire's part to harm him in anyway. Perhaps Rhianna was right about the vampire. He unbuckled his seatbelt and climbed out of the car as the vampire stood back.

Caleb closed the door then turned to look at Rhianna. Her expression showed relief and gratitude. Did she doubt he would welcome her brother into his home? Was she going to be angry with him? He knew she must know everything. Obviously something had transpired on her way over to his place.

"I'll tell you about it later," she said quietly walking over to him. He took her overnight bag and slipped an arm around her shoulder. At least she was talking to him. "Coming, Rafe?" Rhianna held out her other hand to her brother. He moved to take it and they walked into the house together.

Caleb set her bag down in the hallway and turned to her with a questioning look but she shook her head quickly at him but managed a smile, which did reach her beautiful eyes. No trace of anger yet. Perhaps it was a good sign.

"Are you hungry, Rafe?" She turned to her brother but he shook his head in the negative.

"I'd really just like to lie down." It was the same listless tone he'd spoken in the entire drive over.

Rhianna sighed and frowned at him. "Well that's just tough. Is that how you escaped your pack? Did you pretend to be tired and then sneak off the moment their backs were turned? Well you're not doing that to me, Rafe. I've only just found you again and I am not going to lose you. Now get a grip of yourself and act your age!"

Caleb didn't know who was the more surprised, himself or Rafe. The big man's head snapped up and a small smile began to tug at his lips as he regarded his sister intently. "Is it running with a vampire that has turned you into a little harpy?" There was spark of life in his voice for the first time in a long time.

"No, it's having an ass of a brother who also happens to be a part-time wolf," she retorted waspishly. "Really, Rafe. I don't know what to do with you. I don't recognise this person in front of me. My brother is inside there somewhere and I want him back. So have a chat with Wolfie and work out how you're both going to accomplish that."

He blinked at her in surprise and then laughed. It was a harsh sound, his brown eyes narrowing. "You think it's that simple, Rhianna? Just snap my fingers, say hi to *Wolfie*, and everything is going to be okay?" He felt his anger rise and he struggled to dampen it down, aware of the dangerous man at his sister's side.

"It's as simple or as hard as you want to make it, Rafe." Her tone was less abrasive. "My big brother used to tell me that and he was a very wise man. Maybe you should talk to him about it."

She turned to Caleb, slipped her arms around his waist and leaned her head against his chest. "I could really use one of your excellent mochas."

He followed her lead and ignored the burnt out man at their side. He smiled slowly and picked her up so he could give her a long, thorough kiss. "As my lady commands," he answered before he set her feet back down on the floor and escorted her into the kitchen, leaving Rafe alone in the ornate hallway.

He gathered her into his arms the moment they were alone and sat her on one of the kitchen counters, easing between her thighs so he could bring his face close to hers. "You're making him angry," he said quietly, his golden brown eyes searching hers.

"I know." She kept her voice just as quiet. "It's the only time he has a spark of life in him, Caleb. He needs to remember what it feels like to have some fight in him. I'm going to push him hard, love, and I need you to not interfere, no matter how angry he gets with me. I know I'm asking a lot of you but you have to trust me. Rafe will never hurt me no matter how angry he gets."

Caleb frowned darkly at her, his expression turning mutinous. "He's not only Rafe now, Annie. He's a wolf too and he is unstable at the moment. He could accidentally hurt you. You can't expect me to stand idly by and do nothing to protect you."

"Wolfie will never hurt me either, Caleb," she sighed softly. "I keep telling you that but you don't seem to believe me. I'm asking you to have some trust in me, Caleb. I need you to trust me to know what is best for my brother."

He didn't want to argue with her and he could tell from her set expression she would dig her heels in if he pushed her and her first night in his bed would be a distinctly chilly event. He smoothed his frown away but his unhappiness was still etched across his face. "I'll try, Annie," he conceded. "It's the best I can give you. You're just too precious to me, my love. I don't want to lose you when I've only just found you."

She smiled and cupped his face. "It's a start, Caleb. Just count to ten very slowly if you feel your anger taking hold. Rafe told me what happened last night with the Weres. Whilst I appreciate your need to protect me and your sense of outrage at the perceived injustice done to me, I really will be very unhappy if you start a war in my name."

Caleb actually blushed and looked down, his teeth worrying his bottom lip. "I'm sorry about that, Annie." He almost sounded humble. "I wanted to tell you about Rafe, I truly did, but Jared needed to be sure you could handle finding out about me first. It was his intention to put the question of whether or not to tell you the truth to his pack once I'd had the chance to meet with him again after I had revealed myself to you. I didn't quite expect it to happen so soon. I was going to meet with Jared tomorrow. Something serious must have happened to have brought about all this." He raised his eyes and searched her face intently for some clue as to what had happened on her way over to his place.

"I tried to commit suicide by throwing myself in front of a passing car," Rafe said from the doorway and they both turned around and looked at him. He rolled his eyes and snorted. "I am a wolf now. You could at least try and remember I have enhanced hearing abilities. It will make it less embarrassing for both of you when I overhear you talking about me."

"Rafe," Rhianna sighed, trying to hop down from the counter but Caleb kept her pinned with his body.

He growled low in his throat and his hands tightened on her hips painfully. "If you tell me you selfishly threw yourself in front of Annie's car, I am going to beat the living daylights out of you, dog!" he hissed furiously.

"Caleb!" Rhianna gasped, stunned by the onset of his sudden rage. "Count to ten very slowly. Now!"

He ignored her and continued to glare at Rafe, another long hiss coming from his throat, as the other man did not deny his actions.

"Caleb!" She tried to get his attention again but he was totally focused on her brother. She could feel the rage in the tenseness of his body and she was afraid he would give in to it and attack Rafe.

He seemed to pay her no heed so she changed tactics as her fear began to build quickly. She moaned low in her throat and let her body go completely limp. As she started to fall back against the counter, Caleb's head spun around as his arms wrapped around her and he pressed her against his body, Rafe completely forgotten.

"Annie," he groaned, his hand cupping her cheek.

She opened her eyes and caught his gaze with hers. She watched slow realisation dawn in his eyes and then anger flare for a brief moment before his expression slowly cleared and he gave her a rueful smile.

"I suppose I deserved that," he admitted, brushing her lips gently with his. "Are you going to do that every time I lose my temper? I really hope not because you just made my heart stop there, sweet one, and I really didn't like it one bit."

"Counting to ten slowly is the preferred option, but I will use any and all tactics I have to. You have to learn better self-control than that, Caleb. I can't let you hurt Rafe."

"You should have let him pound me," Rafe said darkly, his expression angry. The vampire was right to be angry with him. He had almost killed his sister tonight and there was no excuse for his actions. "You think you feel angry, vampire? You should have heard Annie run her mouth off at me. I've never heard the words fuck and fucking used so many times in a mere handful of sentences before." He sounded oddly impressed, as Rhianna felt her cheeks flush scarlet at the memory.

Caleb regarded him with narrowed eyes, and then looked at Rhianna. "I wish I'd been there to hear it." He rubbed his thumb across her bottom lip thoughtfully. "Maybe you could repeat it for me later on?" He suddenly found himself wanting to hear her utter profanities, preferably, when he was sliding his body deep inside hers. It had been so deliciously erotic when she'd done so earlier.

She flushed scarlet again, knowing what he was thinking of and pushed at his chest. "If you two have finished, perhaps you could get around to making that mocha?" she asked archly.

Caleb slid her from the counter top and turned to Rafe. "Would you like a coffee?" He kept his tone as polite as he could manage. "I can make just about anything you fancy." He was trying his best to connect with Rhianna's brother. He knew it would make her happy and despite wanting to rip the other man's head off for recklessly endangering his love, he felt almost responsible for the desperation he must have felt to try to end his life like that.

"I'll have a cappuccino," Rafe answered slowly as he watched Annie move over to the table and pull out a chair. He followed her and sat down across from her. "I promise I won't try anything like that again." He paused and looked down at the table. "I know I'm a bit of a mess right now but, at the time, I thought you would never know I was still alive. There was nothing keeping me to this life. There is now." He looked up and met her gaze.

Rhianna stared at him solemnly before nodding. "Just don't give up. You can't ever give up, Rafe. I know it's not easy for you dealing with this duality inside of you. Your problem is you see your human side as being separate from your wolf side. When you come to me, you either come as Wolfie or as Rafe. You are not two separate individuals in the same body, you are one. When you can make that connection, find that inner balance, the pain and misery will all go away."

"How do I do that, Annie?" he whispered, his handsome face twisting into a mask of misery. "I've tried but I just don't know how to do it."

Rhianna reached across the table and took his hand in both of hers. "Wolfie needs the wisdom of Rafe and Rafe needs the strength of Wolfie," she told him, her tone firm. "When Wolfie is having a hard time, he needs to reach within himself and ask Rafe to help him and vice versa. You have to learn to trust both aspects of your nature. Stop viewing Wolfie as a monster. I know Wolfie well and he most certainly isn't one. He may be an animal and have some baser type needs, but he is still a lovable creature."

"When did you get so wise, Annie," Rafe asked, a hint of awe in his voice.

"Ironically, I think it started to happen when I lost you," she answered with a wry smile. "I suddenly had to start making difficult decisions without having you there to back me up. I didn't think I could do it on my own, but every time I fell down I would remember something you had said to me and I used that to help me through the rough patch. I've never lost faith in you, Rafe, even when you were gone. Have faith in yourself. You can find your inner peace and I'll be here to help you when you fall."

Caleb set the coffees on the table and sat down beside Rhianna. He had listened into their conversation and his love and respect for his woman grew in leaps and bounds.

"I will be there to help too, Rafe," he offered. "I can help you when you need to confront your wolf side. I would prefer if Annie was not present during those moments. Just as a precaution."

"I would never hurt her," Rafe said fiercely, his expression turning horrified at the very thought of hurting his beautiful sister.

"Maybe you wouldn't," Caleb conceded, "but you must understand, Rafe. She is my life now, the most precious thing in the world to me. I wish to avoid any possible harm coming to her and I wish to avoid any possibility of me harming you because you accidentally hurt her. I would be unable to stop myself from it and then she would hate me forever. If we do things my way, then a large element of risk is removed."

"Caleb," Rhianna groaned rolling her eyes. At least he wasn't threatening to beat Rafe up but still, his over protectiveness was grating just a little.

"No, Annie, he's right," Rafe interrupted her. "Why choose unnecessary risk when there is a safer way to do things? You are precious to both of us. Let us protect you from your overgenerous need to fix this."

She would have argued with them but she caught a spark of hope in Rafe's eyes, and it was the first unforced emotion from him since he had arrived. His shoulders were not so slumped in defeat either.

"Okay, I will bow to both of your superior wisdom on the matter," she sighed softly. "Caleb will help you with Wolfie and I'll help my big brother."

Rafe smiled slowly and nodded his head before he picked up his coffee and took a sip.

Caleb smiled his satisfaction and brushed her hair away from the side of her neck so he could place a soft kiss there. "Did we just compromise?" he asked with a soft laugh and she rolled her eyes and drank her coffee without replying.

Rafe did look tired the more she stared at him. Rhianna knew how he felt. Emotional weariness was just as exhausting as physical weariness. She felt emotionally drained as she sipped at her mocha, the wonderful chocolaty coffee not giving her the adrenaline rush she had expected. It had been a very long day. She'd found out her boyfriend, lover, whatever Caleb was, was a vampire and her dead brother really wasn't dead but was a werewolf instead. It was hard to take it all in.

When Rafe pleaded tiredness again, she didn't argue with him, only nodded her head. He had sworn he wouldn't attempt to take his life again and she believed him. He didn't appear to be as depressed as he had been earlier but then his moods changed in a blink of an eye. Caleb's too. It was hard dealing with two strong alpha males with volatile moods, so she was actually relieved when Caleb took Rafe to show him where he could sleep.

She sat alone in the quiet kitchen and closed her eyes. The peace was blissful and she sighed deeply.

"You looked exhausted, love," Caleb said quietly from her right side and she started in surprise. She must have nodded off because she hadn't heard him return.

Caleb could see the fatigue on Rhianna's face and he smiled ruefully as he plucked her from the chair and cradled her against his chest. It wasn't quite how he had planned his night but he wasn't too upset about it. She was here in his arms when she needed his strength and he was content to be here for her.

"I'm sorry, Caleb," she said quietly. "You didn't exactly sign up for this when you asked me to spend the night."

He strode from the kitchen taking the stairs three at a time. "Hush." He smiled down at her. "You're here with me and that's all that matters, Annie. I don't just want your body, sweet one, though your body is incredibly delightful." He shot her a lusty glance and she laughed as he carried her into his bedroom. Her overnight bag was already on the floor beside the bed as he dropped her onto the thick mattress.

She laughed as she bounced and he smiled as he stared at her. She looked so perfect lying on his bed, her radiant curls fanning across his black pillows. He wanted to follow her down onto the bed and slowly strip her clothes from her beautiful body so he could lose himself deep inside her. He dampened down his erotic thoughts, picked her bag up and put it on the bed beside her.

"I assume my lady requires something from her bag to prepare herself for bed?" he asked, his golden brown eyes twinkling as he raked them over her body.

"You presumed correctly, kind sir," she giggled sitting up and pulling out her toiletry bag. It felt sinfully wicked to have actually packed her bag with the sole intent of spending the night with him. It would be her first time ever sleeping with a man and she was excited and nervous at the same time.

Caleb scrutinized her face for a moment and then sat down on the side of the bed. "If it's any consolation, it's my first time too. I'm just as out of my depth as you are."

She smiled and moved over to him. "Am I that transparent, Caleb? I thought I was acting pretty blasé about it."

He ran a finger lightly over her cheekbone and felt his body stir at the contact. Her skin was so soft and delicate. Every part of her was perfection and he was finding it impossible not to touch her in some manner.

"You've had a very emotional day, Annie. I want to make love to you again." He gave her a crooked smile. "I want to make love to you constantly," he admitted, "but you're exhausted, so why don't you just do whatever little human rituals you need to do to prepare for bed and then climb into bed with me so I can hold you close while you rest. I just want to feel you in my arms tonight. Nothing more."

She sighed softly and smiled at him, reaching up to tuck his hair behind his ear. "That sounds like heaven, Caleb." Rhianna smiled again and gave him a quick kiss before she slid off the bed and headed into the bathroom.

Fifteen minutes later, she came back into the bedroom to find Caleb already in bed, lying in the middle waiting for her. Her breath caught as she took in his naked chest, the light dusting of golden brown hair so tempting to look at. Her fingers itched to curl in that hair, and gently run through it as she felt his hard muscles contract beneath her fingers.

She knew he was naked beneath the covers. She had been wondering what to do about sleepwear and had packed a nightie just in case. She smiled as she imagined his face if she put the little nightie on. She didn't think he'd be too impressed with that so she quickly stripped off her clothes and threw them on the chair closest to the bed.

Caleb feasted his eyes on her naked body as he pulled back the covers so she could slide in beside him. His body hardened and he stifled down a groan. She was just too beautiful for words. It was no wonder he walked around with almost a permanent erection when she was close to him. Her sweet scent filled the room and he pulled her close to him as he reached across her to turn out the bedside lamp.

"You smell wonderful," he breathed into her hair as she pillowed her head across his chest.

"You smell pretty good yourself," she smiled and allowed her hand to lightly run through the soft hair on his chest as she'd been imagining doing.

"Rhianna," he groaned, catching her hand and halting her movement. "Sleep, love, before you drive me insane with need." He tilted her chin up so he could kiss her gently, deliberately keeping the kiss light. If she responded with too much passion, he would lose the tenuous hold he had on his self-control and he didn't want to do that.

She smiled against his lips and closed her eyes. "I love you, Caleb," she whispered softly, as he kissed her on the top of her head and settled down into a comfortable position. "I love you too, Annie," he whispered back as he closed his eyes contentedly

CHAPTER THIRTEEN

Caleb woke slowly and stiffened for a moment before opening his eyes as he felt the soft breath wash across his face. His surprise lasted a fraction of a second before he remembered Rhianna was lying at his side. She was sleeping deeply, lying on her side facing him, their faces mere inches apart. Her hand was clutching his tightly on the pillow between them.

His breath whispered out as he stared at her in wonder. She was simply breath taking. Her beautiful face was relaxed in sleep, her lips slightly parted, her luscious curls half obscuring her face as they tumbled around her. He reached out and brushed the curls away so he could get an unobstructed view of her face. She murmured quietly and shifted closer to him. Her hand tightened on his before slowly relaxing again. His name passed her lips on a quiet breathy sigh and he felt his heart skip a beat.

She was dreaming of him in her sleep. His lips curled in a soft smile as he watched her. He marvelled at just how much she had changed him in the last couple of months. She brought out all his better qualities. Whilst he exalted in the wonderful new feelings she inspired in him, he was also aware of just how much she weakened him too. She was just too important to him. She was his Achilles heel now and he would have to guard against others of his kind trying to take advantage of him, of them possibly trying to use her to get to him.

He carefully disentangled himself so he could get up. He would let her sleep. It was Sunday and they didn't have any plans. He showered, shaved and dressed in a clean pair of Levis and a black T-shirt. He could hear Rafe stirring and he wanted to be there when the wolf came downstairs.

Caleb was making breakfast when Rafe entered the kitchen. The big man had dressed in the clothes Caleb had left out for him. The jeans were a bit too long but apart from that everything else pretty much fit okay. His hair was still wet from his shower and he watched the vampire cook the huge fry-up as if it was a common occurrence for him.

"Have a seat, Rafe. I don't know how much you eat so I just put everything on. I figured whatever you didn't eat Annie would when she gets up. If it's still warm enough." He frowned and looked at the other man. "How do you keep food warm after it's been cooked?"

The big man burst out laughing. He couldn't help it, the expression on the vampire's face was just so comical. "Put one of your ovens on at the lowest setting to heat up." He hunted in a couple of cupboards before he found a clear casserole dish with matching lid. He passed it to Caleb. "Annie likes two sausages, a couple of bits of bacon and an egg," he told him. "The egg takes no time to cook so that can be done when she gets up."

Caleb smiled, nodding his head. "That's the second favour you've done me today."

Rafe was surprised and raised an eyebrow at him. "What was the first?" He was curious about his comment.

"Being here," the vampire replied instantly. "With you here, I don't have to eat human food to keep Annie company when she eats."

The healthy dose of relief in his voice made Rafe laugh again. He watched the vampire apportion out food and sat down at the dining table. "I didn't know vampires could eat human food." His curiosity was piqued even more. He didn't know a lot about vampires and he supposed he should find out as much as he could about the man his sister had chosen.

Caleb grimaced. "We can when we must but it's not a very pleasurable experience for us. Everything tastes pretty bland and unappealing. Drinking though, that's a different matter. For some reason our taste buds work perfectly when it comes to beverages. We can drink anything humans do." He handed Rafe his breakfast and put Rhianna's in the oven as per the big man's instructions. He quickly made a couple of cups of coffee and sat down at the table to watch Rafe eat. "You seem slightly more balanced this morning."

Rafe tensed for a moment and then relaxed slowly. "Being around Annie seems to have that effect on me," he answered before eating some more of his food.

Caleb nodded. "She does the same for me. Most of the time. Sometimes my nature gets the better of me, like last night when I became so angry with you."

Rafe stopped eating again, eyed the vampire for a long moment and then suddenly laughed. "We have the same problem, don't we, Caleb?" he chuckled, "And Annie is our cure."

Caleb hadn't quite thought about it like that before but, as he considered Rafe's words, he realised what he said made sense. Annie was teaching him how to come to terms with his finer feelings and she was trying to teach her brother how to come to terms with his more violent feelings. They were opposites and yet they were the same.

The two men looked at each other for a long moment and then Caleb smiled with genuine warmth. "It would appear we have a lot more in common than I first thought, Rafe."

Rafe returned his smile and nodded his head. Maybe he wasn't so bad. He appeared to genuinely care about Annie.

Caleb headed back upstairs, content to leave Rafe to his own devices for now. He was anxious to be with Rhianna. Knowing she was so close, lying in his bed sleeping, made his heart thump loudly and he found he couldn't stay away from her any longer.

She was still sleeping when he entered his bedroom. She looked so tiny in his enormous bed, and he simply watched her for a moment before he stripped off his clothes and climbed back in beside her. She stirred and reached for him, and he groaned as he pulled her body against his. He was hard and aching for her instantly and he couldn't deny himself any longer.

He teased her lips gently with his, feather light kisses across her soft mouth until she moaned and threaded her hands into his hair to press his mouth harder to hers. Her eyes were still closed but he could sense she was wakening up and his excitement grew as he deepened the kiss. His tongue dipped into her sleepy mouth to taste her wonderful sweetness before he trailed his mouth across her neck and along her collarbone as her hands tightened in his hair and her body arched against him.

"Caleb," she murmured and he raised his head to look into her exquisite face. Lavender eyes smiled sleepily at him and his breath caught in his throat. He didn't think he had ever seen her look more beautiful as she did right at that moment.

"Good morning, my love," he sighed against her lips, lightly stroking her mouth with his as his fingertips trailed down her side, sliding around her back to cup her bottom and press her into his hardness.

"You've showered already," she said with a small smile, feeling the dampness of his hair, "and you've had coffee."

He chuckled and kissed her cheek. "I let you sleep a little longer. You needed it."

Rhianna stretched languidly and smiled back at him, "And now you've decided I don't need any more sleep?" There was an impish expression on her face that caused him to groan and his pulse to race faster.

"Now I've decided I can't wait any longer to make love to you again." Caleb let out a sigh, rolling her onto her back and sliding between her thighs, so he could press against her more intimately. His breath rushed out when their bodies touched and he had to kiss her again.

Rhianna was breathless when he finally let her up for some air, desire sending her blood pressure sky high. "What a fabulous way to wake up," she thought, and then flushed scarlet when Caleb laughed and she realised she'd actually said it out aloud.

"I can make it so much more fabulous," he promised her, his golden brown eyes glinting with desire as his hungry mouth latched onto one of her breasts and he began to caress her tender flesh.

She cried out and arched up against him as he teased her aching body, liquid heat firing through her body and going straight to the juncture between her legs. She watched Caleb's head rise briefly as he inhaled deeply and smiled, and she knew he was scenting her arousal and was pleased with what he scented. His head lowered again and he returned to his teasing, his mouth hot and demanding, building her desire to fever pitch in an instant.

Rhianna wanted to touch him too but he was intent on giving her pleasure and held her body pinned beneath his. She wanted to give him the same pleasure he was giving her and he laughed when she tried to tell him.

"You always give me pleasure, sweet one," he chuckled against her stomach. "Every little moan, every sweet cry and lusty scream fills me with unimaginable pleasure." His hot mouth was trailing slowly downwards and she ached for him to get there, even as she wanted to be the one exploring his body.

"I want to touch you and kiss you the way you're doing to me, Caleb," she moaned and he halted his progress to look up at her with darkened eyes. He rose up above her and kissed her with a long, drugging kiss and then he moved away from her lying on his back and resting his head on his folded arms.

"I don't know how much I'll be able to stand," he admitted, his voice husky, his eyes glittering, "but I'll do my best. You may have your wicked way with me, sweet Annie."

Rhianna giggled at his words and moved over his body sitting up on her knees to look down at him. "Is this the vampire's equivalent of the submissive position?" She teased him with a wicked smile and a low growl emitted from his throat.

"Vampires do not submit to anyone." Caleb's lips twitched as he tried to keep the smile from his face. He couldn't deny his woman what she wanted. If she wanted his submission, he would give it to her, for a little while at least. He hadn't been lying when he said he didn't know how much he'd be able to stand. He wanted her so badly it was all he could do to lie there and let her look her fill.

Rhianna slowly ran her hand over his wide chest, watching the muscles bunch under her touch and hearing the sharp hiss of breath from Caleb. She leaned down and kissed his chest slowly at first, a bit hesitantly, and then her confidence began to grow and her mouth was gliding effortlessly over his skin, her tongue flicked out to tease his hard nipples.

He groaned under her touch and the sounds he made were so heady they emboldened her further and she kissed down his flat stomach, her hands stroking over his hips as his groans turned to soft growls the closer she got to her goal.

"Annie," he growled, her name a warning sound as her breath whispered over his impressive erection but she ignored him and tried to wrap one hand around his girth. His breath hissed out and his hips instinctively bucked upwards, giving her a heady sense of power as she took a deep breath and began to give him the most intimate of kisses, as he had pleasured her the night before.

Caleb thought he was going to die when her mouth touched him. The image and feel of her lips and tongue on his body sucked the breath right out of him. She was a witch, a tempting, teasing little witch who was trying to drive him insane with need. His body trembled hard as he fought to maintain control, fought to give her what she wanted, but it was so hard to just lay there and let her do what she wanted.

He growled again, his breathing became harsh and ragged as her confidence increased, brought on by his reaction to her ministrations. Her mouth engulfed him and he bucked up, trying to muffle a loud roar as pleasure suffused him. Caleb fisted his hand in her hair, pulling it away from her face so he could watch her take her pleasure and return it tenfold.

It was too much for him to endure. With a muffled curse, Caleb flipped Rhianna onto her back, and pressed into her. Her startled expression quickly changed to one of need as she wrapped her arms around him.

"Love me, Caleb."

Her whispered words brought tenderness to his touch as he began to move, sliding deep within her, his mouth and lips trying to touch every inch of her skin. "I do, my Annie," he whispered back. "Now and forever."

CHAPTER FOURTEEN

Jared Hanlon took the steps three at a time as he made his way up to the apartment. His wolf was prowling close to the surface, and he was having a hard time keeping a tight leash on his beast. It was his own fault. He had stayed away from Millie for too long, because of the complicated circumstances involved, circumstances, which had now changed drastically.

Rafe was safe with Annie for the moment, and Annie knew of their existence so claiming his mate would no longer be an issue. The only real problem remaining was his mate. She was being extremely difficult to say the least, and he was fast losing patience with her. Didn't she feel the attraction between them? He had been so sure she had when they'd first met. Her beautiful cobalt blue eyes had widened when she'd looked at him; he'd smelt the first faint hint of arousal coming from her deliciously curvy body, and then, she'd gone and thrown him out. She had actually thrown him out of her apartment!

If that wasn't bad enough, she refused all his calls until he was acting like some mad stalker, even calling her at her workplace so she couldn't scream at him and slam down the phone. A proud smile crossed his lips. She had one fabulous temper on her, his woman. A true Alpha if ever he'd seen one. She would make a glorious wolf and a strong ruler at his side, when he finally managed to get her to submit to him.

He hesitated briefly at the apartment door and looked at his watch. Damn, it was barely seven am on a Sunday morning. If he woke her up, she would be really pissed at him. Pissed and off balance, just the right combination he wanted. Smiling broadly, he knocked loudly on her door.

"You have got to be fucking kidding me," Millicent Cooper groaned, as she heard the loud knocking on the front door. She pulled her head out from underneath the covers and squinted tiredly at the clock. Five past seven! Who the hell was knocking on the door at this obscene hour in the morning?

"Annie!" she yelled, and then, cursed when she remembered her friend wasn't in. She had stayed overnight at Caleb's. Cursing when the knock sounded again, Millie grabbed her robe, pulled it on over her teddy bear pyjamas and scrubbed a hand through her tangled curls. She was going to kill whoever was at her door.

She threw it open, a torrent of abuse ready to tumble from her lips, and found herself staring up at the most gorgeous man on the entire planet. Deep blue eyes raked over her swiftly, and she felt her heart start pounding loudly even as she tried to slam the door shut in his face.

Jared threw a hand out and stopped the door from closing, a smile tugging at his lips at the furious glare on his woman's face. Fuck, she looked so beautiful all tousled and rumpled from sleep. Was she really wearing pyjamas with little teddy bears on them? They were the cutest things ever and made her look as sexy as hell.

"Go away, Hanlon," she growled at him, and his smile just broadened. Most definitely not a morning person, but he would teach her just how pleasurable mornings could be.

"You won't take my calls, so I've come in person, Millie." He smiled. She gasped in outrage, as he pushed his way into the apartment and let the door close behind him. His wolf was crowing gleefully, as it scented his mate. He was sending his human side mental imagines of ripping Millie's clothes off and mating roughly with her, until she screamed her pleasure.

"Get out," Millie hissed at him. "I don't want you here. If I wanted you here, I would have answered your calls. So just get out, or I'm going to call the police and have you charged with breaking and entering." She couldn't believe the arrogance of the ass. Barging into her apartment and smiling his stupid smile at her, as if he wasn't a mad stalker type person.

Her dire threat had him pausing for a moment. She was perfectly justified, his behaviour was appalling, and yet, he couldn't walk away and leave her. His wolf wouldn't let him and he knew once she stopped being so stubborn she would see they were meant to be together. She was fighting the mating pull with everything in her and she would only end up hurting not only him but herself too. "Now, you know you're not going to do that, Millie." His smile never faltered as he slowly started to stalk her.

She instinctively backed away and his wolf sat up, its attention caught. Was she going to run from him? He'd really enjoy it if she did. There was nothing quite like a good chase to get the blood pumping for what was to come when he finally caught her. His wolf would really enjoy it if she ran.

Jared stifled down a groan and had a stern word with his wolf. He was way too close to the surface and almost ready to grab control. He did not intend to let his wolf mate with Millie. Not yet. Not until she knew everything about him and exactly what it would mean to be mated to a Were. But, that wasn't going to stop his human side from taking her. He had waited far too long for her. He barely ate or slept anymore. All he could think about was his Millie, and how he longed to be with her.

Millie felt a little frisson of fear course through her, as she watched the various emotions crossing Jared's face. They ranged from almost feral to deeply tender, but the most dominant was determined. This man had come here for a reason, and he did not intend to leave until he'd fulfilled his goal. She had a good idea what that goal was. A deep stab of desire coursed through her, as she reacted to his overt sexuality, the blatant sensual expression that was now crossing his face.

"Jared," she said, shakily putting a hand out to ward him off, not believing he would pay one blind bit of notice of her. The man was an alpha to his core, which was one of the reasons she'd been ignoring him. Despite the perception she gave, her experience was pretty limited with the opposite sex. She'd always had trust issues because of her unorthodox childhood, so any dates she'd chosen had been with men who weren't a threat.

She was surprised when Jared did pay attention. He stopped moving forward and watched her intently for a moment before he pushed his hands into his tight, very sexy blue jeans. "Millie, why are you fighting this? You know you want it as much as I do. Can't you feel the sexual tension in the room?"

She shook her head at him, silky black curls tumbling around her head. "I don't even know you."

"I can quickly rectify that," he drawled wickedly, taking another step closer and causing her to back up again until she found her back pressed against the far wall. She couldn't take her eyes from his as he took another two steps until she could feel his body heat so tantalisingly close to hers. Her heart thundered in her chest and a shiver of pleasure ran down her spine as she watched his nostrils flare and saw his eyes darken.

"I can smell you, Millie," he whispered. "I can smell how much you want this." His voice was so deep and husky, so sensual that she could only stare at him in shock, as she felt the liquid heat pool between her legs. Oh God, he could smell her arousal? He was just saying that to knock her off balance. Wasn't he? He couldn't really smell her? Her face flushed scarlet, and she moaned as he leaned closer, his hot breath sliding down the side of her face and down to her neck.

"Peaches and cream," he murmured, "and that wonderful musky aroma of a woman in heat. What a heady combination." His lips whispered across her neck, and she moaned again and swayed towards him. Her movement seemed to strike something within him, because he was suddenly pressing his big powerful body against hers, and his lips were crushing hers hard as his hot tongue sought entrance into her mouth.

Fuck, she tasted so amazing, so hot and sweet and tangy. Jared ravished her mouth, as he pressed her body hard against the wall. The first taste of his mate was so heady he thought he was going to lose control. His Millie. His woman. "You are mine, Millie. You were mine from the very first second I saw you, and you always will be mine. There's no point fighting it, baby. Just surrender to the inevitable."

"No," Millie gasped, tearing her mouth from his and pushing at his hard chest. His certainty infuriated her. His blatant possessiveness made her want to deny him. She wasn't some kind of possession for him to own. This exact thing was what had sent her running from him in the first place. His lips were sucking at her neck, and she pushed against his chest again.

"Jared, stop!"

He groaned his displeasure and raised his passion-filled face to look down at her. "Why?" His voice was thick with desire. "You know you want me, Millie, and I want you too. I want you so badly I can't sleep at nights. You're all I think about."

"So I want you," she admitted, but her tone was anything but loving. It sounded as if she was angry about it. "What sane woman wouldn't want you, Jared? You're gorgeous, have a great body, and you're sexy as hell. You're also arrogant, cocky and way too sure of yourself. Just because I want you doesn't mean I'm going to act on it." She wriggled out of his arms, as he gaped open mouthed at her. She pulled her robe securely around her body and headed into the kitchen.

"Millie…" Jared sighed and ran his hands through his hair in frustration. Maybe, he was going about this in the wrong way. He watched her across the room as she calmly made herself a cup of coffee, pointedly not making him a cup. "Do you want to take it slower?" he asked, as he crossed into the kitchen area. "I was willing to take it slower, go on dates and stuff, but you wouldn't answer my calls."

"Jared, you're not getting the message," she answered with a more than a hint of irritation in her eyes. She pointed from him to her and back again. "I. Don't. Want. This. I don't know how to be any plainer with you about it. I don't care how attracted I find you. I do not want to be with you."

He folded his arms over his chest and frowned at her, his displeasure etched plainly across his face. "I'm sorry to hear that, Millie. I'm also sorry to tell you I don't give a damn about it either. You are mine, and there is nothing you can do to change it."

Millie stared at him open mouthed and contemplated throwing her mug at his head, and then decided it would be a waste of a perfectly good cup of coffee. She sipped at the bitter liquid and rolled her eyes. "Are you listening to yourself?" she finally said, her tone icy. "Does that Neanderthal type behaviour normally work for you with women? I can assure you, it is not going to work with me."

Jared grinned a very wicked grin, before he stepped closer to her. "Usually women can't wait to get into my bed," he told her with all the confidence of an Alpha male who was used to getting what he wanted. "They're usually very disappointed when I kick them out of my bed, too." She didn't like hearing that. He could see the spark of jealousy in her eyes, which she quickly tried to hide.

"You are fucking unbelievable," Millie cursed him.

He frowned. "Did you want me to lie to you?" Honesty meant everything to him but he had to consider that his mate might need something else from him. "I will, if you really want me to, but I'd much rather tell you the truth, Millie. I've had a lot of women. I have a very healthy sexual appetite, and I like to indulge it. I'm not going to apologise for my past. I've loved every moment of it, and so have my women."

Millie blinked at him in total disbelief. The arrogant ass was standing in her kitchen telling her about all the other women he'd been with? He really thought this was the right way to go about getting her into bed? Was he completely insane, or just so cocksure of himself he truly believed she was ready to be just another woman in his long line of women?

"You seriously need to work on your pickup lines, Hanlon," she laughed, harshly.

He frowned and pursed his lips, running a hand through his hair. "This isn't a pickup line, Millie; I'm just telling you how it is." Jared sighed. "How it used to be," he amended with a rueful smile. "I haven't been with another woman, since the day we met. Oh, I did try once, but the moment I closed my eyes all I could see was your beautiful face, those stunning cobalt eyes, your soft black curls tumbling around your head. You're the only one I want now."

Millie was surprised to feel a hint of satisfaction he hadn't been with anyone. She didn't know why she believed him when he said it. Yet, she did. He had told her honestly about his previous lifestyle, even though it didn't say much about his character. If he was honest about that, then he must be honest about what he'd said since then. Still, she wasn't giving in to the arrogant ass.

"I'm so sorry to hear about your impotency issues, Jared," she said with a saccharine sweet smile on her face. "You do know you can talk to your doctor about it or buy some Viagra?"

His face turned thunderous for a moment, and then he threw back his head and burst out laughing. She watched warily, as he laughed until tears rolled down his face. Laughter was not the reaction she had been expecting, and it made her feel a little uneasy.

He finally stopped laughing and wiped at his face, his deep blue eyes glinting with humour. "Or, I could just fuck you, Millie," he said, suavely, as the humour died from his expression and hot lust appeared in its place. "I'd much prefer that option."

Jared knew he was being totally outrageous with her, but he couldn't help himself. She had one hell of a mouth on her, and he was enjoying their battle of wills. He had almost let her get the upper hand there for a moment, but he'd managed to deftly turn it around on her. Her shocked expression was priceless to look at, and he prepared himself for getting slapped or something thrown at him. She looked like the type to throw things when she got pissed.

"I want you to get out of my apartment, right now," Millie hissed furiously at him. "How dare you walk in here, treat me like I'm a piece of meat, and then talk to me like that. You have no fucking respect for women at all, do you, Hanlon?" She was livid at him and close to bashing him on the head with something hard. She didn't care what it was, as long as it wiped the smug smile off his face.

"On the contrary, I have a lot of respect for women," he smiled, wickedly. "Especially, when they're lying beneath me moaning my name in ecstasy, as I ravish their beautiful bodies." He saw immediately he'd pushed her too far when her face turned red with anger, and she picked up her coffee mug and threw it at him. He ducked in time, and it hit the wall behind him and shattered.

"Get out!" she screamed at him, but he ignored her, closing the final distance between them and catching her in his embrace, as she struggled furiously against him. He pinned her against the kitchen counter and let her struggle, keeping a firm grip on her, but only just hard enough to make sure she couldn't hurt him or herself with her struggles.

"Shhhh, baby," he whispered, soothingly. "I'm sorry. I shouldn't have teased you like that. Take some deep breaths, and try to calm down. I don't want you to hurt yourself."

"Let go of me," she cried mutinously, as she felt his hardness pressing against her, and her own body starting to react to his closeness. Dear God, she seriously couldn't be finding this macho crap a turn on! "You arrogant fucking ass. Who do you think you are?"

He silenced her with a hard kiss, fisting a hand into her hair to hold her still, so he could ravish her soft lips with his. She fought against him, but he kept up the pressure on her mouth, nipping at her bottom lip, until she finally opened up to him and he could slide his tongue into her moist heat and taste her thoroughly. Her struggles started to decrease, and then, she was kissing him back with a passion that startled him at first.

Her sudden capitulation was unexpected, and he still held her tightly just in case it was a ruse, so she could knee him in the groin or something. She was a feisty one, and he wouldn't put it past her to do just that. She moaned deeply and the hot scent of her arousal assaulted his nostrils, and he knew she was lost in his kisses as much as he was, and he growled and deepened the kiss further, his tongue duelling erotically with hers.

He finally lifted his head and looked down into her passion-filled face. She took his breath away, she was so goddamned beautiful. Her cheeks were flushed with colour, and her lips were swollen and puffy. Her cobalt eyes fluttered opened, and they were dazed and so sexy looking. He smiled slowly and ran his fingers through her gorgeous curls.

"Who do I think I am?" he sighed, softly. "I'm yours, Millie, don't you know that? I'm yours, just as much as you are mine. There is no other woman for me now I've met you. You're all I think about, all I dream about. I'm yours, baby. All you have to do is let me in."

"Jared," she groaned, closing her eyes and trying to get away from the heated look in his. His body was so hard against hers, his words sounded so sincere. He scared the living daylights out of her. She just knew if she surrendered to him, her life would never be the same again.

"Millie, don't fight it," he whispered against her lips. "Don't think, baby, just feel."

His mouth slanted across hers and liquid fire shot through her veins. His tongue licked along her bottom lip and then slowly over her top lip. She was moaning into his mouth, as he teased her slowly and relentlessly. She wanted, no, she needed to feel his tongue in her mouth. Hands that had previously tried to push him away were now pulling him closer, as she stood on her tiptoes and thrust her tongue into his mouth.

He growled, and his mouth became more demanding. His tongue duelling with hers, as his hands moved beneath her pyjama top and slowly began to make their way up to her aching breasts, which were swollen and desperate for his touch. He cupped the soft orbs, almost reverently, before his thumbs rubbed over her hard nipples, and she cried out in pleasure, his mouth sucking in the sound, as she pressed against him.

It was as if she had given him the green light to continue. She had, hadn't she? He was suddenly scooping her up into his powerful arms and striding from the kitchen. She'd left her bedroom door open, and he could see the mussed up bed, so he had fair idea this were her room and not Rhianna's. He laid her on the bed and followed her down, not wanting to break the kiss to give her the opportunity to over think things.

Millie could feel her bed beneath her, feel Jared's body pressing against hers, and she knew she should stop this now, but his kisses were like a drug, sweeping her under his potent spell. She wanted this so badly. There was no point in denying it. She'd wanted Jared Hanlon the moment she'd met him, and her reaction to him had scared her witless.

It just seemed so inevitable that they would end up like this, no matter how hard she tried to avoid it. He was stripping off her pyjamas with strong, confident hands. The hands of a man who had stripped many women in his life. That thought made her feel a strong wave of jealousy and also very vulnerable at the same time, and she stilled under him.

"Millie?" he said thickly, raising his head to look into her eyes, his expression heated and yet concerned at the same time. "What's wrong, baby? If you really don't want this right now, tell me before I reach the point of no return." He would die, if she said no to him. He just knew he would. He wanted her so badly, but she had to want him back.

His expression was so genuine she knew he meant every word. Despite his caveman tactics to get into her bed, there was uncertainty in his eyes, concern for her well-being. All the overt sexuality hid something so astounding she hadn't noticed it until now because she was too busy fighting against him. There was honest need in Jared's eyes. This was more than sex for him, she could see that but her insecurity needed to hear the words.

"Did you mean what you said, Jared?" she asked, shakily. "If we do this, there will be no other women? I can't be just another notch on your bedpost. I'm not that kind of woman." He had no idea just how much she wasn't that kind of woman, and she felt a wave of embarrassment surge through her and fought the urge to close her eyes. She wanted to see his expression, so she could see if he was telling her the truth.

"Baby, there's no one but you now," he sighed, leaning his forehead against hers for a moment and then raising his head again. "I meant what I said. You are mine, Millie, but I am also yours. There will never be another woman for me ever."

She bit her bottom lip nervously, as she searched his gorgeous face intently for what she was looking for and found it. She took a deep breath and felt her cheeks warm as she met his gaze. "I've never done this before, Jared," she said, softly.

She watched confusion cross his face for a moment, and then, he stared at her in shock. "You've never been with a man?" he asked slowly, and watched her face flush red again, as she bit her lip and shook her head. He felt the most amazing rush of love for her and intense male satisfaction of knowing no other man had touched his mate and never would.

He brushed her lips with a thumb, tracing the soft flesh reverently. "You don't know what it does to me to know I'll be your first and only lover, my Millie. I feel like the luckiest man in the world that you are granting me this honour."

She relaxed in his embrace and pressed her lips against his. One minute he was an arrogant ass and the next he was all humble and saying just the right thing. The man was a total enigma, and yet, she was willing to lie here with him, willing to give him her body.

He deepened the kiss and tasted her leisurely, as he finished peeling her pyjamas from her body. He wanted to look at her, his mate, his Millie. He rose up onto his knees and stared down at her beautiful body. She was so perfect in every way. Her breasts were full, her stomach flat and taut. Her scent of arousal was thick in the air, and he could see the first hints of her arousal painting her body in delicious colour.

Millie felt a flush of embarrassment as Jared just sat there staring at her body without saying anything. Was there something wrong with her? Maybe he didn't like her? Should she ask him? She didn't know what to do in this kind of situation. She squirmed in embarrassment, and as his eyes met hers, she sucked in a deep breath at the look of total adoration and lust on his face.

"You're perfect, Millie," he whispered, softly. "Every single inch of you is just total perfection."

She smiled shyly, pleased she met his expectations. How had he managed to get under her guard despite all her attempts to keep him at arm's length? She should still be fighting him and yet she ached to be with him. "You have me at a disadvantage."

Sitting up, Millie placed her hands on his chest feeling the muscles underneath tense and contract. She started fumbling for his buttons and his hands came up and stilled hers, raising them to his lips so he could kiss them and give her a reassuring smile. He could see how nervous she was and wanted to show her how beautiful and natural it was to be with the one person created in the world just for her.

Jared leaned over, gently pressing Millie back down onto the bed so he could give her a long drugging kiss before he sat back up and slowly started to take off his shirt. His wolf was howling his glee, and he needed to get it under control before they went any further. He took his time undressing, as he worked to convince his wolf that now was not the time to mate with her. His wolf wasn't happy about it, and he was almost completely naked before he'd managed to convince him that this first time had to be just his human half and their mate. It was only when he explained to his wolf that he would unintentionally hurt her, did the wolf finally back down and permit Jared to mate with her first.

Millie watched Jared take his clothes off, and her greedy gaze roamed over every single inch of naked skin revealed. She wasn't a small woman, like Rhianna, but she felt small compared to Jared. His chest was so wide and well-muscled, his arms so thick and powerful. He could surely crush her easily, if he wanted to. He stood to take off his jeans, and she had to swallow a gasp. He looked quite big and though she lacked experience with men, she was fairly certain he was impressive by most men's standards. She was just at the point of telling him she'd changed her mind, when he was sliding back onto the bed beside her and gathering her into his arms.

Jared hadn't been unaware of her shock at his size, and he pressed her against him savouring the feel of their naked bodies touching for the first time, as he ran a soothing hand down her back. "Don't be nervous, baby," he whispered against her neck. "We'll take things slowly and if you feel you don't want to do anything, tell me and we'll stop."

His words calmed her, and she let out a long shaky breath, as he trailed little kisses of fire along her collarbone, as he continued to calm her nerves. He moved his mouth back up to hers and parted her lips, so he could explore her mouth again with his tongue. He loved kissing her. She had such a wonderful mouth, so hot and wet and sweet tasting. He could kiss her all night she tasted so damned good, and she didn't seem to be complaining. Her tongue was boldly licking against his, following him back into his mouth, so she could explore as he was doing. His body twitched in appreciation, and he groaned deeply, rubbing against her.

She was so hot, so beautiful, so perfect. She was his, and he was going to make her his forever. He loomed over her, pressing her onto her back so his mouth could start its exploration of her satiny soft skin. Peaches and cream, the headiest flavours in his world. Jared lowered his mouth to her breast and greedily sucked in the taut peak, rasping his tongue roughly over the tight bud and causing her to cry out and arch her back. He did it again and then again, groaning as she moved beneath him, signalling her pleasure at his touch.

He caught the nipple between his teeth and nipped hard and then laved it gently with his tongue, as she cried out loudly. Her response was intoxicating, and he could scent just how aroused she was becoming. He moved to her other breast and tortured it as sweetly as he had the first. Her response was the same, and he smiled a smile of deep male satisfaction that he was pleasuring his woman so completely.

Her scent was calling him, and he soon abandoned her breasts to lick down her flat stomach. His hands stroked against her gently rounded hips, and he detoured to nip gently at both hips. They were round and strong. Beautiful child bearing hips. She would give him many strong pups, and he was overcome with the need to impregnate her, as soon as possible. He wanted to see her stomach swell with his seed. He wanted to be at her side, as she pushed their pups out into the world and completed their family.

He barked sharply at his wolf, forcing him back down. No pups, not yet. It would be a while before they were at that stage. He had so much to tell her, so much she needed to come to terms with before they got to producing young.

He continued on his journey, pressing her legs apart, so he could carry on tasting all the sweetness she had to offer him. She was almost ready for him. She only needed a little more loving to be ready enough to accept him into her body. He groaned and his tongue snaked out to rasp boldly against her sex.

Millie screamed and arched up from the bed. It was the most intimate of kisses and his tongue was so hot and wet lapping against her body. The pleasure that exploded through her caught her off guard, and she trembled from the sheer intensity of it. He licked her again, and she tried to strangle down the next scream, but couldn't quite manage it.

Jared's hands slipped beneath her body, gripping her bottom to raise her up to his questing mouth. He was addicted to her taste and couldn't get enough, her cries of pleasure egging him on. He wanted to feel her shatter in his mouth. He needed to pleasure her until she came apart in his arms and gifted him the sweet nectar of her physical release.

He continued his wicked torture until she was moaning and writhing on the bed, her total abandonment exciting him beyond measure. It was good she was so lusty. Pack life was less inhibited about sex than normal human relationships. Her lustiness would be needed to adapt to their life together in the pack.

His cock was aching painfully to be inside her beautiful body, but he wanted her pleasure first before he took his. Jared luxuriated in Millie's taste until her back arched and she surrendered to the bliss infusing her. As she climaxed, he moved over her body, pressing inside with one quick thrust.

Millie was floating on a wave of pure, unadulterated pleasure, as she felt something hard pressing at her opening. She instinctively thrust upwards wanting it inside, needing it inside her, as another wave of pleasure rocked through her body. She felt herself stretching uncomfortably, felt a sharp sting of pain, which was quickly drowned out by the pleasure. Then she was assailed by a sense of completion, and she felt Jared's lips on hers as he caught her moan of pleasure pain.

Jared held himself completely still, his breath rushing out harshly, as her wonderfully tight body sheathed him, as if it were made for him, and he felt the most intense pleasure he'd ever experienced before. He had to fight hard not to embarrass himself like some untried youth. Millie moaned into his mouth and pressed upwards, and he had to grip her hips tightly and hold her still.

"Don't move," he groaned. "Please don't move, baby. If you move right now, I'm going to lose it, and this will be over with before it's even begun." His voice was thick and uneven, his breathing harsh and ragged as he fought for control.

Millie stilled beneath him and opened her eyes, stunned at his strained expression. She wanted to move so badly, the urge instinctive. Did Jared truly want her that badly he was struggling for control? She found it hard to believe she could affect him this way but it was a heady thought, too. She raised her hands and stroked his long hair back, so she could watch every expression crossing his face. His deep blue eyes opened, and he looked down at her. The smile he gave her took her breath away and sent a bolt of pure pleasure surging through her.

"Yes, you affect me that badly, Millie," he said thickly, as if answering her thoughts. "You are so beautiful, so perfect. I'm trying hard not to lose my head completely here." He took a few deep breaths and closed his eyes, then he moved within her, and she gasped as a thousand tiny jolts of electricity flowed through her body, as he withdrew slowly and pushed back inside.

"Jared," she gasped and arched up to meet him, her legs wrapping around his to pull him back to her. "Oh God, that feels so good."

More in control of himself, Jared chuckled and rubbed his mouth against hers. "It feels better than good, baby. It feels amazing." He groaned, his heart racing so hard he thought it would burst out of his chest. "You're amazing, Millie." His hands moved to cup her breasts, and he suckled on one taut peak, as he slid from her body and thrust back in. Her scalding heat enveloped him, and he growled against her nipple and nipped lightly at it.

Her response inflamed him, as her hands fisted into his hair to keep him at her breast. She thrust upward to meet each of his downward movements. She seemed to know what to do and moved in rhythm with him, no evidence of her inexperience in view. That was how it was between mates, how it would always be. Jared let out another groan and stroked into her body with a long, hard thrust. Her tightness massaged his aching cock, and his next thrust was a bit faster, a little harder, as he tried to climb inside her.

She was heat, fire and passion, and she was his. He staked his claim with hard, deliberate strokes, the word *'mine'* echoing in his mind with every thrust. No one would ever take her from him. He would kill anyone who tried.

Millie thrust against Jared's body, a kaleidoscope of emotions and sensations rippling through her, as he staked his claim. How could anything feel so magical, so right? She cried out, when he thrust harder into her, her breath coming out in little pants, as she strove to meet him halfway. His mouth was on hers, hot and demanding, his tongue thrusting into her mouth in time with his body. It was sinful and wicked and such a turn on. She moaned loudly and pressed harder against him.

She almost wept with disappointment when his body left hers. She tried to make him come back to her, but he laughed huskily and flipped her over onto her stomach, pulling her up onto her hands and knees, as he positioned himself back between her legs. He thrust forward hard, joining them once more. Millie cried out her pleasure, the new position allowing him fuller entry.

Jared appeared to be done with soft and gentle and moved onto hot, sweaty, and sinfully lustful. He gripped her hips hard and began to rock into her hard, pulling her back against him as he thrust into her. She screamed her pleasure again and began to rock backwards, feeling a hot tightening in her stomach, a deep intense need for him to quench the fire burning through her veins.

"Jared," she groaned harshly. "I need..." She didn't know what she needed, but he appeared to know. He wrapped his body around hers, one hand still on her hip, the other supporting his weight on the bed. His teeth nipped at her shoulder, as he increased his thrusts, giving her little time to think or breathe. She was just one mass of sensations, as he took her hard and fast.

The sensations inside her body were spiralling out of control. She was tensing, as she felt her orgasm approach. Her cries loud and lusty, as Jared moved yet again, sitting back on his heels, pulling her back up against his chest, as he held her tightly with one arm around her breasts, the other hand snaked in between her legs to tease her mercilessly.

"Fly for me, Millie. Take your pleasure." His voice was a rasping sound, the timbre adding to and sending her over the edge to her release. Pleasure rolled over her in a hot tidal wave and she cried out, shuddering in his arms.

Millie's climax pushed Jared over the edge and he roared his release, throwing his head back as he danced the ancient dance of love with his woman. Sex had always been a pleasurable activity but this was more than sex. He was joined with his mate, and that connection transcended anything he had ever experienced before. When they truly mated...nothing would be able to surpass the heights they would reach once Millie was finally his in every way possible.

It was hard to control his wolf who was urging him to bite her and claim her for them. His body wanted to react naturally, for his knot to form at the base of his cock to secure him to his mate and let his seed impregnate her. He fought both urges though, knowing Millie needed to know the truth and have time to come to terms with it before he could mark her as his and begin her transformation to becoming a Were.

Jared wrapped both arms around Millie and held her as tiny aftershocks of pure bliss streamed through them. He didn't want to leave her warm body. He knew he had to, that she would be tender with it being her first time, but he wanted a few extra moments inside her before he had to move.

His mouth trailed over her collarbone, up her neck and along her jaw line, as she panted against him. Her glorious body, covered in a thin sheen of dampness, felt so soft and slick against him. He stroked her breast feeling her heart hammering underneath his hand. Jared turned her head, so he could kiss her slowly, and he ran his hands soothingly across her stomach, coaxing her down from her high. Reluctantly, he ended the kiss and gripped her hips, raising her slightly, so his softening cock could slip free.

Millie moaned when he left her. It felt slightly uncomfortable, but she was still sorry to feel him leave her. Being with Jared like this was the most amazing feeling ever, and she didn't want it to end so soon. She felt him turn her body, until she was facing him, her legs on either side of his lap.

"Are you okay, baby?" Jared asked, his voice tender as his lips whispered over hers.

She slowly opened her eyes to see him watching her face intently and smiled. She didn't trust her voice at the moment, and waited for her heart to start slowing back to a normal pace. He kissed her, a long slow, gentle kiss full of love and tenderness, and she sighed softly into his mouth, her arms wrapping around his neck.

"Mine," he whispered, roughly. "You will always be mine, Millie."

She closed her eyes, so he couldn't see her roll them at his possessive statement. He really was an arrogant ass, but he was her arrogant ass. He had said he was hers just as much as she was his. She didn't know exactly what that meant, but she knew it was important somehow.

Jared settled them into her bed and pulled the covers around them. He had so much to tell her, so much to confess. He knew he had to do it, but he was afraid to. What if she couldn't accept him? What if she was angry about Rafe, and his role in the big man's *death*? What if she wasn't prepared to give up her life here in the human world? He knew it wasn't going to be easy telling her the truth. He was certain his mate would have plenty to say on the various issues, and if she reacted as angrily as she had just getting her into bed, then life was about to become exceedingly interesting.

CHAPTER FIFTEEN

"Millie, for the love of God, will you please calm down?!" Jared yelled, as he ducked another flying saucepan and tried to work out the best way to get to his irate mate without allowing her to do him any bodily harm. He was dressed in just his jeans, the only thing he'd taken time to pull on as he chased her out of the bedroom.

He was mentally kicking himself. Maybe, he should have waited to tell her he was a wolf. Coming so soon after their first time together, it was probably too much for her to take in. He tried moving around to her right side, but she tracked him swiftly and another saucepan barely missed his head.

He couldn't stop the wide grin that crossed his face. His woman was an excellent aim. She'd managed to get him with most of her throws. It was only the last two he'd been able to avoid and barely at that. She was glorious, and he felt his wolf try to surface at her aggressiveness. It would be easy to let him out again. He'd tackle her, bring her down and force her to submit.

"You're an animal!" Millie shrieked at him. "You took me to bed, and you're a freaking animal!"

Jared stifled down a deep sigh. "Baby, come on, it's not that bad," he pleaded. "I know it was a bit of a shock me changing like that, but you wouldn't believe me when I just told you. I had to get you to see I was telling you the truth. Didn't you like my wolf? He certainly likes you, Millie. In fact, he adores you, as much as I do." Her final saucepan caught him square on the chest, and he muttered an oath, as he felt his anger starting to rise. This was getting beyond a joke now. The bloody pans hurt!

"You should have told me BEFORE you had sex with me!" Millie screamed. "I deserved the right to make a choice whether or not I slept with an animal!" Frustrated at having no more saucepans to throw, she looked around for something else and came up with the knives in the butcher's block.

Jared cursed when her hand wrapped around the handle of a particularly large carving knife. That was really going to hurt if she stuck it in him. It probably wouldn't kill him, but it would put him out of action for a few days. "Baby, you're not seriously going to throw that knife at me, are you?" He allowed more of his wolf to come to the fore to give him a faster reaction time if she did throw it.

"You just get your things and get out of my apartment," Millie ground out, trying to stop her hand from shaking as she brandished the knife at him. She had exhausted the burst of adrenaline that had overwhelmed her after Jared changed from a man into an enormous black wolf, scaring the complete shit out of her. She knew it was him inside the wolf, could see Jared's eyes staring back at her from the huge beast, but she had still screamed in terror and launched herself from the bed, grabbing her robe and slamming the door shut.

He had followed her of course, but in his man form not as the wolf. She supposed she should have been thankful for that. If he'd bounded out of the bedroom on all fours, she would have quite literally succumbed to her terror and passed out. God knows what he would have done then.

"You know I can't do that, Millie." Jared kept his tone patient, holding his hands up and keeping his distance. "Just put the knife down, and let's talk about this. You know you don't really want to hurt me, and you're really starting to scare me now. You could accidentally hurt yourself with the knife. Please. Put it down."

Millie could feel hysterical laughter starting to bubble up inside her. He really thought he was going to talk her down? The stupid ass really thought she was going to put the knife down and fall into his stupidly sexy arms and tell him she was just fine with having a relationship with a bloody wolf? She was just about to tell him that when she noticed the fear on his face and paused. Jared was afraid? He seriously thought she was going to stab him? She looked closer again and realised, with some surprise, that he wasn't afraid she was going to hurt him. He was more afraid she was going to hurt herself.

It suddenly occurred to her just how insane she must look standing there brandishing a knife like a mad woman, and she slowly put it down on the kitchen counter, as Jared let out a long breath and relaxed slightly, his deep blue eyes full of worry.

He watched her intently for a moment and then took a tentative step towards her. When she didn't react, he moved closer until he was standing right beside her. "I'm sorry, Millie," he said roughly, reaching out a hand to touch her shoulder lightly. "I know I should have told you before we made love; but you kept avoiding me, and I needed you so badly I couldn't stop myself. I had every intention of telling you before we got to this stage, but things just didn't work out that way."

She raised her head and looked at him. He was a wolf, but he was still Jared. He was still the man who had just worshipped her body and taken her to heaven and back again. He was still the man who arrogantly declared she was his even as he happily admitted that he was hers. She really did need to find out what that meant. It probably had something to do with him being a wolf.

"This being a wolf complicates things, doesn't it?" She saw the truth in his eyes, even as his lips tightened slightly, and he nodded his head. She sighed, and he pulled her into his arms pressing her head against his chest. Millie let him hold her. Hell, she needed him to hold her. She leaned against him for a long moment and wallowed in his strength, as she tried to find some inner balance, then she took a deep breath and stepped back.

"I'm going to have a shower and get dressed. When I'm done, you are going to tell me absolutely everything, and you'd better not leave a single thing out, Jared. I need to know just what I've gotten myself into here."

"I promise I'll tell you everything." Jared brushed her lips with his, fighting down a sigh of relief when she not only let him but also returned his light caress. Maybe it was going to be okay, now she was starting to get over the shock of it. He watched her head into her bedroom and set about gathering up the scattered saucepans. He smiled slowly, as he put them away. Lord, his woman was magnificent. A bit scary with the knife thing, but magnificent even still.

Rhianna finished off her well-done breakfast, taking a moment to enjoy the peace and solitude at the dining table. Caleb was off somewhere with Rafe, so she had some time to herself. She had been amazed to see the two men being practically friendly towards each other when she finally let Caleb pull her out of bed. Something must have happened between them while she slept. Rafe had seemed so much better this morning. She felt a little bubble of hope well up inside her. Maybe, he wasn't as lost as he thought he was. Maybe, he just needed to see her to help balance him.

She washed up the dishes that Caleb had left in the sink. He seemed to enjoy cooking as his new hobby, but he didn't have the first concept of cleaning up afterwards. She wondered who cleaned the house, because it was immaculate, and she couldn't see Caleb getting his hands dirty doing it.

There was a loud knock on the front door, and then, it swung open to admit Demetri. The dark-haired vampire looked as gorgeous as ever and smiled when he saw Rhianna walking out of the kitchen. His green eyes twinkled with humour, as he took in her body swallowed up in one of Caleb's silk shirts.

"Now, why am I not surprised to see you here?" he laughed softly, as his gaze ran over her, admiring the view. She really was stunning, and he almost did wish he'd had her first, but the thought only lasted for a second. Then he remembered his friend's manic mood swings and his moping over the little redhead. He could well do without all of that nonsense.

"Good morning, Demetri," Rhianna replied politely. She wasn't quite sure whether she liked him or not. He was everything Caleb wasn't, and yet, he was exactly who Caleb had once been. One minute he was being nasty to her, and the next he was being friendly. She just didn't know how to take him. Today, he seemed friendly enough; if a little out of order eyeing her up as if she were a piece of meat.

"If you're looking for Caleb, I'm not sure where he is right now. He went off somewhere with Rafe. I think they're working on how to help Rafe deal with his wolf or something. Caleb doesn't want me involved in it, so they've probably gone somewhere off the property."

Demetri raised an eyebrow and pursed his lips. Things seemed to have moved on since Caleb's little temper tantrum with the Weres. "I assume we're not going to war with the dogs, then?"

She bristled, and her eyes flashed, before she turned and walked back into the kitchen. "No, you are not going to war with the wolves," she answered tartly, not liking his derogatory tone. She could really do with another coffee and wished she knew how to use Caleb's complicated coffee machine.

Demetri followed the redhead into the kitchen and decided he'd try to be on his best behaviour. She was important to Caleb, so he would try to get to know her better. He saw her staring wistfully at the coffee machine and smiled. "Mind if I make myself a coffee, Red?" Her lavender eyes light up, even as she frowned at his nickname for her.

"You can work this thing?" There was more than a hint of hopefulness in her tone. "I'd kill for a mocha, but Caleb hasn't shown me how to use it yet."

Demetri smiled. This should endear her to him. "Grab the milk out the refrigerator, I'll show you how to use it." He spent the next ten minutes explaining the finer details of how to work the machine and was surprised to find he actually enjoyed seeing the pleasure crossing her face, as she made her very first mocha and sipped at it experimentally.

She really was a rather enchanting little thing. He found himself smiling back at her warmly, feeling oddly pleased that she was smiling because of him, and he blinked slowly fighting down a deep scowl. His eyes narrowed, as he looked at her covertly. Was she some kind of witch in disguise? He didn't like the warm feelings he'd just been experiencing. It was unnatural. Women were only good for two things, their luscious bodies and the hot, sweet life's blood that flowed through their veins.

Rhianna noticed the abrupt change in the vampire and stifled down a sigh. He had been doing so well up until now. He had almost been human when he was showing her how to make the coffee. Now he was back to being suspicious and detached. "You don't like me much, do you, Demetri?" She asked the question even though she knew the answer. He visibly stiffened beside her.

"I don't think much of you one way or the other, Red," he answered tersely, moving away and leaning against the kitchen counter, his glacial green eyes remote as he looked at her. "Caleb seems to like you, so that means you'll be around until he gets tired of you. I can tolerate you until then." He knew his words were blunt and a little cruel, but that was his nature, and if she was going to be around for a while, then she would just need to get used to it.

He saw a flash of uncertainty cross her face, and he actually felt a twinge of remorse but he dampened it down irritably. He was only speaking the truth. Why he should feel bad for doing so was beyond him. His lips tightened, and his eyes narrowed. "What's with the look, Red? You and Caleb haven't discussed the future? That's so unlike Caleb. Usually, he's upfront about most things, except where you're concerned. He's far too busy worrying about your feelings than he should be. You make him weak. You make him vulnerable."

"You think he's weak, because he cares about me?" Rhianna stared at him with an incredulous expression. "You think his life is somehow ruined, since I came into it? What's he missing out on that was so much better? The same life you're living? Tell me, Demetri, when you lie with a woman, do you really know why she's with you? Is it because she's drunk, or she's heard you're the biggest man-whore at the club so she wants to see if it's true? Or maybe she knows you own the club and are rich? Maybe she just wants as many drinks as she can get out of you? Maybe she's hoping you'll spend some of that money on her, and she can get herself a nice expensive gift from you?"

She watched his expression tighten but couldn't stop herself, even though he looked dangerous. "The truth is you will never really know why a woman wants to be with you, Demetri, and that's the saddest thing ever. At least Caleb knows why I'm with him, and that doesn't make him weak and vulnerable, that brings him joy and happiness."

Demetri's eyes darkened furiously, and he pushed off the kitchen counter and took a step towards her before he managed to reign it in. "You've been around less than two months, and you think you know what's best for him?" he sneered. "Well, I've been around for two millennia, Red, and I'll be around to pick up the pieces after you're dead and gone. And just to set the record straight, I don't give a fuck why a woman's with me, as long as I get what I need from her."

Demetri's words struck a chord inside Rhianna, and she tried not to let him see how much his comment had upset her. It brought up the unasked question which had been hovering in her mind since she'd found out what Caleb was. What did their future hold? Right now Caleb said he loved her, and she believed him, but he was ageless and she wasn't. He would stay forever young, and she would slowly grow old. What would happen when she was no longer young and beautiful? Would Caleb still want her? How could he want to be with an old, wrinkled woman when there would be countless beauties out there just dying to be in his arms and in his bed.

Her coffee was suddenly making her feel nauseous, and she put it down, avoiding the dark-haired vampire's all-knowing eyes. "I'm going to get dressed. I'm assuming you're perfectly able to entertain yourself until Caleb comes back?" She didn't wait for his answer. She turned and fled from the kitchen, leaving Demetri frowning as he watched her leave.

He had caught a suspicious glint of moisture in her eyes, as she tried to keep her gaze averted from his. Had he upset her enough to make her cry? Fuck it, he was only stating the obvious! Surely she didn't think her *relationship* with Caleb could last forever? She was human, and he was a vampire. She would age and die, while Caleb would live for eternity, unless someone killed him, which was highly doubtful.

So, why did he suddenly feel like a complete bastard? He felt uncomfortable and furiously angry at the little redhead. Who the hell was she to make him start second guessing himself, to start questioning himself? He straightened his tall frame and strode out of the kitchen. He'd catch up with Caleb later. He had only wanted to find out what was happening with the wolves. The dogs! Fuck! He was even amending how he referred to the Weres because of her. He let himself out of the house just as quickly as he'd let himself in.

Demetri was gone when Rhianna came back downstairs, showered and changed. She was glad. The vampire was obviously bipolar or had some other serious personality disorder. He swung from hot to cold at a flip of a switch. Come to think of it, all the men in her life were like that now. She needed to get away for a bit. Have some time to think and properly digest everything that had happened over the weekend.

Her boyfriend was a vampire, her brother a werewolf. From what Rafe had told her last night, it would appear her best friend was about to be spirited off by Jared Hanlon and turned into a werewolf, too. She was the only *normal* person left in her immediate circle of friends and family, and that meant she was the only one who was going to age and die. The rest of them would live on long after she was dead and buried. It was a sobering thought, and hard to digest.

She considered calling Caleb, and then, opted to leave him a note instead. If she called him, he might be able to tell something was wrong and come back early from whatever it was he was doing with her brother. Rafe needed this time with Caleb more than she did. She found a pen and paper in one of the kitchen drawers and hastily wrote a note before she grabbed her packed overnight bag and headed out.

~~~~

Millie was staring at Jared intently, as he came to the end of his very long story. The one thing that was forefront in her mind was the fact Rafe was alive. It seemed almost impossible to believe, and yet, she had seen Jared change into a wolf. It would appear her adopted brother was now a wolf too and struggling with that fact. "I can't believe Rafe is alive." Her eyes were moist with unshed tears, "and Annie knows? She's with Rafe now?"

Jared nodded, relieved to see she was taking it all quite calmly. His wolf was a bit pissed at her obvious affection for Rafe, but that was only because they hadn't mated yet. Once they did, he would calm down and easily accept the role of brother the large man had in her life.

She looked down at the table and nervously twisted her fingers together. It sounded so easy to turn a human into a Were. Granted Rafe's turning sounded horrific, but Jared said that was only because it was forced. A normal turning, when mating, appeared to be effortless, because the person being turned wanted it to happen. She knew without even asking him that he wanted to do that to her, and she couldn't help feeling a bit afraid. She raised her eyes, looked deep into his and saw his lips tightened at whatever he read on her face.

"Millie, I would never turn you without your full consent," Jared's large hand captured hers and squeezed gently. "I've just explained how unsuccessful forced turnings are. I would never do anything to hurt you. I can't. You're my mate, the woman I love more than my own life. If you decided you never wanted to join with me completely, I would still love you and still be with you." True, he would never father any young, if she didn't truly mate with him, and the Hanlon pack would one day have a non Hanlon Alpha because of it, but he would do anything to keep her in his life, sacrifice just about anything.

He sounded so sincere, his expression earnest as he spoke that she found herself relaxing and even managed to give him a tentative smile. "It's such a lot to take in, Jared. It's a huge decision to make. The pack laws you've just described, they sound so....outdated."

He blinked in surprise. "Define outdated?"

He seemed genuinely interested in hearing her views, so she decided to speak her mind. "You trusted Annie to keep your secret to help Rafe, and yet you don't trust your own pack to. Doesn't that seem a bit odd, Jared? Your pack law states that once a human joins you, they give up their human lives and lose their family and friends, their jobs, everything that defines who they are as a person. Why? To protect the pack? Maybe that kind of restriction was necessary a few hundred years ago, but surely it isn't needed now?"

Jared's automatic reaction was to think of the pack. They had to be protected at all costs, and yet, Millie's simple questions had a certain kind of naïve logic to them. He couldn't argue with the fact they had let Annie know about them and trusted her to keep their secret, because she not only cared about Rafe, but also cared about Caleb, too. He knew each and every member of his pack would sacrifice their own lives to maintain their secret. It wasn't that he didn't trust the pack, it was just they had always done things this way.

Only he and his betas walked within the normal human world. They had various businesses, which they tended to supply the funding for the pack's compound in the forest. It was necessary to take care of so many people. Only his most trusted lieutenants were allowed to mix with humans, but that was only because it was how it had been done by his father and his father before him. Generations of Hanlon Alphas had protected the pack for centuries, and he didn't know if he could do it any differently. It was deeply ingrained within.

"Interesting points," he finally answered, though his tone was doubtful. "I suppose I can understand why you question the pack laws, but it's the way it has to be, Millie. It's the only guaranteed way to keep my people safe."

She worried her lip with her teeth for a moment, and then she sighed deeply and tried again. She could see he was trying to be receptive to her comments, but she could also see his denial, too. "How many of your pack find their mates within the pack?" she asked, watching surprise cross his face.

change of subject surprised him and made him frown. The little he knew of his mate was enough to let him know she was up to something. "Not many. Probably about a quarter."

"So, what happens to the rest of them?" she pressed. "Do they just go through life unmated?"

Jared's frown deepened, and he shifted uncomfortably in his seat. "Unless they're betas. The alpha and his betas can seek their mates within the human community."

Millie stifled down a touch of anger. It seemed so unfair that only a select few could seek out mates when the rest of the pack went without. From what Jared had explained about mating, almost three quarters of his people never got the chance to meet their one special person, the one they could mate with and produce young.

"So, the pack doesn't grow. It stagnates because only a quarter get the opportunity to mate and have children. That just seems so wrong, Jared. Why do you prevent your people from having what you're asking of me?"

Jared stood up abruptly and paced into the sitting room, his wolf howling mournfully at her words. He felt a rush of anger, of denial, and he struggled to dampen it down. Did she really think he was deliberately torturing his people? Did she really think so little of him? His eyes darkened as he struggled with him temper.

He wasn't used to being questioned like this. He was the fucking Alpha for crying out loud. His pack submitted to him. His mate submitted to him. He turned around intent on making her submit and stopped when he saw the tears in her eyes and on her cheeks. She was crying, and she wasn't crying for herself; she was crying for his pack. He knew it without being told. She felt pain on behalf of his people.

His angry words died on his lips as he looked at her, his beautiful Millie, and he felt the weight of her words crushing him. "It wasn't intentional." His voice was hoarse as he jammed his hands into his jeans and looked down at the floor. "You have to understand the overriding need to protect the pack, Millie. It's everything to the Alpha. It's the one law I can't make arbitrary decisions about."

She scrubbed at her cheeks and ran a hand through her unruly curls. "Then, ask the pack. I know things are different in Rafe's circumstances, because he's officially dead, but the rest of the pack needn't give up their human lives, if they don't want to. It's the one major obstacle I have about even considering joining with you, Jared. I like my job. I like my human life. I don't want to give it up to go live in a wooden house in the forest cut off from everything." Her cobalt eyes pleaded with him to understand where she was coming from.

He raised his head and looked at her, his expression guarded. He seemed less like the Jared she knew and more like the Alpha wolf he really was. She wondered what was going through his head. Was he thinking she was rejecting him, because she really wasn't. Was she? He had said he would still love her and be with her even if she decided to remain human. Had he been just saying that in the hopes she would let him turn her anyway? Had he lied when he said that?

Jared's thoughts were in utter turmoil, and he automatically retreated into himself, as he tried to work out what to do. Millie didn't want to leave her human life, and he couldn't not be with her. She was as necessary to him as his need to breathe air. She was bright and beautiful and so very intelligent and sharp. She had cut straight to the very heart of what was a major problem within the pack. A problem he had so clearly overlooked, and for that, he didn't deserve to be the Alpha of the pack. In protecting themselves, they had quite literally stunted their evolution.

The pack would be split by Millie's controversial suggestion. The older wolves would want to stick to tradition, the younger wolves would most likely jump at the chance of being able to walk among humans and seek out their mates. It would be utter chaos and give him the worst headache imaginable. Even worse than dealing with Rafe, which had been his toughest challenge to date as Alpha. Still, the pack had supported him when he asked for their approval to help save Rafe. Maybe, they wouldn't be so resistant to changing pack laws as he thought they would be.

The only thing Jared knew for sure at that moment was that he needed Millie badly, and his pack needed her too. Her keen way of looking at things and reaching conclusions of such staggering importance was direly needed. She was his equal in every way. She was his mate, and therefore, she had a say in how the pack was run, even if he hadn't officially mated with her, and maybe never would, if he couldn't convince the pack to change.

His long silence worried Millie, as did his carefully neutral expression. She had no idea what he was thinking and the longer the silence stretched, the more her anxiety increased. Finally, she couldn't take it any longer and she let out a little sigh, "Jared?"

Her hesitant tone, her worried expression, wrenched at his heart and he smothered down a groan and crossed the room to pull her up from her chair and into his arms. He buried his head in the side of her neck and inhaled her sweet scent deeply, as his lips whispered over her satiny skin. "I'm going to need your help, baby. It's not going to be easy to convince the pack. We're all so set in our ways. Not everyone will understand the need to make changes."

She melted into his embrace and wrapped her arms tightly around his waist. He seemed so unsure of himself, so unlike the arrogant ass he could be, but the vulnerable side to him called at something deep inside her, and she found she couldn't resist it. "I'll be with you every step of the way, Jared. I don't seem to have any choice in the matter. I love you too much to walk away."

He smiled against her neck, as his woman told him she loved him for the first time. He knew she did even though she hadn't said the words before, but hearing them made his heart soar, and he suddenly felt able to take on the whole world if he needed to. He was capable of achieving anything with Millie at his side. They would convince the pack if they stood together. He just knew they would.

CHAPTER SIXTEEN

Caleb sat high in the tree, his sharp gaze watching Rafe in his wolf form as he stalked the wild boar slowly. He was keeping his scent away from the boar to allow *Wolfie* to explore his animal nature without any hindrance. Rafe really was an impressive wolf. He moved with such grace as he came at the boar from downwind.

He used an economy of movements and was on the squealing animal in the blink of an eye. His normal gentle nature reared up, and he silenced the boar with a quick kill. The animal's throat was gone in an instant, and its life extinct a fraction after that. A quick, merciful kill. Other Weres may have relished the excitement of sparring with the boar before they ended its life. Caleb doubted Rafe would ever be like that. He leapt nimbly down the branches, landing lightly on his feet, and headed towards the wolf. Now, the next part of Rafe's lesson.

Wolfie sensed the vampire close and raised his head, a feral growl rumbling from his throat as he rose quickly to stand over his kill. If the intruder thought to take his food from him, he would tear him limb from limb. The red mist of rage clouded his mind, and he roared at the advancing vampire.

Caleb kept on walking towards Rafe. He could see he was completely wrapped up in his feral side. There was no trace of the gentle man in the fierce brown eyes regarding him with rage. Caleb's stride appeared nonchalant, but he was alert and ready to move if the wolf attacked. The whole point of the lesson was to ensure that Rafe didn't attack.

If he could control his feral nature in the face of Caleb's challenge, then the vampire was certain Rhianna would never be in any danger from her brother. It was imperative to Caleb that his Annie was safe at all costs. The wolf growled, a savage rumble emanating from his throat once more and Caleb tensed further sensing an impending attack

If the vampire came one step closer to his kill, Wolfie was going to rip his throat out. He relished the sheer joy he'd experience as his teeth sank into the disgusting smelling creature's neck. He would rip hard and fast and feel the hot blood flowing into his mouth, just as it had with the wild boar. He tensed, his powerful body coiling ready to spring agilely into the air. The approaching man paused a millisecond before he sprang, flying through the air, a snarling blur of dark brown fur.

Caleb was Ancient and able to spot the slight tension in the wolf before it exploded into action. He sidestepped to the left, his vampiric speed taking him out of the animal's way and foiling its attempt to rip out his throat. This clearly enraged the wolf as it took the vampire closer to its kill. Not wanting to infuriate Rafe any further, Caleb took off running before the wolf could halt its forward progression and turn for a second strike. He leapt into the air, catching a tree branch and swinging himself gracefully into the thick canopy of leaves.

Golden brown eyes tracked the prowling wolf as it launched itself against the tree, scrabbling to find purchase to get to the vampire out of its reach. Loud snarls filled the forest as the animal hurled itself repeatedly against the tree, claws raking away the bark on the trunk. Finally, the wolf paced away, growling as it headed back to its kill.

Caleb watched Rafe protect his food, a frown marring his brow. Jared was right about the big man's latent Alpha abilities. Weres were fast but Alphas – they were something else entirely. They had to be the biggest, strongest, fastest wolves to run a pack. The speed Rafe had moved at was a clear indicator that he was born to be an Alpha, whether he wanted to be one or not.

Another thought crossed his mind that made his blood run cold. If Annie had tried this…dear God, Rafe could have killed her without realising what he was doing. There hadn't been any recognition in the wolf's eyes as it attacked him. There had been no sign of Rafe at all. Caleb was glad his woman had seen sense and agreed to let him work with her brother. Despite both Annie and Rafe's protestations, neither of them had the first inkling about how to deal with the wolf half of a newly turned Were.

As Rafe became enamoured with his food again, Caleb slipped back out of the tree and decided to try again. There was no shame in the big man failing the first time. There was a high probability it would take numerous attempts at this before Rafe was able to fully control his animal side. It was just a case of trial and error until he got it right.

The blur of colour was the only warning the vampire got before the wolf careered into him. Caleb spun sharply, cursing himself for being distracted thinking about Annie's welfare that he hadn't been giving Rafe enough of his attention. His palm snapped out and he had to moderate his strength as he connected with the wide chest of the wolf. With a startled yelp, the huge beast flew backwards but not before his jaw raked down Caleb's arm drawing blood.

~~~~~

Blood; hot, metallic, tasty blood filled the wolf's mouth as it flew through the air to land with a hard, thump against a tree. The collision hurt but it struggled to its feet ready to make another lunge at its enemy. A voice sounded somewhere, and the wolf stopped in confusion.

'Best not do that, Wolfie,' the voice said. 'Annie will be really pissed, if you hurt Caleb.'

The vampire forgotten, he turned around wildly to see who had spoken, but there was no one there. The voice was laughing now in his head, and he roared furiously, his confusion growing.

'You're not going to find me behind you,' the voice said, with more than a hint of amusement. 'I'm inside you, Wolfie. I'm your other half, your human side.'

The wolf sat down heavily and shook his head, a low whine coming from his chest. He instinctively knew who the voice was, even if he didn't want to listen to him right now.

'I'm not going away,' Rafe continued. 'I belong here, too, Wolfie. We are one.'

Wolfie whined loudly again and turned his big head to look at the vampire, who was now standing right beside his kill. The desire to rip out the man's throat was still there, but it was muted now. His human side was starting to take more and more control from him, stopping when they were balanced evenly.

Wolfie/Rafe looked at Caleb and chuffed lightly, his teeth baring into a wide grin. This really wasn't as difficult as he had imagined it would be. Oh, he knew he'd failed a couple of times, but something about drawing Caleb's blood had gotten through to him before he could do too much damage. The second that had happened, Rafe had been able to gain enough control to reason with his beast.

His human side could look at his kill with only a modicum of discomfort. His wolf side could recognise the vampire as a friend and dampen down his need to protect his kill. His back hurt where he'd hit the tree as did his chest. But apart from that, things had gone reasonably well for both sides of his dual nature and Caleb didn't look too pissed at being bitten.

Caleb smiled at Rafe when he grinned at him. He walked over to the big wolf and placed a hand lightly on his large head. He felt the wolf quiver fractionally and then fully relax. He could sense the balance within the animal and felt genuine pleasure. He was actually beginning to like Rhianna's brother. He wasn't that bad for a wolf, and he was important to his woman, so he had an added incentive to like him.

"That didn't seem too hard," he said to the wolf, removing his hand and stepping back as the animal shifted, and Rafe's human body uncoiled and stood up quickly. "I expected you to fail a few more times before finding some balance." He wasn't concerned about the bite. He had healed instantly, and he'd let Rafe bite him a thousand times if that's what it took to keep Rhianna safe.

"It was easier than I anticipated," Rafe answered with a slow smile. "Wolfie was a little surprised for a moment, a bit resistant to listening, but I was able to get through to him quite quickly. Sorry about the bite."

"It's a wolf's instinct to see one of my kind as being an immediate threat. The fact you managed to talk Wolfie down and reach a balance so quickly is commendable. I was expecting you to fail at least the first half dozen times we tried this," Caleb told him.

The big man's smile broadened. He was pleased he had surprised the vampire. The surprise was evident in Caleb's tone along with grudging respect, too. Annie's choice in mate was appearing to be a good one. He still wasn't comfortable with his sister dating a vampire, but she was all grown up now. She didn't need him the way she used to. She had Caleb now and he had the pack. They would always be extremely close, but he could now see their lives had moved in completely different directions. At least, they would still be able to see each other.

Caleb tossed his clothes to him, and Rafe quickly stepped into his jeans and T-shirt. He looked back at the wild boar and found he could look at the animal without wanting to heave his guts up. He smiled wryly, as he felt Wolfie's approval deep inside him. "Seems a bit of waste." He nodded his head at the carcass.

Caleb's keen gaze was still intent on the man before him, taking in every nuance of his speech and emotion crossing his face. He smiled and pulled out his cell phone, making a quick call to the Hanlon compound to let them know there was a fresh kill near the stream. Some of the pack would come out soon and claim it.

"Ready to go home, Rafe?"

Rafe looked at him steadily, knowing he wasn't referring to returning to the mansion. The vampire seemed to sense his more balanced state. He was asking him if he was ready to return to the pack. He ran a hand through his shaggy hair and pursed his lips. "Another few days," he finally answered. "I'd like to spend a bit more time with Annie, if you don't mind?"

Caleb smiled and turned to head back towards the mansion. "I meant what I said, Rafe. You're welcome to stay as long as you like. Even when you go back to the pack, you will still be welcome in my home. You're Annie's brother." It was just as simple as that, as far as the vampire was concerned. Rafe made Rhianna happy, so he would always be welcome.

"You're not so bad, for a bloodsucker." Rafe laughed, matching Caleb's long strides, as they threaded their way through the trees.

Caleb threw his head back and laughed, loudly. "You're not so bad, for a dog."

They entered the house from the rear, using the back door, which entered into a large utility room. Caleb stopped and inhaled, discerning instantly that Rhianna was gone. His brow drew down in a frown, as he moved into the kitchen and spotted the note on the dining table.

"What?" Rafe asked, following him inside, seeing him tense.

"Annie's gone," he answered, handing him the brief note that simply said she would be back later. He looked at the two coffee cups, scented Demetri in the room and pulled his cell phone from his pocket.

"What did you say to Annie?" he demanded, when his friend picked up.

"Good morning to you too, Caleb," Demetri drawled. "I only stopped by to see if we were at war with the dogs and showed Annie how to use the coffee machine. Why? What's wrong?"

"She's gone," Caleb snapped tersely. He was sure his friend had said something to upset his woman. He wasn't fooled by the innocence in Demetri's tone.

Demetri laughed softly down the phone. "Well, if you don't know where your little human is I don't know why you would think I would know where she is. Maybe she's tired of you already?"

"What did you say to her, Demetri? You forget how well I know you. Keeping your mouth shut is not a skill set you're particularly good at. Now, if you don't want me to come over there and beat it out of you, I suggest you start talking right now." Caleb's tone brooked no argument, his anger clearly audible.

"Oh, very well," Demetri sighed, wearily. "I may have pointed out the fact that your 'relationship' couldn't last, what with you being a vampire and Annie being a human. How was I to know you hadn't discussed that little 'hiccup' with her? I thought it was fairly obvious myself."

Caleb's breath hissed out angrily, and he seriously contemplated going over and kicking the shit out of Demetri, but he needed to find Rhianna first and make sure she was okay.

"In future keep your opinions to yourself, Demetri," he hissed down the phone. "If you find you just can't manage it, then I suggest you fuck off to some far flung region of the planet for a couple of centuries where I can't track you down and beat you senseless. Just in case I am not making myself clear here, DO NOT fuck with Annie ever again! You hurt her in any way, and I will hurt you back a thousand times worse."

"Fuck, I really hope what you've got isn't contagious, my friend," Demetri chuckled, softly. "I'd rather pay someone to take my head, than fall in love, if I'd start reacting like you are." He chuckled harder when Caleb growled loudly down the phone at him. "Alright! I get the message, Caleb. I swear I will not upset your little human again. Now go find her before you burst a blood vessel or something."

Caleb was so close to crushing his phone, when Demetri terminated the call. Sometimes he hated his friend with a vengeance, and this was one of those times. He knew he'd calm down once he found Rhianna and talked to her, but right at the moment he wanted to kill his friend.

Rafe remembered the vampire Demetri from the night Caleb came looking for him. The vampire had been irritating to say the least. He found it hard to understand what Caleb saw in him. "Is Annie okay?" he asked Caleb. If this Demetri had hurt her in anyway, he would kill the vampire and worry about the consequences later.

Rafe's anger transmitted to Caleb, and he forced himself to relax slightly. "I'm sure she's fine, Rafe. I'm going to head out for a bit and track her down." He grabbed his car keys and swiftly left the house.

~~~~~

"Mmmmm, Jared, what do you think you're doing?" Millie squealed, as she tried to lay out clothes on the bed. It should have been a simple task, but he kept getting in her way, dropping little kisses on whatever exposed skin he could find. It wasn't that she objected to his warm lips brushing against her skin, only he had promised to take her to Caleb's house, so she could see Rafe, and she was really anxious to get there.

"What does it look like I'm doing?" Jared rumbled huskily, his tone light and teasing, as he watched Millie's robe part temptingly, as she moved around the room. He grabbed her around the waist, as she tried to slip past him to get to something on her dressing table.

"Jared, come on." Millie groaned in exasperation, as she tried to pull some clean lingerie out of the pile on the top of her dressing table. She really did need to fold them and put them away. She would have, if she had known she was going to have a man in her bedroom.

"That's what I'm trying to do, baby," he laughed, softly. "I'm trying to come on to you."

He seemed to find his play on words very amusing, and Millie wondered if a smack around the head would convince him to stop thinking with his dick and concentrate on getting ready so he could take her to Caleb's. She turned to give him a piece of her mind, but his big hands stopped her.

One moment she was upright, and the next, she was bent over the dressing table on her stomach with her robe up past her hips, and Jared's thick fingers running over her backside to slide down between her legs. She gasped in a combination of shock and arousal and felt her face flush scarlet, as she immediately became wet at the contact of his hand on her tender flesh.

She winced slightly at the tenderness there and Jared's fingers gentled immediately. He leaned down and planted a soft kiss on the side of her neck, before running his mouth slowly up to her ear.

"Sorry, baby, I forgot you would be a little tender. Let me kiss it better for you." He dropped to his knees before she even registered his words and spread her legs.

"Jared," she groaned, moving to push herself upright, and then, his tongue laved her and the breath whooshed out of her as liquid fire shot through her veins. "Oh!" she gasped hoarsely, and he chuckled against her heated flesh and paused in his ministrations.

Jared had really tried his hardest to leave her alone, to give her time to recover from her first experience of sex, but her scent was driving him wild and the little flashes of skin teasing him, as she moved proved too much for him. He growled his pleasure, as his woman gave up fighting him and began moving her hips backwards, pressing against his mouth.

She tasted so damned good. His cock was hard and throbbing, and he knew he would pay for his actions with his own unfulfilled need, but he had to taste her, had to give his woman pleasure. He loved tasting her like this, bringing her release from the most intimate of kisses.

He could feel her starting to tense, knew her completion was just moments away, and he increased his ministrations. He was so desperate to be inside her there was a ringing noise in his ears as she moaned loudly and shattered against his mouth.

He growled, drawing out her pleasure. This was so worth walking around with a raging hard-on for the rest of the day. His ears were still ringing, and it took a moment for him to realise that the sound wasn't in his head.

"Jared, someone's at the door," Millie suddenly gasped, pushing her body up from the dressing table and looking down at him. Her face flushed scarlet, as she took in his heated eyes and wet mouth. "Oh God, you don't think whoever it is heard, do you?" she asked, mortified.

Jared laughed and stood up trying to position himself so it didn't ache so painfully. He grabbed his shirt and pulled in on but left it unbuttoned. "You get ready, baby. I'll see who's at the door." He dropped a quick kiss on her lips before he ran a hand over his mouth and stepped out of the bedroom.

Whoever it was at the door wasn't going away. Jared could feel his temper starting to rise, as he strode across to the front door to open it. Whoever it was better have a very good reason for interrupting them.

"Jared," Caleb said, not the least bit surprised to see the Were at the apartment. His lips quirked in a little smile. "You missed a bit," he commented, pointing at the other man's face as he stepped around him and into the apartment.

Jared laughed and rolled his eyes, as he wiped at his face again. Caleb had no doubt heard everything in the apartment. Thankfully, Millie wouldn't be aware of that fact. "I was going to call you," he said, as he closed the door. "Millie knows everything, apart from you that is. She wants to go see Rafe. I trust that won't be an issue."

Caleb sat down in one of the armchairs. "That's fine with me. I'm starting to get used to my home turning into Grand Central Station, since I've met Annie." He had hoped to find his woman at the apartment, but knew instantly she wasn't there. Her scent was nearly a day old.

"Sounds like Annie," Jared smiled. He flopped down onto the sofa, stretched out his long legs and re-adjusted himself into a more comfortable position. Caleb's appearance was helping with his frustration problem. "So, how is Rafe doing?" He was suddenly all Alpha.

The vampire smiled. "He'll be back with the pack soon. I think he's ready to come back now, but he needs a little more time with his sister. You'll find him much improved."

Jared quirked an eyebrow in surprise. "So soon? Annie is a miracle worker. She's not only managed to tame you, but she's put Rafe back together again, and all in twenty four hours?"

Caleb's smile widened. His woman really was a force to contend with. "I'm looking for her at the moment. I thought she might be here. Do you think Millie would have an idea where she would go to if she needed some quiet time to think?"

"The Botanical Gardens, by the pond display," Millie said from the bedroom doorway. She had successfully managed to get dressed, throwing on a pair of jeans and a couple of tank tops, one over the other in two different shades of blue. "Did you two have a fight?"

Caleb sighed. "No, we're fine," he answered. "One of my friends said something which may have upset her. I just want to find her and make sure she's okay." He stood up relieved to have a possible location for Rhianna. "I'll maybe see you later, if you're still at the house when we get back." He nodded to them both and left the flat.

"You know there's something about that man that isn't quite right," Millie said, with a thoughtful expression on her face. Her cobalt blue eyes bored into Jared's, as he shrugged as if he didn't know what she was talking about. She would eventually have to know about the vampires, but he thought Rhianna and Caleb would prefer it if they told her.

"He's not a Were, is he?" she suddenly asked and Jared burst out laughing.

"No, he most definitely is not a Were," he smiled, standing up and buttoning his shirt. "Are you ready, yet?" he asked with a twinkle in his eyes. "You do know we're going to see Rafe?" He laughed loudly, when she hit him with a cushion from the sofa.

~~~~~

Caleb stood silently under the shade of a large tree watching his woman, as she slowly paced up and down beside the pond in the Botanical Gardens. Her beautiful face was deep in thought, and he wanted to cross the final distance to her, but was afraid of the upcoming conversation. He sucked his breath in when she suddenly stopped pacing and turned to look directly at him.

She stood there for a long moment, and then she slowly smiled, and he was striding across to her and pulling her into his embrace. "I don't like coming home and finding you gone." He kissed the top of her head. "The house feels so empty without you." He was astounded at just how empty it did feel without her in it.

"Demetri stopped by," she answered quietly, resting her head against his chest and wrapping her arms tightly around his waist.

The mention of his friend made him stiffen before he sucked in another deep breath. "I know, I've already spoken to him. Did he upset you, Annie, because if he did, I'm going to bloody kill him?"

Rhianna couldn't help laughing at the outrage in his tone, turning to look up at her beautiful man. "Caleb, love, you can't go around beating people up just because they speak the truth," she said with a bit of humour in her eyes. "Demetri might be a pain in the ass, but he was only pointing out the inevitable."

She sighed, trying to keep her emotions in check as she rested her head back on his chest. "You're a vampire, and I'm human. You're going to live forever, and I'm going to die."

Caleb's arms tightened around her, and a low groan escaped him. "Don't say that, Annie," he whispered. "I don't ever want to think about you dying. I can't bear the thought of not having you in my life."

She stroked his chest, trying to soothe him even as her hand trembled. "It's something we have to talk about, Caleb. We can't bury our heads in the sand, no matter how much we want to. It's going to happen one day. I'm not sad about dying. Well I am, but only because I know how much it will hurt you. What does make me sad is growing old, while you stay forever young."

Caleb squeezed his eyes shut tightly, wanting desperately not to talk about it, but knowing he had to because she needed to. He let out a long breath and looked down at her, his finger tugging gently at her chin to raise her gaze up to his. "You will always be beautiful to me, my Annie," he whispered, softly. "I will always love you, and I will always want to be with you." He tried to put all of his emotion into his eyes, so she would see it and believe it.

She smiled her beautiful smile, her face glowing with her love for him, and he lifted her up so he could crush his mouth desperately against hers. All his fear of losing her was in the hard punishing slant of his mouth over her soft lips, his hands clutching her tightly to him. He didn't want to lose her ever.

Her gentle response to him slowly soothed him, and his lips softened against hers, as he carried her over to the wooden bench beside the water and cradled her in his lap. His tongue delved into her moist heat to taste her sweetness. Nothing in the whole world tasted as good as his woman. She was sweetness and redemption all rolled into one. He finally released her mouth and cradled her head against his chest, as he stared unseeingly into the water before him.

"Caleb..." Rhianna hesitated, toying with a button on his shirt. "You know how Weres mate with humans. Can vampires do that, too?" She held her breath, when he stiffened against her, her fingers nervously pulling at the button until it suddenly snapped off in her hands, and she looked up guiltily.

Caleb didn't seem to notice. His golden brown eyes were burning like amber, as he continued to stare unseeingly into the water, every muscle in his body locked tensely. He finally looked down at her, and she couldn't read the expression on his face.

"This isn't the life for you, Annie," he finally said, his tone so quiet it was hard to hear it. "This isn't the life I want for you. I should have been less selfish. I should have stayed away from you, but I wanted you so badly I just couldn't. I don't ever want to look into your beautiful eyes and see them become jaded the way it happens to my kind. Something about living for eternity makes everyone change in the end. We forget how to laugh and to love. We become selfish and cold. I would rather die, than see the love for life disappear from your eyes, Annie."

She blinked slowly, a frown beginning to mar her brow. "Isn't that my decision to make? Isn't it up to me how I want to live my life? Can you honestly look at me and believe that I could ever become shallow and unfeeling? Maybe your kind has lost its way a bit, but that doesn't mean you can't change. You're proof of that, Caleb. A few months ago you were like Demetri and look at you now."

"Only because I met you, Annie. I'm not a shining example to wave in the air as a precursor to how my race can evolve. I'm an anomaly, an oddity, not the start of a new breed of vampire. You would have, maybe a few centuries, where you could retain your identity, your personality, if I turned you, maybe a little longer because you would still have Rafe and Millie around you to hold onto your humanity. Then the joy would start to recede, the light would fade from your eyes, hell, you'd probably even start to like Demetri."

Rhianna's lips twitched in a little smile. "That would be a fate worse than death," she remarked dryly, and then she turned serious again. "I'm willing to take the risk, Caleb. I'm willing to believe in our love being strong enough."

He groaned and buried his face in the side of her neck, hugging her tightly. "I'm too scared to take the risk, Annie," he ground out hoarsely. "I can't bear the thought of ever doing anything which would hurt you."

She sighed and stroked his hair with a soothing hand. He was so stubborn sometimes. He worried like an old woman too. She smiled as she cupped his face gently in her hands and brushed her lips lightly against his. "I know what I want, Caleb," she murmured against his mouth. "You know you want it too. We don't have to make a decision right now, we have plenty of time. Just promise me you'll think about it, love."

She met his gaze and saw longing warring with reluctance and her smile widened. It was clear he wanted her for eternity, and she knew, without a doubt, she wanted him for eternity too. It was just a matter of getting him to see things her way, and she was sure she would win the battle. "Come on, love, let's go home," she smiled

CHAPTER SEVENTEEN

Millie couldn't stop touching Rafe. When he had opened the door to them earlier, she had shrieked with joy and thrown herself into his arms, laughing and crying at the same time. Jared's wolf had protested loudly, as his mate wrapped herself around another man. He had tried his best to give her a moment with her adopted brother, but his wolf had won out, and he was soon growling and pulling her away from his beta.

Jared was surprised to see how easily Rafe handled his overt aggression. Usually aggression caused his beta to flinch and turn inward, but Rafe had smiled slowly and lowered his eyes submissively, letting his Alpha know he had no designs on his mate. It was only this submission and the obvious changes in Rafe which enabled Jared not to attack him every time Millie stroked his arm or his cheek, as she was doing right at that very minute. He couldn't stop the low growl, which erupted from his throat as he clenched his hands at his side.

"Mills, will you let up with all the touching?" Rafe suddenly laughed. "You're driving Jared nuts. Any more and he's going to kick my ass, and I'd prefer for that not to happen."

Millie's cobalt blue eyes swung to Jared, and she took in his strained expression and tense stance. "What is your problem?" There was a hint of belligerence to her tone. "He's my brother for goodness sake."

"You have no blood relation to him," Jared answered darkly, taking a step closer to her and shooting Rafe a black look.

"Jared," Millie sighed, trying to fight down her exasperation. "Rafe has been taking care of me since I was a little girl. As far as I'm concerned, he's my brother and that's the end of it. So, stop acting like an ass."

"He can't help it, Mills," Rafe chuckled, putting a bit more distance between them to try to soothe his Alpha a bit. "He'll be like this until you mate with him properly."

Jared looked at his beta in surprise. Rafe was quoting pack etiquette, as if he'd been with the pack all his life. It was coming out naturally, and he could see Caleb was right. Rafe was ready to come back to the pack. This time he would come willingly and become fully integrated. He smiled with contentment. He had managed to do right by Rafe and the rest of the pack, and it had come to a satisfactory conclusion.

He saw Millie watching him intently, and he shot her a wicked smile. He stepped closer and pulled her into his arms, dropping a quick kiss on her upturned mouth before he turned back to Rafe. "I'm calling a pack meeting tonight. I would like you to attend. Will you have an issue with that?"

Rafe shook his head. "I was waiting for Annie to come home, and then, I was going to head over to the compound anyway. I thought I'd hang with Aaron for a while, if he wasn't busy."

Jared's smile widened. He barely recognised the man in front of him; he was so much easier in himself. Little Annie really was a miracle worker. Maybe he should take her to the pack meeting and see if she could settle down all the angry wolves tonight.

The object of his internal musing suddenly appeared through the front door, her vampire firmly attached to her as if they were joined at the hip. Her face lit up when she saw her friends, and she gave Millie a quick hug before she turned to her brother. A long silent moment passed between the siblings, and then, Rafe was scooping up his little sister and hugging her enthusiastically.

"You're about ready to go home, aren't you?" Rhianna smiled, happily.

Rafe nodded. "I am. Jared's just been telling me there's a pack meeting tonight, so I need to attend that. I think I might stay there tonight and see how it goes with a view to staying full time. You're okay with that?"

"I'm okay with whatever makes you happy, Rafe. You know there's always a place for you here, if you need it." She turned to look at Caleb, who smiled his agreement.

"No, I'm pack now, sis." Rafe smiled. "I'll still come by for a visit, though, and I'm sure Jared won't mind if you come visit the compound either."

"You're welcome any time, Annie, but leave Caleb at home," Jared laughed. "He'd only try to start another war, if one of the pack ventured too close to you by accident."

Caleb frowned darkly at the Alpha and then smoothed out his expression when Rhianna tutted lightly at him. "Fine, you can go by yourself," he grumbled, irritably, "but she's your responsibility when she's there, Jared."

"Caleb!" Rhianna rolled her eyes and stepped into his arms. "You really need to work on this over protectiveness, love."

Millie watched the way Caleb and Jared squared up to each other, her eyes narrowing. "So, if you're not a Were, Caleb, what exactly are you?" she suddenly asked. All heads turned to look at her, and Caleb stiffened noticeably.

He looked at the dark haired woman for a moment, and then slowly relaxed. She was going to find out anyway. "I'm a vampire, Millie," he answered and watched her blue eyes grow huge in her head, as she took an unconscious step closer to Jared.

"Werewolves and now vampires, too?" she gasped. Millie swallowed hard. Her gaze turning to Rhianna, who was watching her reaction with a slight smile on her face, "You're okay with this, Annie?"

Rhianna laughed. "My brother's a werewolf, Mills. Having a vampire as a boyfriend is really a moot point after that."

Millie stared at all of them, her face turning pale and a slightly wild look coming into her eyes. Jared frowned down at her with concern on his face, feeling her stiffness against him.

"Mills, why don't you come and help me make some coffee?" Rhianna said quietly, watching her friend intently. "Jared, you can let go of her. She's not going to vanish into thin air." She shot the Alpha a pointed look and their eyes locked for a moment, before he slowly released his grip on his mate with a slight nod of his head.

Rhianna threaded her arm through her friend's and led her out of the sitting room and into the kitchen. She chatted lightly about how beautiful the Botanical Gardens were as they walked, her friend relaxing as her words washed over her.

"Annie, how can you be so calm about everything?" Millie asked when they were finally alone. "Rafe is still alive, but he's a wolf. Jared's a wolf, too, and Caleb is a vampire…why are you just accepting all of this?"

Rhianna smiled at her, trying to project reassurance as she sat down at the kitchen table, waiting until her friend sat down beside her. "Mills, I know it's a lot to take in. Believe me, it was all a bit of a shock to me, too, at first. I forgot how to breathe when Caleb revealed himself to me. The very same night I found out about Rafe and Jared, so I kind of got hit with it all at the same time like you have."

Millie ran her hands through her black curls and met her friend's eyes. "It doesn't seem to bother you, though," she said, almost accusingly. "How can you just accept it without batting an eyelid?"

Rhianna gave her another smile. "Because, I refuse to allow myself to become hung up on labels, Millie. I love Caleb more than anything in the world. I don't look at him and think 'he's a vampire'. I look at him and think of how much I love him, and how much he loves me. With the wolves, it's the same thing really. I look at Rafe, and I see my big brother, and he's not dead anymore, so it doesn't matter if he's a part time wolf. He's still Rafe. He's just got a little extra part to him now. If someone had asked me if I could have my brother back just slightly altered, I would have jumped at the chance. I wasn't asked, but I got that miracle. I can't very well freak out about it, can I?"

Millie stared at her friend, hearing her words and trying to take them in. She watched Rhianna rise and head over to the coffee machine and begin to make coffees. Her thoughts turned to Jared, and how he had swiftly become important to her. She'd been running from him for weeks, knowing instinctively that the moment she surrendered to him things would never be the same again. She just had no idea they would be so extreme.

Could she be as accepting as her friend? What Annie said made a certain kind of sense. Could she look past the labels and just see the people involved? Jared wanted to change her into a wolf, too, yet Rafe's change had been so horrific. He'd barely managed to survive it. What if something like that happened to her? What if she agreed to it and she didn't really want it? What if it didn't work?

She looked up when Rafe wandered into the kitchen. "Caleb's keeping Jared entertained for the moment," he said with a warm smile for her, as he sat down. "You're having a bit of a hard time about all this, Mills. It's understandable."

"I'm scared, Rafe," she swallowed hard. "You're one of the gentlest people I know, and this wolf stuff almost killed you."

He smiled and reached out and took her hands in his. "It's because of my nature that I found it so hard, Mills. You're a lot stronger than I am. You're feisty and tenacious, two very good attributes to make a perfect wolf. The only question you really have to ask yourself is do you love Jared enough?"

Millie looked at him and then turned to look at Rhianna, as she headed back to the table and sat down on her other side. She reached out to clasp her own small hands around their joined ones.

"Who would have thought we'd get the chance to sit like this together again," Rhianna said with a small smile. "Our lives have changed so much in the last few months. Just because things are different, it doesn't necessarily mean it's a bad thing, Millie. You're still in control of your life. You still get to make the decisions on how you live it. There are just a few new variables you get to mull over as you decide what you want to do."

She smiled at Millie before she turned to her brother. "Did I tell you I was opening a bookstore, Rafe? Well, I was supposed to be until you turned out not to be dead. Jared gave me a lot of money, like an insurance policy. I was going to use that for the bookstore, but I suppose I probably should give it back to him now."

Rafe laughed and shook his head. "The money's yours, Annie. You were never meant to know I still lived. It is what the pack does for the bereaved families. Just because you know the truth that doesn't negate the pain and heartache you and Millie have both been through. Jared won't accept the money back, so you go ahead with your dream, sis. You deserve it."

Rhianna smiled a big smile and nodded at Rafe before her keen, lavender eyes turned back to their troubled friend. "Millie named the bookstore for me. Why don't you tell Rafe what you named it, Mills?" Her tone was light and full of innocence as she regarded her friend.

Millie blinked at her very slowly, and then, looked back at Rafe before her head swung once more in Rhianna's direction and a slow smile started to curve her lips. "Create your own Happiness Bookstore," she finally said in an awed tone, as she looked at the petite redhead, whom she'd once thought was the most fragile woman on the planet, with a completely new level of respect.

Rafe laughed, his brown eyes twinkling, as he looked at his two little sisters, because Millie would always be his sister just as much as Rhianna was, no matter what Jared said about lack of shared bloodlines. Rhianna was sitting there with an expression of carefully cultured innocence on her face, and Millie was staring at her with such a stunned expression on hers.

"What?" Rhianna asked, with a shrug when no one spoke for a long time.

Millie suddenly laughed and threw her arms around her friend. "Oh, you are so good, Annie," she laughed. "Sitting there like little miss innocent, pretending you didn't just lead me by the nose right to where you really wanted me to go."

Rhianna hugged her friend back warmly. "I only helped you get there a little sooner than you would have, Mills. You would have done it yourself, once you got over your natural tendency to overthink things."

Millie sat back and reached for her coffee, taking a long sip as she looked at her family. Rafe was a wolf now and Annie...well what was Annie going to be? "Annie, are you going to become a vampire?"

Some of the light died from her friend's eyes though a smile remained on her lips. "Caleb and I have discussed it today, so yes it is open for debate. It won't bother you both if I do? I mean...all this Weres and vampires don't like each other crap?"

Her brother and sister stared at her in shock for a second, and then, both reached for her hands. "You'll always be our Annie, no matter what choices you make," Rafe answered for both of them.

Rhianna sighed with relief, knowing that at least one hurdle was crossed. Smiling, she rose from her seat. "Best get back to the boys then; they'll be wondering what's keeping us so long."

Rafe headed out of the kitchen after gathering up the coffees on a tray, leaving Millie and Rhianna to follow behind him.

"Thank you, Annie," Millie said, quietly. "You're turning into a right little Sage with your words of wisdom."

"I just like fixing things," her friend laughed, as they re-entered the sitting room.

Jared was immediately at Millie's side, staring down at her with concern for a moment, and then, slowly relaxing when he saw her untroubled expression. "You okay, baby?" He hugged her close to his side.

Millie nodded. "I just had a few things to work out. Everything is fine now, Jared."

He smiled his relief and kissed her on the top of her head. "We need to get moving. There's a lot to be done before the meeting."

Millie gave Rhianna another quick hug and then slipped back into Jared's embrace, because she really had no other choice. The man couldn't seem to keep his hands off her.

Rafe left with Jared and Millie to head over to the compound. His Alpha and his mate were sharing loaded glances every now and then, and he felt a growing sense of unease the closer they got to compound. He had no idea what the proposed meeting was about, but he had a feeling it was going to be something important, and he could tell his Alpha was worried about it.

"Jared, you want to clue me in about this meeting?"

"I'll tell all the betas together. I'm going to need you all at my side tonight, Rafe. I know I'll have your support on what I want to discuss. You'll understand why after I speak to the betas. In the event things get ugly, I want you to get Millie out of there, as quickly as possible. I know you'll keep her safe."

Rafe's unease grew, as Millie turned to look at Jared. "I'm not going anywhere without you."

Jared sighed, the sound deep and loaded with exasperation. "Millie, if things turn ugly the last thing I'll need is to be worrying about you. If I tell you to leave, you will go with Rafe immediately." His tone was firm and brooked no argument.

Millie was going to argue with him, but his face was set hard, and she knew she would be wasting her breath. One glance behind her told her Rafe would be just as immovable. He may not know what was going on, but her safety would be as paramount in his mind, as it was in Jared's. She sighed in resignation and folded her arms crossly over her chest. Stupid macho male crap!

~~~~~

Jared watched his betas' faces, as he concluded their briefing as to why he was calling the pack meeting. There were ten men crowded into his large study. Millie was sitting in his office chair with himself on one side and Rafe on the other. To say the betas were stunned was an understatement. Each man wore a shocked expression, but he couldn't detect any outright disapproval. He slowly roamed his eyes over them and waited for some response.

Pete was the first one to speak. He was the shortest man in the room at just five foot nine, and he was overly sensitive about his height. His stocky build made up for his lack of stature when in wolf form. "Boss, the old timers are going to go ape shit," he said, doubtfully. "I was amazed they voted yes to Rafe's sister being allowed to know about us. This might be a step too far for most of them."

There was a murmur of agreement around the room, as the betas looked from one to another. Aaron seemed to be the least worried, but then he always seemed to find something to smile about, no matter how dire a situation was. "It might not be so bad. Half of them have never mated, and this would give them the opportunity. They may surprise us all."

Jared sighed. "That's what I'm hoping for. I'm going to need you to fan out around the room and stick close to some of our less tractable friends, just in case any of them lose it. The children will be present, and I don't want any of them accidentally hurt. I take it none of you have any issues with this proposal?"

Each beta gave him their support. He looked to Rafe last. The tall man was deep in thought, but he smiled widely when his Alpha's eyes met his. "You know I don't have any objections."

Jared frowned slightly. "Rafe, you do understand this cannot apply directly to you and any of the others who have technically 'died'," he asked with a touch of concern.

Rafe nodded. "I know that, Jared, but it will only be for a while, maybe a generation or so, and then I can once more go out among humans again. Millie will be here, and I can visit with Annie any time I want to. That's enough for me." He took a deep breath and looked at Jared intently.

"Rafe Armand is dead, as you've pointed out. It's my wish to take the pack name if you have no objections?"

Jared blinked slowly in surprise. Did Rafe know what he was asking of him? His eyes swung to Aaron, who had been the big man's teacher in all things pack related. The stunned expression on the blond man's face echoed his own and, then, his head turned to look at his Alpha, and he shook his head, signalling that Rafe had no idea what he had just asked for.

Jared turned back to Rafe and pursed his lips thoughtfully. He had always liked the big man, right from the very first moment he'd met him. He had worked hard to keep him sane, until he could come to terms with his new life. He supposed Rafe had been the start of the changes to pack life, too. For some reason, Jared had connected with the big man in a way, which had forced his hand to make decisions he would never have made.

Rafe had no idea what he was asking of Jared. He had no idea that he was unconsciously going to elevate himself into a position he probably wouldn't want. The question was, did Jared want the change in status? Rafe was Millie's brother and the bridge between the pack and the less militant local vampires. He was most definitely an asset to the pack in many ways.

Jared stared at him a moment longer, and then, he suddenly smiled broadly. "Welcome home, Rafe Hanlon," he said quietly and the slight tension still in the room evaporated, as the betas welcomed Rafe back to the pack with obvious pleasure.

"Okay, let's go get this meeting over and done with," Jared announced, and they all filed out of his home and down to the meeting room.

The betas fanned out among the gathered community with Rafe following Jared to the front of the room. Jared positioned Millie to his right, which was closest to one of the exits. Rafe stood to her other side and ran his eyes carefully around the room.

There was a lot of murmuring going on. The meeting was unscheduled; therefore, it was attracting a lot of speculation. A few of the females were eyeing Millie up speculatively, particularly Loretta who was probably the closest to an Alpha Bitch the pack had without actually being one. She had been Jared's preferred bed partner, and therefore Rafe marked her as one to watch when the meeting started.

The room quickly settled down, when the Alpha stood to talk. "I'm glad to see everyone could attend," Jared began with a smile. "I know you are all curious as to why I have called this impromptu meeting."

"Does it have anything to do with the human woman?" Loretta asked, her tone cold. "Has the Alpha finally decided to mate?"

Jared's cool blue eyes locked with hers and a muscle jumped in the side of his jaw, his teeth clenching at her snide tone. "This is Millicent Cooper, and yes, Loretta, she is my mate."

There was a ripple of voices around the room, and all eyes turned to stare at Millie intently, which began to make her feel uncomfortable. Now, she knew what it was like to be an animal in a zoo.

"You're not mated yet, and she's still human, so why is she here?" Loretta persisted, glaring hard at Millie. "Surely, you didn't call a meeting just to tell us you had found a mate? I know it's been a long time coming, Jared, but it hardly warrants a full bloody pack meeting to announce it."

Millie stared back at the woman running her mouth off and felt irritation rise at her derogatory tone. "If Jared chooses to call a pack meeting to announce our joining, what is it to you? Are you jealous, Loretta?" She kept her tone saccharine sweet and was rewarded by a flare of anger in the other woman's eyes.

"Why would I be jealous? I've already had Jared, and I dare say once he tires of you, I'll have him again."

Millie laughed. She laughed so hard she started to cry and had to wipe at her cheeks to get rid of the wetness there. "I'm sorry I took so long to accept you, honey." She turned to Jared, when she stopped laughing. "If I'd known you'd had to resort to that, I would have come to you much sooner."

Jared's eyes widened slightly, and then a big grin crossed his face. He had been concerned about how Millie would cope with the more aggressive females in the pack, and she was handling Loretta perfectly by not letting the stupid bitch get under her skin. He reached to pull her up against him and gave her a very lusty kiss.

"Play nice with the females, baby," he laughed huskily, letting the whole room hear his words. "It's been a long time since they've had a proper Alpha female, so they're a bit out of practice when it comes to showing the due respect necessary." His blue eyes drilled into Loretta, as he spoke, and she held her peace and lowered her eyes, clearly still unhappy.

"I've called this meeting for three reasons," he addressed the room, keeping Millie clutched tightly at his side. "The first to introduce Millie as my mate, which I believe has now been done. The second is to welcome Rafe back home to us." He turned to smile at his beta, and there were loud shouts to Rafe, welcoming him home.

"As everyone can see, Rafe is much healed and ready to be one with us again," Jared continued. "He has asked to take the pack name, and I have agreed, so he is now to be known as Rafe Hanlon. We owe a debt of gratitude to his sister Annie and her partner Caleb Ryder for helping to bring him back to us. I owe a debt of gratitude to you all for voting to allow Annie to help heal our brother."

He paused and let the pack absorb his words and feel his deep pride in all of them. They were basically a good bunch of people, if a little volatile at times. He was proud to lead them, and he hoped fervently they were proud to have him as their Alpha.

"You said three reasons, Jared," Bill Shepherd called out loudly from the back of the room. "What's the third one?"

Jared stiffened at the question. Bill was one of the 'No' voters regarding Annie, and he knew without a doubt he would be one of the loudest No votes to the coming proposal. Millie squeezed his waist soothingly, and he gave her a quick smile before he turned back to the pack.

"When explaining to Millie about pack life, she asked me certain questions," he said, loudly. "Questions I found difficult to answer. One of her first questions was why didn't I trust the pack." There was an outraged roar around the room, and he held his hand up for silence, though it took a minute for the noise to subside.

"She meant no disrespect," he continued when they settled. "She merely wanted to know why I trusted an outsider to keep our secret, when I didn't appear to trust the pack to do so. My immediate reaction was anger. I trust each and every one of you with my life and the lives of all our brothers and sisters. But, the more questions Millie asked, the more I came to realise how much I had failed you as an Alpha."

He held up his hand again, when there was another roar of anger throughout the room. "I have failed you," he said to the suddenly hushed room. "Three generations ago our pack stood at three hundred strong, now we stand at only two hundred strong. The reason for this is the sheer number of unmated among us. Too many of the pack are not having children, and we are slowly starting to decline because of it."

"There's nothing can be done about that, Jared," Bill called loudly. "I fail to see how you can view your leadership as being a failure because of it."

Jared's gaze locked on his. "It is my failure, because I allow it to continue," he said simply. "We all know Rafe's almost pathological need to return to his human life. My Millie also balks at the idea of leaving her human life behind to become my mate. She asked me why it was necessary, and the only answer I could give her was because that was the way it has always been done."

"It's what protects the pack," Bill shouted loudly. He was slowly starting to see where this meeting was heading, and he didn't like it one bit.

"The pack protects itself," Jared argued, talking over him when he went to talk on. "Who says the pack has to protect itself here in this compound? Think of it everyone, the chance to find a mate of your own instead of hoping that one is eventually born into the pack."

The room erupted loudly, people jumping up and shouting angrily at their Alpha, others sitting shell-shocked, as just what he was proposing sank into their stunned brains. Jared let them shout, as he slowly surveyed the room. There were more seated than standing. He didn't know if that was a good sign or not. He hoped it was. Millie was trembling slightly at his side, and Rafe had taken a step closer to her, his big body coiled and ready for his Alpha's command.

"This is outrageous!" Bill screamed over the others, his lined face red with fury. "You only suggest this because of your mate's unwillingness to become one of us!"

His accusation startled Millie out of her fear and she looked at the man for a long moment as the rest of the room suddenly fell silent again. Everyone was still looking at her, most probably waiting for her to run screaming from the room. If Jared didn't have such a tight grip on her, she would most likely fall to the floor. She drew herself up straighter, knowing instinctively that she couldn't be seen to crumble. If the pack thought her weak for one moment, then Jared's leadership would be in jeopardy, and she couldn't let that happen.

"Yes, I don't want to give up my human life," she said truthfully, swallowing down her fear and surveying the room slowly. "I like it, and I don't see why I should be confined here in this compound with the only explanation for it being that's the way it's done. If the pack chooses to remain as they are, then I will make the change, and I will come to live here. I will do so, because that's the only way Jared can have the heirs he so desperately wants. I will do it for him, because I love him."

There was a murmur of approval and she held up her hand to halt it. "But, I will weep, when I do so. I will not weep, because I no longer have my human life. I will weep, because I will be mated to this wonderful Alpha and bearing his children, while three quarters of my new family are doomed to never know the joy I know. There is a finite time for some traditions. It is not wrong to examine those traditions and amend them, if necessary."

The room remained silent when she stopped talking, and she felt Jared's gaze on her, but she was too scared to look away from the faces in the room. She wanted to meet every eye to try to gauge what they were thinking.

"I still say this is outrageous," Bill yelled loudly, when the silence wore on.

"Oh, put a sock in it, Bill," Loretta complained from the front row, causing Millie to start in surprise. "It's all right for you. You're already mated and have had your children. What about the rest of us, the ones who aren't betas and will never get the chance to mate? Our Alpha talks sense."

"She's not Alpha, until she mates properly," Bill shot back, furiously. "She has no right to even be speaking here on this subject!"

"She's Alpha Bitch, if I bloody well say she is," Loretta snapped back, standing up and glaring at him. "I've been leading the females for over three centuries, and if I submit to her, then she is the Alpha and you can just keep your big nose out of female affairs!"

Loretta's unexpected championship stunned Millie. She stared at her, until she turned around and sat down again. The wiry woman nodded in her direction and folded her arms.

"Thank you, Loretta," Millie said quietly, knowing that something momentous had just happened. "All we ask is the pack consider the possibility of leaving the compound to search for their mates or live among humans, if that's what you really want to do. No one will be forced to do so. The option will just be there, if you do want to. New mates will not have to give up their human lives, if they don't want to. It's time to bring the pack into the twenty first century." She tacked her brightest smile onto the end of her words. "And, can we lay off with the Bitch stuff, too?" she asked with a little laugh.

Jared's heart swelled with pride when his woman literally charmed the pack with her keen intelligence and quick wit. Ripples of laughter were going around the room at her last comment, and she was quite literally glowing, as she turned to look up at him to see if she had done okay. She had seen a side to them he hadn't been prepared to show her yet and she had stood strong by his side.

"You are amazing, my Millie," he said softly, cupping her cheek and stroking it lightly. "You would really join with me, if the pack votes no?"

"My life is with you now, Jared. How could I ever deny you the chance to have a complete family? If the pack vote no, I will mate with you properly and give you the children you so dearly want. I will do the same if they vote yes, too," she laughed, softly.

"I love you so much," he whispered, his handsome face full of joy, as he bent his head and caught her lips in a tender kiss.

"I love you too, Jared," she whispered against his mouth, as Rafe coughed discreetly at their side.

"I think the pack is ready to vote, boss," he said, with a little laugh.

Jared and Millie turned to face the pack again and were startled to see so many smiling faces looking at them. Millie blushed scarlet, and Jared chuckled loudly. "So embarrassed over a little kiss, Millie? Just wait until you find out what's involved in an Alpha mating." Her eyes widened slowly, and she opened her mouth to ask, but decided maybe she didn't want to know right now.

"I call the vote," Jared called. "Please stand if you agree with the change in pack law with regards to its segregation from human life." There was a shuffle of feet as people stood.

"Please stand if you are opposed," Jared called and there was another shuffle of feet.

"I declare the vote is in favour of amending pack law," Jared smiled broadly. "There will be a lot of work involved, as we work out the logistics of how we are going to fit in with the humans around us. If anyone has what they feel would be helpful skills to work towards that end then please see the betas. I declare this meeting over."

Rafe smiled, as Jared and Millie mingled with the pack for a little while, and then disappeared back to the Alpha's house. Bill and some of the older ones were still grumbling about the meeting, but the pack had voted, and they would eventually calm down and accept the changes. If they were that set against the idea then they would leave and join another pack.

His brown eyes surveyed the room slowly, and he finally found Loretta staring at him with a speculative look on her face. He cocked an eyebrow at her, and she wandered over, as he perused her with open appreciation. She looked like she might be fun to tussle with.

"So, you're a Hanlon now," she said with a smirk on her face. "Guess that makes you Jared's adopted brother."

Rafe frowned. "How do you work that out, Loretta?"

She gave him a disbelieving look. "You think the Alpha lets just anyone take the pack name?" she asked, incredulously. "He's never allowed anyone to do so before, Rafe. Jared Hanlon was letting the pack know tonight, in no uncertain terms, that you are now officially his brother."

He stared at her in stunned surprised, and then he started to laugh. "I need to learn a hell of a lot more about pack life." He had the distinct feeling he had just let himself in for more than he'd bargained for by becoming Jared's adopted brother.

"I could help you out with that," she said slightly huskily, threading her arm through his.

Rafe looked down at her and smiled. What the hell, she was a good-looking woman, and he was still available for now. He leaned down and fisted his hand in her short, dark hair, bringing his mouth down hard on hers and growling when she met his aggressive kiss with an equal ardour.

"Why don't you teach me, then?" he breathed against her lips, and laughed when she growled her pleasure and pulled him from the room.

～～～

"Jared, what did you mean about the mating with an Alpha comment?" Millie asked, unable to keep her concern from her voice, as they slipped into his house. Her blue eyes sought out his and saw the laughter in them, which made her frown.

"Well..." he sighed softly. "It's more of a group activity, than a private one. Involves the whole pack and takes place outside. We get naked, and I take you in both my human and my wolf form, before I bite you to mark you as mine. When I bite you, I will pass the wolf gene into your blood stream, and then, you will bite me and mark me as yours."

Millie's heart thumped wildly in her chest, as her eyes grew larger and larger the more he talked. Group sex? People watching? Her face paled at just the thought, and she had to swallow hard to try to control her breathing. She could do it, for Jared she could do it. She hoped.

His loud laughter filled the hallway, as he scooped her up into his arms and took the stairs two at a time up to his bedroom, his blue eyes twinkling merrily. "Or, that's how it used to be done, until Ma told Da in not uncertain terms that there was no way in hell she was having sex in front of the pack, and he amended pack law to claim her. I'm not the only Hanlon Alpha to amend pack laws, when necessary."

"You bastard!" Millie shrieked, slapping him hard on his chest even as a wave of heartfelt relief ran through her. "You did that deliberately, didn't you?"

Jared kicked his bedroom door shut and slid her legs to the floor, but kept his arms firmly around her so her hands were jammed against his chest, and she couldn't hit him again. "You were going to agree to it, too," he chuckled lightly. "I could see it in your eyes, baby, and it makes me so proud that you would be willing to do that for me, but it's not required. We can do it right here, right now, in this room if it's truly want you want." He held his breath, as he waited for her answer.

Millie stared into Jared's eyes and felt a second's hesitancy about taking such a huge step. His expression was patient and understanding, but she could read the deep longing in his eyes. Taking a deep breath, she nodded slowly.

"Are you sure, Millie?" he whispered. "You need to be completely sure you really want this. If you're uncertain we can wait a bit longer."

Any lingering doubts melted away and she smiled, "I'm sure, Jared," she said huskily. "But, can I see your wolf again first? I'd like a moment to be with him without screaming the place down and running away."

Jared smiled and moved away from her, quickly stripping off his clothes and shifting the moment he had. He sat down on the floor and regarded her attentively.

Millie stared at the large, black wolf before her and walked forward until she was beside him. She tentatively reached out and touched him on his large head and the wolf rumbled in his chest and butted against her hand making her laugh with delight. "Your fur feels so soft, Jared," she laughed, running her hands over the wolf's head and neck, letting the silky black fur tickle her hands. "You're beautiful."

The wolf rumbled again and was suddenly Jared once more. He rose swiftly from the floor and caught Millie in his arms, his mouth descending to hers to give her a quick, lusty kiss. "Not as beautiful as you, my Millie," he smiled against her lips, as he started to strip her clothes from her body.

"When will I be able to change into a wolf?" Millie was breathless as she tried to stop giggling at his haste to get her naked.

He trailed his lips along the side of her neck, drawing a small moan from her. "It depends on the person. Usually it's straight away, but some people it takes a few days." He picked her up and carried her to the bed, laying down beside her and pulling her naked body flush against his, so he could slant his lips over hers and slide his tongue deep into her mouth and lick greedily at her wonderful sweetness.

God, he could never get enough of her sweet taste. He wanted her so badly, wanted to fully mate with her so badly. He reluctantly dragged his mouth from hers and brushed her errant curls back from her face. "Millie, when we join this time, in the mating ritual, my knot is going to form. It will mean we won't be able to disengage for a little while after we make love. I just thought it best to let you know that ahead of time."

She blinked at him in confusion. "Knot? What's that?"

He smiled slowly at her and leaned down for a gentle kiss. "It's a part of my body that grows to keep me joined with my mate, to help aid conception. I have a certain amount of control over it when my human side is in control, but with the wolf, it's another matter. He will most definitely want to pin you, baby."

Millie sat up and looked back at him. Knot? Pin? Conception? Her heart thudded in her chest, as she felt another moment of panic.

Jared sat up too and kissed her shoulder, running a hand down her back slowly, gentling the rising panic within her.

"Conception, Jared? So soon? I mean...it's not that I don't want to have your children, but we're still getting to know each other. Changing into a wolf is going to be a huge leap for me to begin with, but getting pregnant straight away...." She trailed off trying to work out how to put into words what she was feeling.

"Ah Millie, you worry too much." He couldn't help smiling at her confused expression. "I didn't mean you would get pregnant straight away. I was just explaining the physical side of my anatomy and my wolf. Millie, your body won't be ready for a while. Your whole physiology will be changing. It will take time before it settles down enough for us to be able to produce young. I promise you, baby, I'm not going to turn you into a wolf and knock you up on the same night."

His amused tone annoyed her, and she turned around, her eyes flashing with irritation. "I'm glad you're finding this so funny, Jared. It's not my fault I don't know enough about all of this....wolf crap."

Jared sighed again and lay back down, folding his arms behind his head. "You're right. I'm in such a rush to mate with you, I haven't stopped to think of all the things you need to know first. Maybe tonight is not the night for this. I should let you get used to the pack, learn a bit more about our ways." His wolf practically shrieked his rage, as he uttered the words, but he pushed him down ruthlessly. One moment of doubt in Millie could turn their mating into a complete disaster. He wasn't willing to take that risk. She was just too precious to him.

Millie stared down at him, biting her bottom lip as she met his gaze. She didn't know enough about what it meant to become a wolf, and she loved Jared all the more for realising it and being willing to slow things down until she was ready to fully commit. Her eyes slowly ran over his handsome face, and she sucked in a deep breath, as she saw the total adoration in his eyes as he stared back up at her.

She lay down on her side and slowly traced along his hard jaw, watching a muscle jump at her light touch. He looked so relaxed lying there, but she could feel the tension in his muscles, as he waited for her to speak.

"Thank you for being willing to wait. I know how hard it is for you and your wolf to agree to do that, Jared. Is there anything else I need to know about this mating thing? It's not being videoed to be shown to the rest of the pack at a later date?"

Jared laughed loudly at her facetious comment, rolling his eyes in mock despair. Her own lips twitched in a small smile, and she leaned down to lightly brush her lips against his.

"Then, I'm ready, Jared. I want this as much as you do. I just needed to clarify a few things first. I can learn all the other wolf stuff later."

She was gauging his expression and saw the spark of longing in his eyes as well as the slight hesitancy on his part this time. She kissed him again, winding her fingers into his long black hair and pressing her tongue inside his mouth until he groaned and took over the kiss, rolling over and pressing her back against the bed, as he stroked his tongue into her mouth.

Millie sighed and surrendered to his kiss and the urgency of his hands on her flesh. He cock was pressing against her stomach, hard and impatient as he began to kiss her mouth and neck with a feverish need, his touch wild and untamed. She moaned as her body started to ignite under his hungry touch.

Jared slid slowly down her body, his wolf so close to the surface, so desperate to get his chance to mate with their woman. He nipped down her neck and towards her breasts, latching onto a hard nipple and sucking hungrily on the taut peak before abandoning it swiftly for the other one. His hand moved between her legs and dived into her moist heat, slipping through her silky folds and groaning his pleasure at finding her so wet and ready to be possessed by him.

"I'll be slower next time, baby," he said thickly, sliding between her legs and bringing his mouth up to hers. He pressed into her beautiful body with a quick hard thrust, and she cried out her pleasure and arched against him.

Jared's hands seemed to be everywhere at the same time, as he thrust into her body. Millie moaned and met his thrusts eagerly, her fingers tangling in his hair as he kissed her hungrily. His urgency excited her, and she responded in kind, wanting to be mated to him.

He took her with short, hard thrusts, grinding into her body with a fierce, animalistic need, his breathing harsh and ragged, as his wolf demanded to be let completely free. He managed to hold him at bay for the moment so he could luxuriate in the sheer joy of feeling Millie's tight body sheath his cock repeatedly. He would never be able to get enough of this beautiful woman in his arms.

His wolf didn't want to wait any longer, and he pulled out of her body and hovered over her for a moment, staring down at her exquisite face. Her eyes were dazed with passion as she met his gaze and he smiled and kissed her again, before flipping her over onto her stomach and pulling her onto her hands and knees.

He licked at the join between her shoulder and neck, as he slowly pressed into her body again and groaned his satisfaction at coming home again.

"Jared," Millie whispered breathlessly, as she pressed back against him. "Now?"

"Now, baby," he groaned back, stroking into her body. "Don't be afraid, Millie. He loves you just as much as I do and will never do anything to harm you."

"I'm not afraid," she answered pressing back against him. "Make me yours, Jared."

Jared almost howled at her words, his wolf forcing himself to the fore, no longer willing to wait to claim his mate. He shifted, and then he thrust into Millie's body, his tongue lapping at the spot he would make his mark. He felt her tremble slightly beneath him, as she registered the change against her body, but she was still eagerly accepting him, was still pressing back against him.

With a low growl, his wolf stroked into their woman's body with a fierceness that rocked the bed. His knot began to form, and he pressed slowly into her, being as gentle as he could as he slotted the rigid bump at the base of his cock deep into her body until they were locked together.

Millie felt the hard knot pressing inside, and she stifled a moan of discomfort as Jared pressed relentlessly into her. She had no idea how much of Jared's human side was still in control of his wolf, but she thought it must be quite a bit, because he was being as gentle as he could be with her.

The knot slid home, and she sighed with relief, and then moaned softly when Jared's tongue once more licked the join between her shoulder and neck and he began to rock inside her with short, quick strokes, building her swiftly towards her peak.

Millie's cries of pleasure echoed around the room as she began to come apart, her orgasm crashing over her. Jared bit into the juncture between her shoulder and neck and joined her in her orgasm, emptying himself into her body, as he sucked on her blood before releasing her fragile skin and licking at the bite.

Jared shifted again, as his wolf completed the mating ritual and howled his contentment at claiming his mate. He held Millie close to him and lowered them both gently to their sides as they lay locked together, their breathing ragged and their hearts thumping loudly.

He smiled his satisfaction at seeing his mark on his mate's body. She was his now, but they weren't finished yet. She had to stake her claim, too, but it would have to wait until his knot subsided.

"Wow," Millie said in an awed tone. "I can feel her, Jared. She's right there inside me." She placed a hand to her stomach, as she closed her eyes and felt her wolf start to prowl around inside her head and body, pacing impatiently as she waited to do something.

Jared lightly stroked her stomach and ran his hands up to her breasts, cupping them gently and teasing her nipples with his talented fingers. "Sensing your wolf for the first time is a wonderful experience," he smiled against her neck.

Millie's eyes flickered open, and she turned her head slightly to look at him. "She's impatient for something."

He smiled and leaned forward to kiss her swollen lips. "She wants you to claim me," he said huskily. "She can do it, soon. We just need to wait until my knot subsides."

Millie felt the strange being inside her growl her impatience again, and she stifled down a giggle at the strangeness of it all. It felt weird, and yet, it felt so right too. She was a wolf now. She would be able to change like Jared and Rafe. She still felt like herself, only she was something more, something better. It was the most amazing feeling in the world.

"Jared, she doesn't want to wait," she said with a little laugh. "Can't you make your knot go down faster?"

Jared rolled his eyes and barked out a laugh. His woman really was awfully demanding, but he couldn't stop the thrill of anticipation which went through him at the thought of her claiming him. "Lie still, and be quiet," he said gruffly, closing his eyes and trying to will his body to do what he wanted it to. Ordinarily they could be joined for anything up to half an hour, but if his Millie wanted to claim him, he'd try to accommodate her.

A few minutes later, he achieved his goal, sliding from his mate's body, as she twisted around in his arms smiling excitedly at him. Her cobalt eyes flashed with barely controlled need. His heart skipped a beat as he stared up at her, seeing her wolf prowling close to the surface, his own wolf howling his glee deep within him.

"You don't need to shift, Millie," he said huskily. "I can teach you that later. For now, you just need to bite me in the same place where I bit you."

Millie stared at the join of Jared's neck and shoulder, the spot she had to mark. Her wolf howled her impatience again and gave her a mental nudge to get on with it before someone else came along and tried to take their mate. She smiled wolfishly and licked along the spot as Jared trembled with excitement, his hands coming to her waist to pull her on top of his body, his cock once more standing proud and rubbing against her wet heat.

"Please, Millie," he ground out hoarsely. "Don't make me wait, baby."

She laughed and sank her teeth into him, feeling his blood enter her mouth, as he growled loudly and impaled her on his body. She licked at her bite mark, and then brought her mouth to his, as she began to slide up and down his hard shaft. "Mine," she growled, possessively.

"Mine," he answered with his own deep growl

CHAPTER EIGHTEEN

Millie woke and blinked in confusion for a moment, her eyes taking in the strange surroundings around her before finally turning to the man lying at her side. She smiled as she ran her cobalt eyes over Jared's handsome face, shifting slightly so she could brush his long black hair aside, wanting to fully appreciate the view.

Her Jared. Her mate. She felt her wolf rumble her satisfaction deep inside her as her eyes lit on the mark on his body, their mark which told the world that this beautiful man belonged to them and no one else.

She blinked again, this time in surprise when she realised it was still dark and she could see almost as well as she could in daylight. She could hear better too. Every single sound outside drifted towards her. She could hear the leaves on the trees blowing gently in the breeze, the sounds of some of the pack moving around in the compound. There was even the hungry wail of a child off in the distance, demanding to be fed instantly.

So this was what being a wolf was all about. She had thought it felt amazing last night, just feeling the wolf come to life inside her, but she had no idea all her senses would be heightened the way they were now. She had such a lot to learn about her new life but she knew Jared would teach her everything she needed to know.

Right now her wolf wanted to be free. The compulsion to go outside was so strong she found herself rising quietly from the bed, making sure not to wake Jared as she did so. She was so awake, so alert, so not like how she used to be before she was changed. She had never been a morning person before. Now she was chomping at the bit to get up when it was still dark and run downstairs to greet the sunrise.

Grabbing Jared's shirt, she pulled it on and padded silently from the room and down to the lower floor. She threw open the front door and stood on the threshold taking a deep breath and smelling the heady aromas of forest. She could smell the damp earth, the morning dew seeping into the ground and settling on the leaves of the trees. It smelled so perfect, so wonderful. Her wolf growled impatiently, asking to be allowed to come forward, to run on the damp ground, to race through the tall trees.

Millie smiled slowly a second before Jared's arms wrapped around her from behind and his lips settled on his mark at the side of her neck. His tongue traced fast whirls across it as she leaned back into his embrace with a sigh of pleasure. He was naked and unashamed of it, not caring who saw him as he greeted his mate enthusiastically, spinning her around so he could devour her mouth in a hot, wet kiss.

His body hardened and he groaned softly as he stroked his tongue into her willing mouth, his hands sliding to her ass to pull her tightly against his erection. God, he wanted her so badly he was ready to take her in the doorway and to hell if someone came along and saw them.

Millie moaned and pulled her mouth away, taking a moment to lick at her mark on his body before she pushed against his chest. "I want to run," she said huskily. "Teach me how to shift, Jared. Come run with me."

He groaned his displeasure, much preferring to take her back upstairs and lose himself inside her beautiful body, but she smiled up at him, her wolf prowling close to the surface and he suddenly very much wanted to see just how beautiful she was in wolf form. "Come on," he said gruffly, scooping her up into his arms and striding outside and into the closest cover of trees.

"Do you always walk about naked?" she laughed as he set her down on a patch of wet grass.

"Clothes don't transform," he laughed back, eagerly peeling his shirt from her body and sucking in a deep breath as her beauty was once more revealed to him. He ran his hands lightly over her breasts, tugging playfully at her nipples which had hardened instantly as the cool morning breeze danced over her creamy white skin. "You're so beautiful, baby," he whispered hoarsely, his eyes darkening with need as he lowered his head to suck one taut peak into his mouth and he suckled on it firmly.

Millie groaned loudly and threaded her hands into his head, tugging gently to pull him away from her body even though she didn't want the delightful feel of his mouth against her breast to stop. "We can do that later," she sighed softly. "My wolf wants to run, Jared."

He growled and frowned in annoyance at being thwarted again and then his expression smoothed and he smiled and gave her a quick kiss. "I can't help it if you're too beautiful for me to keep my hands off you," he said cockily and then sighed when she arched an eyebrow at him. "Wolf, run...I get the message."

He sank down onto grass and pulled her down beside him, laughing when she grumbled at how wet the grass was. "Close your eyes, Millie," he whispered softly. "Concentrate on your wolf. Feel her inside you. Let her come to the fore, surrender to her and let her come out."

She blinked slowly and then closed her eyes, feeling inside herself for her wolf. She relaxed and took a deep breath. Jared said to surrender so she did her best not to fight as she felt her wolf start to become more dominant. She uttered a startled gasp, feeling as if she was slowly sinking downwards as the wolf seemed to grow stronger.

"Don't fight her, Millie," she heard Jared say softly as if from a distance. "She won't let anything happen to you, baby. She's as much a part of you as you are a part of her."

She opened her mouth to answer him but nothing came out. She felt her body tremble slightly and then suddenly it was shifting around her and she felt her bones melt and start to change. She yelped loudly in shock as pain blossomed through her body as her bones stretched and her body elongated. She fell forward, yelping once more as she looked down at the long black fur covered paws in front of her.

"Jared," she tried to say but only a long whine came out of her snout because her face was no longer the same anymore and she was incapable of making human speech form in her new throat.

"*It's okay, baby, I'm here,*" Jared said inside her head and she swung her head around to look at him in surprise. "*Yes, I'm talking inside your head,*" he smiled, reaching a hand out to place it soothingly against her jaw. "*We can all talk to each other mentally when we're in wolf form,*" he continued in the same soothing tone. "*As mates, we can do so when in human form too. I will show you when we shift back.*"

Millie blinked at him and nudged against his hand. "*Jared,*" she said experimentally inside her head and he smiled again at her, signalling he had heard her even though he was still in human form. *"Oh, wow!"* she suddenly laughed. *"This is so amazing. Does it always hurt when you change? How can I still talk to you when my wolf is in control?"*

Jared laughed and reached around her neck to brush his face against her glorious black fur. *"You're balanced almost evenly at the moment,"* he explained. *"You won't notice the pain of shifting again. You really only notice it the very first time you shift willingly. After that, it's a simple as breathing, you just do it."*

Millie rumbled deeply and pressed against Jared's body, chuffing lightly when she accidentally pushed him over and he fell on his backside. Blue eyes glinted at him before she turned suddenly and raced out of the little clearing, disappearing into the trees. *"Catch me if you can,"* she called mentally, laughing as she disappeared from view.

Jared's wolf howled his pleasure as he sat on the grass a few moments longer, letting Millie get a head start on him. She didn't stand a chance of escaping him. It didn't matter how fast she ran, he would track her down. He grinned wolfishly as he felt his blood rise. He shifted and set off after his mate.

Millie flew through the trees, her heart racing, her paws pounding on the damp ground. She knew Jared was somewhere behind her, catching her quickly because he was bigger and stronger and much faster than she was. But he wasn't smarter than her. She veered left, towards the sound of running water, breaking cover from the trees and diving into the small stream, running furiously along the waterbed before darting left again and exiting the stream further up.

She laughed and her wolf chuckled along with her. That would slow him down. He would have to stop and check for her scent while she would be able to gain better distance on him. She wove back out of sight and continued on through the forest, spotting a rock formation with practically no vegetation on it. She laughed again and sailed through the air onto the rock, running along the smooth face and then turning right, sailing back through the air to put as much distance between the rock and her landing spot.

"Millie," she heard him whisper in her head and her heart faltered slightly because he sounded so close. *"Neat trick with the stream, baby, but it's not going to stop me catching you."*

She refrained from answering him, knew he was trying to tempt her into giving away her direction. She continued to run, wondering if she could climb up into one of the trees to hide from him. She was just about to ask her wolf if she could climb when a black wolf streaked out of the trees and barrelled into her, knocking her to the ground.

She rolled and came up snarling, shaking her head in anger as she glared balefully at Jared. He snarled back at her and she would have gulped if she could. His snarl was so much more impressive than hers was.

"That's because I'm your Alpha," he chuckled inside her head and she snarled again, angry with herself for thinking the thought when she knew he'd be able to pick it up.

"Oh, you think so?" she thought archly. *"Thought I'd made it perfectly clear how I feel about your macho male crap, oh powerful Alpha."*

Jared lunged for her and she darted to the left, barely escaping his jaws as they went to clamp around the scruff of her neck. She rolled again and came up facing him as he paused slightly, watching her intently.

"But I've never made it clear how I feel about your constant challenges to me," he countered softly and his mental tone made her shiver slightly. *"Submit, Millie."*

"Submit!" she huffed shaking her head. *"Do you intend to teach me how to sit and beg on command too, Jared?"*

His head cocked to the side and he grinned at her. *"What an excellent suggestion,"* he laughed. *"Now, that could truly be fun. Mmmmm, the thought of you begging me makes my body tingle all over."* His irritation flared into something else and Millie shuddered as she watched his eyes darken and her wolf started to rumble her appreciation at the way their mate was regarding them.

She shook her head again. Really, her wolf was that easy? One little word from him and she was ready to roll over and give in to him? Her mental admonishment sparked her wolf's aggressive side. She snarled again and suddenly darted off into the trees, Jared hot on her heels and gaining fast. She had to outrun him. If she didn't, he'd be a complete pain to have to put up with.

Jared brought her down again before she got much further away from him. Only this time, he ensured he landed squarely on her back and aimed his jaws for the scruff of her neck. She howled her frustration as he pinned her to the ground firmly, holding her immobile underneath his strong body.

"You'll never be able to outrun me, baby," he whispered into her mind. *"You can try all you want to but you know I'll always catch you. You're mine, Millie. You always will be."*

Millie grunted her annoyance at being caught so easily and allowed him to hold her down. Not that she really had that much of a choice but she liked to pretend she had some say in the matter. It was so unfair of him using his superior strength and speed against her. She fumed silently refusing to acknowledge his dominance over her. If he thought she was going to meekly start obeying him then he had another think coming.

It took her a moment to realise his jaw wasn't around the back of her neck anymore though his strong body was still pressed against hers. He seemed tense, unsure almost, and his stillness transmitted itself into her and she turned her head slightly to look back at him. *"Jared?"*

He backed away from her, letting her up as he moved further away and sat down, regarding her intently. He shifted unexpectedly turning back to human form, his expression very serious as he regarded her intently.

Millie shifted without even thinking about it, moving over to his side and sitting down beside him. "Jared, what's wrong?" she asked, her voice full of concern, her arms automatically going around him. He turned to look at her and he seemed so uncertain it tore at her heart.

"What did I do wrong, Jared?" she asked softly. "You were reading my mind, weren't you? Damn, you're going to have to teach me how to guard my thoughts if they're going to upset you so much. I don't mean to challenge you, love. I don't mean to make you feel any less of the Alpha you truly are. It's just I've had to rely on myself for so long that it's hard to let go and let someone else take charge. It doesn't mean I don't love you and want to be with you because you know I do. Hell, I let you change me into a wolf. I can't think of any other way to show you how much I love you and need you, Jared."

Jared stared into his woman's beautiful cobalt eyes and reached out to play with an errant curl. Her lack of submission had cut him to the quick. His need for her submission surprised him in its intensity. Yes, it was his alpha streak coming out but he'd known when he'd chosen Millie for his mate that she was strong and feisty and the last person in the world who was going to meekly submit to him. It was why he loved her so much.

He smiled slowly and leaned forward to brush his lips slowly over hers. "I'll teach you how to guard your thoughts," he said ruefully. "That doesn't mean I won't still try and make you submit though," he added. "Perhaps if you're feeling generous you'll soothe my wounded ego and allow me to do so."

Millie sighed and rolled her eyes but she smiled and hugged him tightly. "I'll try every now and then," she laughed softly. "But don't you think it would be so much more fun having one equal partner who can help you shoulder the heavy burden of running the pack? I mean, did your mother submit to your father?"

Jared thought about it with a surprised expression on his face and then he suddenly laughed. "Only in public," he admitted. "And only when it was absolutely necessary. Ma was most definitely the one in charge at home."

He laughed again and pulled his woman into his arms for a long, lusty kiss. "You know, I was so hung up on what I believed an alpha to be, I never considered how my parents did things when they were running the pack," he murmured against her lips, his hands stroking down her back. "Again, you make me look at things from a different perspective, my Millie. I'm so lucky to have you, baby."

She laughed softly and straddled his body, feeling his cock hard and eager as it pressed between her legs. "Just try and remember that the next time I wound your precious male ego," she laughed, slowly moving against his hardness and making him groan his appreciation.

"The sun's coming up," Jared sighed against her lips. "The pack will be waiting to greet their new Alpha Bitch properly." His hands were stroking down her back and cupping her ass as he spoke, completely at odds with his words.

Millie chuckled and rolled from his grasp, leaping nimbly to her feet and smothering a loud laugh at the bereft expression on his face. "Okay, let's head back then," she teased lightly.

"What? You're suddenly going to start listening to me now?" he asked incredulously. This was third time she'd pulled away from him just as things were starting to get interesting and he didn't like it one bit.

"I thought you wanted me to obey your commands, my Alpha?" she laughed impishly and then shrieked when his hand shot out to grab her ankle and jerk her off balance until she fell astride him again.

"I command you to slide your beautiful body onto my cock and show me how much you appreciate being chosen as your Alpha's mate," he said thickly, his blue eyes so dark they were almost black with need. He raised her body and slowly pulled her over his aching length, watching her beautiful face intently as he sheathed himself inside her delicious body.

"You're so stunningly beautiful, my Millie," he whispered roughly, pulling her mouth to his so he could slide his tongue slowly along her lips. She moaned and slowly began to raise and lower herself over his cock, her body trembling with pleasure as he filled her so completely.

Jared pressed his tongue into her mouth, feasting on her sweet taste as he rolled his hips up to meet her movements, his hands sliding to her breasts to tweak at her taut peaks and draw more deep moans of pleasure from his woman. He tugged and twirled the tight buds as he felt his lust start to spiral out of control. He moved suddenly, laying her back in the grass and taking over their lovemaking.

Millie didn't have a problem submitting to him when he was so deep inside her. She longed for him to stamp his claim on her body, she craved it even. She wrapped her legs tightly around his waist to pull him deeper inside her as he set up a strong, hard pace, thrusting into her with long, hard strokes. He demanded everything from her with no holds barred and she gave him everything, knowing that soon she would be riding the most intense wave of pleasure and letting the entire forest know how much she was loving it.

Jared wanted it to last forever but knew they had much work to do and there would be ample time later to be with his woman like this again. They had a lifetime together and he knew they would never get tired of loving each other like this. His Millie set a fire in him which only she could quench. His cock was throbbing inside her tightness, her heat scalding him as her juices coated his aching staff so deliciously. He increased his movements, driving hard and ruthlessly into his woman as her sweet cries filled the morning air and his own deep growls of pleasure joined her in song.

He felt her body tremble, felt her tight canal ripple around his aching hardness and he caught her scream of pleasure in his mouth as she came apart beneath him, grinding her body hard against him as her pleasure washed over her and sent him tumbling headfirst after her a bare second later. He felt his knot start to grow and he groaned as he fought to hold it back even though he wanted nothing more in the world than to be pinned with her on the forest floor.

He roared his release into the air, his body jerking violently against hers as he spilled his seed deep inside her beautiful body. Their bodies ground hard against each other a few moments more before they finally stilled and Jared lowered himself carefully against her, supporting his full weight on his upper arms as he kissed her tenderly and then groaned in despair.

Millie stared up at Jared with a slightly puzzled expression when he groaned as if he were in pain. She smoothed back his long hair from his face. "What?" she asked softly, her heart still hammering furiously from their lovemaking.

He shot her a rueful smile and kissed her lightly before he lowered his head against hers. "Breakfast will be later than anticipated," he sighed. "We're going to be joined like this for a little while longer."

"Jared!" Millie groaned in exasperation. "I thought you said you could control this pinning thing when in human form."

He laughed and rolled to his side taking her with him and sighing his contentment at having her in his arms. "I thought I could," he admitted sheepishly. "It's not my fault you're just too beautiful that I lose all coherent thought when I'm inside your body." He stifled whatever else she was going to say with his lips, giving her a long slow kiss until she was breathless.

When he finally let her up for air she smiled at him and stroked his cheek gently. "I suppose it's not so bad," she whispered softly and then cuddled into his chest as they basked in the afterglow of their love.

~~~~~

Rhianna entered the kitchen and smiled as she saw Caleb indulging in his new favourite pastime which seemed to be fattening her up. He was studiously standing over the stove, stirring a pan full of eggs which were for her no doubt. He had quickly gotten out of the habit of eating with her, realising he just couldn't stomach the food, no matter how much he wanted to please her.

He looked up and smiled when she entered the kitchen and lifted her up to sit on the counter beside the stove. He dropped a quick kiss on her lips and went back to his eggs.

"Caleb," she said tentatively. "You know how we were talking about you changing me into a vampire? Well, I had a chat with Rafe and Millie about it and they're really happy for me to go ahead and I was wondering when would be the best time to do it."

She watched Caleb stiffen and his hand cease his stirring motion. "We've already discussed this, Annie," he said quietly, not looking at her. "I thought I'd made it perfectly clear to you that it wasn't going to happen. Why you felt the need to seek Rafe and Millie's approval is beyond me when I've no intention of turning you."

Rhianna took a deep breath and slowly let it out. "Yes, we discussed it," she admitted. "But I wasn't aware we had reached a decision on it. I know I didn't agree to not being turned because it's something I wouldn't agree to. I want this, Caleb, and you want it too." She tried to keep her tone reasonable but a little of her exasperation crept into it.

Caleb turned his head to look at her and his expression was so carefully neutral she had no one idea what was going through his mind. His golden brown eyes bored into hers intently and then his lips tightened and he looked away again. "I am not turning you, Annie," he said firmly and stirred the eggs again, his big body taut with tension.

"Caleb," she sighed irritably and he swung back to her so quickly she gave a startled squeak. This time his expression was angry, furious even, his eyes flashing amber as he glared at her murderously. She'd only ever seen him look at her that way once before and it had frightened her as much then as it did now.

"Drop it, Rhianna," he hissed furiously. "I allow you great latitude as it is because I love you, but that does not mean I will forever let you have your own way. This topic is not open for debate, now or ever. Am I making myself perfectly clear here? Because I will not be responsible for my actions if I find I have to repeat myself."

The colour drained from her face as she stared up at him wide eyed, biting her inside lip to prevent the tears which were starting to gather. His anger pierced straight through her, but it also made her angry too. Who the hell was he to turn around and use his stupid, mad vampire persona to intimidate her and basically make her shut up? Her anger kicked up a notch and her mouth set stubbornly.

"Oh, you won't be responsible for your actions, will you?" she asked, her lavender eyes flashing furiously at him. "What are you going to do, Caleb? Spank me? Use your damned vampire powers on me? Come to think of it, just what are your vampire powers apart from the obvious ones? Can you get inside my head, control my mind even? That would work out so well for you if you could do that. You could just get inside my mind and make me do whatever you wanted me to. It's so bloody unfair, Caleb. You have no right to deny me what I want and then turn around and go all vampire on me because I don't agree with you."

Her anger shocked him and Caleb took a step back from her as he tried to control his own anger, a feeling of guilt coming over him so strongly that he'd lost his temper with her. He didn't want to fight with his woman but he wasn't willing to give in to her on this point, no matter what she said. "I will not discuss this with you," he said coldly, struggling hard to rein in his temper and deal with the foreign emotion of guilt still overwhelming him.

"Fine," Rhianna spat jumping down from the counter. "If you won't do it, then I'll ask Demetri to do it instead." She didn't really mean it but she wanted to lash out at him because he was disappointing her so much with his unreasonable behaviour.

The expression which came over his beautiful face chilled her to the very bone. For one brief heartbeat she thought he was truly going to hurt her, his face turned so vicious and she realised she was looking at the vampire Caleb truly was, with no hint of the man she loved anywhere in sight.

Caleb quivered with rage, seethed with fury, as his woman blithely turned around and announced she was going to have his best friend turn her into a vampire. It didn't matter that Demetri would refuse her request. It was the fact she was willing to allow some other vampire to sire her that burned his heart to shreds. She couldn't hurt him anymore than she was doing right at this very moment.

He stared down at his beautiful woman and saw her lavender eyes wide with fear and brimming with tears and he could only imagine what she must be seeing in his face. She was seeing him at his true vampiric best, the monster he really was and he was frightening her. A part of him was glad he was frightening her. She really should be reminded what he truly was, what she would become if he gave in to her and granted her request.

"So you want to be a vampire, Rhianna?" he asked dangerously quietly. "You want to be this?" He pointed at his face, baring his fangs at her, not one trace of human compassion or love anywhere in his expression.

Her face paled even more, her eyes silently beseeching him not to scare her this way and suddenly the breath hissed out of him in a long tortured gasp and he spun on his heel and raced from the kitchen, slamming out the front door and disappearing into the night.

Rhianna bit her lip. She'd pushed Caleb too far and now he was gone, running away from her. He was probably scared he would hurt her. For a moment she had thought he was going to and she felt guilty for having that moment of fear. She knew he would never hurt her, not deliberately so. She just wished he believed it of himself too.

She stared down at the burning eggs in the pan and sighed softly. She threw the entire pan into the sink, eggs and all. She wasn't feeling very hungry anyway. She took a few deep breaths and headed out of the kitchen, seeing the front door lying wide open and shivering slightly as the cool breeze wafted inside.

She knew Caleb was close by somewhere. He would never leave her alone and vulnerable in his home with his door wide open for anyone to walk in. She considered calling him and then decided not to. She was still annoyed with him and he probably wasn't too impressed with her either at the moment. Some time to let tempers cool was most definitely the best thing.

~~~~~

Caleb watched her hover at the open door, a deep scowl on his face. He was riddled with feelings of guilt but he was still angry at her too. She was being so unreasonable, so stubborn and single-minded, and downright bloody annoying.

So why was he the one skulking outside like a four year old in a temper tantrum? Why did he ache to go to her and promise her anything she wanted if only she would smile her beautiful smile at him and welcome him into her arms? Being in love was one of the hardest things he'd ever had to do in his very long life.

His scowl softened as he watched Rhianna peer into the darkness and then turn and start to walk up the stairs, leaving the door open for him to come home to her. He sighed deeply and raked his hand through his long hair. It was pointless fighting against his woman. She was always going to win, no matter how much of a fight he put up. She had enough faith for both of them and he had no option but to trust her judgement. Making up his mind, he headed back towards the house just as his cell phone rang.

~~~~~

Caleb slammed open the bedroom door and stormed into the room. "I'm going to fucking kill him," he roared furiously. "When I get my hands on him, I'm going to rip his fucking head off."

Rhianna looked up from where she was lounging on the bed, her book falling from her hands as she blinked at him in surprise. "Who are you killing now?" she asked quietly, trying to fight down the small smile tugging at her lips. He was prowling around the bed, their disagreement clearly forgotten by whatever had upset him.

She sucked in a deep breath as she watched him. God, he was glorious when he was angry, especially when he was angry with someone other than her. His amber eyes blazed with fury, his hair flowing wildly round his head as he moved. She felt a little shiver run down her spine and a deep warmth begin in the very pit of her stomach.

"Bloody Demetri!" he growled. "Beth just called to tell me Demetri has decided to take a few days off to attend to some personal business. I'll bloody give him personal business! He knew damned well I wanted to spend this week with you. He knew he was already skating on thin ice after his last little dig at you. You would think he'd have the bloody sense to try and get back in my good books, but no, not Demetri. He pisses off, so I'll have to go into the office this week, when I really wanted to spend it with you instead."

She watched him stomp around the bed, his fury at his friend reaching almost fever pitch. She couldn't stop her smile growing wider, as he started telling her just what he intended to do to Demetri when he got back from wherever he was. The more he ranted, the hotter she became and all traces of their earlier disagreement flew from her mind. She finally gave into the urge to unbutton her jeans and slip them off when his fangs came out. She was lost the moment she saw those wickedly sharp teeth.

Her scent hit Caleb like a ton of bricks, and he blinked slowly, turning his head towards the bed. His mouth dropped open, as Rhianna crawled into the middle of the huge bed and wiggled her thong-covered backside at him.

"You going to do something with those teeth, love, or are they just for show?" She laughed as he growled and dived onto the bed, trapping her body underneath his and scraping his fangs lightly against the side of her neck.

She was supposed to be mad at him. Didn't woman withhold their sexual favours when they were mad at a man? He didn't take long to ponder it. She was aroused and wanting him, and he wasn't about to let such a blatant invitation slip past because he didn't understand the subtle nuances of being part of a couple.

"Witch!" he groaned thickly, quickly shredding her little tank top and then snapping the sides of her thong and throwing the ruined items to the floor. Her deep musky scent flowed over him, and he groaned again, all thoughts of Demetri gone from his head.

Her sudden arousal had come out of nowhere, and he was reacting to it instinctively, and more wildly than normal, because of their recent argument. His usual self-control appeared to shatter somewhere between her wiggling her ass at him and uttering those words about his fangs.

All that mattered was being with her, his precious Annie, the other half of his soul. For however long they had he always wanted to be with her like this, kissing, touching, loving one another. Caleb dampened his wilder side and set about showing her how much he loved her, licking and kissing her body in slow, languorous strokes until she purred for him, surrendering to his touch.

Their lovemaking was slow and sensual, a meeting of spirits as if both wanted to show the other how sorry they were for their part in the earlier argument. Kissing Rhianna deeply, Caleb worshipped her body with his until she cried out her pleasure, tumbling him along with her, their bodies dancing together in the ancient language of love that required no words.

Rhianna smiled, snuggling close to Caleb as her heart continued to race and she sought to bring her breathing under control. He had told her without words just how sorry he was and how much he loved her. There would be many times they would argue over the years, but the making up would soothe any pain. Rubbing her cheek against his skin, she kissed his chest, as his arms wrapped tightly around her.

"Are you okay, love?" he asked softly.

She purred deeply and rubbed her softness against him. "That was delicious," she sighed, and he chuckled, his hand stroking through her tangled curls as she lay across his chest.

She smiled and kissed his chest. "You just look so incredibly sexy when you're angry," she giggled. "The moment your fangs came out, I just couldn't help myself."

Caleb laughed with her and kissed the top of her head. "I wasn't complaining," he admitted, contentedly holding her tightly against him. He closed his eyes and savoured the feel of her body in his arms. Lying with her like this gave him a feeling of true peace. His beautiful woman tamed the monster inside him with a whispered word, a slight touch of her hand, her lips twitching in a secret little smile. She was his redemption and he would be lost without her.

"I'm sorry about earlier, Annie," he whispered, and he felt her still against him for a moment and then she raised her head and looked intently into his face.

Her lavender eyes met his and he sucked in a deep breath as he stared into perfection. She was so beautiful with her lips swollen from his kisses, the slight flush of her passion still in the smoky depths of her eyes, and the faint flush of red in her cheeks.

"I'm sorry too, Caleb," Rhianna sighed. "I didn't mean what I said...about asking Demetri." He quietened her by placing a finger on her lips, his golden brown eyes intent on hers as he slowly stroked her soft mouth until he was sure she had gotten the message and wouldn't continue with that line of conversation any further.

She smiled and raised herself higher so she could press her lips gently against his. The sheet fell away from her and his eyes travelled slowly down her slender neck to the swell of her beautiful breasts, his marks colouring her creamy skin so erotically he felt himself start to harden again.

"Annie," he groaned, cupping her face gently in his hands. "I find I can refuse you nothing, sweet one. I'll give you what you want, baby. I'll make you mine forever, I promise you I will, but we need time together so I can guide you through the changes. Can you wait until Demetri returns?"

He knew he was being so incredibly selfish, but he also knew he would never survive without her by his side. Her beautiful face lit up with such joy that he forgot to breathe for a moment as he stared at her in wonder.

"I love you, Caleb. I can wait for Demetri to return, as long as I know that it will only be a little while longer." Rhianna kissed him again, and then slid her body completely on top of his, causing him to stifle down a deep groan as she pressed her heat against his already hardened cock.

"I should refuse you," he whispered softly. "I should tell you no and be satisfied with just one life time with you, my Annie, but I can't bear the thought of never seeing you like this again, of never holding you and loving you and hearing your sweet cries as you shatter so beautifully in my arms."

She smiled her beautiful smile at him, and his breath caught once more before he groaned and ground her mouth hard against his as he crushed her tightly to him. "I love you, my Annie," he whispered, his voice thick with emotion. He sighed and settled her along the length of his body, her face buried in the side of his neck as she slowly stroked his chest.

He wanted to lie like this forever with her, to forget about the outside world and the trials of daily life, but thoughts of Demetri were plaguing his tired mind and he inwardly cursed his friend.

He had a good idea of what his friend was up to right now. They had called him first and he had refused. He knew they would call Demetri next. The fact he was now gone was a clear indicator Demetri had agreed to their request. If his actions upset Annie in any way he would seriously kick the shit out of him, friend or no friend.

Rhianna stirred in his arms, lifting her head to peer at him sleepily. She stroked his face lightly and settled back down against his chest. "Sleep, Caleb," she murmured softly. "Whatever you're fighting with Demetri about will resolve itself eventually. Stop thinking about him and rest with me, love."

He chuckled and trailed his fingers through her riot of curls. She always seemed to know what he was thinking. Kissing her head gently, Caleb snuggled Rhianna closer, once more wrapped in her loving spell. He'd deal with Demetri tomorrow. Tonight there was only his Annie in his heart and in his mind. He closed his eyes and drifted slowly into sleep.

Coming Soon

The Assignment
Book Two in the Fighting the Inevitable Saga

ABOUT THE AUTHOR

I have been married to George for almost 15 years, and he has been my love, my support, and my best friend for even longer. We weren't blessed with any children, though I am incredibly close to my beautiful nieces and nephews, and my gorgeous great niece Maddison.

I live in Edinburgh, Scotland and class myself as being Scottish though I was born in England. I have lived here most of my life now, so Edinburgh is most definitely home.

I work in Finance and write, write and write some more in my free time. My dream is to one day be a full time author so I can do what I love most.

Made in the USA
Lexington, KY
01 May 2016